Arion Golmakani

Solacers

We are what we think

Solacers

a Memoir
Arion Golmakani

RED CORN POPPY BOOKS, 2011

Copyright © 2011 by Arion Golmakani.

ISBN -10   0615445268
ISBN -13   978-0-615-44526-7
eBook:
ISBN -10   061548042X
ISBN -13   978-0-615-48042-8

For bulk order and other information please contact publisher at www.redcornpoppy-books.blogspot.com

Printed in the United States of America
FOURTH PRINTING FEBRUARY 2012

For Kia, my mother & Momon Bozorg

I dedicate this book to all the orphans and
all the oppressed women of the world

Acknowledgment

My deepest gratitude:

To my aunt Sarvar, may you find living just as joyful on the other side as you did here in this world.

To all the Rahimis for sharing your home with me and having me as a member of your family, and to Rahim for being a wonderful older brother to me.

To Jamshid and Hooshang Golmakani for being my summertime brothers and solacers in Mashhad and in Golmakan.

To Morvareed for sharing your home with me in Abadan.

To the Badieis for sharing your home and bread with me and treating me as if I were a member of your family.

To Molouk, one of the gentlest and most beautiful souls I have had the privilege of being with, albeit for such a short time. May you forever rest in peace, my dear.

To Ibrahim Noroozy, my Abadanian older brother, to Bahram Honar, Masood Qolampoor, Parveez Qazian, Qolam Benrashid, Shahbaz Behdan, Feerooz, Noric and all my other wonderful friends in Ahmadabad and the Palm Date Grove of Braim in Abadan. You were the best friends anyone could have. I will never forget you.

To Mr. Haydari, my algebra teacher at Bozorgmehr high school.

To Sarah, I will always cherish our private moments on the edge of Arvand Rood, when life was simpler.

To everyone in the 1973 class of 28 of the old Iranian Navy in Hassan Rood.

To the Zareefs for your kindness and generosity.

To all the dovish and wonderful Baha'i folks that I had the privilege of crossing paths with. I read somewhere that the truth is the greatest good and love is the highest truth; you epitomized both.

To Mr. Naser Malek-Motiei for paying for my train ticket to Tehran to visit my mother.

To my beautiful wife for being my number one fan and best friend.

To all of my children for choosing me as your father.

To Baba, may peace be upon you wherever you are.

To my brothers Mehdi, Mohsen and Hussein and my sisters Mehri, Maasumeh, and Nasrin for being such loyal fans to your older brother and for all the love you have shown me. I will always love you.

To Elizabeth and the rest of the McLallen family for taking me into your home, for your generosity and for being my first American family.

To Mohammad Mousavi for being my friend for life.

To my good friend Larry Henry, our days at the Chaparral Club in Lackland AFB are still fresh in my mind.

To Virginia Chambers for giving me my first job, mentoring me, and being a wonderful sister. You have the elegance of a queen.

To Larry and Cindy Youse, I never forget how wonderful you were.

To all my brothers and sisters at the 1979 and 1980s Grand Finale Restaurant.

To Sheryl Davis.

To all my friends at the old Trumps in Cincinnati, especially Raylyn for hiring me and teaching me the art of tending bar.

To my brother Mark Gabbard for pulling for me and championing my professional growth at Circuit City.

To all of my friends at the Circuit City Stores, I will never forget any of you.

To Anthony Amico for being a great and loyal friend.

To Dr. Eric Anderson and Dr. Morleen Getz Rouse of College Conservatory of Music for being so wonderful and kind.

To Robert and Linda daCosta for being my family.

To Michael Jennings, Sarah Andrews, Katherine Massaquoi and Diane Alexander.

To Mike and Pia Vammino for your friendship.

And to Dr. Ahmed Nasrullah for inspiring me to write this book.

Prologue

❖

When I first began to put in words what is now the content of this book— my account of growing up in Iran— I did not give much thought as to why, what for, and why now, after all these years, am I writing them? I wasn't thinking about any great purpose my story was going to serve, who its audience was going to be and how it was going to improve or impact their lives, if any. It wasn't my intention to avenge or to vilify places and people with my pen, or to help myself find closure. And definitely, I did not write this book to save the world. The world does not need to be saved if people take care of what is on their own plate and in front of them. If the world needs any saving it should be from the zealous folks who believe it is their responsibility to save it. History shows those intentions often had disastrous consequences.

Writing a book about my childhood was the last thing I wanted to do. I am not into mental regurgitation of events, especially the unpleasant ones. In 2003, after a complex brain surgery, I lost a good portion of my eyesight and became grounded. That provided me with the opportunity to sit, keep my eyes closed, and gaze with my mind at the road of life. After a year or so of this, one day I began to slowly tap away at my old computer's keyboard and painstakingly, one word at a time, write. My intention was to put my story in a book and throw it out into the ocean of life for anyone who wishes to pick it up and read it.

This is not a book about Iran or the Iranian people, for I hardly qualify as an expert in either. This is simply my story, which happened to take place in Iran, though it could have taken place anywhere. I think of my life in Iran as a short journey on a very narrow path with a limited view; therefore, I can describe here only what I was able to see and not all the things that I was not in a position to experience and missed. The Iran that was the stage for my life no longer exists. Like the waters of a river, the Iran that I swam in as a child has long passed through and been replaced with a new one.

Out of respect for the privacy of those folks who played a role in my Iranian life, I have changed their names and locations in this book.

Solacers

a memoir

Arion Golmakani

American Heritage Dictionary:

1. **Solace** *v* Comfort in sorrow, misfortune, or distress; consolation.
2. **Solacer** *n* One who comforts, cheers, or consoles, as in trouble or sorrow.

❖*Chapter One*

L ike a gentle wind Baba zigzagged through the scattered, early evening traffic. He rode his bicycle with the grace of a nobleman riding on the back of a horse. His upper body remained upright and motionless as he pedaled. Without looking at his legs it was difficult to tell he was riding a bicycle. Even the frigid winter air that smashed against my numbed face like a leather belt seemed incapable of disturbing his thoughts and bringing him back from wherever they had taken him. Every now and then I turned my head around and looked up at him, hoping to catch his glance, but to no avail. Baba's small brown pupils had taken his soul to a distant horizon far beyond the city structures in front of us. I wondered if he was thinking about me. I wondered if, had he had the means to care for me, he would not have gotten rid of me.

Sitting in front of Baba, I gripped the cold chrome handlebar of his bicycle tightly with my bare hands, which had already turned purple with cold. Winters were brutal here. My ears were trapping the frigid wind and allowing pain and cold to penetrate deep inside my head. I was too timid to let go of the handlebar and cover my ears with my hands. I wished I had a hat, the kind that came all the way down and over the ears. With my chapped lips squeezed tightly together, I was squinting and holding my breath for as long as I could at a time, in an attempt to keep the cold out. I was being taken back by my stepfather to a foster home I had just run away from. I missed my mother and my baby brother Mehdi already.

I loved Baba. He was my mother's husband and the closest thing to a father figure I ever came to know. My mother called him Mansoor Aqa—Mr. Mansoor—but I preferred calling him Baba, Farsi for daddy. He was the first to introduce me to all the things

1

that were wonderful in life back when I was little: cinema, Pepsi-Cola, and ice cream. In his early twenties, Baba was a relatively tall and handsome man with broad shoulders and a John Wayne attitude. Men with dishonorable intentions wouldn't dare follow my mother home from the market anymore, or frighten her at odd hours of the night by serenading her from the alley next to our home—not after Baba came into our lives. He was fearless and strong and could take on more than one man without ruffling his perfect hair. I had seen him in action a few times. He spoke very softly but, if a situation arose, he was lethal with his fists. A tailor by trade, he had the appearance of the movie stars of the 1950s black-and-white films that he used to take me to see on Fridays.

Before Baba, the only men I knew were my mother's brothers and father, who were from the countryside and dressed and spoke a certain way. They wore suits made from inexpensive fabrics that, after a few weeks of wear, began to sag and bulge around the elbows and the knees. The sleeves of their jackets never seemed to reach their wrists, and after a few washes the hems of their pants would no longer hang past their ankles. They did not believe in ironing clothes, thinking it would reduce the life of the fabric. Baba, on the other hand, always wore new clothes made from European fabric, perfectly pressed at all times. My mother used to say, "You can slice a melon with the creases on Mansoor Aqa's trousers." Besides my birth father, he was the only man I personally knew who wore a necktie and starched white shirts. Baba had a thin, perfectly trimmed mustache that was an indispensable part of his upper lip. His face was neatly shaved and splashed with European aftershaves, his hair greased and combed backward and to the side at all times.

I oftentimes overheard the other women in the house muttering while doing their laundry or washing dishes by the fountain; why, with so many eligible virgin girls in the world, would a handsome young bachelor like Mansoor Aqa travel from Orumiyeh clear across the country to Mashhad and marry a divorced woman with a child? My mother fervently believed that Baba showing up in her life was the direct result of her prayers being answered by Imam Reza. As for myself, I was just grateful for Baba being in our life—the "hows" and "whys" of him choosing my mother didn't matter to me at all. He altered our uncertain and droning existence from the very first day that he set foot in our lives, introducing us to color when gray was all that my mother and I were accustomed to. He possessed all the attributes that a six-year-old boy like me wished for in a father; he was strong, fun, and loving.

On both sides of Naderi Avenue, under the dark ultramarine sky of early evening, strings of hanging lights and buzzing mantel lanterns lit up the sidewalks. Beneath them merchants laid out a masterful display of seasonal fruits and sweet-smelling baked and deep-fried goods. Pyramids of shimmering sweet lemons, oranges, persimmons, pomegranates, and large soft dates colored the sidewalks, enticing the taste buds of hungry pedestrians rushing home. The dense cold air, saturated with the delicious aromas of sugar, rosewater, and cardamom escaping trays of various native sweets, filled my lungs. Just seeing the mounds of syrupy fritters and baklavas on display at the storefronts and on top of wooden pushcarts hurt my jaws. I could swear all these treats were winking at me invitingly as Baba pedaled past them. I remember when he first married my mother, on Thursday evenings Baba always came home with a box or a bag of some treat under his arm—be it pastries, sweets, or fresh fruits.

I'd been very hungry earlier that day. My mother was so busy worrying how Baba was going to react when he came home and found me there that she couldn't think of anything else, much less feeding me. A few hours before it was time for Baba to return from work, she became uneasy, walking around the little room, murmuring to herself, and praying. The last time I ran away from a foster home, Baba was not at all pleased. The frowning faces of my mother and Baba and the deafening silence around the next morning's breakfast *sofreh*—a tablecloth-like sheet of plastic or fabric spread on the floor and used to serve food on—told me that they'd had another fight over me while I was asleep. Despite Baba's insistence that my mother be firm with my birth father by sending me back to the foster home, my mother was reluctant. She just wanted her son to be with her and didn't care much about the principle of things or teaching her ex-husband any lessons.

My heart fell when I heard the distinct sound of Baba's footsteps coming from the adjacent narrow foyer. His face turned crimson when he walked in through the door and found me in his

3

home again. He looked disappointed, mostly at my mother for her indecisiveness. My mother's face shrunk into a look of anguish as she softly said hello to Baba.

After a brief pause and contemplation—without taking his shoes off and sitting down, as he often did when he returned home from work—he threw his hands into the air and said in his sweet Turkish-Tehranian accent, "I can't do it, Soory *joon* (dear Soory). I am only a tailor, working like a donkey just to pay the rent for this little matchbox we live in—and to fill my wife and children's bellies." He refused to touch the cup of hot tea my mother had placed for him on a small chrome tray on the rug.

"You don't seem to get it, Soory. Alireza's father should be taking care of Alireza. He has the means; I don't. Every time this boy runs away and comes here and you don't object, you are indirectly telling your ex-husband that it is all right for him to be an irresponsible bastard."

My mother stood like a sad little orphan, looking down at the patterns of the shabby red Persian rug covering the floor, and softly said, "He is just a child. God would not be pleased with me if I tell my own son he cannot come here. What can I do, Mansoor Aqa?"

"I have said a thousand times and I say it again, take him to his father's home and leave him at his doorstep. The pimp would have no choice then but to take care of his own son. As God is my witness, Soory, I love Alireza like my own son, but it burns my ass knowing that man collects a good and easy salary from the military on the first of every month while I have to feed his flesh and blood. I, a perfect stranger from Orumiyeh who six days a week sits behind a sewing machine and earns his every *rial* needle by needle with his fingers. Do you think God is pleased with that?"

I was not the subject of a new discussion that evening. The two of them had been down this path many times before. In fact, my mother had been on the receiving end of similar remarks and advice from others besides Baba for a long time now, often right in front of me.

"Take Alireza to his father," they would say to her. "Why should you sacrifice your marriage and youth for his kid while he's enjoying life in the arms of his new wife?"

4

Standing submissively with her back against the damp wall of their small and dimly-lit room, her hands in front of her one over the other, my mother didn't utter another word. Her head was hung downward, her lips puckered, and her eyebrows pulled together—a silent display of protest as well as a gesture of reluctant surrender—a gesture I knew all too well by now. Baba was the man and this was his home. That was how she saw it and that was how she had been taught by her parents to see it. She was a woman—and women had no voice where she came from. She was lucky to have found a young and handsome bachelor wanting to marry her, willing to take her and her son into his home, she always told me. This man who could have chosen a virgin with dowries that could fill two large rooms had chosen her instead, and for that she could not be ungrateful.

Through the entire discussion, I was curled up in the corner of the room, sitting on the floor next to the crib of my baby half brother Mehdi and hugging my knees. I gazed in envy at Mehdi's chubby, rosy cheeks as he peacefully slept while my fate was once again being debated. Purposely, I tried to make myself appear less significant, hoping that would sway Baba's heart and he would change his mind about taking me back to the foster home. But I knew it was too late for that. I wasn't welcome here anymore. In fact, I knew that, as long as my birth father was alive, I was not welcome anywhere. For someone in my situation, having a father alive and well was a big liability.

My father's professional and subsequent financial success after divorcing my mother was only the icing on the bitter cake of animosity that everyone on my mother's side had baked for him. Divorcing my mother was the real catalyst of their anger, however, and in many ways the main source of my misfortune. In my parents' village, everyone knew everyone else. It seemed that half of the people of the village were related to my mother and the other half to my father—in one form or another. And those who were not related to either side had ties to my father's new wife, who was also from the same village.

Assad Banafsheh—Assad, son of Banafsheh—had divorced the daughter of Qolumali Qassob—Qolumali, the butcher. In a society where the motto for the bride was "Go to your husband's home in a white dress and leave only in a white shroud," divorce

5

was the kiss of death for a woman, as it inevitably brought shame upon her family. A divorced young woman was often viewed as a rejected product and a liability to her parents and for that, my father was not forgiven. Emotions ran high, especially on my mother's side, where my father was deeply despised. This was bad news for me. I looked like my father, grinned like my father, and was, without question, my father's son—as I was reminded regularly by my mother's relatives. And to my father and his side of the family, I was the son of Soory, a name that was not uttered kindly by my father and his mother in particular. My presence seemed to peel at the scabs of the wounds caused by the divorce, on both sides.

I wanted to promise Baba that night to eat very little from now on, to be a good boy and listen to my mother. I wanted to promise not to pee in my bed anymore. But it was too late for that. His mind had been made up for over a year now. Once again it was time for me to leave. Like a puppy that kept running away from the animal shelter and back to the only master it knew, I too kept coming back here to the only home I knew.

Baba signaled with his head that it was time to go as he walked firmly toward the door. In the dark and narrow foyer I put on my little black rubber shoes that my aunt Sarvar had gotten me from the gypsies in exchange for a small sack of dried mulberries and two rials. Feeling homesick and anxious already, I couldn't bear the pain of separating from my mother again. I wanted to cry and beg her to let me stay, but didn't. That would only have salted the wounds of her heart even more, and I could not stand seeing my mother suffer. A droopy goodbye look was all that I could muster for her as I walked out the door and followed Baba into the dark alley. Like my grandfather's sheep when he took one of their lambs away for slaughter, my mother stood motionless outside the doorway and watched as Baba and I disappeared around the corner on his bicycle. Her eyes spoke of the same helplessness I used to see in the eyes of those sheep.

On my signal Baba turned into a narrow side street and then into an old alleyway where my latest foster family, chosen by my birth father, lived. Fearing potholes and the gutter that ran in the middle of the dark alley, Baba stopped the bicycle and we walked the rest of the way, which wasn't but a few hundred meters.

6

"Are you sure you know where they live?" Baba asked. I nodded yes. Reluctantly, I took him to the house. Walking the bicycle up to the door, he grabbed the door knocker and gave it a few slams. Minutes later the sound of approaching footsteps could be heard from the other side of the heavy wooden door. The door's left panel opened, its old hinges squealing under its weight. A man I knew all too well appeared in his pajama pants, with a military blanket folded in a triangle over his shoulders to keep him warm.

"*Salam* (Hello)," he said to Baba with a questioning look. Before Baba could introduce himself, the man noticed me half hidden in the dark, against the brick wall of his house, away from the door and Baba. I was staring at the man like a startled, featherless baby sparrow that had fallen out of its nest and was about to be touched by a human.

"It's you!" he said somewhat unhappily, yet sounding relieved at the same time. "Where have you been, boy? My sons have looked for you everywhere!" Then he turned his attention back to Baba and asked, "And who are you, mister?"

"Salam, aqa." I am his mother's husband," Baba replied as he extended his hand. "I understand his father has placed him in your care, so I brought him back."

"Yes." The man nodded unhappily as he shook Baba's hand. "He ran away from work early this morning and we were worried what to tell his father if he never came back. It is not right, *aqa*. His father is a military man and could cause trouble for us if we lose his kid, you know."

"I am sorry, it will not happen again. He's only a child and doesn't understand any better. Please forgive him," Baba assured the man, while giving me a punishing look. "He has promised he will stay with you and be a good boy."

"I hope so. Okay then. Thank you, mister, and thank God he is found. Come on, kid, let's go inside, it's freezing out here," the man said as he shook Baba's hand. Baba and I exchanged a brief glance as he lifted his bicycle and turned it around. Then he disappeared into the shadows of the night. The man immediately closed and latched the door behind us and began hurrying across the tiled courtyard.

7

I followed, longing hopelessly for my mother, Baba, and Mehdi.

Chapter Two

I was born in the spring of 1956, in the city of Tehran, to a young couple from a northeastern Iranian village in Khorasan Province. My father was an army enlisted man, stationed in Tehran at the time. By my second birthday he was transferred to the city of Mashhad, just south of their old village. Mashhad, with a population of a few hundred thousand at the time, was the capital of Khorasan Province and also the home to the shrine of Imam Reza, the eighth of the twelve imams of Shi'a Islam. Literally translated, the word *Mashhad* means "a place of martyrdom." Soon after their move, my father fell in love with a girl from his old village, divorced my mother, and married the young woman. At that point I was almost three and my little sister Shahnaz was a few months old.

I heard my mother's saga piece by piece as I was growing up, some of it from her own lips and some from friends and relatives. Shortly after the divorce my grandfather rented a small room in a large, centuries-old house near Imam Reza's shrine where we would temporarily live, pending my father's decision as to what to do about my sister and me. According to my mother, her parents offered to have her move back home but she declined, too ashamed to go back and subjugate herself to the gossip and the inquisitive stares of the villagers. A young and beautiful woman returning home, especially after being divorced by her husband, was sure to spark endless speculation in her small village.

My grandfather was able to pay our rent for only a couple of months at most. He was an old farmer with very few resources, with a wife and four of his own children still living at home to take care of. Life in the village was not easy and required the participation of everyone in the family in order to make ends meet. For food, my grandparents and my young aunts and uncles relied on a small patch of farmland, a few apricot, mulberry, and walnut trees, and a handful of sheep. For everything else, they bartered their goods and worked to make money. My grandfather served as the village's part-time butcher, and my grandmother made and sold soap bars and *rooshoors,* amongst other things. Rooshoors were round pellets the size of a small walnut, made from sheep's brain. These somewhat oily pellets were very popular in Iran, especially amongst women, for use in the shower to moisturize and prepare the skin for a better scrub. My grandmother, according to many women, made the best rooshoors in her village. She even had some customers in Mashhad.

My grandmother, whom we affectionately called *Modar Joon* (dear Mother) was the real pillar of the family. She was a tough, no-nonsense lady and a savvy homemaker who did not believe in such a thing as a free ride for anyone, including children. If you could walk, you could work, she believed, and so three of her four children who were still living at home worked at weaving rugs at a shop in the upper village. They worked there six days a week except during harvest time. Every Thursday evening they brought their pay home and handed it over to Modar Joon. From their earnings she gave them each a few *shahis*—a shahi was one twentieth of one rial—to spend at the village general store, provided she was in a good mood and they begged her long enough.

I remember the massive mulberry tree that stood just outside of my grandparents' front door and shaded the entire house, in addition to providing the family with an ample amount of berries every year. My grandmother used some of the mulberries to make molasses, and the rest she sun-dried along with the apricots harvested from their little orchard on the outskirts of the village, sacking the fruit for use during the long winter. The dried fruits and walnuts were a great source of energy and a favorite snack and treat for her children and visiting grandchildren.

My father was the main reason for my mother's decision to stay in the city. She was in love with him, and despite the divorce she could not accept the fact that he was no longer her husband. Somewhere deep in her heart, she believed it was only a matter of time before my father came to his senses, and she wanted to be near when that happened. She only needed to wait and be patient until the novelty of my father's new bride wore out. Sooner or later he was sure to miss his children and first wife, a young woman one hundred times more beautiful than his new wife, my mother thought. But that day never came, and the pressure of being responsible for two small children and having no income began to squeeze my mother into a tight corner. For a little while she was barely able to make ends meet by selling, piece by piece, the few items of gold jewelry she had managed to hide from my father at the time of their divorce. But once her last gold bracelet was gone, she began to panic and sought the guidance of her elderly father as to what to do. My grandfather's advice was that her only solution was to find my father and demand child support from him.

I was too little at the time to remember those days in their entirety, but over the years, my mother's cries of injustice and tales of suffering filled in the blanks for me. Some years later, when I was five or six, she told me one particularly harrowing story that will always live in my memory. Her own words tell it best:

"Your father took everything away from me at the time of divorce. He put me out on the street with you and your little sister in my arms and the clothes that I was wearing and nothing else. I had managed to hide away a couple pieces of gold jewelry for a rainy day, and after the divorce, I was able to sell them and use the money to take care of you and your little sister Shahnaz. Our situation became grimmer with every passing day. I could not get a job with two small children to take care of and no one to leave them with. All my relatives lived back in the village at the time, and I was all by myself in the city. Under the circumstances, your father held the key to our salvation, but he refused to talk to me. He did not respond to numerous messages and pleas for help that I left for him with friends and relatives. Finally, I was left with no other alternative but to muster the courage that I needed to go and confront your father." This was a brave step for a frail-hearted and unassertive woman like my mother. "I was well acquainted with your father's temperament and knew how brutal he was with his fists from past experiences, but I was desperate and had no other choice. My father, aunt, and uncle all advised me to go to him and give him an ultimatum; either pay child support or take the

11

children. I thought he and his new wife would not be interested in wanting to raise two small children and would probably agree to pay child support instead. How stupid I was."

"One late afternoon, I took my last two *toomans* that I had stashed away for emergencies, grabbed you and your sister, got in a taxi, and went to see your father. He and his new wife were staying with his brother Mohammad at that time. I wish God would have paralyzed my legs that day, my dear Alireza," she sighed with this thought, and then paused for a long while, dazed, with her eyes fixated on a distant point—a point perhaps deep within her soul—before continuing with her story.

"We got there right around suppertime. Fatimah, your uncle Mohammad's wife—what a wonderful and kind woman she was—opened the door and invited us inside. I went in and waited by the door in the foyer with Shahnaz in my arms and you standing by my side. If Fatimah hadn't answered the door, I would not have dared to go inside. Your uncle Mohammad came out and greeted me while taking you in his arms and kissing you. Fatimah, with a visage that clearly indicated she was feeling sorry for us but was helpless to do anything, stood against the wall and watched. Finally, your father came out, and when your eyes fell on him, your face opened up with a big smile—like a flower that has seen the sun. My heart dropped in fear but I did my best to appear strong. He asked Fatimah to take you and Shahnaz inside while he and I went outside to talk, without even acknowledging you or answering my hello. I was hesitant to hand over my daughter, and it became obvious that she didn't want to leave my arms either; crying, turning, and twisting her little body in protest as she lay wrapped in her swaddling. Fatimah gave me a look of assurance that I shouldn't worry and, with that, I handed my daughter to her, kissed you and told you that I'd be right back.

"Outside, standing by the steps, I talked, explaining our situation to your father, telling him how I was having difficulty feeding and clothing the two of you. I told him about needing rent money since my father could not afford to pay indefinitely. His only response was that he didn't have any money to give me. Out of desperation I began crying and pitifully begging him for help, swearing him to God and Imam Reza to have a heart and do the right thing for his children. He was obligated in the eyes of God to

12

support his children, I told him. When none of my pleas seemed to sway his mind, I gave him the ultimatum that if he was not willing to give financial support for his children, then he needed to come and take them, though of course I didn't mean it.

"With a sour face and a harsh voice that he was trying to keep low, he grabbed my arm and said, 'Let's go somewhere else and talk.' I needed to get my children first, I told him. 'They will be all right inside,' he said. Once we reached the main road, without saying a word to me, he waved down a taxicab and told the driver to take us to Quchan Gate Square. He sat in the front with the driver as I sat in the back. If I wished to resolve the issues I had no choice but to go along.

"As you know, I am not the most assertive person in the world. In fact, when it comes to many things, especially men, I am very submissive. In general I see most men as predators and I am afraid of them. If I wasn't desperate, and if it wasn't for my father and relatives convincing me to go and talk to him, I wouldn't have been riding with your father in that taxi that evening. Feeling like a kid who was in trouble and wasn't sure what was going to happen to her, I was very anxious. The sound of my heart pounding under my *chador* was so loud that I thought for sure the driver could hear it. Did you know that your father never laid a hand on me until he met that woman and decided to divorce me for her? It all started when I refused to go along with his demand for divorce. But that night I was not his wife anymore and he had no reason or right to touch me, I thought, trying to reassure myself.

"By the time we arrived at Quchan Gate Square, it was completely dark outside. Your father paid the driver, got out, and began walking in a hurry northbound on Naderi Avenue. I followed. In those days the square was pretty much the edge of the city. Past the square, a few stores and residential homes were scattered here and there and not much of anything else. The foul smell of Qara-Khan Canal was overwhelming. The canal entered the city from the north and ran down the center of Naderi Avenue, splitting it into two halves. Before entering the city, it was an irregular snake-infested waterway with rough banks and various depths. The clear water turned murky and foul once it made its way through the city.

"I paced behind your father, while holding onto my chador, and didn't dare ask where he was taking me.

"Looking at him walking in front of me, knowing that he was no longer my husband, crushed my heart. Despite everything that he had done to me, he was the father of my children and I loved him still. Every page of my short history as an adult, was filled with his name. After leaving my father's home, he was the only man I came to know. We had three children together, and because of that I felt some sort of entitlement to him and his life—so much so that I couldn't easily let go. I guess more than anything, it was the feeling of being discarded and replaced that broke my heart the most. The awful feeling of rejection, being told that I was not wanted, and the thought of him going to sleep at night in the arms of another woman was eating me from within. I'll never forget how much I cried on the night of his wedding. With Shahnaz in my arms and you by my side, I stood behind some trees at a distance and watched the bride and the groom at the outdoor wedding and wept.

"On this fateful night after I'd given my ultimatum, your father was walking fast, complaining and criticizing my family and me about anything he could think of. He became more belligerent and loud with every step we took farther away from the city limits. Young and gullible, I honestly thought we were going to someone's home to sit and talk things over. Maybe I was wishing for him to somehow miraculously change and suddenly turn around and say, 'My dear, I am very sorry for everything. I have made a big mistake—please forgive me! Let's just go back get the children and go home!'

"Instead, he accused me of trying to embarrass him by showing up at his brother's home with the children in my arms. He said that I was overdramatizing things because I was jealous of his new wife. Finally, he began fuming and threatening me, promising to do this and that to me and my family if I didn't leave him alone.

"'I will kill both children before I give you one shahi,' he said, clutching his teeth together furiously and waving his fist in my face.

"He was deafened by anger. And I, feeling hopeless and all alone in the world, sobbed and reluctantly followed him, stopping only when he would stop and turn around to bark at me some more. I didn't have the nerve to ask where we were going, fearing

14

that would stoke his anger even more and ruin my only chance of securing any child support. We'd passed the last streetlight a while ago. The paved sidewalk had ended and was replaced by a hardened dirt path along the canal. It was difficult to see the canal clearly in the dark, but I could smell it on my left. I began to get a bad feeling in my stomach. Something was telling me he had not brought me there to talk about the children. I was contemplating turning around and running back toward the city, but didn't. I was hoping he would eventually calm down and give me ten or twenty toomans. That would have been enough to pay my rent and feed you two for a month. He wasn't an easy person to get a hold of, you see, and I didn't have the means to be chasing him every day, so reluctantly I kept on following him.

"Finally he reached a boiling point, and without any warning he turned around and began punching and kicking me mercilessly. Mothers in my village had always taught their daughters never to tell their husbands not to hit them, because flogging a wife was within the husband's rights. They were told to find ways to convince their husbands to hit them less severely. But he was not my husband anymore and did not have the right to hit me. I began screaming, but there wasn't a soul around to come to my aid. The more I screamed the harder he punched until I was knocked down to the ground. He twisted my long hair around his fist and dragged me toward the canal. I gave up trying to hold on to my chador dragging behind me, got myself up somehow, and followed him before the weight of my body could rip my hair and skin from my skull. With every step he twisted my hair tighter around his hand, pulling me closer as I held tightly to his wrist. Suddenly a cold and eerie feeling came over me—I felt as if I was about to die. He pulled me to the edge of the canal with my hair still wrapped around his hand and forced me to look down into the deep darkness in front of me. He knew how terrified I was of the dark and of heights. I couldn't see the bottom but the acrid odor stung my eyes.

"'Are you going to come around my family and embarrass me again?' he asked angrily.

"'No, sir,' I sobbed.

"'Are you going to go around my base and talk to my colleagues about child support again?'

15

"I shook my head no.

"'I didn't think so,' he said as he released my hair and kicked me in the stomach, sending me flying into the canal. I screamed as I fell.

"Worse than the fall was not being able to see what I was falling into. I was petrified and thought my heart was going to stop for sure. Ever since I was little I was afraid of the dark. When I lived at my parents' home, I would not go to the outhouse alone at night and my sister, Sarvar, used to tease me about that. That was not all. I could not swim either. If the fall didn't kill me, I was sure the water was going to. The word 'swimming' did not exist for women where I grew up. For girls in our village, our only experience with open water like rivers and creeks was limited to doing laundry, washing dishes, rugs, and sheep. And that I did while fully covered with my chador wrapped around me and secured around my neck. The girls and open water were forbidden to mix in our village. During the hot days of summer, whenever we passed the river and saw the boys, including our own brothers, jumping and splashing in and out of the cool, clear water, I oftentimes wondered what that must have felt like—how it felt to have the silky, cool, wet substance wrapped around one's bare skin. 'It is a travesty that God created rivers for the swimming privilege of men and sheep only,' my sister Sarvar used to shake her head and say sarcastically. She loved the water so much that my mother joked about her being a fish in another life. In the summers after my father and brothers left for work, she would take off all of her clothes and jump into a little fountain we had in the corner of our courtyard. I used to worry and warn her that she was going to hell if a man ever walked in and saw her like that. She'd just laugh and splash around with joy. Sarvar, while younger than me, was the bravest of all of my siblings and closest to me.

"'*Ya Zamene Ahoo* (O Guarantor of the Deer), I too have small children to return to,' I prayed to Imam Reza as I fell. Legend has it that while Imam Reza was traveling through a forest, he saw a hunter about to kill a captured deer. He noticed the deer pleading with the hunter to be allowed to return to her fawn and feed it one last time, promising to return promptly, and the hunter refused. Imam Reza stepped in and personally guaranteed the deer's return, and the hunter set the deer free.

16

"You may not believe this, my son, but when I realized your father was going to push me into the canal, I was afraid I was going to die, but it wasn't the dying that I was afraid of. It was the sudden awareness that my children were going to be left motherless that ripped through my heart. All I could see at that moment were my children's faces. After the humiliating divorce, you two were the only reason I had for living. The thought of me dying and my children falling into the hands of a stepmother was unbearable.

"Before I could finish my prayer, I plunged into the water. Panicking, I swung my arms and legs in every direction. Miraculously, I felt the slimy bottom of the canal under my feet while my head remained above the water. 'Thank you, God,' I whispered.

"The thick and sticky mud swallowed my shoes as I struggled to drag my body out of the water. Feeling my way in the dark, I got out of the water and quietly crawled over against the tall bank of the canal, where I sat still, covering my mouth. I could see your father up on the edge of the cliff still. He paced back and forth for a few moments, scanning the bottom of the canal, and then disappeared into the darkness. The faint moonlight bouncing off a patch of cloud was not enough to reveal the bottom of the canal for him to see what became of me after I fell. He probably thought I was dead or was about to die, and tomorrow they would find my body, the case would be closed, and he would never have to deal with me again.

"Once I felt comfortable that your father was no longer around, I pulled myself out of the canal and began limping toward the road and the city. Suddenly a cold fear swept through me; what if his plan was to erase his past with me by killing me *and* my children? What if he was on his way to kill them right now? Disorientation and fear of being alone at night and in the middle of nowhere soon gave way to panic, and I began running toward the distant streetlights. As I was running, I was slapping my face, pulling my hair, and sobbing and condemning myself for leaving my children in the first place. I was begging God to look after my children for me.

"With my hair all out of place, my dress and pants wet, muddy, and ripped in several places, and without any shoes and chador, I looked like an insane asylum escapee. I was certain that I was going

17

to go to hell for being so exposed, but I hoped God could understand my circumstance and make an exception this one time. The few men that I crossed paths with kept their distance after seeing my condition.

"Frantically, I looked around for a taxi as I made my way back to Quchan Gate Square. My plan was to get home, change, and then go and pick you and your little sister up from your uncle's. During the day, Quchan Gate Square was packed with horse-drawn carriages, and sometimes even one or two black-and-white taxicabs waiting around to pick up passengers arriving on buses from out of town. But at night the place was deserted. For the most part, the entire city went to sleep shortly after dark.

"I touched the corner of my headscarf that was dangling from my neck, searching for the money I had wrapped and tied there earlier that evening, and to my surprise, it was still there. A taxicab finally appeared on the road, and the driver hesitantly agreed to take me home. I was terrified of being alone in an automobile with a strange man and at that hour of the night. Every time the taxicab passed under a streetlight, I could see the driver's eyes studying me in the rearview mirror.

"'Would you like me to take you to a hospital or the police station instead, lady?' the driver asked, breaking the silence.

"I shook my head no, muzzling the sound of my weeping. He was probably thinking that I had been raped. Going to the police would not have helped me—it would only have infuriated your father more. What I needed was a stronger family, one that could stand up to your father on my behalf. Unfortunately my father was old and frail, and my brothers were all too young, except for one, and he was married to your father's only sister and couldn't and wouldn't help me.

"To my delight, like a miracle, I found your grandfather, may God rest his soul, sitting and waiting for me in our little room as I opened the door. It was as if God had sent my father to the city to solace me at my loneliest moments that night. With my head down I muttered, '*Salam, aqa joon* (Hello, dear father).'

"Before I could say another word he was up on his feet, anxiously asking what had happened and where the children were. He wrapped his arms around my shoulders and kissed and rubbed my head comfortingly as I let all the tears lumped up in my throat explode on his shoulder. I sobbed and told him everything.

"Ironically, despite being a part-time butcher, my father had a dovish personality. Since *hammoms* (public bathhouses) were not open that late, your grandfather, God rests his soul, quickly heated some water, had me sit in my underclothes inside a laundry pan in the middle of the room, and began to wash me with a sponge. He poured the warm water slowly over my head, one bowl at a time, and gently washed away the blood and slime from my hair and face.

"I was embarrassed to be washed by my father. That was the first time he had ever seen me partially dressed. That was also the first time he had ever washed me. I can say with certainty that it was probably the first time any father from our village, under any circumstances, had ever washed his own daughter. But apprehension quickly gave way to a warm sense of belonging and being loved. There weren't many intimate moments between the fathers and daughters in my village, especially in a family as large as ours. I closed my eyes for a moment and imagined myself as a little girl back in my father's home in our village. I imagined sitting in a large gleaming crystal bowl under the warm sun and my father was pouring water over me from a golden pitcher while my sister Sarvar danced in a circle around us. The pitcher never seemed to run out of its glittering water.

"My father went outside to smoke his pipe and to give me privacy to get dressed. Soon I was ready to go get you and Shahnaz and bring you home, but my father advised against it. He thought it was late and best to let you stay at your uncle's for the night, and promised to accompany me to get you two first thing in the morning. He tried to convince me that I needed to rest and assured me that nothing was going to happen to my children overnight. That after all, the man was your father and no father would harm his own children, no matter how angry or callous. With that, my father put some mercurochrome on my cuts and advised me to go to sleep. We could not find a taxi that late in the night anyway, he reminded me.

"I spread my mattress on the floor for your grandfather to sleep on, and I slept on your little mattress next to him. After the divorce I had very little of anything to accommodate my father any better that night; the few things that I had were all courtesy of my parents.

"As soon as I closed my eyes, your scent, coming from your little pillow, rushed into my head and I began to have a panic attack. It suddenly hit me that my children were not there next to me and, at that thought, I covered my face with your pillow and wept. Remembering your father, the canal and the events of earlier that evening, and worrying about you and your sister kept me awake and fueled my anxiety and tears. Having finally lost control and fearing that I was going to wake my father, I quickly left the room and continued crying on the steps in the courtyard. I felt like I was being buried alive and needed to scream and escape for air, but that would have awoken the landlord and the other tenants living in the house. Unable to take it anymore, I ran outside into the alley and entered an old abandoned building next door and let loose. I struck my head and face in self-condemnation as I wept. Crying your names, I scratched the surface of the walls until my nails were bleeding and numbed. After a little while my father's silhouette appeared in the doorway. He walked over, hugged me, and begged me to stop and return home. 'I am a mother and it hurts me to be without my children,' I sobbed. 'I miss them very much and worry I may never see them again, aqa joon,' I cried.

"With a sad voice he said, 'I understand, *dokhtaram* (my daughter). I am a parent too. How do you think I feel seeing my child in this situation and suffering like this?'

"He wrapped his arm around my shoulder and took me out of the abandoned and empty house.

"The next morning I had the tea brewing before my father and I started our morning prayers. That morning I prayed fervently, adding my own thoughts and words; sort of a down payment for getting my children safely back. I missed having you sitting across from me and playing with my praying tablet as I prayed.

"Shortly after sunrise, my father and I were outside in a taxicab going to your uncle's home on the other side of town to pick you and your sister up. Your father would have been gone to work by that time—to avoid any confrontation, your grandfather thought it was best if your father wasn't around when we arrived. Your uncle's wife Fatima answered the door and let us inside. She offered us hot tea as she inspected my cuts and bruises with sympathetic eyes. I declined the tea and immediately asked for you and Shahnaz. She went into another room and came back holding your hand. I leaped and picked you up into my arms, squeezing you as if I hadn't seen you for a thousand years, sinking my face into the depth of your neck and filling my lungs with your sweet baby scent. You too were elated to see me, and when I asked you where your sister was you said, 'Shahnaz gone bye-bye, *Momon* (Mommy).' My heart suddenly fell.

"I looked at Fatimah and asked—with a visage that begged her to say it wasn't true—where my daughter was. I prayed you were mistaken and she was still asleep. My breasts were filled with fresh milk, a reminder that I hadn't fed my baby since yesterday. The whole world seemed to be coming down upon me when Fatimah dropped her head down and didn't say anything. I handed you to your grandfather and ran to the adjacent room she had brought you from, looking for your sister, but she wasn't there; neither was the bag containing her clean diaper cloths and backup bottle.

"'Where is my daughter?' I cried, as I ran from room to room looking for her. There was no trace of Shahnaz anywhere. I returned to Fatimah, held her hands, looked her in the eye, and begged her to tell me where my daughter was.

"'I don't know, Soory joon. Early this morning Habiballah came over and together with Assad wrapped the baby in a blanket and took her away. I am sure she is going to be all right, Soory joon, don't worry.'"

My father had two brothers. The nicest one was Mohammad, Fatimah's husband, and Habiballah was the other one. My mother's story continued.

"We waited until late in the afternoon for your father to return, but he never did. My father had to catch the afternoon bus to the village, so we finally had to leave. 'The man is her father, *Dokhtaram*, he's not going to do anything to his own daughter,' my father reassured me.

"Fearing your father might take you away as well, the next morning I took you over to my brother Zabih, who had recently moved to Mashhad, and left you with him before going back for Shahnaz. But there was no sign of her, not that day, not any other day after that. She vanished without a trace. I did not see your father again for six or seven months after that. You would not believe how many pairs of shoes I went through looking for my daughter. Seven days a week, from dawn to dusk, I sat in front of the army base where your father was stationed, or in front of his brothers' home, and waited to try to get ahold of him.

"No one from your father's side would ever talk about Shahnaz after her disappearance—it was as if she had never been born. My breasts bursting with milk were a constant reminder of my daughter's absence. It was killing me not knowing what happened to my baby. A thousand unpleasant thoughts would cross my mind with every passing day that I didn't have her in my arms. What if he had abandoned her in the mountains and the wolves had gotten to her? What if he had sold her to the gypsies? What if he buried her alive somewhere? The 'what ifs,' like termites, were eating away at my sanity for the longest time, my son."

Sadly, my mother never had a picture of my little sister in her possession. And my father denied her existence when I confronted him about her some years later. I remember when I was almost a teenager, my cousins and I were visiting a relative in my mother's village one night. While I was eating dinner my eyes caught a small black-and-white picture sitting, unframed, in a niche. I got up, grabbed the picture, and looked at it for a long time. There we all were, my mother and father sitting next to each other, with me on my father's lap and Shahnaz on my mother's. When the relative asked me if I knew who those people in the picture were, without turning around and revealing my tear-soaked eyes, I nodded "yes."

I wished I could keep the photograph but, given my circumstances at that time, perhaps it was best for it to stay where it belonged, in the past.

Chapter Three

My mother and father were born and raised in a small, lush oasis-like village named Golmakan in the foothills of the Hezarmasjed Mountains near the city of Mashhad. Their village was truly the land of milk and honey. It was blessed with an abundance of fruit and nut orchards, natural springs gushing everywhere out of the ground like liquid crystal, and many sparkling streams originating from the mountaintop. The sky there was a brilliant blue during the day, a velvety black meadow of twinkling stars at night. More than anything else, however, it was the inhabitants of this beautiful village that made the place special. Like most country folks, they wcrc hardworking, hospitable, and kind, especially to those visiting from the city. Simplicity and innocence was the essence of what made their lives beautiful and gave them grace.

The greater village was composed of three different sectors: the lower, the middle, and the upper village. Each was independent of the others, with its own squire, shepherd, general store, rug-weaving shop, and mosque. Each village also had its own center where a bus traveling between the city and the village picked up and dropped off passengers twice a day.

Following an ancient practice and for reasons of safety, the adobe homes were all built in clusters attached to each other. A network of irregular and unpaved alleyways provided access to the homes. All the farmland and the fruit orchards sat scattered outside of the village, surrounding the homes for many square kilometers.

The aroma of freshly baked breads was always present in the village air, along with the smell of dried bushes and timber burning in the in-ground clay ovens. Roosters crowing, donkeys braying, a dog barking here and there, the chirping of countless sparrows in the bushes and treetops, and the baaing of lambs all combined to create the symphony of daily life there. Each day's end brought the spectacular sight and sound of the herd of sheep and goats returning from the pasture with their udders bouncing from side to side, bursting with fresh milk. They baaed, announcing their arrival as they hurried home to their hungry babies, who baaed back impatiently within the adobe walls of every home. The animals' hooves rumbled and caused a cloud of dust, which rose into the air against the backdrop of a setting sun—truly a magnificent vista.

My mother was from the middle village, one of eight children in her family. She had an older half brother and half sister from her father's first marriage and five younger siblings. Like all the girls in her village, she was uneducated and was raised under strict Islamic rules. Her childhood training was focused entirely on helping her develop the skills necessary to become a good wife someday. When she was growing up, the idea of education for girls was still foreign in the countryside. The more homemaking skills a girl had by the time her parents decided she was mature enough to marry, the better were her chances of attracting a good suitor. Being blessed with natural beauty and having a wealthy and honorable family was always a plus. My mother was blessed with both beauty and an honorable family.

At the age of thirteen, my mother accompanied an acquaintance and her teenage daughter on a trip to Gorgon, a city near the Caspian Sea in northern Iran, to visit her older half brother. The lady's son and my mother's brother had recently enlisted in the army and were about to graduate from basic training. This was my mother's first long-distance journey out of her village. According to her, during the visit, the two young men each took a liking to the other's sister and decided to marry them right then and there. Banafsheh, the acquaintance, was delighted with the prospect of marrying both a son and a daughter at the same time, and she sent a telegram to my grandparents, asking them to join her in Gorgon. A week later, with everyone's blessings, my mother married Assad Banafsheh and my uncle took Fatimah, Banafsheh's daughter, to be his wife. At the time my mother was still a minor and so by law could not be given away in marriage. For the time being and to bypass the law, the adults decided to use a provision in Shiite Islam known as *siqeh*, which allows for a man to temporarily marry a woman for as little as twenty-four hours and up to ninety-nine years. Historically, the practice of siqeh was mostly used in Iran and by pilgrims in shrine cities like Mashhad. The argument was that the traveling pilgrims had sexual needs, and temporary marriage offered a legal way of satisfying them. The next day my grandparents returned to their village, leaving their thirteen-year-old daughter behind in the hands of her husband and God. Banafsheh, on the other hand, a widow and with no more children left at home to return to, stayed in Gorgon and took up permanent residence with her daughter and my uncle, her new son-in-law.

My mother gave birth to her first child in Gorgon and lost him to a mysterious illness two years later while she was visiting her village. I was born in Tehran, the Iranian capital, some two years after the death of my mother's first child. My sister who would later vanish was born in Mashhad just before my mother's divorce was final.

I cannot help but to think of my mother's marriage as one aching ride on a roller coaster. She left her village, married my father, and gave birth to three children in three different cities across the country, lost two of her children, one to death and one to destiny, and returned back to where she started from by the age of nineteen. Her only mementos from the journey were me and a broken heart. Quite an adventure for a simple country girl who had known nothing about the world outside of her village before the day Banafsheh took her along to Gorgon.

Chapter Four

In 1958, seven years after my mother first left her village, she was living an uncertain life, one day at a time, in a diminutive rented room in Mashhad with me, her only reminder of her brief marriage. Life gave her so much so quickly and then took it all away in the blink of an eye, as if it was all just a bad dream. If she was to speak of her saga to a stranger, she had nothing in her possession except for me to substantiate her story—not a photograph, a dress, or a piece of jewelry. The bitter and difficult journey that takes some unfortunate people a lifetime to make, my mother completed before her twentieth birthday. The poor woman was just too young to be cursed with carrying the wounds of so many losses: her marriage, her husband (the first man she ever loved), and two of her children. Many women of her age were still living in the comfort of their fathers' homes, attending school and dreaming of a fine future. My mother's future was sealed in her past. Now, she was a destitute single mother, too ashamed to return to her village and too poor to live in the city. Her life was filled with heartless and empty moments in a culture that was still struggling to define itself when it came to women, especially divorced ones. It was an uncertain and difficult time for her, to say the least.

At that time, divorce was an awful stigma for a woman to carry, regardless of her age. "There must have been something wrong with her for her husband to let her go," people often assumed. Regardless of the truth, a divorced woman was viewed as a product that had been returned to the store by an unsatisfied customer after he'd broken the seal and opened the box. Very few families, especially the reputable ones, would have wanted such women for their sons.

My mother was totally out of luck when it came to finding a good and desirable husband. Not only had she been divorced, she had also given birth to three children, and that was a lot of mileage for any woman, according to the standards du jour. The only things still in her favor were her exceptional beauty and physical attributes.

She was an attractive lady with a set of perfectly aligned pearl-like white teeth that sparkled with every opening of her mouth. Her kind and romantically sad half-smile melted the hardest of hearts. Without gazing and venturing deep into her bottomless warm brown eyes, it was difficult to tell what a terrible hand life had dealt her thus far. In her situation, however, her beauty was sometimes more of a liability than an asset.

Being an extremely religious person, my mother covered herself with both chador and headscarf, but she still managed to turn the men's heads wherever she went. On the days we went to the market, I remember unemployed young men following us around from one vegetable stand to another. They pretended to be shopping by amateurishly examining the produce while, from the corners of their eyes, they scanned my mother's every move nervously and with lust. Without my mother asking, married middle-aged merchants, delighted by her presence in their stores, often offered her discounts on merchandise, a gesture reserved only for those customers who are willing to haggle. They called me *amoo joon* (dear nephew) and offered me an apple, a lollipop or a pack of Roster brand chewing gum for free, to which my mother would always say no. They would nervously smile and with a stuttering voice tell her that there was nothing in their store worthy of her, whatever that meant. She was too afraid of God and going to hell and too simple to know how to take advantage of such circumstances.

Young Iranian men, much like their Italian counterparts, never missed an opportunity to follow and harass a beautiful lady when they saw one. Some women may have found the experience flattering, but not my shy mother. She viewed most men as predators and was afraid of them.

I will never forget one night when my mother and I were awakened by the sound of a drunken man roaring her name in the alleyway and proposing his love. She tiptoed out of our room and I followed behind her, to investigate the late-hour disturbance. From between the cracks of the old wooden door I saw a man leaning unsteadily against the light pole and looking directly at our door. He was wearing a black bowler hat tilted sideways, holding a bottle in his hand, and his jacket dangled over his shoulders. My mother was trembling like a dove that had seen an eagle. We silently waited in the darkened courtyard behind the door until the man finally went away. Inside our room, my mother, all shaken up, cried and asked God to find her a husband soon.

We lived in a small rented room in a large brick house near Quchan Gate Square that year. It was a typical Iranian brick house with a tiled courtyard and a rectangular fountain at its center. Living quarters faced each other on two sides of the courtyard, and tall brick walls stood on the other two sides. The eastern wall housed an old, heavy wooden entrance door that opened into a narrow alleyway, and the western wall separated the next house and was used to hang laundry from. Sheikh Aliakbar, the landlord, and his family occupied all the rooms on one side of the house and rented the other section to my mother and another small family.

Every house in Mashhad had a fountain as its center of gravity. Often a home's only source of water, the fountain played a pivotal social role—the equivalent of an office water cooler—especially if the home was shared by more than one family, which was usually the case in the middle- to lower-income neighborhoods. A couple of goldfish swimming around and an upside-down L-shaped brass faucet or a hand pump to supply fresh water for cooking and drinking were characteristic of every fountain. Recipes, news, and gossip were often exchanged and spread by women squatting around the fountain washing dishes, doing laundry, or preparing vegetables and herbs for cooking. In multifamily homes, some teenage boys and girls exchanged forbidden glances by the fountains, fell in love, and arranged for secret rendezvous while pretending to be washing their hands or getting a drink of water. By the fountains, some women spoke ill of an absent tenant or picked a fight with another, and some devoted men nullified their ablutions—Muslims' ritual washing of their hands, face, and feet before praying—by furtively lusting over the partially exposed neckline of a neighbor's wife as she filled her tea kettle. If only the fountains of Mashhad could talk!

There were plenty of women by the fountain in Sheik Aliakbar's home who could start talking about her if a suitor did not come along soon, my mother feared.

The house's only toilet stood in the farthest corner of the courtyard, away from the living quarters. I read somewhere many years later that in order to measure how cultured a society is, one should look at how they treat their toilets and their dogs. In the working-class segment of the society that I was growing up in, both toilets and dogs were considered impure, and were therefore always neglected. They were often boring and colorless little structures, with a Stone Age design that was unfriendly to small children and old folks with bad knees, built as far away from the rest of the house as possible—and for good reasons too. The lack of any ventilation system or flushing mechanism often made for an atrocious sight and scent, especially during the hot days of summer. For many children like me, wetting my mattress at night and dealing with the consequences the next morning was a much better alternative to crossing a dark courtyard in the middle of the night, dealing with all sorts of shadows and imaginary monsters, and going to the toilet. And to complicate the matter even more, a bulky and heavy copper ewer, designed for high-traffic toilets, was the only means available to transport water from the fountain to the toilet for sanitary use. I could not carry the ewer even when it was empty. For all the logistical difficulties that I just mentioned and for other reasons unknown to me, I was a chronic bed wetter and suffered greatly because of it.

A light blue, double-panel wooden French-style door facing the square courtyard served as both an entrance and a window to our little room. Inside, the walls had a slight hint of azure blue, left perhaps from the time when the home was first built. A naked light bulb dangled from the ceiling, casting a harsh and impudent glare over the room at night. A small plaster shelf extending outward from the wall held a Koran wrapped in a green velvet cover, my mother's praying pouch, and a small unframed handheld mirror. The shelf was the only decoration on the otherwise bare walls of our room. No picture of anyone or anything hung anywhere. At

29

the time, photography was still a technology limited to the professionals and the sophisticated. Some people at least had a color poster of Imam Ali, or Hussein, the king of Iran, or at least the word "God" written in Arabic posted on their walls, but not us; we couldn't afford any of them. If any of us were to die the next day, there would be no photographs, or anything else for that matter, to suggest that we ever existed.

The few basic things my mother now owned to make the room a home were given to her by her parents, including a tattered rug that covered the floor we sat and slept on. All of my mother's worldly possessions were kept in a little walk-in closet known as the trunk room. A modest sleeping set, two small pots and pans made of aluminum, a kettle and a teapot, a couple of inexpensive glass teacups, a portable Aladdin kerosene space heater (used mostly to cook on), a few utensils, and my mother's two or three sets of extra clothes—they were all kept in the trunk room. The china teapot had a large red rose printed on it and was mended in few places, I remember.

In the life of a tenant, the trunk room was far more than just a closet; it also served as a dressing room, a pantry, a place for children to play or be sent for a timeout, and a sanctuary for anyone seeking a private moment. Above all, it was a prop room. Everything that was needed to transform a room into a dining room, a bedroom, a living room, or a kitchen, for instance, was kept there in the trunk room. I took great pleasure in hiding and playing in ours.

Every morning my mother completed her ablution at the fountain, filled the kettle with water and placed it on the Aladdin to come to a boil while she prayed. By the time she was done fulfilling her obligation to her God, the water would be boiling. She made and drank her tea and waited behind the window for the last male occupant of the house to leave before she started her work, weaving wool. She would not take her first break until mid-morning when I woke up and she stopped to feed me breakfast. The porch under the wooden canopy in front of our room was where she set up her business and went to work with only a small tattered rug to sit on, a wooden spinning wheel, and a large sack of wool. Six days a week she toiled, and in the process found peace in the humming of her spinning wheel as she sang softly and turned

30

wool into yarn. Her songs seemed to intertwine with the fine wool and form into threads. I spent my days playing with other children in the courtyard, taking naps, or sitting next to my mother and watching her work. She hummed heart-wrenching, melancholy folk melodies that spoke of her broken heart, her missing daughter, an unfaithful world, and the beloved village she had left behind, all as she spun the wheel with one hand and gently released the fluffy fine wool with the other. My mother loved to sing and made up most of her lyrics as she went along. Whenever possible, she inserted my sister's name or *khodaya* (my Lord) in among the lyrics. I loved my mother's soothing and sad singing voice, especially at night when she softly murmured lullabies that contained my name as I drifted into sleep.

She was paid once a week. Every Thursday evening a short, skinny man with a thin mustache dropped off a new sack of sheep wool, collected the finished yarn, and paid my mother for the completed work before he left in a hurry.

I did not have any toys and for a long time wanted a red plastic toy bus I had seen at a convenience store near our home. Every Thursday night, as my mother counted her pay, I would ask her if she would buy it for me, and every Thursday night, without fail, she would say no. The little bus cost two rials and that was way too much money to spend on a toy, she would say. I understood and, as disappointed as I was, I didn't bring the subject up again until the following Thursday night.

When there was no wool for my mother to weave, she cracked and seeded almonds, walnuts, and apricot pits to make money. I liked the nut-cracking job the best; I was allowed to eat the damaged nuts. My mother worked hard at whatever task she could find, but still her earnings barely covered the rent. If it wasn't for my grandmother bringing bread and drained yogurt from the village once every other week, I am not sure what we would have done for food. We ate bread and hot sweetened tea for breakfast, bread and drained yogurt for lunch and dinner. Eggs, meat, and rice were luxuries we could not afford.

Despite the lack of money, we had some elegant-looking clothes that my mother had sown or woven from inexpensive fabrics and yarns. Being blessed with my parents' good genes— they were both very attractive people—and groomed and dressed properly and tastefully at all times, I looked more like the children from the upscale parts of town than the children where we lived. According to my mother, I was her crown jewel that she guarded with her life and was never willing to give up. And I was crazy about my mother, the only person in my life.

I don't remember seeing my father at all during that time.

❖Chapter Five

F
ridays were the weekends, and my mother closed shop and didn't work on that day. She wanted to work but chose not to on account of all the men living in that house being home for the weekend. As a devout Muslim, she wouldn't be caught dead without her chador in front of strange men, and weaving yarn from under a chador was not practical.

The entire house and neighborhood became alive and festive on Fridays. Our landlord considered music to be sinful and did not permit radios in his house, but we could still hear Mahvash, an iconic female singer, singing on the radio in the adjacent house.

By midmorning, men and their sons returned home from *hammom* (a public bathhouse) with their hair puffed up to triple its regular volume and their faces glowing red from steam and scrub. The women, who did their hammom-ing during the week, stayed home and did nothing but cook a special feast for their beloved husbands.

When in season, just before the weekend, women purchased eggplants and squashes from traveling peddlers who sold their produce from donkey backs and wooden pushcarts going through the neighborhood. On Friday mornings, women brought out baskets and trays lined with peeled and salted slices of eggplant and set them in the sun to sweat some of their moisture and bitterness away in preparation for frying. Meanwhile, the air was saturated with the aroma of lamb chunks being fried with onion and various herbs and spices such as fenugreek, cinnamon, and turmeric. Just before noon, the heavenly fragrance of basmati and jasmine rice steaming with Kermanshahi butter and saffron began to join in and drive any hungry person mad. The sheep of the Kermanshah region were said to graze on mountainous meadows containing some of the most aromatic and flavorsome vegetation, hence producing one of the most sought-after butters in the country.

While for most people Fridays were days of epicurean feasting, relaxation, and visiting friends and family, my mother and I spent half of each Friday in hammom getting cleaned and the other half looking for my father or going to Imam Reza's shrine. On that day, with her faith in Imam Reza and her focus on finding my father and softening his heart, my mother embarked on the mission of finding her missing child. She feared my father in her bones, but that didn't deter her from standing at the army base's gate for hours at a time, looking for him. Unfortunately for my mother, he was not the easiest person to catch. If Houdini had an Iranian brother, it would have most certainly been my father. Over time, constantly eluding his creditors had made him a master in evasion. No one could get a hold of him if he didn't want them to. My mother used to say, "He could even swindle the devil if he wanted to."

Our Fridays started long before the neighbor's rooster opened his beak. Right after a hasty prayer, my mother would put my shoes on, grab the hammom supply bundle she'd prepared the night before, and off we went to get cleaned. The bundle, a substitute for a bag, was a large cloth holding a towel, clean clothes, and a bag containing her body washing and scrubbing supplies. No one took bathing more seriously than my mother.

Usually we were the first to arrive in hammom, while it was still dark outside and I was half asleep. My mother wanted to get there as early as possible to maximize the amount of time she could spend scrubbing herself. Since I didn't have a father, she had no choice but to take me with her to women's hammom. As long as the boy was under the age of four and none of the customers objected, most women's hammoms allowed bringing little boys in.

Excluding the front foyer where the cashier was located— often the same person as the manager of the hammom—the public hammoms basically consisted of two main sections: a large dressing room with some mirrors installed on the walls, and a large bathing room. Almost all the surfaces in the bathing room were tiled—the floor, the walls, the benches, and even the pools. Before it became mandatory for hammoms to install showerheads, patrons used two

34

separate pools to wash and rinse themselves: a small one for rinsing off soap, and a larger one with hot and clear water for the final rinse. There were faucets around for people to get water from during the washing process. I remember women's hammoms being always crowded and loud, with the tiled surfaces intensifying the noise level even more.

My mother would find a secluded corner, as close to a water faucet as possible, place the contents of her bag neatly on the floor, and go to work. Her tools were a twisted and scentless bar of soap made by her mother in the village, a course scrub mitten, a sponge, a rooshoor, a double-sided wooden comb, a chunk of foot-scrubbing lava stone, and a small bowl. I was first. She wanted to get my cleaning out of the way so she could savor working on herself. She began by using the rooshoor and scrubbing my body mercilessly with the coarse mitten, starting from my face and ending at my toes, several times over. Then using the sponge and the bar of soap, she washed my entire body, including my hair. My grandmother's homemade soaps, probably best suited for use on large farm animals, lacked subtleness. They burned my skin and stung my eyes every time. My mother was even less subtle than her mother's soap when it came to washing me. While scrubbing me furiously, she would lift, twist, and bend my body parts around as if I were boneless. Halfway through the process I would start crying.

Hissing between clenched teeth while giving me the look of death, "I don't want to hear a *jeek* (a small sound) out of you," she would say when I began to annoy her with my nagging. There was always a tug-of-war happening between us as she lifted my arms and turned and twisted my body around trying to wash me, leaving my private parts exposed, and I in turn struggled to keep them covered. Conscious of the curious eyes of the little girls present in the hammom, I kept lowering my arms or turning in order to cover myself. Frustrated, each time she would slap my buttocks and yank me back to position.

Needless to say, it was a painful and humiliating experience for me almost every time. I passionately despised going to hammom with my mother; her brutal cleaning techniques aside, I was embarrassed standing exposed amongst a group of naked little girls and women. Hungry, tired, and bored, I would nag and cry, wanting to go home. Some women brought oranges and other

35

suitable fruits, depending on the season, and rewarded their children with them after they were done, but not my mother. To quiet me down, she would point to the other children around us and say, "Boys don't cry! The girls are watching and wondering what kind of a boy you are!" It was more likely that they were wondering what kind of a boy comes to women's hammom, I thought.

In later years, I came to understand that my mother suffered from some kind of an obsessive-compulsive disorder. She scrubbed both herself and me until our skin was nearly gone and, just when I would think she was done and we were going to go home, she'd start all over again. Despite my mother's best efforts to leave early, we spent anywhere from four to six hours in hammom each time we were there. Most women with one or two children were in and out of there in one hour. She was already banned from the hammom closest to where we lived for spending too much time and using too much water there. Here too she had been warned not to stay longer than a reasonable time proportionate to the five rials she paid to get in.

After leaving hammom we went home first, where my mother gulped down one or two cups of hot tea, one after another, as she hurriedly shoved bite-size pieces of bread with drained yogurt, similar to cream cheese, into my mouth before we embarked on going to find my father.

The army base where he was stationed was located on the opposite side of town on the outskirts of Mashhad. On the way to the base we often stopped at my uncle Mohammad's first. He was my father's next-door neighbor and his house was attached to my father's house, separated only by a tall brick wall. He was able to tell my mother whether my father was on duty at the base that day or not, hence saving us a trip. My mother was forbidden from knocking at my father's door on account of his new wife getting upset easily. She was breast-feeding her newborn baby and distressing her would have soured her milk, we were told.

Uncle Mohammad was a taller-than-average man and spoke very little. He was thin and handsome, with a warm and soothing voice. His trimmed mustache, green eyes, and full head of reddish hair groomed military-style made him look like a British safari man, especially when he was driving around in his Land Rover, wearing his khaki Department of Agriculture uniform. Like many professional middle-class Iranian men, he and his necktie were inseparable. I don't ever remember seeing him not wearing it, even when he was in his pajama bottoms at home. Of all my father's relatives, Uncle Mohammad was the nicest to my mother and me.

Out of concern over ruffling my father's feathers, my uncle never invited us into his home when my mother and I paid him a visit. During every visit we stood by the front door of his house while my mother, with a sad and desperate tone, begged him to talk to his brother on her behalf. She'd detail the difficulties of our life, how little money she made weaving wool, how much she missed her daughter, and how she needed financial help to feed and clothe me.

"Alireza is of your own blood. God will not look kindly upon you all on the Day of Judgment for abandoning him the way you all have," she would tell him. My mother's tearful pleas of desperation and the sorrow in her voice made me sad as I stood next to her and listened. My uncle always responded by looking empathetic, but only rarely said anything.

I have no idea why we even bothered going there. Our trips were always a waste of the soles of our shoes—nothing was ever accomplished by making the long trips to my uncle's house and the army base. Perhaps that was my mother's desperate way of holding on to her past. At the time I did not understand much of what was going on except that my mother was always unhappy and we couldn't stay home on Fridays to cook, eat, listen to our neighbor's radio, and have fun like everyone else. I did not know my father all that well, and what little I knew of him came from listening to my mother and her relatives talking about him.

"I have to pee, Mommy," I muttered right after we left my uncle's house on one of those infamous Fridays.

"Why didn't you say anything when we were still at your uncle's?" she asked, bulging her eyes and puckering her brows at me.

I looked down and shrugged my shoulders. Except for in the parks, there were no public restrooms anywhere in the city, and there were no parks near where we were. My mother, frustrated with her situation, said, "You are the source of all of my problems, did you know that? If I didn't have a kid, some man would have

37

married me by now and I wouldn't have to suffer anymore. No man wants to take a woman to his home and marry her when she's got a kid attached to her tail." At this point she was talking to herself. My mother, despite her love for me, always reacted harshly toward me when she felt cornered and overwhelmed. Who could have blamed her after what she had been through?

I just had to hold it until we got to a secluded area, she ordered me. I didn't say anything and trailed her. At the first side street, she grabbed my hand and yanked me behind her. Next to a small locust tree she squatted on her heels, pulled down my pants, held my *doodool,* as she called it, aiming it at the base of the tree, and ordered me to pee. Under the circumstances, I couldn't pee, and that frustrated her even more.

"Hurry up! I don't have all day to wait for you and your father to pee on my life."

Embarrassed, I asked to do it by myself. She squeezed her teeth together, frowned and hissed, "No! You will get it all over your pants. Hurry up and pee. Believe me, no one around here is interested in looking at your little date-fruit pit."

After a few smacks on the back of my head, I was able to do my business and we were once again on our way to the army base.

"I am tired and hungry," I said as I walked behind her.

Without stopping, she turned her head around and silently gave me a look of death. Fridays were long and tiring. After being physically abused by my mother for six hours in hammom, I was ready to take a nap in the afternoon.

"I am tired and hungry, Mommy."

"I heard you the first time. We will eat as soon as we get to your father's base. Now be a good boy and don't harass me," she said, without stopping or turning around.

I heard her crying and murmuring things to God as she walked ahead of me.

A short while later we turned into Ahmadabad Avenue, a long, verdant road that ran north and south and extended beyond the city limits. The avenue was symmetrically lined with mammoth, mature shade trees on both sides. Mashhad's piercing summer sun seldom penetrated the dense and lush crowns of the trees that provided cool, comforting shade to an occasional pedestrian below. In some areas, tall brick and stucco walls and massive solid iron

38

gates veiled the houses of the fortunate people residing there. Along some parts of the avenue, continuous long walls blocked the undeveloped land from view and added charm to the road's romantic and picturesque setting. As with most of the older streets and roads in the city, a natural brook ran alongside the trees. Peppermint and wildflowers covered the banks of the brook during the spring and summer.

It was impossible to be a young adult and not think of falling in love while walking under the long line of trees on this secluded road, especially in autumn, when the area echoed with the crunching sound of pedestrians' feet treading the leaf-carpeted sidewalks, releasing the musky scent of the leaves. The avenue in autumn was always a spectacle, with its colorful tall trees that ornamented the romantic road with their oranges, yellows and reds, and the hullaballoo of the hooded crows griping about the coming of winter as they circled over the trees. And Ahmadabad Avenue was even more majestic in winter with its delicate, snow-covered canopy of trees.

Eventually we made our way to Golkari Square, nicknamed for all the flowers the city planted in its round center. A narrow band of white smoke could be seen escaping the open grill of a small popular kebab café to our left. The aroma of charring ground-lamb kebab mixed with the smell of burning lump coal, defeating my last effort to be a good boy and control my hunger as my mother had asked earlier. It had been a long time since she and I had anything but bread and cheese to eat.

My mother paused in front of the café's open window and stared with obvious envy at the skewers of meat and tomatoes sizzling and hissing away over the grill. I asked to be lifted up so I could see better. A thin man stood behind the grill, rapidly fanning the charcoal with one hand and rotating the skewers with another. He wiped the perspiration from his forehead with his sleeve and greeted my mother.

"*Befarmaeyd* (please come in)," the man said as he pointed with his head to the open tables inside the place. At that hour, with the exception of a man seemingly waiting for a carryout order, the place was empty. My mother swallowed her saliva and shook her head no without opening her mouth or taking her eyes off of the kebabs. She was not the type that would give in to her body's desires. I, on the other hand, was willing to trade king and country for one skewer of what was on display in front of me. Looking at the kebabs and the stack of fresh *nan* (flat bread) next to the grill brought on a huge growl from my stomach. In front of the café next to where we were standing there was a white metal cooler filled with ice and frosted bottles of soda. Even though I had never had a soda before and had no idea what it tasted like, the orange ones sure looked good.

My mother put me down and we began to walk away.

"I am hungry, Mommy," I said, as I pulled at her chador.

She sighed dejectedly and replied, "Me too, *pesaram* (my son), me too …"

We circled the square and sat on the ledge of a shallow creek coming down from Koohsangi, a stone mountain a few kilometers up the road. My mother spread a handkerchief containing a little nan and drained yogurt mixed with rosemary flakes on the ground, and we ate. I kept looking at the café on the other side of the square and following with my eyes the delicious white smoke escaping the grill, watching as it ascended and disappeared into the dense branches of the shade trees. My mother usually didn't eat much, but she always brought along some nan and cheese in case I became hungry.

She sat quietly and gazed with a long face at a distant point beyond the square and the tall trees, and perhaps even beyond the city and this world. The whisper of the gentle afternoon wind chiming through the branches of the trees and the constant sound of water gurgling over the rocks had my mother oblivious to the Friday bustle around us. I watched with great interest as the one-rial buses, horse-drawn carriages, and black-and-white taxicabs, all bursting with happy people, went up and down Koohsangi Avenue. In all of our trips to the army base, I had never seen sunlight touching the ground here on Golkari Square or Koohsangi Avenue, thanks to that band of massive trees spreading their branches above. No matter how hot it was everywhere else, it was always cool and pleasant here in Golkari.

When we'd finished eating, my mother led me to the guard kiosk at the gate of the army base. After telling the guard who we were there to see, we stood on the sidewalk near the gate and waited. I watched the guard in the kiosk giving a few turns to the crank handle on an army green telephone, exchanging some words with someone at the other end while looking at us the entire time. I think all the guards knew our story. They all knew we were wasting our time and that my father would never come to the gate, but to make us feel better, they pretended to be trying.

We waited under the shade of a small tree as my mother wetted her fingers with her saliva and moved my hair out of my eyes and to the side. Every time a soldier slightly resembling my father appeared from a distance, my heart began to pound. I couldn't remember when I'd last seen him, but I knew his face from a photograph I had seen at my grandparents' home in the village. As far back as I could remember, I heard my mother saying God, Imam Reza, and my father were our only hope, so I believed if only he would come to the gate, all of my mother's sadness would disappear and she would smile again. But he never came.

My mother was crouching on her heels against the tree with her tired eyes locked on the gate of the army base. She had gone back and talked to the guards at least four times in the past few hours. Who knew, perhaps my father was at home with his wife and new child, enjoying his day off, listening to the radio and sipping on cups of hot tea. As Persians said, my uncle probably sent us after black chickpeas—on a wild-goose chase.

"I am sleepy, Mommy," I said, putting my head on her lap.

"I know, pesaram, I know."

With that my mother decided to call it a day. She got up, picked me up into her arms, and we began our long walk home to the other side of town. The sun was almost gone, taking with it the remains of another long and tiring Friday. With the palm of her hand, my mother held my sleepy head over her shoulder against the curve of her neck while whispering a sad lullaby as we traveled home on the long and empty sidewalk.

"Khodaya," followed by a long sigh, was the last thing I heard coming from my mother before I fell into sleep in my favorite and most secure place on earth.

I loved my mother more than all the two-rial toy buses, kebabs, and shiny red tricycles in the world.

Chapter Six

A long year slowly went by and there was no improvement in our situation. There was still no news of my lost sister and no sign of my father or any financial help from him. My mother continued doing odds-and-ends jobs to pay the rent and buy basic food for the two of us. There weren't many decent jobs available to women back then, because women were not considered to be a part of the country's workforce. Cleaning, cooking, and taking care of children for other people, or doing what my mother did, weaving wool and shelling nuts, summarized the kind of work an uneducated woman could find. There was always rug-weaving work to be found, but my mother could not take those jobs because that meant she had to find someone to leave me with.

During the summer my mother put her culinary skills to work and went into the business of making tomato paste and pickling vegetables for the wealthy housewives in upper-class neighborhoods. Tomato paste was an essential ingredient in Persian cooking, and pickled vegetables were served with most meals. My mother and I spent countless long days in an area called *Koye Doktorha* (the Doctors' Quarter) boiling, seasoning, and jarring baby eggplants, pearl onions, garlic, mixed vegetables, or cucumbers in vinegar and spices. Some days she just made tomato paste, washing and sieving boxes and boxes of fresh tomatoes by hand and reducing the pulp and juice into paste in huge, heavy copper pots over an open fire in the middle of someone's courtyard. Too little to help, I sat nearby and listened to my mother hum or took short naps under a quince or apple tree while she worked. At the end of each day my mother was paid with cash and often given a small jar of her own product for us to take home. We also hauled the discarded tomato seeds and skins home, where my mother pressed them into round balls and set them in the sun to dry for use as fire fuel in winter.

In the beginning, on the days when my mother wasn't working, we combed the city searching for my sister, often going back to the same orphanage home, police stations, and morgues. As more time passed, however, and the hope of finding Shahnaz began to diminish, my mother shifted her focus from searching for my sister to praying for her. She started going to the shrine regularly and took me along. By now I was three years old and beginning to know my way around the city well, thanks to all the walking we did.

A few times a month my mother dedicated an entire Friday to visiting Imam Reza's shrine. We lived only a couple kilometers away from the shrine on the opposite end of Naderi Avenue,[1] the

---

[1] Naderi Avenue was named after King Nader, a ruler of Persia in the eighteenth century. Some historians refer to him as the Napoleon of Persia because of his military genius. King Nader was born to a semi-nomadic Turkish tribe in the northern parts of Khorasan Province. His father, a poor peasant, died while Nader was still little. Nader and his mother were later taken into slavery by marauding Uzbeks, but he managed to escape and joined up with a roving group of bandits while still a boy; he eventually advanced to become their leader. Later he and his men joined the king's forces to fight the invading Russians, Ottomans, and Afghans.

Eventually he defeated and drove out the Afghans from Isfahan, the capital of Persia at the time, and Khorasan Province. He also managed to force out the Ottomans and the Russians from the western and northern Persian territories. It took Nader three times to finally defeat and kill the famous Turkish general Topal Osman near Kirkuk, conquering the city of Baghdad in the process. After taking Baghdad from the Turks, he went back to settle the score with the Afghans. Nader invaded and conquered Afghanistan and in the process took control of northern India as well as some other lands. Eventually he gathered a vote of no confidence against the ruling king and became the new king of Persia in 1736. Once in power, he moved the capital from Isfahan to Mashhad. They say he was the last great military leader to come out of the Middle East in modern times.

main artery that connected Quchan Gate Square to the shrine. Anyone traveling to Mashhad from the north had to go through the Quchan Gate. All the buses coming and going to and from the villages and small towns in the northern part of the province were stationed there.

On Fridays the square swelled with buses dropping off large crowds of country folks coming to town to conduct business, visit relatives, or go to the shrine and the cinemas. During the first half of the day, the sidewalks of Naderi Avenue were packed with people headed south; the women and older men walking to the shrine, the teenage boys running as fast as they could, like a flock of birds, toward downtown and the cinemas. In the late afternoon the direction of the flow was reversed. Just before the sunset, everyone who had come to town in the morning was already aboard buses and on their way back to their villages, until the next Friday.

While my mother cherished the destination, I enjoyed the journey to the shrine. The hustle and bustle of Naderi Avenue and the variety of shops along the way never ceased to amuse me. The air was saturated with the hubbub of automobile horns, bicycle bells, traffic policemen's whistles, and peddlers' jingles announcing their goods, along with the bells laced around the horses' necks clinking in sync with the pounding of the animals' hooves as they drew passenger-filled carriages along the paved road.

At that age, my stomach was always in my thoughts, and Naderi Avenue delivered the most spectacular array of food. Up and down the avenue peddlers sold edible goods on wooden pushcarts or large wooden trays carried over their heads. It started in spring when they sold freshly picked sweet and juicy mulberries, unripe little sour green plums, and green almonds—served with salt on the side—for people to snack on. During the hot summer months, in addition to all the available seasonal fruits, pushcart vendors also sold homemade ice cream and frozen rice noodles served with the choice of sour cherry or lemon syrup topping. In autumn, oranges, pomegranates, date fruits, and persimmons sweetened the taste buds of the passersby. During the winter the peddlers converted their pushcarts and sold hot creamed rice pudding, steamed beets, and boiled fava beans. To lure the pedestrians into their stores and not to be outsold by the peddlers, the store owners too displayed their goods on the sidewalks in front of their stores. The result was an enticing array of mouthwatering sights and smells year around.

More than anything else, my favorite part of the entire journey to the shrine was watching an old portrait photographer at work next to the Office of Taxation. He photographed his subjects on the sidewalk as they stood against a dark gray fabric hanging from the wall. His entire shop consisted of a small suitcase holding his supplies, the gray backdrop, and a large wet-plate camera mounted on a wooden tripod. After taking each photograph, he buried his head under a thick black skirt that hung from the back of his camera and emerged a little later with the images of his subjects immortalized on a wet piece of photo paper. I would have given anything at the time for one peek under the black skirt of his camera. The process was pure magic to me. On every trip I begged my mother to have the old man take our photograph—but she refused. She thought two rials was too much to spend on a little photograph. In retrospect, if she only knew what life had in store for the two of us, she probably would have seized the opportunity and had the old photographer take our picture together. My mother, like the rest of her family, did not believe in self-indulgent activities that required spending money, like taking the bus instead of walking everywhere or once in a blue moon treating ourselves to an ice cream sandwich.

The majestic gold and turquoise domes of the shrine soared into Mashhad's deep blue sky, along with two tall minarets that flanked the great mosque of Goharshad. At noon a *muezzin* called people to prayer in a melodious voice from one of the minarets, and periodically throughout the day, men in uniforms blew long brass horns from the minarets, adding to the imposing presence of the place. The structure emanated hope of justice and redemption not only to my mother but also to many ordinary and less fortunate people who felt they had been wronged. It spoke of the existence of a higher system of righteousness that was aware of both the oppressor and the oppressed. For many deprived people like my mother, divine justice was all that they could hope for, and for them, the shrine stood to symbolize that justice.

The massive fifteenth-century compound had many verandas, courtyards with large fountains, and seemingly endless beautiful

45

fretworks of tiny mirror and ceramic tiles inlaid in every wall of every vast prayer hall. Each hall was made comfortable by wall-to-wall hand-woven Persian rugs covering the floor and lit by immense chandeliers hanging from the towering ceilings above. The air inside was saturated with the fragrance of rose water that was sprayed periodically by the shrine's servants. Visitors were spread out everywhere on the floors, praying, crying, reading the Quran, listening to sermons, talking, or just plain napping.

My mother followed the same routine each time we visited the shrine. We first took off our shoes and placed them together against the wall amongst hundreds of other pairs of shoes. Then my mother kissed the colossal brass door and said a prayer as we entered her favorite prayer hall. Once inside, we sat in a secluded corner where she perhaps thought she could have the best chance of having Imam Reza's undisturbed attention, and prayed for the longest time.

During this entire time, I just sat next to her and entertained myself by running my fingers over the patterns of the rug, pretending to be pushing a toy automobile on the tracks, watched the people's feet as they moved around us, or took naps. Once my mother was ready for the grand finale of her visit, we headed toward the tomb. With me in her arms she made her way to the tomb's chamber and merged into a thick wall of people circling the tomb, inching her way closer to the center with each turn. Once she reached the golden cage protecting the tomb, my mother locked her grip on a section of it and did not move. We were pushed, shoved, and elbowed repeatedly by the crowed of believers, each also forcing their way in to touch the golden cage. My mother held on tight to the bars and did not let go. She cried her heart out as she clutched and kissed the bars over and over while begging Imam Reza for help.

"*Ya Zamene Ahoo*, have mercy on me. Please bring me back my daughter, please open some doors for me, I beg of you," she lamented over and over. My sister's disappearance stood for all the things that my mother felt she had lost. It symbolized the martyrdom she felt inside and the martyr she wished to be. The justice she sought there was as much for herself and her broken heart as it was for my missing little sister. In unity with her, I remember leaning forward in her arms and placing small kisses on

46

the cold surface of the golden bars caging the tomb. I actually thought Imam Reza was there inside the golden cage and could see and hear us but we could not see him.

Eventually red blush blossomed like peonies all over my mother's white tear-soaked face and she went into a convulsion of hiccups and sobs. It was then that she finally let go of the bars and dragged us out of the thick layers of people mercilessly pressing against us. She feared passing out there and leaving me defenseless, getting crushed under the sea of churning bodies. It always scared and tormented me to watch her wail out of control that way.

My mother rested sitting out of the way against a wall for a little while and recomposed herself before we left and sat by the fountain in the courtyard. There she fed me some nan and creamed yogurt as dozens of pigeons circled under our feet in front of us, begging us to share our bread with them.

Sometimes, on our way to or from the shrine we ran into Moosa, one of the many admirers of my mother. He transported passengers between the shrine and Quchan Gate Square on his convertible horse-drawn carriage. Moosa was a tall, twiggy man in his thirties. A thin and sad-looking beard of fine curly hair covered patches of his sunken face here and there. Anytime we walked to the shrine or back, my eyes scanned the street for his carriage. It was certain that if he spotted us on the sidewalk, he'd stop and insist on giving us a ride, whether there was enough room on his carriage or not. When his carriage was full he oftentimes insisted on rearranging his passengers to make room for my mother and me. If needed, he would even ask them to put their children on their laps. He called me *amoo joon* (dear nephew). Anytime a strange man liked a woman and had intentions toward her, he referred to her kid or kids as amoo joon, I learned. I was ecstatic when occasionally Moosa would place me next to him on the driver's seat and allow me to grab a part of the long reins and pretend that I was controlling the horse.

My mother, however, found Moosa repulsive and did not wish to even give him the time of day. She always warned me against getting his attention if I happened to spot his carriage on the road. Poor Moosa was an unattractive opium addict with, as my mother used to put it, lips like a camel. He was infatuated with my mother and even though he knew he didn't stand a chance of ever gaining

47

her affections, he stopped every time he saw us and insisted on giving us a ride to wherever we were going. On rare occasions when my mother finally gave in to his persisting pleas of invitation and my jubilant reaction to riding in a carriage, she would spend the entire ride wearing a sour face and looking in another direction.

Chapter Seven

O ne day my grandmother came to town in what appeared to be somewhat of a hurry. She brought along a large kerchief filled with all sorts of dishes, teacups, and other things usually used in entertaining important guests. It was a common practice for some people to borrow dishes from one neighbor, silverware from another, and teacups with matching saucers from yet another to impress important company, often those visiting from out of town. But my mother never had anyone except for her parents, brothers, and sisters visiting us. Curiosity was killing me as to who was coming, but I dared not ask Modar Joon, my grandmother—she could not stand snoopy children— and my mother was in a sulk at the time for an incident a few days earlier in which she'd had to pay a policeman five toomans, almost what she made in a week weaving wool, in order to get me back.

That incident had begun when my mother left me alone at home while she went to the butcher shop right up the street from where we lived. She wanted to be quick, she said, and did not feel like taking me along, despite my whining and insisting on going with her.

"I just need five minutes to myself without having you attached to my tail. So be a good boy and don't leave the room until I get back. I promise you will not die without me."

That was easy for her to say. She was the air that I breathed, and truly I did not believe that living without her was at all possible. With her I was always in paradise and it didn't matter if we had nothing, ate only nan and yogurt, slept on a straw rug, and the girls laughed at me for going to women's hammom. As long as I had her, I did not need anything or anyone else.

Reluctantly I promised to be a "good boy" and stay in our room while she was gone. But my promise was only as good as my attention span at the time. It wasn't long before I began missing my mother, so I immediately put on my shoes and went to look for her. There were only two butcher shops on all of Naderi Avenue: one near our home and the other farther up by Statue Square. I checked the one near our home first and she wasn't there, so I kept on walking to the next one.

I didn't find my mother at the second butcher shop either, so I began to head back home, when suddenly seeing the old photographer in action snapped my attention. He was taking a picture of an old country man, and I could not help but stand around and watch. I had always wanted to see the entire process from beginning to end, but my mother wouldn't let me.

It wasn't long, however, before a policeman approached and asked me what I was doing there and who I was with. I was looking for my mother, I told him. He grabbed my wrist with one hand while playing with the tip of his bushy mustache, raised one of his eyebrows, and asked with an intimidating tone if I was lost. Scared and with a lump in my throat, I shook my head no. He then asked if I knew where I lived and I told him yes.

"Okay, kid, let's go and find your mother," the policeman said and asked me to lead the way and show him where we lived.

I knew my mother was going to kill me for leaving the house, but I didn't have much choice at that point except to do as I was told.

Once we arrived at my house, the policeman refused to surrender me to my mother— who was all panicky, apparently from coming home and not finding me there— unless he was paid for finding me. Despite her repeated pleas for forgiveness and mushy stories of being a single mother with no real income, he did not hand me over until he was able to extort five toomans from her. Left with no other alternative, my mother had to borrow the money from her landlady and pay the policeman off. Originally he wanted twenty toomans for allegedly finding me and bringing me home safely, but like everything else, even extortion was up for haggling.

The policeman folded the bill and placed it under the lining inside his cap and casually walked away, but the memory of what he did never left. My mother and I stood in the narrow alleyway in front of our house, speechless, I with my head remorsefully down, looking at my feet, and she in a daze with her eyes on the end of the alleyway where the policeman disappeared. Perhaps she was calculating in her head how many extra sacks of wool she had to weave in order to pay the landlady back.

I was certain my mother was going to punish me once we were inside, but instead she chose not to speak to me for a while. It was more painful to have the only person in my life not speaking to me than to get spanked.

Not long after Modar Joon arrived, both she and my mother went to work diligently cleaning and tidying up our little room. The following morning, my mother had already left for hammom by the time I was awake. It was the first time she had ever gone to the hammom without taking me since I could remember. The air in our little room was tense that day. Modar Joon was running around like a chicken with its head cut off, dusting, arranging, and rearranging the few belongings that my mother had. While my mother was still at hammom, Modar Joon and I made a quick trip to the market where she bought some fruits and pastries. At home she immediately washed the fruits and arranged them on a platter that she placed high on the shelf next to the box of pastries which, not unexpectedly, was well out of my reach. I was still afraid to ask Modar Joon what was going on as her answer was always the same: "It has nothing to do with you. A child should not be so nosy." Unlike my grandfather, who was like a dove, Modar Joon used very little diplomacy and discretion when she spoke to her children and grandchildren. Whatever she said came out of her mouth without any regard for their feelings.

It was way past noon by the time my mother eventually returned from *hammom* and endured a brief argument with her mother over her being gone for so long. Soon after her arrival, my mother worked on hiding away her weaving equipment and supplies while Modar Joon went to work scrubbing my hands, head, and face by the fountain, using her infamous harsh homemade soap. Now I knew where my mother had gotten her brutal scrubbing techniques from. I cried the entire time during the rough wash, but Modar Joon, I guess calloused over time by raising as many children as she had, was not swayed in the least by my tears.

As the evening neared, Modar Joon finally decided to tell me that we were going to have some very important guests coming over soon. She also gave me some advance warning about the things I should not do in front of the guests, like reaching for the pastries or asking for some. "Nobody likes a gluttonous child," she said as she gave me a mild sample of her famous killer frown and rounding of her eyes. Modar Joon had prominent high cheek and brow bones, resembling those of a warrior, making her large eyes appear sunken deep into her bony face, hence giving potency to her expressions of disapproval. One thing was for sure—I wasn't about to disappoint her this evening, but it wasn't until a few years later that I understood what she was trying to accomplish by warning me against behaving gluttonously.

For the rest of the afternoon, Modar Joon crossed her legs while sitting on the floor in front of my mother and worked diligently on my mother's face. I sat and watched as she transformed my mother by plucking and thinning her eyebrows with the use of strings, accentuating her eyes and eyelashes with kohl (black powder), whitening her face with ceruse (a skin-whitening cosmetic), and applying rouge to her cheeks and lips.

The last of the daylight was slipping away behind the western brick wall. Atop a charcoal-burning samovar near the window, black tea was brewing in a china teapot decorated with large rose patterns. Next to the samovar on the floor, four teacups sat on their saucers on a round silver tray, waiting. A small glass bowl filled with sugar chunks that Modar Joon had chopped earlier was also on the tray. She had placed two bolster pillows, borrowed from our landlady, against the wall facing the entrance door where the guests were going to be seated. Someone very important must be coming to visit us, I thought. I had never seen our little room so propped up and perfectly staged before.

The sun was completely gone and the sky turned a pale azure. My mother, seeming restless, was standing against a wooden pole on the veranda, when suddenly the door knocker sounded. It was an unfamiliar knock.

"They are here!" Modar Joon shouted softly and anxiously. With her chador fluttering like a large bird, she jumped out of the room and onto the veranda. She and my mother murmured something in a hurry as Modar Joon rushed to answer the front door. I stood up, attached myself to my mother's leg, and fixated my curious eyes to the canopy covering the main entrance across the courtyard. "Stand up straight," my mother told me. I was happy when she said that, knowing we were on talking terms again. Modar Joon emerged first from under the canopy, immediately followed by a man and a woman I had never seen before. The woman was a little younger than Modar Joon, and the man was quite young. He was wearing a very nice suit and a tie.

"Saaaalaaaaam, Soory joon," said the lady to my mother with a Turkish accent while smiling ear to ear through her loosely held chador.

"Salam, Roqyya Khanom, welcome," my mother answered softly, as she bowed her head.

"This is Mansoor, my cousin. He is here visiting from Tehran," the lady said as she introduced the young man. "And this is Soory joon that I have told you so much about, Mansoor joon."

"Salam," he said as he politely nodded to my mother.

"Salam," she uttered delicately in reply, all the while looking down and blushing, with little sweat beads covering her upper lip.

Turning her attention to me, the lady bent down, kissed me, and then complimented me on how much I had grown since the last time she saw me.

My mother smiled proudly.

According to my mother, the lady was friends with Modar Joon and lived only a few alleys away from us. What brought her and Modar Joon together in the first place was Modar Joon's rooshoors. Apparently she had been a customer of my grandmother's for a while. Thinking back, I remembered seeing her and my mother talking at hammom once. But I didn't think she was here to buy rooshoors that evening.

The young man picked me up into his arms, kissed me, and talked to me for a little bit before Modar Joon directed everyone into the room.

Once seated on the floor, the grown-ups talked, drank hot tea, and nibbled on the various fruits and pastries. I sat politely next to my mother and didn't touch or ask for anything. Not once did

Modar Joon or my mother have to give me a bad look while the guests were there.

The next day my mother explained that the young man was a possible suitor for her. She also explained what that meant for the two of us. If everything worked out, he would be a husband to her and a father to me, she said, and we wouldn't be alone anymore.

A few evenings later Roqy Khanom and her cousin were back again, pleasantly talking, drinking hot tea, eating pastries and trail mix, and smoking ghalyan (a waterpipe used for smoking tobacco). My grandfather was absent once again, on account of being very ill and unable to walk. Halfway through the night I eventually fell asleep on the floor next to my mother with my head on her lap.

The next morning my mother informed me that she was engaged to Roqy Khanom's cousin. I didn't know what that meant exactly, but I was pleased to see my mother happy and smiling for the first time since I could remember.

On the first Friday after my mother's engagement to Mansoor Aqa, as usual she dragged me to *hammom* while it was still dark out and I was half asleep. Thankfully we were there for only about two hours as opposed to our customary four to six hours. After returning home, all morning long, my mother seemed to be pleasantly restless, trying on different headscarves and viewing herself in her little book-size handheld mirror. She was uncomplicatedly beautiful, like a verse in an Omar Khayyam poem or a blossom on one of my grandfather's apricot trees in spring. For the first time her romantically sad eyes were shimmering, perhaps with hope or love or something else that I was still too young to understand. According to her, Mansoor Aqa was going to take us out later on that day. I had no idea what going out with a man entailed. For as long as I could remember, I had only been going out with my mother, and those excursions were not at all fun. But since my mother was excited about the day ahead, so was I.

After she was done dressing me up and combing my hair, I sat outside in the veranda across from our room, glued my eyes to the front door, and waited for Mansoor Aqa to arrive. It was midmorning when I heard him knocking—three slow yet firm slams of the doorknocker against its base. I had memorized the knocking of every occupant of the house, and his was like no one else's. Of course with so many people living in that house, the door was always open during the day, but as was customary, Mansoor Aqa did not enter until I ran out front and greeted him.

"Salam, Mansoor Aqa."

"Wow, that was quick. Salam, Alireza joon. How are you?"

"Fine."

"Is your mother home?" he asked, smiling.

"*Bale* (yes), Mansoor Aqa."

"Well, can I come inside?"

"Bale, Mansoor Aqa."

We walked in together, and for the sake of propriety he decided to wait for my mother out in the courtyard. Considering our landlord was the religiously zealous Sheikh Aliakbar, that was very thoughtful of Mansoor Aqa. I was sure everyone living in that house was already monitoring the situation from behind the curtains of their windows. And Mansoor Aqa seemed to realize that. The last thing my mother needed was for her reputation to be tarnished by having a handsome young man walk into our room, and tarnished it would have been, even though they were now officially engaged. The tenants and the landlord had already been informed of this new development in my mother's life.

Mansoor Aqa was wearing a necktie and a two-piece suit like no suit I had seen any man wear in and around our working-class neighborhood. He smelled fantastic, and his shiny hair was perfectly trimmed, greased, and combed to the side and back. Everything about him was new, exciting, and different to me, including his shimmering shoes. My mother's relatives rarely let go of any shoes; instead they just kept changing the soles until the uppers looked like mutilated rawhide and could take no more repairs.

With a smile as broad as his shoulders, Mansoor Aqa greeted my mother when she finally stepped out of the room, and soon the three of us were in a taxicab going somewhere he called Arg. Right away I fell in love with the way Mansoor Aqa talked; it was like no one else I knew. He spoke with a sweet and classy accent that I later learned was a combination of Tehranian and Turkish. Back then, people from Mashhad were famous for having one of the most unpleasant accents in the country.

As I learned some years later, Arg Avenue, or Arg as the area was commonly referred to, was in essence the downtown of Mashhad, an upscale and glittering shopping and entertainment district in the heart of the city. What one could find in Arg existed nowhere else in the city. All of Mashhad's nine cinemas, fine hotels and restaurants, chic boutiques, and some of its finest European-style pastry and ice cream shops were located in Arg. The jewel of Arg, however, was the gated European-style Melli Park, situated right in the middle of all the actions. Mansoor Aqa and my mother talked it over and decided to go and see a film. A film—what was that? I asked Mansoor Aqa, and he told me that I just had to wait and see.

My first cinematic experience was nothing short of magical. The large and colorful posters hanging outside above the theater's entrance, the crowded theater's salon, the comfortable seats, the cold carbonated beverages sold by men walking up and down the aisles, and above all, the moving picture in front of me, were all part of a world that I could not have imagined existed if it wasn't for Mansoor Aqa that day. During the picture show he bought my mother and me each a bottle of ice-cold Pepsi-Cola, my first soda. The Pepsi filled my eyes with tears and my body with thousands of little tickles. I could not help but compare that Friday with the Fridays when my mother and I went out. It was unquestionably better than going to the shrine, listening to my mother and everyone else around her lament and say things in Arabic that I did not understand, while getting crushed under a sea of people. My grandfather always said happiness germinates more happiness, and misery germinates more misery. I had no idea how my mother was expecting to find happiness when she only looked for it in places of sorrows and sobs, one Friday after another.

After the film, Mansoor Aqa took us to a fancy kebab restaurant for a late lunch. He ordered me my own plate with two kinds of kebabs and a skewer of grilled tomato on top of a mound of steaming long-grain basmati rice. The rice was garnished with a raw egg yolk placed in the center of its peak, and the kebabs were sprinkled with zesty ground sumac. To drink I had another bottle of Pepsi, while my mother and Mansoor Aqa drank *dooq*—a mint-flavored yogurt drink. I had never had that much food placed in front of me before. Not knowing how temporary or permanent

56

this newfound life of luxury was going to be, I did not take any chances and ate as much as I could and then some. I was bloated and had difficulty walking when we left the restaurant. As Modar Joon would have said, my eyes were bigger and hungrier than my stomach when it came to food. My mother touched my tightly packed belly and joked about where I put all that food, and she and Mansoor Aqa laughed.

Mansoor Aqa walked us over to Melli Park, where my mother and he sat on a bench and talked for a long time, while I took a contented nap on my mother's lap, with a smile on my face, I am sure.

By the time I woke up, the sun had already set and the park was crowded with people dressed in stylish clothes, strolling around on the paved pathways that ran everywhere in between beds of flowers and freshly mown grass. Couples and small groups were chatting and laughing as they walked; some men were smoking cigarettes and some women cracking toasted melon or pumpkin seeds with their teeth. Mansoor Aqa and my mother were sitting slightly closer to each other now and seemingly were more comfortable with one another. He suggested that we should go for a walk around the park now that I was awake, and my mother agreed.

The park was lined with tall, mature trees and landscaped with beds of colorful perfumed flowers, evergreens, and perfectly manicured grass. A long and narrow rectangular fountain ran in the center of the park, from one end to the other. A small art gallery and an alfresco café were tucked away hidden at the very end of the fountain on the opposite side of the park. In the center of the fountain, thick jets of water, illuminated by submerged colorful lights, forcefully shot high into the early evening sky, cooling the air with their mist. The colorful jets of water resembled giant popsicles against the darkened sky. For a few rials, visitors could have their photographs taken there by professional photographers and mailed anywhere in the country.

Unlike Naderi Avenue and the shrine circle where all women wore chador and most people had frozen looks on their faces, here in the park and on Arg Avenue, there was no sign of chador and everyone seemed happy. Not only did people dress differently around here, they also behaved differently. The place was filled with laughter and the cheery chatter of people who seemed to come from a different world than the one my mother and I lived in. I wondered why my mother did not know about this place and, if she did, why we hadn't been coming here on Fridays.

On the way home, lying on the back seat of the taxicab with my head on my mother's lap, I was reviewing the day's events and wondering if this was what having a father was like. I will never forget that Friday.

About a week later my mother and Mansoor Aqa stood shoulder to shoulder against the bare plastered wall in our little room and became husband and wife. My mother was wearing a silk head scarf, a white pair of shoes, and a cream-colored dress that was made out of heavy cotton fabric and reached just below her knees. As for Mansoor Aqa, he always looked like a groom, wedding or no wedding. I remember I was sitting on the carpet on the floor, just across from my mother and Mansoor Aqa, watching and nibbling on pastries. A handful of relatives and neighbors present at the ceremony stood around the room and clapped their hands to the sound of music coming from a gramophone that Roqy Khanom had brought over. My grandfather was not there due to his illness, and that had my mother saddened.

According to my mother, a month earlier, Mansoor Aqa, who was here from Tehran to visit his cousin just for a few days, ran into my mother in the alleyway and immediately fell in love with her. As luck would have it, his cousin Roqy Khanom happened to be friends with Modar Joon through purchasing rooshoors from her; hence she knew my mother and had seen her naked at the neighborhood's hammom. When Mansoor Aqa asked for his cousin's advice, she approved of his intentions and vouched for my mother's having integrity and a beautiful body. Back then, as part of investigating a girl prior to requesting her hand in marriage, it was not at all uncommon for a man to have a woman relative follow the girl to hammom and check out her physical attributes. But, though he'd been told the details of my mother's body, Mansoor Aqa was never told about my missing sister and dead brother, and I was warned never to mention anything about either one of them to him.

❖Chapter Eight

Modar Joon's initial worry that Mansoor Aqa would take her daughter to some faraway land after the wedding proved to be unfounded. Immediately following the wedding, Mansoor Aqa found a job at a tailor shop and settled in Mashhad for good. And within weeks after that we were all forced to find a new place to live.

Sheik Aliakbar, our landlord, was no longer interested in renting a room to my mother now that she was married. Sheik Aliakbar was a man of God, and Mansoor Aqa, a cinema-going and radio-listening handsome young man, just did not fit into his world. People like Mansoor Aqa were different, and different is always viewed as a threat by callow souls. A few months of Mansoor Aqa's living at the Sheik's house could have opened the eyes and ears of his wife and young daughters, and before he knew it, they too would want to listen to the radio, go to movies, and more dangerously, learn to increase their expectations of their men. Anything and anyone that could open the eyes and ears of women, was a danger and therefore, forbidden. The more the women were kept in the dark and away from the outside world, the easier it was for men to control them.

With Mansoor Aqa's arrival, our life pivoted in a different direction. We were no longer adrift at the shrine or the army base on Fridays, searching for hope and miracles. No more lamenting and tears. My mother now had a man to erase her tears and take away her fears. The wool-weaving and nut-cracking business also disappeared from the stage of our life.

Right after marrying my mother, Mansoor Aqa took out a small bank loan—using a rug that his cousin gave him as a wedding present as collateral—and purchased a bicycle. Bicycles were the primary mode of transportation in Mashhad until some years later when Mopeds began to arrive. For every automobile, there were a few hundred bicycles on the roads back then. The bicycle gave Mansoor Aqa the wings that he needed to explore his new city, and he went everywhere with it. He hardly knew anyone here in Mashhad, and so he often took me along; I couldn't have been happier.

Too little to understand the criteria involved in qualifying a man as someone's father, I almost immediately adopted Mansoor Aqa as my father—or more accurately, I assumed that he was my father. He was my mother's husband, lived with us, took me places, and was kind and affectionate toward me, so that must make him my father, I assumed. I remember every evening just before it was time for him to return from work, I sat by the window of our second-floor room, fixed my eyes on the front door across the tiled courtyard, and waited for him to walk through it. Sometimes my mother allowed me to wait for him outside by the front door. I was always ecstatic when his silhouette, pedaling on his bicycle, appeared at the end of our narrow street. He never came home empty-handed—a kilo of pastries, a melon or whatever fresh fruits were currently in season—there was always some treat under his arm and a broad smile on his face when he walked through the door.

Because of Mansoor Aqa, Friday became a day of fun and festivity for us, just as it was with most of our neighbors. If we did not go out somewhere as a family on that day, my mother, renowned for her culinary skills, cooked some of her best dishes for her new husband. Usually after lunch, Mansoor Aqa took a quick nap before getting dressed and going to Arg to see a film, taking me along, of course.

My mother always chose to stay home when going out meant going to the cinema. She was no fan of cinema, not only because she had been told it was sinful but also for its hefty cost (hefty only to my mother) of ten to fifteen rials per ticket. With that much money she could buy a kilo of meat, a few kilos of potatoes or eggplants, and make a couple meals, she argued. She was raised to be thrifty and also to fear God in her bones. Despite Mansoor Aqa's repeated appeal for her to come along, teasingly assuring her

God was not going to punish her for going to see an Indian film (which were well-known for being family oriented and morally sterilized) my mother would not come with us. There was no way she was going to risk burning in hell someday, she'd argue. "That one time was more than enough for me," she would say, referring to the first time Mansoor Aqa took us to the cinema. As with most of her relatives who followed their religious learning blindly and without truly understanding it, it was the fear of God, rather than the love of God, that propelled my mother to make the choices that she made. She tried to do the right thing but often for the wrong reason.

My fondness for Mansoor Aqa grew stronger with every passing day. The more time we spent together, the more I realized he was like no one else I knew. He was a strong and classy man, and now that I look back, very mature for his age. He handled himself like a prince in exile, without any wealth yet with a lot of style and grace. With what little money he made, he was always extravagant, a definite shortcoming for someone whose spending often surpassed his earnings. Despite his almost nonexistent education, he was an intellectual and insightful man.

I remember when I was finally banned from the women's hammoms in our area, and my mother had no choice but to impose on Mansoor Aqa to take over the responsibility of washing me once a week. According to the old lady in charge of the last hammom my mother and I were going to, I was too old to accompany my mother there. Apparently some women had complained that I had stared at them inappropriately. I remember my mother confronting me and warning me about staring at the women before. It was true, I did stare at them, but for an entirely different reason than what I was accused of, and for that I had to blame Lulu.

You see, whenever I misbehaved or didn't do what I was asked, my mother threatened to call Lulu on me. Lulu was an imaginary monster used to frighten children when they were bad. Every child had his own version of Lulu in mind, I am sure. Mine was a dark and hairy thing with no clear physical description. I was petrified when, a year earlier and for the first time, I saw in a hammom what I thought was the Lulu itself. This specific hammom was somewhat older, with a large bathing room that, if I

61

am not mistaken, could easily accommodate about forty or fifty people at one time. The misty and dimly lit bathing room had an eerie feel to it, especially when it was still early in the morning and not fully occupied.

I remember a tall, slender woman with unusually white skin and long, wavy black hair that reached to the floor where she was sitting—which just happened to be across from my mother and me. The uncommon combination of her physical attributes—bushy black eyebrows, dark, sunken eye sockets set in a narrow, long face, strangely black hair contrasting with her snow-colored skin, a large meaty mole above the corner of her upper lip, and thin, long legs—drew my attention to her from the moment she walked in. While she was busy washing herself, a part of the customary bathing shawl that she had wrapped around her waist suddenly slipped away, revealing a bushy black thing hiding in the darkened depth of her scrawny crotch. I thought I had finally seen the infamous Lulu for sure and was terrified, and began nagging and crying and wanting to go home, for which my mother spanked me a few times. From that day forward, without ever actually telling my mother, I feared for my dear life from the time we entered a hammom until we left. Therefore I took no chances and kept an eye on the crotch of any woman who sat close to my mother and me. And for that I was finally banned from women's hammom before I reached the age of four.

Like everything else, Mansoor Aqa even went to hammom with style. I remember well the very first time that my mother asked him to take me to hammom with him. As much as I hated hammom, I was ecstatic at the idea of finally going to a men's hammom like other boys. The night before, my mother had packed and readied everything she thought Mansoor Aqa and I were going to need.

The hammom that Mansoor Aqa took me to was completely different from the ones I was used to visiting with my mother. This place had a large reception area with both men and women, mostly young, sitting on metal folding chairs and waiting. They all seemed to be reading something: magazines, the newspaper—Mansoor Aqa's favorite—or books. Mansoor Aqa was given a number at the desk, and we sat and waited with everyone else. I was holding onto our kerchief full of the stuff that my mother had packed and didn't ask any questions. I had become so accustomed to my mother shushing me all the time and telling me that it wasn't polite for a child to ask so many questions that I decided to leave a good impression on Mansoor Aqa and keep quiet. But inside I was dying to know how in the world all those men and women were going to bathe together.

Once our number was finally called, we followed the attendant down a long, narrow, brightly lit corridor that was decorated with tiles and greenery. Up and down the corridor stood these narrow metal doors facing each other, all of them numbered. The man opened one of the doors and Mansoor Aqa went in and I followed. Mansoor Aqa told the man something and then closed the door and began to undress and asked me to do the same.

I was expecting a large dressing room and a crowd of men and boys, but instead I found myself in a room not much bigger than an average bathroom with a tiled bench, a couple of hooks to hang clothes on, and a large mirror mounted on the wall. There was another small metal door inside this room that I assumed led to the bathing area. Gauging from the little dressing room, I pictured a very small hammom packed with people on the other side of this mysterious door. Mansoor Aqa could not stop laughing when I finally asked if there were a lot of people washing themselves on the other side of that door. He explained that we were in the private cubicles section of our neighborhood hammom. Here customers were charged ten rials per hour, unlike the ones that my mother and I went to where she paid five rials and could stay almost as long as she wished. That explained why there were also women waiting in the reception room.

Before entering the shower room, Mansoor Aqa grabbed only his razor out of the large bag that my mother had prepared and left the rest behind, including Modar Joon's yellow bar of soap. I was puzzled how he was going to wash the two of us without any tools, but then I remembered it was not polite to ask questions. The shower area was a cozy little place covered with white ceramic tiles and had a bench, a faucet, and a showerhead. If only my mother could see this place, I thought.

Mansoor Aqa turned the shower on and we began to soak ourselves, I in my underwear and he with a traditional *long* (a bathing shawl) wrapped around his waist. People in general were very shy about anything concerning their bodies and sexuality. No one ever stood completely naked in front of someone else, regardless of their relationship—although husbands and wives excluded, I am sure. Even two sisters who shared a room would not undress and change in front of one another, for example.

Just as I was watching Mansoor Aqa and mimicking his moves, there was a knock at the door, followed by the voice of a man announcing his entry. Startled, I looked up at Mansoor Aqa with my eyes opened wide. But, before I could say anything, a man also wearing a long and carrying a metal bowl walked in and said hello. I was quick to learn that he was a *dellock*—a body washer. I had seen female dellocks in women's hammoms before. For about five rials they washed and scrubbed people, and for an extra fee they also gave a hearty massage.

The man's bowl contained everything he needed to scrub and wash both of us. I'll never forget the little individual packages of the metallic-yellow shampoo that the man used to wash our hair with. I had never had my hair washed with shampoo before and did not even know what it was until that day.

Afterwards, the man had Mansoor Aqa lie on his stomach and began folding and unfolding Mansoor Aqa's body parts, pounding his back and twisting his neck in a very rough manner. Mansoor Aqa called it a massage, but it looked more like a torture to me. Soon after the dellock finished up and left, and just when I thought going to the hammom couldn't get any better, there was another knock at the outside door and Mansoor Aqa, without hesitation, asked the person to come in. It was the same attendant we saw when we first arrived, carrying a small tray in his hand. On the tray stood two frosted bottles of orange soda, a large and a small one. My eyes popped wide open in disbelief. Who would have imagined life and hammom could be this fantastic? I leisurely finished my soda while watching Mansoor Aqa shave his face.

Let me tell you, nothing tastes as good as a cold soda after you've been inside a hot and steamy room for a while. In the front lobby, Mansoor Aqa settled our tab at the desk, and we went home with our pink faces glowing. After that experience, I would never go to hammom with my mother again, even if I'd been allowed back.

❖*Chapter Nine*

We were now renting a slightly larger room in a newer house, not far from where my mother and I used to live before. The rent was somewhat higher here, and from the very beginning Mansoor Aqa seemed to have difficulty coming up with the entire amount at the beginning of each month. With the way Mansoor Aqa splurged, and also with summer being a slow season for tailors, the situation did not seem to have any chance of improving anytime soon. I overheard, once or twice, Hajji Sinichi, our landlord, talking to Mansoor Aqa about the past-due rent.

I should explain that our new landlord had proudly adopted the prestigious-sounding title Hajji even though technically it did not apply to him yet. Like most folks in the Middle East, Iranians loved giving and receiving titles: Mr. Engineer, Mr. Boss, Mr. Doctor, Hajji (one who had been on pilgrimage to Mecca, which our landlord had not), Karbalaey (one who had been on pilgrimage to Karbala in Iraq), Mashhadi (one who had been on pilgrimage to Mashhad), for example. Titles that revealed one's level of education, professional position, power, or religious devotion—which incidentally at the same time spoke of one's wealth since it was costly to go on pilgrimage—often preceded people's names. In those days, without question being a Hajji was much more prestigious than being a Mashhadi, for example. In Iran almost anyone could afford to go to Mashhad, but to go to Mecca required sophistication and money. The Hajj, or pilgrimage to Mecca, is currently the largest annual pilgrimage in the world and, as the fifth Pillar of Islam, is an obligation that every able-bodied Muslim with the means to do so must carry out at least once in their lifetime. Our landlord had not yet fulfilled this obligation, but since he had

65

already put a deposit down and was on the list of a future group to go to Mecca, his wife and tenants went ahead and called him Hajji Aqa, a title he did not seem to mind at all.

Very late one summer night we were awakened by a knock at the front door, followed by the voice of a drunk-sounding man coming from the street. In a challenging tone the voice was calling on Mansoor Aqa to come outside. My mother was first to jump and sit up in bed, startled. Having lived so long without a man around, she still tended to become jittery at the slightest sound coming from outside at night.

Mansoor Aqa, who was also awake by now, told my mother to stay calm and began to put on his shirt and leave the room to go and answer the door. My mother, clearly frightened, pleaded with him not to go and to let one of the other tenants or the landlord answer the door. Before she was finished with her sentence, he had already left the room. I watched him from the window, crossing the ghostly, moonlight-drenched courtyard. My mother, without turning on the light, rushed to the window and stood next to me with her face appearing bloodless under the wedge of moonlight seeping through the curtains. This was the same petrified look she'd had on that night when a drunken man sang her name from the alleyway next to our old home. Suddenly we heard scuffling sounds coming from the other side of the front wall and door. I was terrified for Mansoor Aqa.

There were two other families, including Hajji Sinichi, living in that house, but peculiarly none of the lights in their side of the house came on. They seemed to sleep through all the commotions. It wasn't long before I saw Mansoor Aqa stepping back into the house, quietly closing the door behind him, and walking back across the courtyard. I let out a sigh of relief.

When he walked into the room, his always-perfect hair was ruffled and his upper torso was slashed in several places; the slashes were bleeding through his white tank-top undershirt. My mother covered her mouth with both hands, let out a silent scream and then hit herself on the head with the palms of her hands—a gesture Mansoor Aqa detested. When my mother reached for the light switch, he grabbed her wrist and shook his head no. Not a sound came out of him to indicate that he was in any sort of pain; there was just a frozen frown on his face, showing that he was

66

angry. I was told to go back to sleep as my mother tended to his wounds. His cuts were apparently not deep enough to necessitate going to the hospital. The next morning as Mansoor Aqa was leaving for work, he instructed my mother to go and look for a new place for us to live and told me not to speak to anyone of what had happened the previous night.

At the time, when it seemed as if my mother and I had no one else in this world, I had come to celebrate Mansoor Aqa's arrival into our life and view him as an invincible citadel of sanctuary. I'd come to idolize him, having seen him fight once or twice before and knowing how strong and lethal he could be. Seeing my idol cut up and covered with blood had me frightened and worried. I did not want anything or anyone to take him away from us.

I remember Mansoor Aqa always stood up to the bullies, oftentimes on someone else's behalf. My mother was learning to be nervous when we all went out together. There was always a chance that a hoodlum—one always appeared to be standing at every street corner—could look at my mother the wrong way or make a wrong remark and draw Mansoor Aqa into a quick brawl. My mother rationalized his behavior by attributing it to his Turkish background. "He is a Turk and cannot help himself," she would say.

The Iranian Turks were stereotyped as being overzealous when it came to protecting their women's honor. But in my opinion the truth lay someplace else. Looking back now, I believe that more than anything it was seeing too many John Wayne films that led Mansoor Aqa to behave like a superhero at the slightest provocation. My theory cannot be too farfetched, since he grew up fatherless and without the influence of an adult male in his life.

Despite Mansoor Aqa's clear instruction that no word of what took place that night should be told to any relatives, a few days later, Rahbar, my mother's tall and handsome cousin, showed up at our doorstep, riding on the back of his beautiful and shiny brown Turkmen horse and carrying his Brno rifle over his shoulder. Cousin Rahbar, as we all called him, was a Golmakani folk hero in the flesh. Women of his village and the surrounding villages secretly wished to be with him, and men wished to be him.

Judging from his conversation with my mother, word of what had happened had reached Golmakan, and Rahbar had been riding nonstop since the crack of dawn to come here and find the culprit responsible for knifing his cousin's husband. Somehow news always seemed to get to Golmakan fast and spread even faster.

If you were a Golmakani—from the village of Golmakan—or even remotely related to one, you were sure to find almost the entire village behind you in times of conflict, and Mansoor Aqa was now related to the Golmakanis. Tribalism was still alive and well in Golmakan; you messed with one and you had messed with them all. It was not at all unusual to find a large truck and the village bus loaded with Golmakani men, carrying wooden clubs and shovels and going somewhere to fight on behalf of one of their own.

I remember that bright and sunny summer day as if it were only yesterday; Cousin Rahbar sat me on the back of his horse and walked around the block on the blacktopped street as he and my mother talked. Since my mother did not know who was behind the attack, there wasn't much he could do except make sure his presence served as a warning to whoever was watching.

The next day Abbas Pahlavan—Abbas the Champ, another one of my mother's cousins—came by after also hearing the news. He was a world wrestling champion and a hero of all the Golmakanis as well as many Iranians. After having a few cups of tea and talking to my mother for a little while, he too took to our street in a show of force. There was no way that the men responsible for knifing Mansoor Aqa, if they lived on our street, would not have been wetting their pants upon seeing the bigger-than-life Cousin Abbas. I remember all kinds of men approached Cousin Abbas and shook and kissed his hand as he strolled up and down the street that day. While he clearly enjoyed this adoration from his fans, he made sure that everyone knew that my mother was his cousin.

All this happened while Mansoor Aqa was at work. He was not told about the support he had received from his new Golmakani relatives because my mother did not want him to find out that she had gone against his wishes and told her sister about the incident. A week later my mother found a room in the Pole-Khaki area, near where my biological father lived, and we moved.

A few years later I learned why Mansoor Aqa was attacked that night and by whom. According to my mother, two ruffians were paid by our landlord, Hajji Sinichi, to deliver a rent-past-due warning to my stepfather that night when things got out of hand after Mansoor Aqa slapped one of them. Hiring ruffians to act as debt collectors and to settle scores was not an uncommon occurrence.

Chapter Ten

O ne sunny and bitterly cold day in January of 1961, I accompanied Mansoor Aqa to the hospital to bring home my mother and my newly born baby brother, Mehdi. I remember on the way home the baby was sleeping on my mother's lap, wrapped warmly in a blanket, wearing a hat and a little sweater that my mother had made for him during her pregnancy.

Mansoor Aqa, smiling from ear to ear, sat in the front with the taxicab driver. His chest expanded with pride as he told the driver how the birth of his son made him the first among his siblings to have a boy. His older brother had three daughters before he finally gave up and left his wife for another woman in hope of a son, he told the driver. And here was a bull's-eye for Mansoor Aqa on his first try. Unlike Mansoor Aqa, his brother was educated, and as a result had an easy and good-paying job teaching at a high school in Tehran. And for that, Mansoor Aqa had deep resentment toward his brother. He saw the birth of his son as the universe's way of balancing things out a little in his favor. Seeing Mansoor Aqa so happy and knowing that she had something to do with it made my mother beam with pride as she let out sighs of happiness while looking at the road ahead and listening to her husband brag.

Sitting in the backseat of the taxicab and listening to Mansoor Aqa, I remembered my mother used to tell me how proud my father was when I was first born.

"I cannot tell you enough how gratified your father was when you were born, pesaram. He did not want anyone near you, fearing they may give you germs or something. Worried that you may catch a draft, he did not allow any windows to be opened when you were in the room. And who could have blamed him after the sudden and unexpected death of your brother Parveez? I could not get pregnant for a long time, no matter how hard we tried and how many doctors we saw after your brother died. Finally, it was Imam Reza that answered our prayers and gave you to us. Your father's oblations and my prayers paid off, and I became pregnant with you. To show his gratitude to Imam Reza, your father named you after him: Ali-Reza. Having a son again had your father walking on clouds. He showered me with kisses and gold jewelry."

I had heard the story often enough to know it by heart, and each time upon hearing it again, I would smile and feel good, knowing that there was a time when I had a place in my father's heart.

As if in celebration of Mehdi's birth, Old Man Winter had decided to decorate the city in white and silver. Snow and ice a few days old covered the treetops and the edges of buildings everywhere, glittering under the sun like ornaments. I too was happy and celebrating in my heart my little brother's arrival. Through him, I was now forever bonded to Mansoor Aqa.

After the birth of my little baby brother, going to Arg and the cinema with Mansoor Aqa became a thing of the past. He rarely went anywhere anymore and spent the bulk of his free time at home and with the baby. From very early on, Mansoor Aqa began to teach Mehdi to say *baba*—papa in Farsi. Of course Mehdi was still too little to utter any words, but I was not. I was four and a half at the time and almost immediately began to call Mansoor Aqa Baba.

Now that she had a child, securing her fairly new marriage, my mother's only dream was to have a home of her own, just like her two younger sisters. A dream that under their circumstances only a miracle, like winning the lottery, could fulfill—and Baba played the lottery religiously. Every Wednesday night at eight o'clock sharp he sat on the floor with his one lottery ticket in his hand, glued his ear to the radio, and listened to the drawing only to be disappointed once again.

Financially things seemed to be getting worse for us. We were changing residences almost every four or five months. Often we were forced to move because Baba had fallen behind in the rent payments. He was not making enough money and clearly was struggling to keep up with all the expenses that were associated with being married and having a family. And as if things were not difficult enough already, every bicycle that Baba bought was stolen; without a bicycle it was difficult for him to go to work. In addition, my mother gave birth to her second child with Mansoor Aqa. I was there when her water broke as she was cleaning our tiny trunk room and, with the help of one our neighbors, she delivered her baby right there.

To ease the financial burden on her husband somewhat, my mother was eventually able to convince Baba to put aside his pride for a while and allow her to resume weaving wool and cracking apricot pits again. Despite the extra money that my mother brought in, her frugal ways of running a home, and her unique ability to stretch every rial, the financial pressure did not seem to dissipate much.

Deciding to live in Mashhad after marrying my mother had not turned out to be such a good choice for Baba. According to him, the business of sewing men's suits was not as lucrative and constant here in Mashhad as it was in the larger and more sophisticated city of Tehran, where he had lived for many years. And unfortunately for him, he did not know any other profession and lacked any kind of formal education that might qualify him for a better-paying job with the government, the nation's largest employer.

Norooz season (the Persian New Year) and the last month of summer just prior to the reopening of schools were Baba's best earning periods. But, despite working overtime in those more lucrative interludes, he was left to struggle for the rest of the year. He lacked the discipline to save and to budget his earnings appropriately. Considering his age, twenty-some years old, that was not at all surprising.

As things worsened, I found myself the subject of a new and less than happy conversation. Thinking I was asleep, my mother and Baba began whispering my name at nights while in bed on the other side of the room. These whisperings centered on how to go about getting child support from my father—a subject that had been all but forgotten since my mother met Baba. The buzz from the relatives indicated that my father was doing well for himself; hence my mother felt mounting pressure to take some action.

Finally one afternoon, while Baba was at work, my mother left my two little siblings with a neighbor, grabbed my hand, and off we went to see my father about getting child support for me. This time, unlike in the past, she went straight to my father's house and rang the doorbell. My father himself opened the door wearing a pair of shiny black army boots, green army pants, and a white tank-top undershirt, indicating that he had just returned from work. His brother Habiballah, the one who was involved in the disappearance of my sister, was also there, standing behind him in the doorway. Standing on the sidewalk next to my mother, I raised my head and looked up at my father at the top of the stairs with my heart pounding in excitement. This was the first time I'd seen him since I could remember. From what I'd heard about him, looking at him invoked both fear and love within me. I was searching his eyes for any sign of paternal affection toward me. He did cast a brief and indifferent gaze at me before turning his attention to my mother and asking her in a cold tone why she was there. My mother, in an innocent and submissive tone, told him that she was here to ask for child support; she did not bring up the subject of my missing sister.

They exchanged some more words before my father asked her to come inside. While she still held my hand, the two of us went up the stairs and into a corridor. He closed the door behind us and glanced at me once again with the same indifference before turning his attention back to my mother. I was too young to understand half of what they were saying. Soon he was snarling at my mother, calling her names and shaking his fist in her face. They exchanged a few more words before my father suddenly went into a rage. He grabbed my mother's hair and used it to drag her down to the floor, repeatedly kicking her in the process. I immediately ran to my mother's side, grabbed my father's leg, and made a futile attempt to stop him. Before I knew what happened, I found myself flying across the dimly lit corridor and hitting the wall. By now Habiballah had joined his brother, kicking and punching my mother. I sat dumbfounded on the cold marble floor with my back against the wall, petrified and crying helplessly as I watched the two men banging her head against the floor. Then we were thrown outside and I heard the front door slammed shut behind us.

My mother found it difficult to maintain her balance as we began to walk back home. Once we reached the creek close to our house where she did laundry once a week, she sat on a large rock under the shade of a tree, handed me a small handkerchief, and asked me to get it wet for her so that she could clean the blood off of her face. I served as her mirror, pointing to where the blood was, as she wept and complained to God about his unjust world.

As we walked the rest of the way home, my mother ordered and begged me at the same time not to say a word to Baba of what had happened. She was afraid, and rightfully so; if Baba found out, he'd for sure kill my father and go to jail for the rest of his life, and that would have been the end for my mother. As much as I wanted Baba to know what had happened so he could go and grab the two brothers and slam their heads against the wall and the floor, I painfully kept what I'd witnessed to myself. Once we arrived at home, my mother covered some of her bruises with makeup, and for the ones that she could not hide, she made up a story for Baba, telling him that she had slipped and fallen. Keeping what happened to my mother a secret while at the same time hungering for revenge was one of the most difficult choices I have ever made in my life. Knowing Baba, one word from me about the incident would have certainly brought about some sort of an end to my father, to Baba, and to my mother's new life.

I couldn't look in my mother's eyes for a while after that incident. I felt responsible for what happened to her and guilty for being my father's son.

Soon I was beginning to inadvertently pick up bits and pieces of conversation that were taking place all around me. Perhaps the conversation had been there all along and I only now was old enough to understand it. My mother and Baba, various relatives who came to visit, and sometimes even the neighbors, all seemed to be talking about me.

"It is not as if his father is dead." "His father should be raising him." "Poor little boy. He has been abandoned by his own father." "Poor little orphan, what is going to become of him when he grows up?" "Take him to his father's house and leave him at his doorstep. It is his kid, why should you have to be the one sacrificing your marriage?" "Poor Mansoor Aqa, he has committed no sin to be stuck with raising somebody else's child."

I began to sense that I did not belong anywhere and no one seemed to be trying very hard to claim me. I felt like an intruder that nobody knew what to do with. Before Baba, when my mother used to wish and pray for a good man and a home, I automatically assumed that her prayers were for both of us. I presumed that my mother and I were a package and whoever ended up wanting and marrying her was also going to want me.

"I don't want to go, Momon," I pleaded with my mother, but it was too late. A small kerchief containing some clothes for me was already waiting by the door. I was being sent to live with my father, just for a little while— an arrangement apparently negotiated between my father and my mother by relatives. It would be different if my mother had said I was going to *visit* with my father for a while, but to live? The word "live" had a devastating connotation to me. It was difficult for me to understand how this could be happening. The only parent I knew was my mother, and I always thought she and I were inseparable. How could she send me to a man that she had been speaking so ill of for as long as I could remember? A man I knew very little about?

"I promise not to ever wet my mattress again, Momon, please …" I had this notion in my head that besides being an extra mouth to feed as economic hardship beleaguered my mother's marriage, the main reason I was being sent to my father was because I wet my bed at night, regularly. Each morning, long before the sun rose, my mother already had my pants and my little cotton-filled mattress hanging from the clothesline to dry, announcing to the world what I had done. I remember standing in humiliation just outside our doorway, watching my mother stripping me naked, grumping and squeezing her teeth together in anger, whispering, "I am embarrassed that every morning Mansoor Aqa has to wake up to the sting of your urine."

She washed my pants and rinsed only the area of the mattress that was stained with pee and hung them, all before Baba got up. But it was impossible for Baba not to notice my wet pants and wet little mattress hanging on the wall across from our window where he stood and shaved his face every morning before going to work.

Not wanting me to see her tear-soaked eyes, my mother looked the other way, pretending to be rearranging something on the niche, and said, "It is a good thing that your father has agreed for you to spend some time with him. Every boy needs a father."

"But Baba is my father."

"Yes, but it is also good to get to know your real father."

That evening when Baba came home from work, my mother served him a couple cups of hot tea, which he drank without changing into his pajamas as he usually did, and then he asked my mother if I was ready. My mother nodded yes with a despondent look on her face. They both looked at me, and Baba asked if I liked the idea of visiting my real father for a while. With a large lump in my throat and my lower lip hanging in protest, I shook my head no. If it wasn't for my recent encounter with my father in the hallway of his house, I probably would not have been as reluctant. I had no interest in getting to know the man I saw so brutally attack my mother not very long ago.

My mother kissed me and whispered some last-minute advice in my ears:

"Don't drink a lot of water or eat any watermelon at night, even if they offer it to you. Watermelon makes you pee your bed. Be sure to use the bathroom before you go to bed at night. Be very polite and always say hello, good morning, and good night, pesaram. Nobody likes a gluttonous boy, so do not touch any food unless they offer it to you. Don't give any excuses to anyone to punish you, pesaram."

"But I don't want to go, Momon," I whispered with my head down.

"I know, pesaram, but who knows, you may like your father. You are his son and he loves you."

A little later I was riding in front of Baba on his bicycle, holding on to the folded kerchief containing my earthly possessions and going to my uncle's house, where I was to be dropped off. My father was going to pick me up later that evening, I was told. Baba tried to calm my anxiety by telling me how no one could truly replace one's real father and how this stay could be a good opportunity for me. What I wanted to hear the most, however, was when he would come back to take me home. I couldn't help but cry as he pedaled farther and farther into the early evening twilight and away from our home. I did not know at that moment that there were going to be certain words in the world that would never have the same meaning in my life as they did in the lives of everyone else. The word "home" was one of them.

76

In a last attempt to sway Baba's mind as he went up the steps at my uncle's home and reached for the doorbell, I told him I was sorry for peeing in my bed. Baba rubbed my head and smiled without saying anything.

Beebee-Fatimah, my uncle's wife, opened the door, smiling, indicating she was expecting me. My eyes, however, were glued to Baba as he said goodbye, got on his bicycle, and pedaled away, disappearing into the night.

❖ Chapter Eleven

More than a week passed at my uncle's home, and still no sign of my father coming to pick me up. During the days, as I played in my uncle's courtyard with my cousins, every now and then I could hear the crying of a child and the voice of a woman coming from the courtyard of the adjacent house on the other side of the wall. That was my father's house, and according to my cousins the voice of the woman was that of my stepmother and the baby's crying belonged to my infant half brother. Even though I had never met her before, hearing her voice sent a chill down my spine.

Finally, one early evening my father came over and took me to his home next door. He said very little to me but thanked his brother's wife Beebee-Fatima for looking after me. My cousin Mehri, her face covered with a sympathetic and sad smile, handed me the kerchief containing my change of clothes.

"Don't worry, Alireza, my brothers will come over tomorrow to take you outside and play, okay?" she said, winking at me.

"Okay." Mehri was my uncle's oldest daughter, about eight or nine years of age at the time. Like an angel, she took me under her wings while I was at their home, looked after me and assuaged the pain of being away from my mother. She had inherited her mother's amiable tenderness. With her long, wavy reddish hair, freckled white skin, and green eyes, she resembled a biblical character sent here just to solace me during those difficult first few nights of my motherlessness. Mehri said that I should not worry, but I was more than worried; I was terrified thinking I was going to be staying with my father and his wife. All the tales that I had heard growing up suggested stepmothers were cruel and jealous people who stopped at nothing to rid themselves of their stepchildren. And as for my father, I had witnessed his brutal nature firsthand and knew that he was responsible for my sister's vanishing. What if I too disappeared like my sister and never saw my mother, Baba, and my baby brother Mehdi again?

My legs began to tremble as I followed my father up the front steps into his house—the same steps my mother and I had taken only a month ago, moments before she was viciously beaten. Once inside, I closed the door behind me and took my shoes off. The stone-tiled floor of the narrow hallway felt ice cold to the soles of my bare feet. A flashback, and then a sudden feeling of panic and melancholy swept over me. I wanted my mother more at that moment than any other time that I could remember. An overhead light fixture cast pale and ghostly fluorescent light, giving the corridor a cold and surreal appearance. I clenched the kerchief that held my belongings tightly against my chest. It smelled like home and my mother. The spirit of my mother was there, flung on the floor in front of me, screaming soundlessly as she extended her hand toward me and whispered for help. For one brief moment I thought of turning around and running away. But where to? I had nowhere else to go.

I followed my father into a living room. "*Salam, khanom,*" I said nervously to a lady sitting on the floor against the far wall. Without raising her head, she lifted her eyes and eyebrows, looked at me from afar, and asked how I was doing.

"Fine, *mercy, khanom* (thank you, lady)."

Her gaze made me feel as if she was studying me, perhaps trying to gauge from my look how beautiful my mother was, or possibly how much I looked like her husband—a right, she perhaps felt, reserved only for her children.

Then she abruptly turned her head away to tend to an infant she was holding on her lap and said nothing more.

When it was bedtime, I was shown where to sleep: on a child mattress that was already spread for me in another room. I had never slept in a room all by myself before. I missed my little baby brother Mehdi and my mother. As I lay there alone in the room, it felt as if I'd been left behind in a foreign and hostile land somewhere far away. My father hardly spoke to me the entire night before I went to bed—a good thing, I assumed. If tonight was any indication, I did not believe my father had any plans of getting to know me. If anything, he was probably planning on getting rid of me. I heard him and his wife speaking in Zargary once or twice. People often spoke in Zargary in the presence of children when they did not wish to be understood. Zargary was a speaking language only, created to be used in private conversations. The letter Z was inserted into each spoken word here and there, hence confusing a listener. There were no set rules in where to place the letter Z as long as the word felt natural to the tongue. The word "book" in Zargary would be pronounced "bozok" and the word "comeback" would be "cozombazak," for example. I knew of Zargary from hearing my mother and grandmother speak it, but did not understand it at the time.

After I cried in my pillow for a while, I fell asleep and had a vivid and soothing dream, in which I found myself sitting on a high plateau overlooking a lush green meadow of tall wheatgrass that danced with the wind. Sitting on a smooth boulder next to me was a man with a kind and friendly smile on his face. He looked very masculine, with an ancient Greek warrior's body and a *himation* draped over his bare shoulder and across his waist. His perfectly trimmed white beard matched his short and somewhat curly white hair. While I did not recognize this man, he felt very familiar and close to me. Everything about him conveyed a reassuring and unmistakable message of solace. The next morning I found myself profoundly affected by the dream; I could not get it out of my head for many days to come.

Like a garden missing its gardener, I was not doing too well after what seemed to be a month or so of being at my father's home. My hair and nails had grown long, my scalp was itching, and I was in dire need of a good scrub and wash. I looked like the little beggar boys my mother and I used to see hustling the pilgrims around the shrine on Fridays. If it wasn't for my cousin Mehri washing my clothes once or twice next door, they would have rotted on my body by this time. My feelings were also in disarray.

Before I left home, I was under the assumption that I would be staying with my father only for a little while. I was now very homesick and did not know what to do. There was no news from my mother and no indication at my father's home that my presence there was going to be permanent. My unwashed extra clothes were bundled in the same kerchief I brought them in, sitting next to my shoes by the front door in the foyer. I was afraid of asking my father and did not know what to do or who to talk to about going home. I was certain that I knew how to find my way home and considered running away once or twice, but each time the memory of the policeman who took me home and demanded money from my mother dampened that idea.

Here at my father's, no one talked to me much or told me anything about any plan concerning me. My father seemed to always be at work, except on some Fridays, and when he was home he slept a lot. I was afraid of approaching him, and he didn't show much interest in talking to me. My stepmother, Zahra Khanom, only spoke to me when she needed me to go to the store for her or walk her baby in my arms when he was sleepy and crying.

Zahra Khanom was an average-looking woman with a round and chubby face. She rarely smiled at anyone, and when she did, the smile was often cold and empty. A permanent frown or an empty stare seemed to be her only two facial expressions. At the time she had two children, a toddler daughter and an infant boy. All I can remember now about the baby boy was his overly large belly button—the size of a golf ball—and the fact that his mother fed him beaten raw egg yolks mixed with sugar almost every day.

More than feeling sorry for myself, however, my heart went out for my mother. I could not imagine what she was going through without me. Before she met Baba, I was her companion, her solacer, and according to her, her reason for living. I could hear her singing sad folk songs, inserting my name in the lyrics and crying, as she did during the first years after my sister's disappearance. Having grown up in this land of eternal victimhood, like many others in her shoes, my mother viewed herself as a martyr. Everything, good or bad, was God's will. Dragging God into their personal affairs was an excuse for many folks, like my mother, to wash their hands of their responsibilities and cover their incompetence. Under the circumstances and knowing my mother, perhaps it was best that she blamed God and not herself.

Besides going to stores for Zahra Khanom, I left my father's street only once the entire time that I stayed at his home. My stepmother took me along once as she went to visit her younger sister who lived on Naderi Avenue near the shrine.

Once we arrived at her sister's, I took my shoes off in the foyer and walked up the stairs and entered the room my stepmother had already gone into. I remember the room being crowded with women, mostly Zahra Khanom's sisters and mother. There was a sudden and simultaneous silence as the women's attention turned to me, followed by a murmuring between them as they looked at me out of the corner of their eyes—looks that were intensified by the black eye makeup they all seemed to be wearing. It appeared as if the murmuring was about whether I looked like my father or not. There were no introductions for me. I guess none were needed since everyone already seemed to know who I was. Like a soldier who has all of a sudden found himself alone behind the enemy lines, my heart lurched and I felt sickened. If any of those women were to ask me any question at that moment, I was sure to explode into tears.

Eventually the women all left the room to participate in the family activity of making *aush* (Iranian noodle soup) in the little courtyard below. I was told to stay in the room and look after Zahra Khanom's baby. After everyone left, a teenage girl resembling Zahra Khanom came over, touched my face, smiled at me and said, "You are very cute. Let me know if you get thirsty or need to go to the bathroom, okay?"

"*Chashm, khanom,* (yes, madam)," I replied, smiling back.

At lunchtime everyone gathered on the floor around the sofreh in the living room and ate the hot noodle soup they had just made. My stepmother took me to another room and handed me a small copper bowl filled with the noodle soup and returned to join her mother and sisters in the living room.

I had never before had anything so foul-tasting as that bowl of aush given to me by my stepmother. It was a slightly warm, slimy, and thick substance that did not resemble or taste like any noodle soup I had ever eaten before. Aush was a popular national soup served during religious rituals and other important ceremonies and sold in restaurants and on wooden pushcarts out on the streets. Unless someone lived under a rock, it was impossible for any Iranian, regardless of age, not to know what aush should taste and look like. But I was too hungry to be picky, so I ate the entire contents of the bowl regardless of the awful taste. A little while later the teenage girl who I learned was my stepmother's sister came by, saw that my bowl was empty, and asked if I cared for more. I nodded yes. She took the bowl and returned a little later with it full, steaming hot and smelling like a true aush should, garnished with sour whey, fried garlic, onion, and mint. Looking back now, I cannot help but to believe that the first bowl of the soup my stepmother gave me was intentionally tainted to taste the way it did.

Finally, one fine afternoon, the universe felt sorry for me and decided to pleasantly surprise me. Bored and unhappy, I was sitting on the edge of the fountain in my father's courtyard, gently paddling the water back and forth with my hand in an attempt to attract the little goldfish swimming below. Zahra Khanom was sitting on a folding chair a few meters away with her son on her lap, feeding him a beaten egg yolk and sugar out of a little bowl. Suddenly, Aliakbar, my oldest male cousin from next door, accompanied by his younger brother, walked into the courtyard and asked Zahra Khanom if I could go outside and play. She said no. I cannot recall now why she objected but, nevertheless, she did. After some begging and pleading, Aliakbar was able to persuade her to let me go with him, but for just a little while. He pretended to need a third person for the game he and his brother were going to play. Once outside he grabbed my wrist and began running to the end of the block, stopping in front of the neighborhood's convenience store located on the corner of the street. Before taking me inside, he asked me to close my eyes and I did. Once inside I opened my eyes and could not believe my good fortune; my mother was there waiting for me.

Over the course of my life, I have had many reunions with various loved ones, but this one I will never forget. I ran into my mother and locked my arms around her neck. Nothing had ever smelled as wonderful and secure to me as did the scent of my mother that day. My mother used to say that she could pick her child out of a group of a thousand children with her eyes closed by simply sniffing behind the ears of every child; now I knew what she meant by that. She kissed my head, my face, and my hands and neck over and over while the two of us cried. Like a puppy who had found its mother, I was wriggling with joy. She wiped my tears with her kisses while she kept repeating in a rhythmic way, "My beautiful boy, Mommy's life, Mommy's breath, I hope to die for you a thousand times, pesaram. I hope God takes my life and adds it to yours, Ali joon. Mommy's beautiful flower, what have they done to you, pesaram? Isn't anyone bathing you, my dearest?" she cried after seeing the shape I was in.

My cousin reminded her that I could not stay for very long. She pulled herself together, squatting in the corner of the store, unfolded a piece of wax paper containing a slice of baklava and began feeding it to me in a hurry.

I touched her wet and crimsoned face and asked her about Mehdi and Baba. They were fine, she told me. Mehdi missed me a lot, she said. "He walks around the house with his bottle in his mouth, calling your name and looking for you." Then her demeanor changed, becoming more tense and hurried. "We don't have much time. I have to go back and get Mansoor Aqa's dinner ready before he gets home. I have to leave before your father shows up and finds me here near his home," she said, looking around nervously.

I gave her an "I understand" look as she kissed clean the pastry crumbs from the corners of my lips and bombarded me once again with kisses that were hard and loud. She then paid the shop owner for the baklava and gave my cousin five rials for arranging the meeting. Our brief reunion was over. I stood on the corner of the narrow street and watched my mother go, walking backwards and looking at me while shaking her head from side to side and crying.

I don't remember ever feeling as bad for anyone as I did for my mother that day and at that moment. Even though every cell in my body was screaming her name and asking me to run after her and beg and cry for her to take me home, I couldn't. She must have had a good reason for not mentioning anything about my going back home with her. Asking her would only have salted her wounds even more. I knew that, as she walked home, she was most likely crying and hiccupping and blaming it all on God. Poor God. Poor Mother.

❖Chapter Twelve

J ust as my father knew little about me and my life as I was growing up, I knew even less about him, and most of what I did know was secondhand information, often tainted by the feelings and personal opinion of the individual conveying it. He and I were never together long enough at any given time to get to know one another—in the few dozen encounters we had over the course of our lifetime, he always seemed to be in a rush, going somewhere.

My father was a handsome man, somewhat shorter than average. In his home village of Golmakan, everyone knew Assad, son of Banafsheh. He was famous for being clever, a quick thinker, fearless, glib-tongued, a hoodwinker, and some other flattering and not so flattering adjectives, depending on whom you talked to. He was known as someone who could get almost anything done, and for that he was given the nickname of King's Cousin. In the minds of many villagers, only a cousin of the king had enough clout to be as influential as Assad was perceived to be.

But his story was a hard one. His mother, Banafsheh, had given birth to a total of eight children, of which only four had survived—three boys and one girl. Shortly after the birth of her daughter Fatimah, when my father was nine, Banafsheh's husband passed away. Being long disowned by her powerful father for disobeying his wishes and marrying her now deceased husband, she was left destitute. According to relatives, even though my father was the youngest of three boys, he took upon himself the responsibility of being the breadwinner for his family. I never found out why he, and not his older brothers, decided to shoulder such a heavy burden.

According to my cousin Jam, who was practically raised by Banafsheh and knew her story better than anyone, when she was young Banafsheh had fallen in love with a handsome young peasant who worked as a sharecropper on her father's land. Her father, the headman of the Upper Golmakan, when approached by Banafsheh with the idea of marrying the young man, adamantly forbade the union. Banafsheh, madly in love and left with no other choice, packed her things and ran away from home in the middle of the night. She rendezvoused with her lover at the edge of the village, where she got on the back of his horse and the two of them rode away into the night, not to be heard from for many years to come. The father, shamed and heartbroken by what he perceived to be a treachery, issued a ban prohibiting the young couple from ever returning to Golmakan. Some years later, however, when Banafsheh sent a message to her father asking for his forgiveness and permission for her and her husband to return to the village, he conditionally agreed, granting them permission to return to the village as long as they never crossed his path or asked him for anything.

The death of her husband some years later did not change Banafsheh's standing with her estranged father. She had very little choice but to place her hopes on little Assad, my father. The young boy took on odd jobs in the farms and orchards in and around Golmakan, reaping grains and picking fruits and vegetables to support the family. The job that paid him the most was working on a poppy farm where, for a few rials a day, with a razorblade in hand he slit poppies in the early morning hours. He went home with his fingers cut and bleeding every day. Since the ideal time for slitting the poppies and extracting their opium was just before sunrise, little Assad was compelled to get up and go to work long before the rest of the villagers were even awake. Every morning he would have to walk a distance of a few kilometers in the dark and on dangerous mountainous paths to get to the hidden poppy fields. Newly enacted laws had made opium and opium-related activities illegal in the country, and little Assad sometimes got caught in the crossfire between the government's forces and the opium growers or smugglers.

At the age of twelve, Assad gave up the dangerous poppy work and went into the business of selling small household goods. Using the family's donkey, he rode to the city where he purchased his goods, mostly pots and pans, and then sold them in Golmakan and the surrounding villages. This part about his life my father actually told me himself once, I'm guessing for no other reason than to emphasize that life was not easy for him either.

When some years later the army came to his village seeking to recruit and enlist any young man with some reading and writing skills, my father seized on the opportunity and signed up. As a boy he had learned to write and read his own name and a few other words by attending Quran classes on Fridays. At the age of sixteen he and his best friend, Abdul, my mother's older half brother, enlisted in the army and left their village for good.

I am no psychologist, but I cannot help but wonder what role my father's harsh past and lost childhood played in shaping the man he later became. I wonder if the razorblade from his poppy-slitting days left bleeding wounds not just in his small fingers but in his heart as well.

Chapter Thirteen

My father was standing and shaving his face in front of a mirror by the living room window. At the time very few homes were equipped with modern bathrooms; with sinks, mirrors and lights, therefore, most men shaved their faces by the window where they could take advantage of natural light. During my entire stay at his house, this was the first time that I'd known him to still be home and awake so late in the morning. Being a military man, six days a week he left for work long before the sun came up or anyone else was awake at the house; on his day off he slept in and would not have been stirring at this hour. I happened to be sitting in the room that morning, and when I saw no objection in his face, I decided to stay and watch, hoping he may talk to me. I used to enjoy watching Baba shave and giggled when he winked at me through his mirror. The fluffy mound of shaving foam on Baba's face never ceased to amuse me; it looked like a sweet dessert.

I sat and watched from the middle of the room while my father shaved with an electric razor. Despite my limited and less than pleasant experience with him thus far, instinctively I still yearned for his affection. Feeling lonely and insecure, I was also hoping to find some comfort in a conversation with him. He twisted and turned different parts of his face as he ran the razor over the surface of his skin. I watched his expressions in the mirror with glee. Once as he puckered and twisted his lips sideways, perhaps in an attempt to accommodate his razor, I thought he was smiling at me, so I smiled back. My father suddenly stopped his razor and turned around. Looking at me coldly, he snarled, "Why are you smirking, you son of a bitch?" With his eyes rounded and bulging, he stared at me, as if he was waiting for my reply. Dumbfounded by his harsh reaction, I didn't know what to say or do. Like a hot piece of metal that had been pulled out of the fire and submerged into a bucket of cold water, my smile and the hope of connecting with my father sizzled away fast.

"I am sorry, Aqa," was all I could think of to say. I was shocked and heartbroken, not only by his uncalled-for and unkind reaction but also because no one had referred to my mother as a whore before and at the time I did not understand calling someone a name could only be a slur and not necessarily a statement of fact. I could not get what he called my mother out of my mind for a long time.

Once he was finished shaving, my father told me to gather my things and be ready to leave soon. His words were music to my ears; I was finally going home to my mother. I had nothing to gather but my kerchief that held an unwashed pair of pants and a shirt. I put on my shoes in a hurry and waited by the front door for my father to get dressed. Just as we were leaving, I reluctantly stuck my head into Zahra Khanom's bedroom and said goodbye before I ran outside and got into my father's Volkswagen Beetle. She pretended to be sleeping and did not answer.

This was my first time inside a private automobile. I'd never known anyone who owned an automobile. According to our relatives, my father had made history by being the first man from Golmakan to own an automobile. Sitting in the backseat, like a patriot returning home from exile, I eagerly devoured with my eyes all the familiar places and landmarks as they passed by my window. As my father drove closer to where we lived, I began imagining being embraced by my mother and baby brother Mehdi and my heart began to pound faster. My father did not speak a word, and I was not one to dare to ask any questions. Just as rapidly as my heart began to pump when we neared our neighborhood, it began to slow down and almost stop as we passed the area. I did not understand. Why didn't he turn into our street? Where was he taking me? A thousand questions and worries started to rush through my head as hope of going home faded away.

Always in autumn, the parts of Mashhad where the roads were lined with tall, massive trees turned both beautiful and melancholy. As striking as the orange, red, yellow, brown, and green foliage that colored the streets and blanketed the sidewalks was, it silently spoke of a sad separation and an end. The gray sky and the musty scent of fallen wet leaves hinted that summer was over and winter was about to move in. When I was little, I used to think the crows raucously calling overhead were screaming at the trees for their inaction as the wind snatched the foliage away from their arms. Why weren't they stopping the wind, why didn't they care about their foliage? the crows seemed to be cawing.

This particular morning was one of those typically nippy and gray autumn days.

Once my father drove past the Saadabad football stadium and headed east, I knew for sure he wasn't taking me home.

"You have passed our street, aqa," I softly said to him.

He briefly looked at me through the rearview mirror and said nothing. Thinking he did not hear me the first time, I repeated my remark.

"You are going to stay with my uncle for a while," he told me.

"But I want to go home, aqa. I miss my mommy."

He did not reply.

Disappointed, I rested my head against the automobile's door, gazed at the gray sky, and asked no more questions. I wanted to cry, but I was too ashamed to do so in front of my father. At the time I did not know that my days of living with my mother were forever over. Those days had actually come to an end back on that evening when Baba took me to my uncle's. I was now and forever only a specter of my mother's past. My grandfather used to say that a child needs the shadow of at least one of his parents over his head. Going forward, the only shadow I seemed to have over my head was my own.

My father dropped me off at his uncle's house, exchanged a few words with them, and left without saying anything to me. I had never met my father's uncle before, but I knew the area where he lived like the palm of my hand. We used to live in an alley across the street from him, where my mother delivered her last baby in the trunk room. My aunt Sarvar also lived just a few blocks up the road. Returning to a familiar neighborhood and knowing that my aunt lived close by warmed me from within somewhat.

After about a week, my father returned and took me across the street to someone else's home. These people were his cousins, according to my father. We used to live just a few doors down from them in the same alley. My father did not stay for very long, and just before he left, he thanked the young couple and assured them that this was only a temporary arrangement until he could come up with a permanent solution for me.

Mashhad's notoriously cold and long winter had arrived early and settled in. I, on the other hand, still had no idea what was going to become of me. I was not fully acclimated to this new life and had no clue when things were going to go back to the way they were, if ever. The only thing that seemed certain was my father's authority. It was clearly he, and he alone, in charge of my fate. I missed my mother very much and wanted to go back to her but I didn't feel I could make such a demand. Most children of that age become angry and act out when they don't get their way, but I couldn't. Anger is often caused by failed expectations, and I had been gradually indoctrinated into not having any expectations. It was difficult to have any sense of entitlement and to get angry when I was made to feel my whole existence was one big burden on others. I did all my crying for my mother when I was in bed or alone. I do remember telling my father once about wanting to go home, to which he responded with a cold, half grin.

A few days after I was transferred to my father's cousins, two men came by and told the lady that they were there to take me away per my father's instruction. The lady handed me my kerchief and said goodbye without asking the men any questions. Outside, the two men claimed to be friends of my father's as we walked on the snow-covered sidewalk toward the main road. They were taking me to Golmakan, my grandparents' village, and were going to look after me for a while, they said.

At the Maydoneh Bar area—Mashhad's only wholesale fruit and produce market—we boarded the morning bus to the village. The bus was fairly empty. Golmakan, a mountainous village, was often buried under heavy snow during the winter, and therefore hardly anyone who did not live there traveled to Golmakan during that season.

I followed the men to the back of the bus and took a seat next to a window. The two men sat together on the seat across the aisle from me. They hardly said a word to one another—and nothing at all to me. I had been to Golmakan many times before. In the past my mother, and sometimes my grandparents or my uncle Zabih, had taken me there, but never in winter.

Soon the assistant driver cranked the engine with a handle from the outside, the bus started, and we were on our way. The entire landscape was covered with snow, marked by scattered trees here and there. One, two, three ... I began counting the white kilometer stones on the side of the road as they rushed by my window. I could only count to three. I wondered why my father would want me in Golmakan at this time of the year. None of the events of the past few months had made any sense to me—why should this trip be any different? But it wasn't as if I had anything better to do. At least now there was a chance that I could see my grandfather and spend some time with him. I loved my grandfather very much.

The bus eventually stopped to refuel. I watched as the two men walked off the bus and to the edge of the station near the road. One of them seemed to be listening, while the other one smoked a cigarette, talking and waving his hands the whole time. I turned my attention to the two measuring glass jars on the station's only pump and watched them take turns filling and emptying with the translucent reddish gasoline. Soon the bus was on the road again and on its way to Golmakan. It wasn't long before the bus turned off of the main highway and headed west toward the mountains, where the village nestled in the foothills.

My recollection of the events of that day are somewhat hazy now, but I do remember that once the bus neared Golmakan, just before entering Lower Village, the men asked the driver to stop and drop us off on the side of the now snow-covered gravel road—way before the bus was due to reach its first regular stop. Once off of the bus, I followed the men through a vast snow-covered meadow where the snow was almost up to my waist. After walking a good distance, we arrived at the ruins of an ancient structure. In a country as old as Iran, these structures were a part of the landscape everywhere. The two men entered the ruins and began building a fire using some partially burned wood they had found, saying that we were going to rest there for a little while.

Outside of the semi-roofless structure, there was snow covering the rolling hills for as far as the eye could see. I heard water gurgling nearby and followed the sound to a narrow stream meandering through the snow. The heads of young peppermint could be seen poking through the snow on the edges of the stream.

From a distance, through a large opening that suggested there used to be one massive door there, I watched the two men as they sat by the newly built fire and appeared to argue. The younger man, in his late teens or early twenties, seemed to be doing all the listening, and the older one, in his late twenties, did all the talking. They didn't seem to worry about me going anywhere.

After a while the younger man called me back and offered me a piece of flat bread rolled with drained yogurt. Suddenly I came up with an idea and told the men to wait as I ran out back to the stream. Moments later I returned with a handful of peppermint and offered it to the men to have with their food. The younger man was delighted and took some out of my hand and placed it inside his rolled bread. As he did so, the two of us made eye contact for the first time. If it wasn't for the temperature being so cold and all, I could have sworn I saw tears in his eyes after I offered him the mint. The other one was not eating and therefore declined my peppermint offer. They exchanged a brief look with one another as the younger man bit into his bread.

Sitting there and observing, I came to the conclusion that the younger man was definitely from Golmakan; I could tell not only from his accent but also from hearing him tell the other man about the area. I also felt that there was a disagreement between the two of them over something. It appeared as if the younger one had reneged on a promise and the older one was trying to remind him of that and convince him to follow through, smoking cigarettes the entire time.

From my many previous visits to Golmakan I knew that all the homes were built in clusters up in the village. Given that knowledge, I was not sure what we were waiting for here in the middle of nowhere. I chose not to ask, however, as I was under the assumption that my father was going to show up at any moment. After I was done with my food, the older man told me to go back outside and play for a while, and I did.

After what seemed a long while, the younger man called me over and said that we were leaving. The sky was overcast, so I had no idea how late in the day it was, but all things considered it must have been very late in the afternoon. To impress my companions with my ability to know the way back, I ran ahead of them toward the snow-covered gravel road. And it was there that the three of us waited for the afternoon bus to take us back to the city.

Back in Mashhad, we got off the bus in the Maydoneh Bar area and the younger man asked if I knew how to get back to my father's cousins' from there. Once I said yes, both of them quickly disappeared around the corner. It was dark by the time I arrived at my father's cousins' home.

The memory of that cold winter day's trip has always been a conundrum to me. Over the years, I've been able to reach only one conclusion, and that is a chilling one: Was I supposed to vanish that day, perhaps under circumstances similar to my sister Shahnaz's disappearance?

❖Chapter Fourteen

Aday or two after I was taken to and from Golmakan by the two men, I learned that my mother had been living in the same alley, just a few doors down from where I was staying, all along. Apparently my family had moved back here and was re-renting our old room for a while. If it wasn't for my mother's landlady seeing me out in the alley and recognizing me, there was a very good chance that my mother and I would not have crossed paths there at all.

For the rest of the time that I was being looked after by my father's cousins, I spent the days with my mother and my baby brother. Every morning right after I woke up, I stood by the front door of my father's relatives and waited for Baba to leave for work. Once he left and disappeared around the corner, I ran to my mother and stayed there until it was time for him to return. Even though Baba had no objection to my daily visits, he was concerned that the practice could turn permanent and once again he would get stuck with raising someone else's kid. He used to put it this way: "If you let the camel's nose into the tent, the rest of it is sure to follow."

In my heart I knew that Baba cared for me, but at the same time he was unwilling to let my father escape his obligations. I remember that I fell asleep at my mother's once or twice, and each time when Baba came home and found me there, there was a big argument. My mother did not have the heart to wake me and send me away, she would say, while Baba argued her actions were only making matters easier for my father. All my mother wanted to do was to follow her deeply ingrained instinct to be a mother—a concept that no man, including Baba, could ever understand.

Luckily my mother did not have to worry about dealing with Baba's objections for very long. Soon I was taken to another home in a different part of town.

On one particularly cold winter evening in 1962, my father was behind the wheel of his Volkswagen Beetle, once again driving me to someone's home as I sat in the back and held the same old kerchief containing my same old extra change of clothes on my lap. More than a year had passed since Baba first took me to supposedly "spend some time" with my father, and I had been relocated a dozen times thus far. I usually did not ask any questions, and my father did not offer any explanations, except for this time. The family that he was taking me to could well be the one "we" had been hoping for, he said in a somber tone. There was a very good chance that they were going to keep me for good, he added. I believed otherwise. My father seldom honored the promises he made, and it did not take long for people to realize that and send me back to him.

My father's sharp and professional appearance and his ability to charm people, together with his good looks, often hoodwinked the smartest of people. He wore a suit and tie, spoke well, and drove an automobile, but behind his sophisticated façade there lurked a bamboozler. Thus far I had been kicked out of most homes that my father had placed me in, each time because he breached his promise. In every new place that he took me, he gave the people a small amount of money up front and promised to make a monthly payment of thirty toomans (about four American dollars at the time) going forward. That was a rate he had calculated to be a fair compensation for feeding and looking after me; everything else, like shoes and clothes, he was going to provide. Of course he never came back and I was let go. I could not believe this time was going to be any different, and frankly I didn't care either. Nothing short of running back to my mother's arms was going to make me happy, and that did not seem possible.

I remember once, out of curiosity, asking my father why I could not just stay with him. It wasn't a good idea, he said. Zahra Khanom was pregnant and she did not need the extra stress. A few years later, my stepmother's abomination for me grew to the point that I was completely forbidden from coming near her, hence forever eliminating any chance of my finding a permanent home at my father's. She even went a step further to erase me from their lives. Iranian law at the time required children to be listed on the parent's birth certificate. Upon the parent's death, the children listed automatically inherited the deceased's wealth. According to relatives, once my father became very wealthy, my stepmother bribed the officials at the office of vital records to have my name permanently removed from my father's birth certificate.

By our cultural definition I was now officially considered to be an orphan—even though both of my parents were still alive—a categorization that was fanned even more by my mother's side of the family in an effort to invoke and keep alive the memory of an injustice they felt my father had brought upon them by divorcing their daughter. It seemed as if labeling me an "orphan" somehow served as a reminder to God that they had been wronged and hence were entitled to divine redemption. What my mother's relatives believed and felt was not at all that unusual. In general, the lower segment of Iranian society often saw itself as a victim, a concept they seemed to not only enjoy but, in a twisted way, welcome. Victimhood meant martyrdom, and martyrdom was as good as an IOU from God.

Being labeled as an orphan drew plenty of sympathy my way but did very little to improve my situation. I felt rejected, abandoned, and without a home, and no amount of verbal and facial sympathy was enough to change that. In the eyes of everyone, I was my father's "seed," and that somehow was being held against me.

My father parked his automobile on Naderi Avenue just a block north of the shrine, and we walked the rest of the way. As usual, rushing to get this over with and get back home, he walked in a hurry down a narrow side street and then an old alley. I trailed him, with somewhat of a lesser intensity, however.

He stopped in front of a large wooden door and sounded the doorknocker. It was freezing outside, I remember. A thin, middle-aged man with a full head of salt-and-pepper hair opened the door and invited us in after an extensive customary greeting. I followed the two of them across the tiled courtyard and up a set of stairs into a living room saturated with the scent of steamed rice and brewing hot tea. Across from the doorway on the other side of the room, two teenage boys and a girl about eight or nine years of age

97

sat under a *korsi,* a low wooden table covered with a large, thick quilt. A charcoal pan placed under the table provided enough heat to keep an entire family warm all night. Cotton-filled mattresses and pillows were usually arranged around the table, where as many as twenty people could sit or sleep. For many low-income families, setting up a korsi was more than just a tradition; it was the only way to survive the cold months of winter, especially in the rural areas.

Inside, despite the man's and soon his wife's insistence, my father declined the invitation to stay for dinner or even tea. And with that he handed the man a twenty-tooman bill and said goodbye, promising to come back at the beginning of the month with the first full payment. The man quickly handed the money over to his wife and walked out of the room to see my father off. The whole process could not have taken more than a few minutes.

The entire time I stood by the door and studied the children from afar. This was my first time in a home with teenage children. After my father left, the woman looked at me from across the room and whispered something to the girl, who then came and took my kerchief out of my hand and walked me over to the korsi, where I sat for the rest of the evening and eventually went to sleep.

Soon after my father was gone, the girl spread a plastic sofreh on top of the korsi as the woman brought out a large round copper tray filled with a mound of steamed rice mixed with chickpeas. She placed the rice on top of the korsi and handed everyone a piece of flatbread to eat it with. There were no utensils. Once she gave the signal, everyone began to dig into the rice as if they had not eaten for weeks. For many, rice and bread were on opposite ends of the affordability spectrum when it came to food. Bread, subsidized by the government, was very affordable, and hence an indispensable supplement to every meal served in most Iranian homes. For large families with middle to low incomes, it was difficult, if not impossible, to fill everyone's bellies without bread. Rice, on the other hand, was a luxury.

The teenage boys, sitting on their knees around the *korsi,* used their fingers and a small piece of bread to scoop up rice from the tray and put it in their mouths with amazing dexterity. I had seen people eat without using utensils in my grandparents' village before but did not know how to do it myself. By the time I managed to

98

somewhat get the hang of eating with my bare hand, there was nothing but a puddle of grease left on the tray, and that too was wiped dry by the two boys in no time. As soon as they were done eating, the woman and her daughter took away the empty tray, and not long after that the man and his two sons lay in the same spot where they were sitting and went to sleep under the quilt. The woman had prepared rice that evening only to impress my father, I learned the next day.

The first few nights in a new place were always difficult for me. I often could not go to sleep, and even though technically I had no home, I felt very homesick. More than anything, I missed my mother and my baby brother Mehdi. I guess in a way, they stood to symbolize home to me. That night was no exception—I was awake the entire night, crying silently into a pillow saturated with the scent of strangers.

Just as fast as the family gorged on the pile of rice the night before, the next morning they swooshed down cups of hot tea, one after another, before all but the woman left for work. The boys placed lumps of sugar in their mouths and poured the steaming hot tea from narrow-waist glass cups into little saucers, then blew vigorously at the hot liquid as they hurriedly took quick sips. I never cared for tea all that much.

I spent the entire day sitting by the window and watching the snow fall in the courtyard as the woman went about straightening the room and preparing dinner and the korsi for the evening ahead.

Closest to my age out of everyone in her family, the girl took a special liking to me and quickly became my solacer there. The next morning, as soon as I was awake, she informed me that I was going to go to work with her and her brothers that day. After a quick breakfast of sweetened hot tea and bread, she helped me put on my shoes with the tenderness of an older sister and whispered in my ear, "Don't worry. God is great," as we all left the house. Perhaps she had seen the turbulence in my eyes and felt sorry for me. Sometimes I wished that there were only women in the world and no men.

The two boys led the way, taking small but fast steps through the ice- and snow-covered alley and then onto Naderi Avenue. The girl, carrying everyone's lunch in a kerchief and at the same time holding on to her little chador, followed her brothers, and I was not far behind, with my hands under my armpits to keep them warm. Like most working-class children, I had no hat, gloves, or warm coat. Our final destination was a rug-weaving shop. As soon as we entered the place, I recognized the scent of wool and lint from when I used to visit my young aunts and uncle at the rug-weaving shop where they worked in Golmakan.

The younger boy and his sister joined another teenage boy and girl on a wooden scaffolding up in front of a partially completed rug and waited while the older boy went to the back of the shop, apparently to speak to the owner about my working there. I stood next to a large black cylindrical heater and kept myself warm and waited. The place was depressing—a long and narrow, poorly lit shop with an unpaved floor. A lone light bulb dangling at the end of a lint-covered electrical wire hanging above the uncompleted carpet did little to illuminate the rest of the place. I prayed for my story not to end here and this way—I had seen how children my age were treated in the rug shops of Golmakan. They were worked twelve hours a day six days a week, and at the end of each week, their parents were paid. I remember when a child fell behind in the knotting, the blueprint-reader would ask the child to extend his or her hand to receive a lash on the palm for not being fast enough. The blueprint-reader delivered the lash with a steel comb used to comb out the yarn after each row of knots was completed to tighten the weave. At age six I was terrified, thinking a similar future awaited me here.

It didn't take long for the older boy to come out of the dark end of the shop, climb the scaffolding, and get to work. He was the leader of the weavers, it appeared. With the blueprint of the rug hanging in front of him, he began chanting colors and knots as he himself reached above and pulled a pistachio-colored yarn down from a spool hanging over his head and began to weave. I spent the day doing small chores and getting acquainted with the people and the place.

That evening the older boy informed his father that Hajj Aqa, the shop owner, had decided to allow me to work as a helper. According to him, I was to do odds and ends around the shop until I could learn to weave. Whatever little money I was to earn was of course going to go to the family, per agreement with my father.

100

Through this entire conversation I sat and listened, as no one cared to ask how I was feeling about the arrangement.

I was up most of the night, not only because I had not gotten comfortable with the new people and the new environment but also because I was worried about the possibility of becoming a rug weaver for the rest of my life. Not having been around any schoolchildren, I knew nothing about going to school and what it meant, but at the same time something inside of me was saying that rug weaving was not in my script. There was nothing wrong, of course, with weaving rugs as long as the choice was made by the person doing it.

In the following days, the boys' efforts to convince me to learn weaving failed. I was afraid once I learned to weave and the family began making money through my labor, I would have been stuck there forever; therefore, I simply refused to learn. I did anything I was told to do, like sweeping the floor, making and serving tea, and going to the store, but I refused to touch the weaving knife. There was always a very good chance that my father would renege on his promise and I would get kicked out of this home too if I could only hold out long enough. I hoped that the next home might turn out to be more promising.

One night, as everyone was sitting under the korsi, one of the boys accidentally knocked over a pot of hot tea that was brewing over the charcoal pan and spilled the boiling liquid over my foot. I suffered third-degree burns and, by the next morning, I had a blister the size of a turkey's egg over the surface of my right foot. Since I could not wear a shoe, I was spared from going to work that day. By mid-morning there was no one left in the house but me. The children and the father had already left for work, and the woman had gone off to the store. It was at that moment that I suddenly decided to go and visit my mother. I was in desperate need of a familiar face and had been thinking of her relentlessly since I was brought here, more so after what happened to my foot.

I remember as usual it was bitterly cold outside and the sidewalks were covered with ice. Despite the fact that I could not put on any shoes and had no way of protecting my foot, I was determined to see my mother that day. That meant traveling the entire length of Naderi Avenue, from the shrine to the Maydoneh Bar area where my mother lived, with one bare foot. Besides being utterly homesick, I also knew there was a good chance that I would not get the same opportunity for a while.

By the time I made it to the alley where my mother lived, my shoeless foot was frozen and completely numb. When I'd left my temporary home over an hour earlier, the blister was wobbling from side to side, but now it had turned into solid ice and was not moving. The rest of my body was not faring any better, as on that day I wore the same summer clothes I'd been wearing when I'd left my mother's home for the first time over a year ago.

To prevent causing any further friction between my mother and Baba, I decided to eavesdrop under her window out in the alley before knocking at her door. I wanted to make sure Baba was not home that day. Sometimes he would stay home if the weather was bad and there were no orders for him to work on at the tailor shop. Unfortunately I heard his unmistakable voice coming from the other side of the wall, and so I decided instead to go see Modar Joon, my maternal grandmother, who lived a couple blocks up the road. She and her two youngest children were now living in a rented basement room near my mother and my aunt. After my grandfather passed away, Modar Joon moved to the city and only went back to her village during the spring and summer.

Modar Joon broke out in tears when she saw me and the condition that I was in. I had never seen my tough grandmother cry before. She warmed some water and tended to my foot as she cursed humanity, accused God of being callous, and wished for Assad, son of Banafsheh, to burn in hell.

It was late in the afternoon by the time I was warm enough to head back to where I came from. My grandmother could not drain the frozen blister, so, to make my trip a bit easier, she fabricated a sandal out of a piece of cardboard and tied it around my foot using rug-weaving yarn. Before I left, she put a handful of toasted apricot pits and dried mulberries in my pocket and prayed for God to look after me. I wished she had given me one rial instead, the cost of bus fare. But Modar Joon was very poor and needed my teenage uncle and eight-year-old aunt to work at a nearby rug-weaving shop to supplement the income she made from her rooshoor and homemade-soap business—just to cover the rent for her little room.

It was just as well that Baba was home that day. If I had been able to go to my mother, she would have become hysterical and, as she used to say, her milk would have turned sour, and that wouldn't have been good for my little sister.

The first of the month came and went, and as I predicted, my father never showed with the payment he had promised the people who were looking after me. Agitated, the family began applying more pressure on me to learn to weave so at least they could collect my earnings. I refused and tried to run away from the shop a few times. Each time I was caught, brought back, and tied to a pole. Finally, one early morning I successfully ran away and went directly to my mother's. We had a jubilant reunion as my mother showered me with her loud kisses and my baby brother Mehdi was unable to contain his joy. My mother told me how much she cried when she learned what happened to my foot. Unfortunately, since she had no idea where I was staying, she could not come and check up on me, she said.

It was nice to be home again and by home, I mean wherever my mother, Baba, and little brother were. Like a long-lost sailor at sea who finally finds his way home, I could not think of anything more soothing than seeing the familiar faces of my mother and little brother again. I was even excited to see my mother's worn rug, portable heater, samovar, and sofreh again.

That night when Baba returned from work and found me there again, he was not happy at all, especially when he learned of the circumstances for my visit. He was firm about doing the right thing and returning me to where I ran away from. My mother pleaded with him to let me stay just that one night, but Baba, afraid of setting a bad precedent, stood by his principles. And so it was that Baba took me outside on that cold early evening in the winter of 1962, set me in front of him on his bike, and zigzagged through the light evening traffic like a gentle wind as he pedaled me back to my latest foster home.

❖Chapter Fifteen

I t was an early evening in June of 1963, and once again I found myself sitting in the back seat of my father's Volkswagen Beetle, holding the same old kerchief—marked clearly with the passage of time—on my lap with my few changes of clothes wrapped inside it. I had just turned seven, but I did not know that at the time. I hardly doubted that my father knew the exact date of my birth either. Commemorating and celebrating birthdays and anniversaries was a Western phenomenon practiced mostly by the educated and more sophisticated segment of the society. Remembering significant dates often required the ability to read, understand, and follow a printed calendar of some sort. Most of my relatives could not read or write. To keep track of things they used the lunar calendar, and for that all they needed was the moon and a clear sky at night.

My father had just picked me up from the home of a distant relative of his where I had been staying for the past few weeks. We did not exchange any words. He was in his world and I was in mine. As usual, he offered no explanation as to where he was taking me and I asked no questions, knowing he had no answers. Questions like: What has been my crime to be condemned to this vagrant existence and at such an early age? Why couldn't I have a home like his children and my mother's children? While I never stopped longing for a place to call home, after two years of wandering from place to place, I had come to accept my circumstances as normal and it didn't matter where I was being taken anymore. At that age I was like water that had been spilled from a fallen pitcher onto the ground; all I could do was follow the gravity and hope for a depth large enough to hold me for a while, until such time that I could grow into a stream of my own and carve my own path through life.

Sometimes I imagined that I was a traveler from some faraway world, just visiting here all alone, and my father was reluctantly going to be my contact and facilitator for a little while. To me he was more a foreign figure of authority than a father, and I am certain to him I was more an obligation and an inconvenience than a son. I never expected to be loved by my father, like Mehdi was by Baba. If it wasn't for some shared resemblance, and the fact that he was introduced to me as my father, I could have never known the two of us were related. Under the circumstances, the most I could hope to receive from him was a little nurturing; the most basic instinct present in all living creatures.

My father drove into an unpaved residential side street off of Sardodvar Avenue and parked his automobile against the wall in front of a house. I recognized the area from the days when my mother and I used to come here and stake out the gate at the army base, looking for my father. I remember I used to mispronounce "Sardodvar" and that always made my mother giggle.

It was completely dark outside. My father rang the doorbell, and a boy about my age opened the door and timidly invited us in. I could tell from the boy's face and the fact that he invited us in without asking any questions that we were expected. Inside, across the lengthy courtyard, on the other side of a fountain, two women were striding to greet my father by the front door as they adjusted their chadors over their heads. After a lengthy greeting, the older woman directed my father into a room and I followed. My father was invited to sit against a large pillow seemingly arranged for him alongside the wall on the floor. I sat across the room from him next to the door in spite of the pleas of the younger woman to move in closer. Having your guest sit by the door was considered impolite and poor hospitality.

The room seemed to be used both as a bedroom and a living room. On the upper section of an army bunk bed in the back of the room lay two boys on their stomachs, with their hands arched under their chins, watching my father and me with interest. The boy who opened the door for us sat on the bottom bed with his eyes on me. A fourth boy, older than the others, sat on the floor next to the two women.

105

Of all the homes that my father had taken me to, this was the first time I saw him take his shoes off and stay for a cup of tea.

My father and the older woman seemed to be doing all the talking while everyone else in the room listened. This was always my least favorite part of the transition, especially if there were children my age present. They talked about me as if I were some puppy in an animal rescue facility, my father trying to sell the prospective adopters my attributes: he eats very little, he is a good boy, very obedient, and does as he is told. All the while I'd be wishing for an invisible hand to come from somewhere, sweep me away, and put an end to the shame and the pain I was made to feel in front of those strangers.

Shortly after he finished his second cup of tea, my father got up, thanked the ladies while casting one of his charming smiles, and promised to return at the beginning of the month. As he said goodbye, he discreetly handed the older lady a twenty-tooman bill and assured her that he would do all that he could to find me a permanent home as soon as possible and take me off their hands. He briefly glanced at me, as if saying, "Look what I have to go through because of you," and said nothing before he left.

The first nights there were much like the first nights at all the other homes that I had been taken to before: sleepless, awkward, worrisome, and melancholy. Almost two years had passed since I lived with my mother or spent time with anyone on her side of the family. The archive of my mind contained no fresh memories of a pleasant place or a friendly face; hence thinking of my mother and others to whom I was once dear, and imagining being with them, was my only solace. Thinking of the days when my mother and I first met Baba and he used to take me everywhere on his bicycle. Imagining being with my grandfather in the apricot orchards of Golmakan—his soothing voice, his kind, sun-toughened face, the familiar scent of burning tobacco that saturated the air of the wheat meadow when he smoked his pipe, his laughter and blaming the crows when he expelled gas, the braying of his donkey—these memories were all lullabies to me.

The next morning I had one of my best breakfasts since Baba first married my mother and moved in with us: freshly baked hot Barbary bread from the bakery around the corner, with thick and grainy grape molasses, creamy Bulgarian feta cheese, and hot tea.

As I was eating I could hear boys yelling and chasing each other in the courtyard. The oldest boy from last night was sitting next to me at the sofreh and cheerfully watching me eat. He was spreading molasses on small pieces of bread and placing them on a plate in front of me with a big smile across his face.

"Do you like the breakfast?" he asked joyfully.

"Yes, thank you, aqa," I said quietly and apprehensively while looking down. No one had been this nice to me in the past few years.

"My name is Kia, but you can call me *dadosh* (brother) if you like. All the boys that you saw in this room last night call me dadosh."

"Yes, aqa." I nodded.

"No. No aqa! Either Kia or dadosh, alright?" He smiled and rubbed my head affectionately.

Once I was finished eating, we left the room and went into the courtyard, where Kia introduced me to the other three boys and the two women from the night before. I was not accustomed to being included or introduced. I was used to people talking about me, sometimes right in front of me, as if I were deaf or dead. Sometimes it took days for me to learn the names and the relations of the people I was placed with, but not today.

Later that day, Kia took me out for a walk around the neighborhood, and it was then that he patiently explained everything about his somewhat unorthodox family. He also talked about the arrangement between his father and mine as it related to me. According to Kia, my father and his father knew of each other from working in the same building at the army base. For whatever reason, Mr. Rahimi, Kia's father, had agreed to have one of his wives look after me while my father looked to find me a home. My father had agreed to pay Mr. Rahimi thirty toomans for every month that I stayed with them, the first payment of which he prorated and made last night.

Mr. Rahimi had three wives, two of whom I met the night before. Ozra Khanom, Kia's mother, was the first and the oldest of the three, and Rana, about twenty or so, the third and the youngest wife. I did not meet Maryam Khanom, the middle wife, for a while. The oldest and youngest wives shared this house together. Kia was his father's oldest son and Ozra Khanom's only child. Rana was the mother of Mr. Rahimi's youngest child, his only daughter, at the time. The other three boys present in the room last night all belonged to Maryam Khanom, the middle wife, and lived with their mother in a different home somewhere by the mountains just outside of the city limits, Kia said. The three boys were there visiting that night. Apparently they came to the city once a week and stayed with their father for one or two days. At the time, however, Mr. Rahimi and his unit were deployed somewhere near the border with Afghanistan and no one was certain when he was coming home.

From the very first day it was clear which one of the wives I was going to be staying with. Maryam already had three boys of her own and was pregnant with her fourth child. Rana had an infant to take care of and was deemed too young and inexperienced to look after me. In addition, she was the wife that Mr. Rahimi resided with, and Mr. Rahimi did not care for a stranger to be living with him. Staying with Ozra Khanom, or as all the children called her, Momon Bozorg (great mother), was the only logical choice. The way it seemed, Kia was not going to give me up to any of his mother's rival wives anyway, even if they had wanted me. I later learned that he had always wished for a little brother of his own, and here was his chance.

I had found myself a new solacer, it seemed. Kia, fifteen years old at the time, took a strong liking to me right away, as if we had known each other for thousands of years, and soon I seemed to become an indispensable part of his life. He took great pleasure in looking after me as if I were born his brother. We went everywhere together, sat next to each other at mealtime, and at nights slept with our mattresses spread together on the floor. As much as he cared about his half brothers from his father's second wife, Kia still felt an emptiness in his life that I seemed to be able to fill.

More than anything, he seemed to enjoy playing the role of a big brother and a mentor to me. He'd deepen his voice and say in a serious tone things like: You should always wash your hands with soap and water before each meal; Never chew food with your mouth open; Always say hello when you enter a room. After two years of being neglected, I enjoyed all the attention that I was receiving and could use the etiquette lessons.

I still had not met Mr. Rahimi and was not going to for a while.

108

❖ Chapter Sixteen

I had not seen or heard from my mother now since that night in the winter of 1962 when Baba took me back to the rug weaver's home.

At the beginning of the new month my father took an unprecedented step; not only did he come back as he said he would, but for the first time in our two-year history, he came through with making a second payment on my behalf. Perhaps he was turning over a new leaf, or maybe the realization that Mr. Rahimi was his equal and knew where to find him was the motive. Whatever the reason, I was thrilled. Mr. Rahimi's home had become my favorite of all the places my father had taken me thus far, and if I was not going to go back to my mother, there was no other place that I preferred to be than here and with Kia.

Mr. Rahimi finally returned home in the middle of July. I was not allowed to meet him right away, however, because he was suffering from some sort of an illness.

Without actually meeting Mr. Rahimi, I already had mixed emotions about his return. I feared his presence could disturb the fragile stability I was enjoying in his home and with his family. For a while now an unsettling theory had been forming in my head that men were not at all interested in children, especially if the children were not of their own blood. Based on my short life and limited experience, I did not have a very positive view of men thus far and, like my mother, I feared them. Up until then, excluding my grandfather, almost all the men I had come across had done more harm than good to me and to those I cared about. My father and his brother were responsible for the disappearance of my sister and the savage beating of my mother. Baba, as wonderful as he was to me in the beginning and as much as I still loved him, was partially to blame for what was happening to me, and you already know the stories of the policeman and Hajji Sinichi. I was beginning to conclude that men were here to take away and destroy while women were here to give birth to new lives and create. As much as I wished to keep an open mind, Mr. Rahimi was a man, and that was one big strike against him already.

For the next two weeks, I was told to go about the house quietly as Mr. Rahimi was still not feeling too well. No one but Momon Bozorg and Rana was allowed to go into his room. Mr. Rahimi was apparently suffering from some sort of skin lesion that he had acquired during a recent military operation.

Finally one day Momon Bozorg decided that it was time for me to meet the man of the house. I knew very little about this mysterious Mr. Rahimi at this point. No one seemed to ever talk about him while he was gone, and there was no photograph of him on display anywhere in that house for me to see what he looked like. His inconspicuous return and then the long isolation only added to the enigma. I had never known any man who had more than one wife and one home before. Baba, my hero, had difficulty maintaining one family, so in my seven-year-old mind I figured this Mr. Rahimi must be superhuman.

Momon Bozorg tiptoed quietly into the room where Mr. Rahimi had been kept, and I followed behind her. She lifted her index finger to her nose as if signaling me to be quiet as we approached a white metal bed that was veiled by a super-fine white net canopy hanging from the ceiling like a mosquito tent.

"Salam, aqa. Alireza, the son of Mr. Golmakani, is here to say hello to you," Momon Bozorg said softly to the man lying on the bed as she waved to me to move closer.

I quietly crossed the room and walked through a section of the canopy Momon Bozorg was holding open for me and whispered, "Salam, aqa."

Lying in front of me was a gigantic naked man covered from head to toe by a layer of clear gel-like substance. A very thin and translucent fabric, saturated with the same ointment, was laid over his groin. At one end of the bed a metal table fan was running, turning side to side and gently blowing air over him.

Dumbfounded by the unexpected image and the sheer size of Mr. Rahimi, all I could hear was the sound of the fan and my own heart. I had never seen any human so immense before and could not believe I was standing next to one now. Everyone in my family was short and petite except for Baba, and even Baba was little compared to the man lying here in front of me. I swallowed my saliva and stood there motionless as I remained attached to Momon Bozorg's leg as tight as I could. Mr. Rahimi took his half-opened eyes off of the ceiling and slowly rolled them my way for a very brief moment, then groaned like a wounded lion and closed his eyes. Momon Bozorg signaled with her head for me to leave the room. I was only too glad to comply.

Soon thereafter Mr. Rahimi was able to slowly come out of his isolation and walk about the house a bit. The big man easily dwarfed anyone and anything that stood next to him. The expansive width of his shoulders appeared to equal that of two ordinary men, and his thick mustache, unusually large head, broad forehead, and prominent brow bones only added to his dramatic and overwhelming figure. I could not imagine any man being able to withstand staring into Mr. Rahimi's eyes for more than a second. Still intimidated by Mr. Rahimi's substantial physique and deep, overwhelming voice, I kept my distance from him as much as possible.

Then one day, I was sitting in the courtyard by the fountain when I heard Mr. Rahimi calling me from a room upstairs.

"*Pesarrrr* (boy)."

I ran upstairs and into the room where Mr. Rahimi always sat on a mattress placed for him on the floor, against the wall.

"Salam, aqa."

"Salam. Take five rials out of my pants pocket hanging over there and go to the store and get me a pack of Eshno cigarettes," he said without looking at me.

"Chashm, aqa."

I took the money out of his pocket and bolted out of the room. I ran as fast as I could to the store, purchased the pack of cigarettes, and returned just as fast. I felt this was my first chance to make an impression on Mr. Rahimi, and I wanted it to be a good one. And from the look on his face when I handed him the pack of cigarettes, it appeared that I succeeded.

"You are very fast, boy!" he said casually and again without looking at me.

"Merci, aqa," I said, standing in front of him, perspiring and breathless. I was very pleased that he had noticed my effort. His sons, the ones from his second wife, came down to visit him once a week and often stayed for a few days, but luckily they were not there today and the opportunity to serve him was mine. "Pesar!" I heard Mr. Rahimi calling me again later that afternoon. I ran over and stood at attention in front of him waiting to see what he wanted me to do for him. He looked bored, as if being cooped up in the house was taking its toll on him.

"How old are you, boy?"

"I am not sure, sir. Either six or seven."

"Do you know what year you were born?"

"No, sir, no one ever told me."

Seeming a bit baffled, he asked, "Do you know the alphabet?"

"No, sir."

"Do you know if your father is planning on putting you in school?"

"No, sir."

"I hope that he does, because nothing can help a child more than an education. There are two types of blind people in this world: those who don't have eyes and those who cannot read."

With that he paused a little, lit a cigarette and said, "Go tell Rana to give you a piece of paper and a pencil and bring it here to me."

"Yes, sir."

I was gone and back in a flash with a piece of paper and a pencil in my hand. And just like that on that fine summer afternoon, Mr. Rahimi began to teach me the letters of the alphabet and the basic numbers. He spent a few minutes each day, writing, showing, and telling me about one number and two letters. I then used a couple of blank pieces of paper and practiced what he showed me on my own for the rest of the day. By the time Mr. Rahimi was fully recuperated and returned to work, I knew all the letters of the alphabet by heart and could write them for Mr. Rahimi. I could also write and count to twenty. Mr. Rahimi was clearly impressed with the outcome.

Our conversations were always very brief and limited to the letters and numbers of the day. Mr. Rahimi never asked any personal questions about my parents, me, or where I came from, and I would not dare ask him anything. He often said very little to anyone. He reminded me of a magnificent male gorilla who sat quietly at a distance, indifferent to the activities of his tribe around him, and said or did very little.

According to Kia, his father was the eldest son of a powerful tribal leader. Up until the early twentieth century, in the absence of a strong central government, most of the Iranian countryside was ruled by tribes and gangs of bandits. After an army officer by the name of Reza Khan overthrew the last king of the ruling Qajar Dynasty and declared himself the new King of Persia in 1925, he began an ambitious program of dragging Iran, sometimes by force, out of the dark ages that it had fallen into during the last century through the mismanagement of the Qajars and into the modern world. Reza Shah (King Reza) made his first priority bringing law and order to the country and building a new army and a strong central government.

As the young central government became organized and grew more powerful, it began to expand and exert its authority throughout the country. Eventually the tribesmen were reluctant to lay down their arms, but as long as they could prove that they could read and write their own names, they were permitted to join the new army, and many did, including the then young Mr. Rahimi.

As to why Mr. Rahimi had three wives, he was just following the practice of his elders, Kia told me. Back then having multiple wives was a common survival practice in the tribal societies. The main reason for such practice was to ensure every woman was looked after and taken care of. More often than not, a husband in a traditional tribal setting was a provider and a protector to a woman rather than her life partner in the romantic sense. And with the number of women, for various reasons, often exceeding that of eligible men, it was only logical for men to take in more than one wife. In addition, a tribe was often only as strong as the number of its male members, and the best way to maintain that superiority was by ensuring every woman had a man and was producing babies, preferably boys.

In keeping with his ancestral tradition, Mr. Rahimi had married three women without divorcing any. According to Kia, before his mother became Mr. Rahimi's first wife, she was married to a man from a different tribe. After her husband was killed in a gun battle with the Rahimis' tribe, Mr. Rahimi's father asked his son to marry the young widow, and he did. Within the first few years of their marriage, Momon Bozorg gave birth to a set of twins who unfortunately died soon thereafter due to some illness. Kia was born some years later and now held the title of Mr. Rahimi's oldest son and Momon Bozorg's only child. Momon Bozorg's aged and gray visage made her look more like a grandmother to Kia than his mother.

Soon the last month of summer was here, and with it began a conversation at the Rahimis' home about a subject unfamiliar to my ears: school. I'd heard of school, but since I had never been with any family who had school-aged children before, my knowledge of it was very limited. Kia, impressed by the fact that I was able to learn the letters of the alphabet and the numbers so quickly, initiated the discussion of signing me up for school and sought his parents' approval. Even though I was worrying about my father not coming through with the monthly payment that was already due—which would perhaps result in my expulsion from Mr. Rahimi's home—the conversation about me going to school was music to my ears. More than anything, the talk of school gave me hope that the Rahimis were intending to keep me for a while longer.

With tenacity Kia was finally able to convince his mother to let him enroll me in school, while his father wished to stay out of any decisions regarding me. Kia was adamant about not only keeping me as his little brother but also sending me to school, and Momon Bozorg was not about to break the heart of her only child. Now all he needed was my father's permission and, of course, my birth certificate, if I even had one. The school acceptance age was seven, and Kia seemed to think I was old enough or close to it.

It was almost mid-month, and my father had not yet shown up to make the thirty-tooman monthly child support payment. Unbothered by that, Kia, with his mother's blessing, embarked on the mission of finding my father in the hope of getting his permission along with my birth certificate. Naturally, I accompanied him.

Mr. Rahimi was no longer working in the same building as my father, but he gave Kia some ideas as to where to look for him. Kia was a clever boy and knew how to convince the guards at the gate to let us into the base. Of course, his father being a staff sergeant with a very recognizable last name was a big help too. After a week of running around the massive army compound under the hot summer sun, following to no avail the clues we were given by different soldiers as to my elusive father's whereabouts, we finally spotted his automobile as he was driving out of the base one afternoon. Perhaps fearing we were there to collect the past-due child support, he tried to evade us, but Kia was able to catch up with him as he was forced to slow down at the gate.

Without giving Kia's proposal any thought, my father dismissed the idea as bad and a waste of everyone's time. I was standing nearby and listening as he lowered his voice and told Kia that kids like me, with no caring mother around, did not stand a chance of ever succeeding in school. "He will probably grow up a street kid, a criminal, or a drug addict," he told Kia. "The best thing to do for him is to put him to work at a bicycle-repair shop or a rug-weaving place somewhere, so he can earn his keep," he said. School was not for me, he proclaimed. Needless to say, I was saddened by his words. He spoke as if I were only a social statistic and not his son. His cold and brutal prediction of the gloomy future in store for me was disheartening, to say the least. And with that he drove away.

Kia put his arm around my shoulder and to cheer me up said, "Don't pay any attention to what your father said. He is very wrong about you. My father thinks you are very intelligent. He said that he knows of no one that could learn the alphabet and numbers as quickly as you did."

A bag of emotions burst inside of me, forcing out uncontrollable warm tears. Embarrassed, I veiled my face with the back of my arm. I was crying not so much because my father believed I was not worthy of going to school or because of his unkind and callous words. I was crying because his words reminded me how alone I was in this world.

Kia suddenly stopped, removed my arm from my face, looked into my eyes, and said, "Listen to me, Alireza. I promise that I will put you in school this year, dadosh joon He placed a kiss on my forehead and began to tickle me until I started to giggle.

The young and wonderful Kia, may the creative force of the universe always be with him, was more determined than my father. As he promised, Kia did not give up, and for many more days to come he stalked and harassed my father at the gate, with me standing at his side, watching. All he wanted from my father was my birth certificate now. He was no longer interested in getting his permission. Finally one day Kia's perseverance paid off and my father surrendered. It was a beautiful, sunny mid-morning when my father pulled over where Kia and I were standing by the gate, handed my birth certificate to Kia through the open window of his automobile, and drove away. It was there and then that I learned I had turned seven years old back in June. Kia added that I was a Gemini, and when I asked him what that meant, he smiled and said it meant that I was going to do well in school. I was very happy. The events of the past few weeks, the conversations, and the focus about me going to school all had me thrilled.

❖*Chapter Seventeen*

Hope and purpose are wonderful antidotes and nourishment for a wilted soul.

With the submission of two black-and-white headshot photographs of me, my birth certificate, and a couple of toomans, Kia was able to get me enrolled at the local elementary school. I was now officially a student.

For the first time I began to notice an aspect of the city I'd been oblivious to up until then. A sudden surge of activities spurred up the neighborhood at the end of what seemed to be a lazy summer. Many people with school-age children were returning home from their summer vacations. Boys and girls, holding their mothers' hands, were going in and out of various shops in a hurry in preparation for going back to school. Barbershops, tailor shops, and shoe-making shops were all very busy at that time.

I remember accompanying Momon Bozorg and taking a pair of used children's shoes to an old shoe repairman on Sardodvar Avenue. The shoes were for me. After a bit of haggling, the old man agreed to make the little shoes as good as new, in his words, for one tooman. She paid the man in advance and went back home, leaving me behind to wait for the shoes. I sat on the sidewalk next to the old man—a sidewalk shoe-shiner who made his money mostly from polishing boots and shoes for the soldiers—and watched his brown prune-like hands replace the soles, nail new heels, color the shoes black, and replace the laces with some from a pair of worn army boots he had in his wooden box.

"Here you go, boy. *Mobark bashe* (blessings)," the old man said in his country accent as he handed me my new shoes.

I was amazed with the result. The shoes originally looked as if some wild animal had slowly chewed on them for a long while; they were colorless, worn, and had holes on their soles where someone's toes once used to rest. I felt sorry for the original owner, whoever he was.

In addition to the shoes, Momon Bozorg had come across some free fabric, just enough to make a school suit for me. It was mandatory for boys to wear both trousers and jackets to school. On that very same day, Kia and I took the fabric to a nearby tailor shop where I was measured for my new suit. The suit was going to be ready on the day before school started. I couldn't wait.

On the last day before school was to begin, Kia and I both received haircuts, went to hammom, and picked up my school suit from the tailor shop. That evening Kia stitched a strip of white plastic over the collar of my new jacket (it was mandatory for elementary school boys to have a white strip of fabric of some sort sewn on their jacket's collar to identify them as students) and had me put it on and model for him and Momon Bozorg. Seeing the look on my face as I checked myself out in the mirror filled his face with glee and his mother's eyes with tears. I could not wait to see the look on my mother's face when she saw me in my school suit someday. Life could not get any better than this.

That night I probably would have gone to sleep with the school jacket on if it were left up to me. All that night, I tossed and turned in my bed thinking about what school was going to be like and how delighted my mother was going to feel when she learned her son was now a student. I felt very lucky and all grown up.

The first day of school was finally here, and I could not have been readier. I was the last to fall asleep the night before and first to wake up that morning. By the time Kia got out of the bed, I was sitting on the window's niche with my face washed, wearing my new gray suit and holding on my lap a new notebook and a box of coloring pencils. I kept the eraser, the pencil sharpener, and my very first pencil in my coat pocket. The exciting scents of the blank pages of the notebook and the coloring pencils are still fresh in my mind.

Kia was starting sixth grade, the last year of elementary school for him. He was a member of the school police unit; therefore, it took him much longer to prepare and put on his uniform. Words are not adequate to describe how I felt that morning as I walked proudly to school side by side with Kia. Covered with Goosebumps, I felt very important walking next to him in my new gray suit with the white collar; announcing to the world I was a student. I looked at every passerby, searching in their eyes for envy. High on joy, I lost myself that morning and completely forgot who I was and where I had come from. Kia had on a perfectly pressed gray uniform with a white leather sash going over his shoulder, across his chest, and attaching to his white belt. A red armband saying "Police of schools," a shoulder cord, a white beret, white plastic shoe covers secured over his perfectly polished black shoes, and a real police whistle were also part of his uniform. He walked like a general, looking serious and stiff with his eyebrows pulled together, a look that demanded respect from all the little boys walking on the same sidewalks and going to the same school as us. Many of the smaller kids were accompanied by their mothers that morning.

Mothers said their goodbyes at the door as some younger boys cried, refusing to enter the building, and others joyfully ran inside. Kia gave me a few quick pieces of advice by the school's small entrance, as he loved to give advice, and then quickly split to meet up with the other school police. The school was a converted residential house with a small courtyard and a large shade tree spreading its branches overhead. Instead of the customary fountain in the center of the courtyard, however, there was an L-shaped water pipe with a faucet soldered at the end of it.

A man wearing a suit and tie stood at the top of the stairs leading into the building and seemed to be monitoring the children in the courtyard. Suddenly, with a hammer in hand, he began to pound on a rectangular metal plate that was dangling from a wooden arm mounted on the brick wall next to him. Reacting to the sound, most children ran and stood in columns facing the building and the man on the stairway. Not knowing what to do, I stood idle with a dozen other kids my age and looked on. A couple of boys were still crying, wanting to go home. The man, who by now had replaced the hammer in his hand with a twig, asked all the boys to gather in front of him at the bottom of the stairs and then introduced himself as the school's assistant principal. He welcomed everyone in a kind and caring tone as he went about completing the

119

orientation process. Soon we were all standing in different columns according to first our grades and then our heights, with the tallest kid in the back. I landed somewhere in the middle.

Once in the classroom, I shared a desk with two other boys. For the first time that day I heard my full name uttered in front of a group when the teacher began conducting a head count.

"Alireza Golmakani?"

"Present!" I said, mimicking the other children. My voice was quivering and my skin itching with goose bumps at hearing my full name spoken so formally and in such a setting. Later, when the teacher asked if anyone knew the letters of the alphabet or the numbers, I was one of the few to raise my hand enthusiastically and with pride.

During the recess some of my joy dissipated when a couple of older boys walked by, giggling, and calling me a *soopoor*—a street sweeper. In the excitement of the day I had failed to notice that I along with a dozen other boys were all wearing the same exact suit made of the dreaded gray fabric that the street sweepers and garbage collectors wore. The fabric, a donation from the communist Soviet Union, was mostly used to make uniforms for the sanitation workers. The leftover material was given to orphans and other needy people for free. I suddenly remembered Baba, being a tailor, talking to my mother about that same fabric some years back. "The Russians are never going to win the heart of the Iranian people by donating that trash they call fabric. It is not even good enough to make a donkey blanket out of. I pray no one I know has to ever stoop so low as to wear that communists' rubbish," he would say.

Fortunately the suit itself ensured that the boys' ridicule was short-lived. After just a few washes, the gray communist fabric shrunk tremendously and eventually disintegrated—and that was the end of my first suit. Once my original school suit was gone, a lady friend of Momon Bozorg gave me one of her son's old suits that had gotten too small for him.

Classes were overcrowded in our school, and after one week there I was transferred to another school. Kia attempted to prevent the school from separating the two of us but was unsuccessful. I remember the assistant principal, with a list in his hand, going from classroom to classroom one afternoon, calling a set of names from each classroom and asking them to form a line in the courtyard. The list included me. We were walked in a single column to a new school a few streets away. My new school was about the same distance from Mr. Rahimi's home as the old one, and I did not mind walking there alone. It was the separation from Kia that had me heartbroken for a little while.

❖Chapter Eighteen

A month after I started school I went to visit my old family. My mother and my little brother Mehdi were overjoyed to see me when I walked through their door flaunting my first-grade textbook and other school supplies under my arm. We had not seen each other since last winter. They had since moved down the street, and I had to get their new address from their previous landlord. It was an emotional reunion, filled with hugs, kisses, and tears, as usual. My mother knew through the grapevine that I had been placed in a good home and that I was alright, she said, but she did not have any name or address to come and visit me. Baba was also very glad to see me when he came home that evening. He was especially happy when he learned that I had been placed in a stable home and was going to school. Since it was the weekend and I had no school the next day, I spent the night at my mother's and Baba did not seem to mind at all. He was very emotional that evening as he lectured me about the values of education and the good fortune of having the opportunity to go to school, while many still couldn't.

Baba was just a baby when his father passed away. His mother never remarried, instead devoting her entire life to raising him and his older brother and sister. He considered the biggest calamity of his life to be the day he was permanently expelled from elementary school when he was only in the second grade. According to Baba, apparently he had a habit of wetting his pants while at school and, after a few warnings, the school authorities decided to let him go for good, a decision that scarred him for the rest of his life. Sullenly he often wondered how differently his life would have turned out if only he'd been given the opportunity to stay in school and continue his education.

"Left with no other alternative, after I was kicked out of school for my 'crime against humanity,' my mother had to leave me alone at home and go to work," Baba told me. "There was no one else to look after me since my brother and sister were both at school during the days and we had no relatives nearby for my mother to leave me with. She left me in our little rented room with some bread, cheese, water, and a urinal bowl for me to do my business in, padlocked the door from the outside, and went to work. I was locked up in that room six days a week, from morning until my brother and sister came home from school late in the afternoon. I spent the days playing alone in the room, standing on an old wooden trunk behind our small window and watching with envy the children play outside in the alley, or taking naps. My old classmates who lived in our alley still went to school every day, and every day I watched them and yearned to go with them. They often came to our window after school, talked to me, and gave me candies and gum through the window bars."

When Baba's mother came to Mashhad for the first time to meet my mother, the ensuing conversations often turned to Baba and his childhood. Each time his mother cried and defended her action. She had no other choice, she told my mother in her broken Farsi. It was either that or the entire family facing eviction and starvation, she would say. After her husband passed away, she had to find work and reluctantly left little Younes—for some reason she called Baba Younes instead of Mansoor—by himself at home. In spite of her many pleas, the school refused to take him back, and she did what she had to do to feed her children and keep a roof over their heads. By the time he finally stopped peeing in his pants, Baba was a few years behind and it was too late for him to return to school, according to his mother.

Baba was exceedingly bitter about that life-changing event and directed some of his anger toward his older brother for being more privileged than he was. What little reading and writing he knew came from his brother teaching him at home. Now as an adult, Baba rarely missed reading the daily newspaper and doing the crossword puzzle.

Visiting my mother became a weekend ritual for me. All week long I looked forward to the weekend, when I could go and spend the night with my mother and, more importantly, with Mehdi. On Thursdays as soon as the bell announcing the end of school sounded, I bolted out of the building and ran all the way across town to Maydoneh Bar, where my mother lived. Often Kia gave me ten shahi (half a rial) or even a rial to buy a snack for myself at school. Taking a page out of Baba's book, I saved that money and bought Mehdi some snacks so I wouldn't be empty-handed when I went to visit my little brother. I enjoyed watching Mehdi drool while anxiously searching my pockets for goodies as I walked into the house on Thursday afternoons. In anticipation of my arrival, he waited outside by the front door, and the minute he spotted me turning into their street, his pacifier fell out of his mouth to dangle by a string from his chest as he ran to greet me. I hugged and kissed him while he searched my pockets for treats. I loved my little brother very much. For me, he was the sum of everything that I loved about having a family. I was practicing on him what I was learning from Kia: how to be a good older brother.

On Fridays the entire Maydoneh Bar area was bursting with all sorts of fun activities. I used to take little Mehdi for a stroll there to look for street performances. There were all sorts of shows competing for handouts from the people who were there to browse or shop at the open market. One performer promised a battle between his snake and rodent—a battle that never actually took place. Another one lifted heavy objects with his teeth or had a small automobile drive over his chest. The most popular show by far was the reenactmr of the bloody battle between Shemr and Imam Hussein. As clichéd as the reenactment was, Mehdi and I enjoyed the brief sword fights between the two characters while the grown-ups, mostly folks from the countryside, sobbed over the tear-jerking story of the battle.

Our favorite activity of the day, however, was sharing a freshly made ice cream sandwich, and the best part of that was watching the man make the ice cream right there on the street. We waited next to his wooden pushcart on the sidewalk as the ice cream man spread rock salt over crushed ice in the large outer barrel of his ice cream maker that was fitted in a hole in the center of his pushcart. He then assiduously twisted and turned the inner metal barrel that was filled with fresh cream (delivered to him from the countryside), sugar, vanilla, and a few drops of rosewater. When the ice cream was finally ready, Mehdi and I were usually his first customers.

Mehdi drooled every time as the man made the sandwich by taking out a round metal mold and using its rim to cut a piece out of a sheet of vanilla wafer, then scooping the heavenly ice cream into the mold over the wafer, and finally topping it with another cutout of wafer. Watching the expression on my little brother's face and the sparkles of joy in his light honey-colored eyes as the ice cream sandwich took shape made me smile with delight.

"*Duo qaran* (two rials)," the man would say each time, without looking us in the eye, as he handed me the fat ice cream sandwich.

We took turns eating the sandwich until it was gone. Seeing Mehdi's little pink lips forming bites over the edge of the oversized sandwich with great pleasure and knowing that I bought it for him was the highlight of my visit.

Mehdi was over three years old now and still using a pacifier. I had seen the frustration on Baba's face whenever Mehdi stood in front of him and passionately sucked on his chubby pacifier. Despite Baba's many threats and promises, Mehdi would not relinquish his little plastic companion. Every Friday as we spent time together, I made it my mission to try and persuade him to give up the little plastic thing. I thought accomplishing that was an older-brother thing and would surely boost my standing with Baba. Finally one day in the ecstasy of eating an ice cream sandwich, Mehdi agreed to let go of his pacifier for good. Ceremonially I unpinned the string of the pacifier from his shirt and threw it into the Kale-Qara-Khan Canal, where I knew it was impossible to retrieve it if he changed his mind.

We were barely through the door when my mother's eagle eyes noticed the pacifier was missing from where she always pinned it to Mehdi's shirt. She was not at all pleased when I proudly explained, like a grown-up, what I did to it and how he was not going to need it anymore. My mother grumbled about how much she had just paid for that new pacifier to replace the one Baba had thrown away a week earlier. I assured my mother that Mehdi was a changed boy and he had given me his word not to ever ask for it.

About an hour or so after we returned home, Mehdi began nagging and crying, asking for his pacifier. When I reminded him

125

of his pledge to me, he looked the other way and cried some more. Before I went back to Mr. Rahimi's that day, my mother, clearly disappointed with me, gave me some money to go to the store and buy him another one.

❖Chapter Nineteen

Another Thursday came and, as usual, as soon as the school's last bell sounded, I was outside and running toward my mother's home on the other side of town. When I finally arrived there a few hours later, I did not find Mehdi waiting for me outside as he usually did. The front door was unlatched, and I walked right into the courtyard, where I found him sitting on the edge of the fountain, quietly sucking on his pacifier. His eyes popped open with glee when he saw me walking in, and he immediately jumped up and ran to me, smiling ear to ear with his pacifier dangling from his shoulder. He wrapped his little arms around my waist and sighed with relief. I could tell he had missed me. A week was a long time to be apart for both of us. My mother told me that during the week, every morning Mehdi would ask if that day was Thursday. I don't think he understood why I was not staying with them permanently. According to my mother, he withered every Friday like a little flower as we kissed goodbye and blossomed back again on Thursdays with one little kiss from me.

My mother was standing in the doorway to their little room with her shoulder and head leaning against the doorframe and drooping. She stood there looking at the two of us with a cheerless face. I walked over to her and gave her a hug. Her eyes were red and it was obvious that she had been crying. She locked her arms around me and began kissing me nonstop, just like the day she visited me at the neighborhood store next to my father's house. I suddenly took notice of the room behind her—almost everything was packed.

"Are you moving again, Momon?" I asked.

She continued kissing me and nodded her head yes.

"Are you going back to the Poole Khaki area?" I asked with excitement. That would have been great since it was much closer to Mr. Rahimi's home.

"Ali joon, what am I going to do, modar? (In this case the word *modar* (mother) means 'my child' or 'baby.') I don't know … Why doesn't God just take my life and end it all at once instead of killing me piece by piece, Ali joon?" my mother asked in a subdued voice.

She moved inside the room and painfully moaned and sobbed for a while until she withered on the floor against the wall. After all these years, my mother's tears, melancholy, rhythmic chants of injustice still shredded my heart as I stood by her and watched helplessly.

She finally came around, and her lips slowly began to utter words that seared my soul. They were moving away to Tehran, she said, and there was no need for her to tell me that the move did not include me.

As much as the events of the past two years had prepared and toughened me for a day like this, I was still not ready to give into the idea of not having a mother at all. I could not envision a world without her and my baby brother. At my age and my level of understanding, it seemed she was moving to another world, a faraway galaxy beyond the reach of my imagination. I was in excruciating pain, as if a large hand had reached deep inside my chest, grabbed hold of my heart, and was squeezing it.

Mehdi was sitting on the floor next to my mother and me, sucking on his pacifier in slow intervals, looking at the two of us and sighing the entire time.

Darkness was slowly crawling up the western wall and devouring the last of the daylight like a hungry snake when Baba came home, smiling and carrying a large bag under his arm. He had brought home kebab and rice for dinner. We ate in silence. My mother sat at the sofreh with a frown and did not touch any food. Baba advised her to stop looking gloomy and eat. He told her that she was upsetting me and making things more difficult. She gave him a cold stare and did not reply.

The next day my mother and her family walked under a Quran held up by my aunt Sarvar at the front door. They then got into a

128

taxicab as a neighbor and a friend of my mother splashed a bowl of fresh water on the sidewalk behind them for good luck. My mother's brother Zabih and I accompanied them to the bus station.

At the bus station, my mother handed my baby sister to Baba and pulled me off to a quiet corner of the roofless, gravel-floored garage. She crouched on her heels in front of me, cupped my face in her hands, and looked directly into my eyes and said, "I hope you and God can forgive me, pesaram. I don't know what else to do. Baba cannot find a good-paying job here in Mashhad and thinks he can do better in Tehran. I promise you that I'll be praying for you and thinking of you every moment of every day, Ali joon."

She began to weep out of control and talk to Imam Reza again. "Ya Zamene Ahoo, I leave my child with you to look after."

It took Baba and my uncle Zabih a while to convince her to unlock her arms from around me. I could not think of anything to say to her. After a long and tear-soaked goodbye, my family boarded the bus as it began to depart.

Uncle Zabih and I stood there at the side of the bus and watched as it pulled away. My mother was sitting by the open window with Mehdi on her lap. Her eyes were fixed on me while my eyes were fixed on Mehdi who was, of course, sucking on his pacifier and looking at me with a droopy face. As the bus was pulling out of the gate, I saw Mehdi's little hand extend out of the window and release his pacifier onto the ground. After the bus left I ran and picked up the little pacifier and put it in my pocket.

❖Chapter Twenty

Despite having Kia in my life, I had great difficulty dealing with the sudden loss of my mother and Mehdi. I was slowly learning to accept and handle living apart from them, so long as I knew they were here in the same city and under the same sky as me. But to a seven-year-old child living in a remote corner of the world in the era before the Internet, satellite television, and wireless communication, the world seemed vast and the physical distances immense. Whether my mother moved to the planet Mars or the city of Tehran, the emotional impact of it was the same. She might as well have died, for that was exactly how I felt after she left.

To deal with this sudden loss, I continued going back to Maydoneh Bar on Thursdays after school and spent the night at my aunt Sarvar's home. Even though I had been living at the Rahimis' and with Kia for four or five months now, I still could not get my mother out of my mind that easily, and going back there helped me slowly wean myself from her. On Friday mornings, before I headed back to Mr. Rahimi's home, I browsed around the neighborhood where my mother used to live, and recalled memories of the past. I watched the stale street performances and bought steamed sugar beets from the ice cream man who, in concession to the season, had changed his product line.

"Dou qaran," he'd say as he handed me a fat steaming slice of the deep purple beet. I hoped he would recognize me, his loyal Friday morning customer, and ask about my little brother. How could he not notice my immense loss and offer a few comforting words?

Some Fridays I just sat across the street from the house where my mother last lived, arched my hands under my chin, and watched the small iron door open and close as people went in and out. I imagined my mother sticking her scarf-covered head out, looking to the left then to the right before calling my little brother and me inside for supper on Thursday nights. Once or twice, when the door was left unlocked, I walked across and peeked through the slim opening, wishing to see Mehdi sitting on the edge of the fountain waiting for me.

To save money and also to be with all of his children and wives, Mr. Rahimi decided not to renew the lease on the house we were living in. In the spring of 1964, he packed up and moved Momon Bozorg and Rana to his house by the mountain where his middle wife and her four boys were already living. Maryam Khanom had little choice but to surrender two of her rooms to Momon Bozorg and Rana.

Perhaps the birth of his new son also had something to do with the move. A few months earlier Mr. Rahimi's middle wife, Maryam, had given birth to her fourth son. The boy was born with a cleft lip, and that had his mother devastated. Being a zealously religious woman, she was convinced that her son's deformity was God's way of punishing Mr. Rahimi for his sins. Mr. Rahimi frequently consumed alcohol, an act forbidden in Islam.

Kia was against the move, but there wasn't much that he or his mother could do. We'd been living in a nice and modern middle-class neighborhood in the city, a stark contrast to where we moved. The new location was more like a small hamlet in the middle of nowhere. I was transferred to a newly built school not very far from the house we moved into, but Kia decided to finish the remaining few months of sixth grade at his old school and commute the distance.

Our new home was located outside of the city limits in the foothills of the Hezar Masjed mountain range. The land, mostly barren and gray, was dotted with small thorn bushes here and there and provided habitat for a variety of grasshoppers, rodents, poisonous snakes, scorpions, and anything else that crawled. Wild dogs, foxes, and jackals also freely roamed the foothills. Mr. Rahimi's cob (mixture of mud and wheat straw) and sun-baked mud-brick house was the last structure at the end of a dirt road at the bottom of a hill, amongst a few other scattered homes. At the top of the hill, just to the left of his house, was a row of wells, looking like giant ant holes leading down to the subterranean water canal. There were often a few fat snakes lying by the mouth of the wells, waiting for the unsuspecting pigeons to fly out. Electricity and city water had not made their way to Mr. Rahimi's road yet.

The house seemed to have been hastily built and was only partially finished. This was not an uncommon practice, especially outside the city limits where the arms of the building inspectors could not easily reach. Some mavericks, often to avoid the expenses of obtaining permits and hiring professionals to build the house, erected their houses in the middle of the night with the help of family and friends. The building inspectors rarely came that far out of the city, and when they did, it was difficult for them to tell if a building was an existing one or a new construction since they were immediately occupied. There were no inspectors who could not be bought for a few hundred toomans anyway.

A tall cob wall wrapped around the rectangular yard, with a rudimentary homemade wooden door serving as the only entrance. The rooms were built at the far end of the unpaved courtyard, opposite the front door. A narrow graveled path ran through the center of the yard between the front door and the living quarters. One had to walk through a covered veranda to reach the house's three rooms. Hand-woven rattan rugs covered parts of the hardened dirt floor of the veranda, where everyone gathered during the early evening hours when it was too hot to stay indoors. The boys used the veranda as a sleeping area at night.

Each wife and her children occupied one room. Naturally Mr. Rahimi lived with his youngest wife Rana and their daughter, with a second child on the way. Maryam and her four boys occupied the largest room in the house, and Momon Bozorg, Kia and I lived together. We all shared a primitive outhouse located at the farthest corner of the yard away from the living quarters.

A grapevine and an overproducing quince tree decorated the unpaved and uneven adobe courtyard. During the early summer, the juices from the sour grapes were used in salads and in cooking and the grape leaves were utilized to make dolma—stuffed grape leaves. In the winter some of the young shoots of the vine were cut and turned into charcoal for use in qalyan. The quince tree produced fruits the size of a small melon. Maryam used the fruit and made delicious quince preserve every summer. Being the first inhabitant of the house, she naturally claimed the grapevine and the quince tree as her own, and no one dared to pick any fruits without her permission.

Living in an adobe home with dirt floors, an unpaved yard, and no running water or electricity took some getting used to. For drinking and cooking we purchased one or two buckets of water a day from a horse-drawn water truck that made a daily trip through the area, and for everything else there was a stream nearby. After water, kerosene was the second most important liquid here; we needed it for everything from cooking to illuminating the rooms at night. I was responsible for hauling water and making weekly trips to the kerosene store for our household—Momon Bozorg, Kia, and me.

Momon Bozorg purchased a hen turkey that first year, and as soon as it was ready to brood we collected as many eggs from the neighbors as we could and placed them all under the bird. Twenty days later there were all sorts of little fluffy chicks following the turkey around the yard. Their presence attracted many uninvited creatures into the house. All day long crows and stray cats came and went, hoping to catch a drifting chick. Sparrows came to eat the chicks' feed, and snakes came and waited behind the tomato plants to catch the sparrows. My job was to make daily trips to the army depot and collect discarded bread from the mess hall's trash to make feed for the birds. The army depot was located in the middle of nowhere, surrounded by nothing but dirt, rocks, thorn bushes, and empty rifle pits. It was visible at a distance from the top of the hill next to Mr. Rahimi's home. Momon Bozorg used to go and stand on the hill to make sure I did not get attacked by wild dogs on my way back. The smell of bread in my sack, often tinted with the scent of meat, attracted the wild dogs to me almost every time. At home, after drying the whole-grain army bread under the sun, Momon Bozorg crushed it and sacked it to use as feed for her birds.

The unusual character of the house and the way it was put together spoke more of Mr. Rahimi's personality than anything else. He did not seem to be shy about how he wanted to live his life, and nothing seemed to bother him all that much, especially how others viewed him and the choices he made. Mr. Rahimi had three younger half brothers by his father's second wife. Besides sharing the same father, the only other thing that Mr. Rahimi had in common with his brothers was his last name. In stark contrast, the three younger brothers each had only one wife and led a seemingly more organized, thoughtful, and successful life. Like many professional middle-class Iranian families, the life of the younger Rahimis bore a strong resemblance to the Cleaver family from *Leave It to Beaver*; everyone always dressed, spoke, and conducted themselves properly.

❖Chapter Twenty-One

I t had been almost two years since my mother and Baba packed up and moved away, and I had not heard from them since. But through Ali Aqa, my aunt Sarvar's husband, I knew that my mother was alright. I also knew that she had given birth to Baba's third child. My father also seemed to have vanished. I knew for sure that he had not made any payment to Momon Bozorg since the summer of 1963, but that did not seem to jeopardize my stay here, thanks to Kia. As long as he was around, my place with the Rahimis seemed secure regardless of my father's neglect.

The past few years of living with Kia and Momon Bozorg had been the most turbulence-free time of my childhood. Besides missing my mother, and the apprehension of always knowing that I was not Momon Bozorg's real son, life in general was good. Momon Bozorg did not have much, and that was just fine with me because I did not need much. I was more than content and grateful for having a roof over my head, the opportunity to go to school, and two wonderful strangers who were willing to share their bread with me.

Kia in particular played an immense role in shaping the man I later became. He was almost a parent to me, teaching me right from wrong, manners, how to be responsible, and to respect others. He pushed me to do well in school, even giving me extra writing or math assignments to complete. He taught me such basics as how to chew my food properly and hold my spoon and knife, how to sit, and when to speak or hold my tongue in front of an adult or a guest. At all times, he emphasized integrity, honesty, and gratitude, as did his mother. But one of Kia's biggest contributions—one that continued to shape my personality long after he was no longer in my life—happened without him ever realizing it.

One Friday evening in 1965 Kia took me to Arg, where we saw a black-and-white film called *Mootalaei Shahre Ma* (*The Blond of Our City*), starring Fardin, the superstar of Iranian cinema at the time. Fardin and the character he portrayed left an indelible impression on me.

Fardin was cool and strong, both physically and internally, in every role that he played. His trademarks were his perfectly sculptured hair, kind and trusting eyes that were always shimmering with life, and a priceless dimpled smile. In every film he defeated evil and forgave those who had done him wrong (often his father who abandoned him at an early age—which of course resonated strongly with me). Fardin's characters stood for decency, integrity, forgiveness, fearlessness, and defending the truth and the weak. To them, righteousness was the greatest wealth of all.

A couple years later, after Kia moved away from home, I started spending every rial that I came across going to cinema and watching Fardin's films. In Kia's absence, the charming and witty actor became my surrogate father. During the summer when I had no one to be with and no place to go, I would often spend an entire day in a movie theater, watching the same film over and over and memorizing the lines. One of the most significant things I learned from Fardin's films was that there is a unique pleasure embedded in forgiveness that can never be found in revenge. At the end of every film he looked into the eyes of those who had done him wrong and forgave them. This was a powerful message to a boy at my age and in my circumstances—a message that taught me how to travel lightly on the road of life by not carrying any grudges. Carrying a rancor was like carrying a bag of trash on my shoulders, and its stench was only going to irritate me, I learned. Soon, I would need that message more than ever to keep from losing myself in the depths of misery and despair.

❖Chapter Twenty-Two

Summer of 1966 marked the beginning of a new and vexing chapter in my life. That was the year Kia, my solacer, champion, and protector, left home. After receiving his elementary school certificate, Kia decided not to go to school anymore, and as soon as he was old enough to enlist in the armed forces, he joined the gendarmerie and was sent to Tehran for a year of training. A few months later, as soon as school ended for the summer, his mother too packed and locked up everything and left for Tehran. She wanted to be near her son and to, as she put it, lessen the pain of *qorbat* (foreign land) for him.

Momon Bozorg was going to be staying with her relatives in Tehran and could not take me along, she said. We did not discuss what was going to become of me while she was away—she had gotten used to me going to my relatives on the weekends and during the holidays. The previous summer I'd even gone to Golmakan, my ancestral village, on my own and spent a few weeks there with Modar Joon. Naturally Momon Bozorg assumed that I had my entire mother's side of the family looking after me; therefore, she was not too worried. Since my father had failed to keep his end of the bargain and had made no payment to her in the past few years, she was under no legal or moral obligation to be concerned about my welfare anyway.

Ironically neither Momon Bozorg nor Kia ever met any of my relatives except for my father. The two of them had certain assumptions about my relatives, and my relatives had their own hypotheses about the Rahimi family, all based on the information they received from me. Each side assumed that I was in good hands and fully taken care of when I was not with them. When I

137

speak of my relatives here, I am only speaking of the ones on my mother's side of the family; I hardly knew and rarely interacted with anyone on my father's side.

I said goodbye to Momon Bozorg and left for Maydoneh Bar to catch the afternoon bus to the village of Golmakan. As might be expected from a ten-year-old boy, I had no specific plan as to what I was going to do or where I was going to stay while Momon Bozorg was away. I figured I would go and visit my grandmother, Modar Joon, for a while and see what happened from there. Modar Joon was a petulant and stubborn woman but nevertheless, she and my aunt Sarvar were the only two relatives I felt close enough and comfortable to go to.

In a small kerchief I carried an extra change of clothes and in my pocket, a five-rial coin, given to me by Momon Bozorg before she left. I took a window seat at the back of the bus and sat and waited for the other passengers to arrive. The soothing and familiar scent of my ancestral village—goat cheese, milk, fresh mulberries, bread, wool, rugs, country folks—lingering in the bus teased my senses. I was not asked to pay any fare last summer when I took this bus to Golmakan and I was not asked again this time, and I knew why. Everyone on that bus, including the driver and his assistant, were Golmakanis, and from the sympathetic look on their faces when they glanced at me, I could tell that they knew who I was: the orphaned son of Assad Banafsheh. The people of Golmakan were very compassionate folks and were never going to allow the assistant bus driver to ask me for any money. As much as I appreciated keeping my five rials, I was not at all happy about being looked upon with sympathetic eyes—it always made me feel pitiful and small, and I hated that. For all the years that I took the bus to Golmakan, I was never asked to pay any fare. I remember once, some years after this journey, a young new assistant driver did ask me to pay, only to be eyeballed and discouraged by the passengers.

Golmakan was heaven on earth, an oasis of solace and nourishment. If it was up to me, I would have spent the entire summer there, especially since my cousins from Gorgan were also there visiting at that time. They were the children of my mother's half brother and my father's sister. Even though they were related to me through both my father and my mother, I considered them to be my cousins from my mother's side of the family.

I prayed for Modar Joon to be in a good and welcoming mood; otherwise I'd have to return to Mashhad and go to my aunt's. Since I had been placed with the Rahimis, whenever I visited relatives I'd been able to return to Momon Bozorg and Kia when I'd had enough of one place or felt that my hosts had had enough of me, but not this time. For the first time in my life I was left completely on my own, with no place to go if things did not work out at my grandmother's or my aunt's.

My stay at Modar Joon's lasted a little over a week before I began to feel she'd had enough of me and I decided to go back to Mashhad and try my aunt Sarvar for a while. After my grandfather passed away and with two children of her own still living at home, Modar Joon did not seem to have the means or the patience to have any other kids around. The other issue was me. Ever since I was very little, I could not stay anywhere if I felt unwelcome, or take anything if it wasn't offered to me with a genuine smile. I could have gone and spent a few days with my cousins from Gorgan on the other side of the village, but it wasn't worth the trouble. Beebee Banafsheh, my fraternal grandmother and my cousins' caretaker, could not stand the sight of me for reasons unknown to me at the time, and I was always very uncomfortable around her.

Of all my relatives, Aunt Sarvar was the only one who showed me a smiling face no matter how often I knocked at her door. I had been visiting her regularly on the weekends and during the holidays ever since my mother moved away. She was like a mother to me and treated me like one of her own sons. Aunt Sarvar and my mother were the closest of all of their siblings, both in age and affection. In my mother's absence, I became the beneficiary of my aunt's adoration for my mother. She always displayed great respect for me and often used me as a good example to follow when she lectured her children about life, school, and studying. My petite aunt Sarvar was a hardworking woman with a very strong personality. She selflessly dedicated her entire life to taking care of her large family. Seven days a week, from dawn to dusk, untiringly and with a permanent smile on her face, she went about washing diapers, baby buttocks, clothes, and dishes, in addition to cooking, cleaning, and everything else that needed to be done at her home. A savvy homemaker, she used her husband's small income to feed and clothe her entire family and even put a few toomans aside for the rainy days. Her only entertainment and break came when she hosted a monthly *rozeh khani*, a sermon-like religious chanting performed by a Muslim cleric (a practice that originated from a type of theatrical singing common in seventeenth-century Persia). As a devoted Muslim, she enjoyed inviting a group of women friends and relatives to her home to hear a rozeh khani she'd hired a mullah to perform. Besides being a religious ritual, the rozeh khani served as a social gathering for the women. It was usually the case that before and after the mullah's arrival, women sat around on the floor, smoked qalyan or cigarettes, drank hot tea, and chatted about everyone and everything.

Early on the morning of a rozeh khani, my aunt would sweep the rugs in her small living room, fire up the charcoal-burning samovar, and place the contents of a few packs of domestic cigarettes decoratively on plates, then she would wait for her guests to arrive. Meanwhile, her daughter or one of her sons would chop a loaf of sugar into bite-size pieces and put them into bowls for the guests to use with their tea. My aunt claimed she had one of the best singing mullahs around. He could make a stone cry, she would say, an attribute of a good mullah. A rozeh khani in essence was a party, prevalent in the lower class and the religious segment of society, where instead of music and dancing, there was chanting by a man and lamenting by others. It may be hard for someone unfamiliar with such customs to imagine that people would actually pay to be made to cry, but one of the criteria used to measure the quality of a good mullah was his ability to chant heart-wrenching religious stories of martyrdom and make his audience cry. Being somewhat handsome and having a pleasant voice didn't hurt either.

Aunt Sarvar's husband, Ali Aqa, was a freelance assistant bus driver. He offered his service to any cross-country bus line that needed an assistant to accompany the driver on a specific trip and went where the road took him, sometimes for weeks at a time. He handed every rial that he made during his trips to my aunt, and in return, my aunt treated him like a little king.

Ali Aqa's lifelong dream was to become a bus driver someday. Unfortunately, his illiteracy pretty much killed his chances of passing the written test of the driving exam and, therefore, of realizing his dream. In addition to being illiterate, Ali Aqa was also very petite in stature, and that made it physically very challenging for him to drive a big bus with standard transmission. If not for his little black mustache, thinning hairline, and often unshaven face, it would have been difficult to tell him apart from a boy.

My mother and Baba's fights and frictions over me were still fresh in my mind. To avoid creating similar circumstances between my aunt and her husband, I stayed away from her home as much as I could during the days until late at night when it was time to go to sleep. Every morning I quietly slipped out of her house, long before anyone was awake, and returned late at night just before they were about to go to bed. That way my aunt was not compelled to feed me anything and her husband could not have any reason to complain. Because of my father's better social status and his apparent financial success, it was hard for anyone to justify taking care of me for any long period.

The summers past had gone by quickly, so I figured this one would too and soon Momon Bozorg would return and I would go home. Until then, I could tough it out with little food if I had to, as long as I had a place to sleep at night.

Three weeks into the summer, one early morning as I was about to leave my aunt's home, she called from another room, "Alireza, I am going to need you to do something for me today, khaleh joon (dear nephew). Be sure to come back here around noon."

"Chashm."

As usual, I spent the morning hours in and around the Maydoneh Bar that day and just before noon, I headed back to my aunt's. As soon as I walked in through the door, she handed me a bucket and asked me to go to the public fountain and bring home some water for her to make tea. Upon my return, I saw a man standing in the middle of her little courtyard.

"This is Cousin Osta Habib (Master Habib)," she introduced the man with a smile on her face.

"Salam," I said to the man. I had never met him before, but I knew of him from hearing my mother telling the story of her tooth-pulling ordeal to relatives some years back. As she told it, when my mother was a teenager, Osta Habib, with the help of two

141

other men holding her head, had pulled her wisdom teeth using a pair of carpenter pincers. She cursed him thereafter for the two weeks of agonizing pain that she endured following the extractions, she said. A barber by trade, Osta Habib, like many other barbers in small towns and villages, made additional money by pulling rotting teeth, setting broken bones, and circumcising boys.

Aunt Sarvar, with a kind and motherly look on her face, said to me, "Khaleh joon, you are now ten years old and almost a man. It is time for you to be circumcised, and since I have chosen you to be my son-in-law when you grow up and I love your mother dearly, I feel it is my duty to do the honor and initiate the process. So what do you think?"

I listened to my aunt and looked at Osta Habib, while the thought of a knife touching me sent chills down my spine. Seeing the fear on my face, the man quickly reminded my aunt that he was only there for consultation that day and did not have the time or the tools to do the actual procedure. Somewhat relieved by what he said, I nodded my head in agreement and said okay. My aunt placed a loud and enthusiastic kiss on my face and winked at Osta Habib. I was hopeful that in a few weeks it would all be forgotten and I would not have to face the man's blade.

"Why don't I measure Alireza while I am here so I know what tools to bring the next time," said Osta Habib, looking at my aunt. My aunt thought it was a splendid idea. The man then looked at me and I reluctantly and bashfully nodded in agreement again. With that he signaled me to follow him into a room, for more privacy, I thought.

I walked behind him through the narrow corridor and into a small room where my little cousins and I slept at night. He closed the door behind us and pointed to a child's cotton mattress and a pillow, already spread on the floor, and asked me to lie down on my back and pull my pants down to my knees. Osta Habib did not bother turning on the ceiling light and, having come from the bright and sunny courtyard into the somewhat dark room, I could hardly see what he was doing. The only light in the room came from a small window facing the adjacent alleyway. In a way I was glad that he did not turn the light on. I was very apprehensive and embarrassed while lying there in front of a stranger with my pants down. With the door closed, the strong odor of urine coming from

142

the rug, courtesy of my littlest cousins who ran around the house pants-less all day long, was overwhelming. Osta Habib knelt on the floor next to me and inserted the end of a pencil-like stick inside the foreskin of my penis, pulled the skin up, and held it firmly in place around the stick with his left hand.

"Where did I put my marker?" he said as he patted his shirt pocket while looking around the room. He then reached under my pillow and said, "I may have left it here under the pillow," still holding the stick and the foreskin tightly in place. Suddenly he pulled out what I believed to be a shaving blade from under the pillow and, before I could react, cut the extra foreskin in a swift and circular move. I was both shocked and in agonizing pain. More than anything I wanted to be angry, but I lost that right when I became homeless in the summer of 1961. Being homeless and an orphan obligated me to be grateful for everything I received, even if I didn't want it. Getting angry would have meant being ungrateful, and that could jeopardize my stay at my aunt's.

Osta Habib cleaned and bandaged me up in a blink of an eye and, with an air of victory, called to my aunt who was standing in the hallway behind the door.

"*Mobarake dokhtar khaleh* (congratulations, Cousin)! Your sister's son is now a man!"

I had not had the opportunity to be a kid yet, and here the man was announcing my manhood.

As he was leaving, I could hear him giving my aunt some instructions as to how to care for me for the next few days.

"Thank you, Cousin Habib! God bless you in heaven for helping an orphaned child."

Aunt Sarvar entered the room and immediately turned the light on. She was glowing with glee as she knelt next to me and placed a bunch of loud kisses on my sunken cheeks. She looked skyward and sighed in gratitude. "I wish my sister was here to witness this moment, Alireza joon." She then ran to the next room and returned with a pair of new underpants in her hands and proudly said, "I picked out the fabric myself and had Sultan Khanom sew it for you, khaleh joon." She then went on to explain how she had met up with my father last week and convinced him to pay twenty toomans to have me circumcised.

"I gave ten toomans to Cousin Habib, and with the rest I bought the fabric for these pants and two kilos of grapes to sweeten our mouths in celebration. Do you like the pants, khaleh joon?"

I shook my head yes, while in my heart I absolutely detested the girlish and glitzy pants.

The next morning, under the inquisitive gazes of my little cousins, I had my first breakfast in a long time—sweetened hot tea and bread. My youngest cousin, three or four years old at the time, asked if I had been a bad boy. His mother told him no. "Then why did they cut Alireza's doodool?" he asked, and with that everybody burst into laughter, including me. Little boys in my family were often threatened with their penis or their ears being cut off when they misbehaved.

Following breakfast, my cousins went outside to play while I lay on the mattress in the little room at the end of the hall. A few hours later I heard the sound of music coming first from the alleyway, then from my aunt's courtyard. Aunt Sarvar rushed into the room excitedly and asked me to come outside. I knew what was going on and refused. She did not take no for an answer and grabbed my wrist and playfully dragged me out and into the courtyard where I was hailed by a group of children clapping their hands to the sound of a drum and a *mizmar*—a woodwind instrument—played by two street musicians. With my aunt standing behind me and clapping in euphoria, I reluctantly stood and faced the crowd and the music. The majority of the kids gathered there in the tiny courtyard were girls my age. I knew of most of them. They all lived in the same alley as my aunt and had been watching me with curiosity as I came to visit her on the weekends over the past few years. I had heard my aunt brag to their mothers once or twice about my grades and my aptitude for learning.

I felt naked standing there wearing a bathing shawl as if I were in hammom. I could swear they were all staring at my crotch; I prayed that the ground would open up at that moment and swallow me in.

On the third day following the circumcision, I felt uncomfortable imposing upon my aunt any longer and decided to leave her house for a while. Before I left, she placed my wounded penis inside a very small, specially designed nosebag, courtesy of Cousin Osta Habib, filled the bag with some sawdust-like substance, and secured it around my waist using strings. I can only assume the substance was to keep my wounds dry by absorbing any moisture, including blood. Despite my insistence on foregoing the new pair of pants, at least for now, hoping that I would never have to wear them, she was firm that I was a new person and therefore needed to wear the new pants to symbolize that. So, wearing the contemptible pants made from a fabric only a newlywed country woman could appreciate, I walked slowly and painfully with my legs spread apart to the other side of town to visit my two cousins from Gorgan who were back from Golmakan and were staying in their father's home here in Mashhad.

My mother's older brother, the one who joined the army with my father and later became his brother-in-law, was still stationed in the town of Gorgan near the Caspian Sea. He owned a home here in Mashhad, renting part of it out while keeping a couple of rooms for when his children came here for summer vacation. Every year he sent three of his children, accompanied by his mother-in-law Banafsheh, my paternal grandmother, to Mashhad for the summer holiday. Beebee Banafsheh, as all of her grandchildren called her, often took my cousins to Golmakan for them to enjoy the pleasant climate and the bounty of fresh fruit and dairy products that the village had to offer. After taking her daughter to Gorgan and marrying her to my uncle, Beebee moved in with them and never left. She practically raised my cousins and, according to them, she did more mothering for them than did their own mother.

Mentally and age-wise, I was closer to my two male cousins from Gorgan than any other relatives. We shared many similar interests, including cinema. The fact that they were here only for the summer made me want to be with them even more.

After my cousin Jam had a good laugh teasing me over my newly acquired exotic pants, we went to Arg and saw an Italian film, courtesy of Jam in honor of my circumcision. My cousins and I loved going to cinema more than anything. And going with Jam was always a fun adventure. First he haggled with Beebee for the money and permission to go to cinema, and if she didn't budge, which she usually did not, he nagged her into submission. A little less than a year younger than I, Jam was a master at haggling. He quibbled with everyone and over everything. Haggling was a way of life in Iran and Jam, at the age of nine, was well on his way to becoming one of the best. People here haggled over everything: shoppers with shop owners over prices, passengers with cabdrivers over the fare, students with teachers over grades, traffic violators with the police over their fines. Even the panhandlers wrangled with the good Samaritans over how much of a handout they should get. I was the exact opposite of Jam when it came to quibbling. I was so bad that sometimes the merchants, who were conditioned to haggle, were put off by the fact that I did not offer a lower price, and they themselves lowered the price for me—"Just because you seem to be a good boy, I am going to give you a discount."

At the cinema, Jam would buy one balcony ticket at the cost of twelve rials and use that ticket to negotiate and get both of us into the eight-rial section. Ushers often gave in and let us through, a savings of four rials for Jam. And that was just the beginning. Before the feature film started, all cinemas play the King's Anthem, and for that it was mandatory for the audience to stand at attention. While everyone stood motionless, on Jam's signal the two of us would slip into the loge section—first class—in the back of the theater. Loge was the most expensive section of any cinema, with cushiony and comfortable seats. Once the film started and the seats were eventually all filled, Jam, in a whispering voice, would begin advertising, "Seats for sale!" to folks who were arriving late and needed seats. Like many other things in Iran, there were no rules or logic to selling tickets at the cinemas. Regardless of seating capacity, as long as people wanted a ticket, the cinemas sold it to them. During the first week's showing of any popular film, not only were the seats all filled, but also the aisles and the floor. There were always some adult men there with their wives or girlfriends who were glad to pay a few rials for our seats. After a bit of haggling, Jam would sell the seats to the highest bidder and we'd move back to the eight-rial section up front. Young country men, day laborers who could not find work that day, and elementary school students, like us, were the likely customers in the eight-rial section. We often ended up watching the film while either standing up against the wall or sitting on the bare floor way up front under the screen with our heads tilted upward.

146

While I loved both Jam and his older brother Hooshang dearly, Jam was more than just a cousin to me; he was my best childhood friend and solacer. We met for the first time in the summer of 1965 and had been the best of friends ever since. Every year I waited anxiously for the summer to arrive and bring with it Jam. His love for me was unconditional. There were times when even I was too embarrassed to be seen with me, like that day I was wearing my new exotic pants, but the loyal and wonderful Jam was never bothered by my physical appearance. He walked proudly, shoulder to shoulder with me, as if I were a prince.

That night after the cinema, tired and in pain from all the walking, I accepted Jam's offer and with Beebee's permission stayed at my cousins'.

❖*Chapter Twenty-Three*

Amazing how heavy and onerous time can become when one has a lot of it and no way to spend it. The summer of 1966 seemed to drag on ever so slowly. Loneliness, constant hunger, and boredom made every hour of every day weigh a thousand tons.

Only ten years old and without any money or a permanent address to go to, I led the life of an alley cat. During the day I purposelessly wandered the city streets and at night, I hoped for someone, out of the goodness of their heart, to open their door and allow me to lay my weary head down in a small corner of their home. And if I was lucky, every now and then they would even place a bowl of food or a piece of bread in front of me.

Unfortunately life had conditioned me to exercise discretion excessively and forego brazenness. I cannot tally how often I went hungry nor can I imagine how much less painful my childhood would have been had I practiced just a little assertiveness at the times that I was most in need. Perhaps it was my inherent pride and not the absence of audacity that condemned me to lead such a difficult childhood. I guess in a way they are both one and the same. For some unknown reason I felt as if I were a king, with a correspondingly huge pride. It was because of that pride that I never begged for anything, refused to touch anyone's food, and asked no one for help. In the absence of Momon Bozorg there weren't many people I could stay with. With the exception of my aunt Sarvar—whose home I went to only to sleep at night so I wouldn't wear out my welcome with her—my relatives didn't seem to be all that thrilled to have me around. And as for the Rahimis, I did not have much of a relationship with the other two wives and therefore had no expectation of them. Without Momon Bozorg and Kia there, I was just a familiar stranger to the Rahimis; hence, I chose not to impose on them.

My cousins from Gorgan were in town until just before schools started but I did not see them all that often. They were usually busy visiting relatives in Mashhad or in Golmakan. One of those relatives was my father, of course. According to my cousins, my father had a summer home in Golmakan built on top of a secluded and scenic hill, overlooking a vast cherry orchard also owned by my father. My cousins, being my father's nephews, were chauffeured by him to the village every now and then where they spent time at his summer home. I was not aware of the exact location of my father's summer home in Golmakan and even if I was, I did not have permission to get near it on account of my stepmother. Even when my cousins were home in Mashhad, I was made to feel unwelcomed by our grandmother Beebee, and because of that, I preferred to limit my visits there.

After Momon Bozorg was gone, I had nothing to do but to wander the streets of Mashhad. Since I was not being charged for the bus ride, I also made a day trip to Golmakan once or twice a week. I enjoyed riding the bus, and the trip provided me with the opportunity to bathe in Golmakan's river and also to pick some apricots to fill my belly.

When I did not go to Golmakan, I slept at my aunt Sarvar's at night and hung around the Maydoneh Bar area during the day, often for the entire day. Maydoneh Bar, only a few blocks from where my aunt Sarvar lived, was Mashhad's only wholesale fresh fruit and produce market. One could smell the sweet scent of famous Mashhadi melons and golden grapes from far away. All morning long, fresh produce arrived from the surrounding countryside. Up until just before noon, the inside of the open-air rectangular compound was a madhouse, swarming with pickup trucks, taxicabs, and Mopeds going in and out as store and restaurant owners from all over the city came to purchase supplies. Outside of the compound, street vendors set up shop alongside of the road and sold fresh fruits and vegetables to the public. I could never go bored or hungry there. There was always a discarded apple, a pear, a few loose grapes, or a slightly soiled broken melon fallen from a truck or a donkey cart for me to find and eat. And

149

across from the compound on the other side of the Qara Khan Canal lay a vast undeveloped area where seven days a week I could find all sorts of activities to watch and keep myself entertained. There were always one or two street performers, more on Fridays, entertaining folks. I could spend an hour watching young men, crouched on their heels, gambling at the far end of the field next to a wall. My grandmother called them hoodlums and detested the way they dressed; the backs of their leather shoes were always folded inward and placed under the heels of their feet while their jackets loosely hung over their shoulders. I guess it was cooler to hang the jacket over the shoulders than to actually wear it. There were country men selling livestock and gypsies reading palms, extracting blood from people's backs for good health, and selling or bartering handmade crafts. Farther up, where the water of the canal was still somewhat clear, boys could be seen swimming as women did laundry and washed rugs. Down from the women and children, there were always a few men washing sheep. Young day-laborers, here from the countryside, sat around in their own groups with their shovels and picks resting on the ground next to them, all the while chatting, sharing a melon, and hoping that tomorrow would be better day.

My father was now driving a French Citroen and living in a nice, big house in an upscale section of the Maydoneh Bar area, about a kilometer or so from where my aunt lived. To go to my aunt's from Mr. Rahimi's place or my cousins', I had no choice but to pass his home. Many times I walked by his children as they played outside. They had no idea who I was, and I never approached them. I ran into him once that summer as he was getting out of his automobile in front of his home.

"Salam, aqa."

It had been well over two years since we'd last seen one another, and I had grown and changed somewhat. It took him a brief second to place me.

"Salam? Alireza, is that you!?"

"*Baleh, aqa* (yes, sir)."

I was certain that he knew all of my mother's relatives lived nearby on the other side of the Maydoneh Bar and therefore was not surprised to see me there. He looked at his wristwatch a few times, indicating that he was in a hurry, as he briefly asked how I was doing and why I looked so grubby. I gave him a quick summary of my situation, saying that Momon Bozorg was gone and I had no permanent place to stay and was starving. I was also tempted to tell him all about my unhealed circumcision wounds when he asked why I was standing funny, but I was too shy.

"Why aren't you staying with your aunt until Mrs. Rahimi returns? Your aunt is not dead, is she?" he asked, as if insinuating it was my aunt's duty to look after me.

My voice was quivering and my left knee trembling out of control as I stood nervously in front of this man with whom I indisputably shared common facial features that suggested we were related. I explained that I did sleep at my aunt's home at nights but I was uncomfortable eating their food. He reached into his pants pocket, pulled out a crisp five-tooman bill, and handed it to me. I could not believe my eyes. I had never been given that much money before, not even during the Norooz holiday when everyone handed out cash to children. The thrill of holding a five-tooman bill in the palm of my hand overwhelmed my thinking circuitry and paralyzed my tongue. I could no longer hear a word my father said, and by the time I had finally pulled myself together, he was already gone into his house. I spent the entire amount in one day; going to a few cinemas and buying sandwiches. I could have bought enough bread with that money to feed me for ten days If only I had inherited my mother's money management skills. I felt guilty and depressed after I had no more money left.

It was now over a month since the circumcision, and my wounds were not yet healing. In fact, the area around the circumcision was infected and inflamed, perpetuated by all the walking I did every day, and it was painful. The lack of proper hygiene and medical care was also to blame. At the time the only person that I felt comfortable enough to go to with such a private problem was my cousin Jam. I was too embarrassed to go to my aunt Sarvar because that would have required pulling my pants down in front of her.

Once or twice a week Jam snuck out a bottle of mercurochrome and some cotton balls from his house, we walked to a secluded section of Koohsangi Avenue where there was a running creek to wash our hands afterwards, and used the medicine to tend to my wounds. Almost anyone can tend to a cut on someone's leg or a wound on someone's hand, but nursing a penis? That takes a big and spiritually enlightened person, and little Jam was exactly that. He had a heart as big as an ocean and a mind as open as the sky above. Being young and naïve, we both feared my penis was going to rot and fall off and did everything we could think of to prevent that from happening. I had no idea how I was going to urinate if it ever fell off, and that had me worried and crying when I was alone.

As the summer was nearing its end, in anticipation and hope of Momon Bozorg's return from Tehran, I started going to Mr. Rahimi's neighborhood a few times a week. I was only assuming that Momon Bozorg was returning, since when she left she hadn't said when or if she was coming back. It was a long trip from my aunt's to Mr. Rahimi's home and back, especially given the condition I was in, but I was desperate and had no other way of learning of Momon Bozorg's return. She did not know where any of my relatives lived; therefore, she could not have come to get me even if she'd wanted to. Plus, I missed Momon Bozorg, Kia, and our little room very much.

In the final two weeks of the summer, worried that school would start without me, I began going to Mr. Rahimi's neighborhood every morning, only to return disappointedly to Maydoneh Bar just before nightfall. The first day of school was right around the corner, and I was getting anxious. What if Momon Bozorg decided not to come back? Her absence during these past few months emphasized how alone I was in this world and how I had nowhere else to go if it wasn't for her. Clearly I could not go to school if she did not return. I wasn't even sure where I was going to live. The days when my father took responsibility for finding me a home seemed to be long over. I was all on my own now. I wished I could stay at Mr. Rahimi's home during those last two weeks so I wouldn't have to make the long trip every day, but that wasn't likely. Maryam Khanom never invited me into her home. As a matter of fact, for all the years that I lived with Momon Bozorg at Mr. Rahimi's home, I do not remember even once having a meal at Maryam Khanom's. And Rana Khanom and I rarely spoke.

There was absolutely nothing to do and hardly anyone to talk to around Mr. Rahimi's neighborhood, and that made the days long and dull. The scorching sun kept most children indoors until late in the afternoon. Every now and then, a person would hurry by at a distance or a boy could be seen running and using a stick to roll an old bicycle rim on the dirt road. Sometimes the only sign of life on this vast barren land seemed to be the grasshoppers, the scorpions, and the little lizards that occasionally came out of one hole, rushed by, and disappeared into another. I took a lot of naps wherever I could find some shade—next to a wall or under a tree by a nearby creek.

At the end of each day while the sun was still out, I walked to the nearby army depot and waited for the soldiers to finish their supper. Trash from the mess hall was discarded just outside the fence, and I could always scavenge a few unsoiled pieces of bread to eat before heading back to Maydoneh Bar. Sometimes I took some extra pieces back with me to have for breakfast the next day. I would hide the bread behind a cement light post or a rock near my aunt's home only to find it gone the next day. There were plenty of stray dogs hungrier than I. Hopefully they appreciated my efforts.

Upon my arrival at my aunt's, I used to wait in the alley outside of her front door and eavesdrop to make sure they were finished with their dinner; only then would I knock at the door. During the summer, my aunt and her family ate out in the courtyard, and I could tell from their conversation and the smell of food and melon or watermelon saturating the narrow alleyway whether they were finished eating or not.

I dreaded being out on the street after dark and felt very vulnerable. In a city that had no television station, for many people nine o'clock was bedtime, even during the summer. Most people were home by eight o'clock to listen to *Story of the Night*, a popular nightly radio drama, and asleep by nine. The streets were eerily empty after dark, and an anxious feeling of melancholy and loneliness took over me and turned my stomach. I guess more than anything I worried over the uncertainty of not knowing whether I would have a place to go to on any given night. Often when it was late and I was still searching for a place to sleep, I would cry quietly and think of my mother or have a monolog with God to keep myself company as I frantically paced through the empty streets. Oddly enough, during that entire summer and many similar summers in the future, my aunt never asked where I had been or

153

what I had been doing when I knocked at her door late at night. Like an outdoor cat, I was usually let in by one of my little cousins. Once I'd been admitted, I tiptoed into a designated corner and apprehensively went to sleep. The awful feeling of homelessness and the shame that it brought tormented me greatly. I always felt like a burden on others.

I will never forget one particular evening in that summer of 1966. I remember going to Mr. Rahimi's neighborhood once again to learn of any news regarding Momon Bozorg's return. Late in the afternoon I ended up chatting and playing with some of my old school friends and neighborhood kids, including two of Maryam Khanom's boys. In the excitement of being with my friends, I lost track of time. It was only when Maryam Khanom stuck her head out of the front door and called her boys inside for supper that I realized the sun had already set. I was praying that for the first time in our mutual history Maryam Khanom would invite me in and offer to let me spend the night at her home.

"You better go home too, Alireza, it is getting late."

With that, they said good night, went inside, and closed the front door behind them. A feeling of panic rushed over me as I suddenly realized how late it was and how far I had to travel to get to my aunt's home. With the circumcision wounds still bothering me, I began to pace toward the city.

My cousins' home was closest to Mr. Rahimi's place, almost on the same route as my aunt's, so I decided to go there first and see if I could spend the night with Jam. Ordinarily I would not go there at night on account of Beebee. Her never-ending, often veiled hostility toward me made me feel uneasy and unwelcome. Usually when I went to visit my cousins, I waited for them out in the courtyard and hardly ever touched any food at their home. Once or twice when I was pressured by my cousins to stay and eat with them, Beebee laced every little bite I took with her poisonous sullen stares. I remember sitting at the sofreh and timidly reaching for the food, swallowing only with great difficulty under her paralyzing glare. I preferred dying of starvation to going through such emotional torment. I remember meeting a lady once who claimed to had been Beebee's landlord during the time when my parents were having marital difficulties, just prior to their divorce. According to the lady, on one bitterly cold night in the winter of

1956 my father brought me over and dropped me off with Beebee to look after me. I was barely a half year old at the time. The landlady described in vivid detail how she used to watch Beebee from the corner of her window as Beebee changed my diapers out in the frigid snow- and ice-covered courtyard. To avoid soiling her hands Beebee would wipe my buttocks by rubbing them on the snow while holding me by my ankles and underarm, the lady said. She remembered her house's only water faucet being frozen at the time and all the occupants had to break the ice covering the fountain in order to get water to use for washing; Beebee apparently did not want to deal with that. Years later, when my cousin Jam and I both became adults, he attributed Beebee's distaste for me to my mother. According to him, Beebee and my mother never got along and Beebee endured many beatings by my father over that.

When I arrived at my cousins', I found the front door unlocked and tiptoed right into the courtyard. In an attempt to gauge Beebee's mood before going inside, I stood in the dark behind a tree just outside of my cousins' living room window and watched. I was hoping to find Beebee cheery; otherwise, there was a very long walk ahead of me to my aunt's home.

At the time a middle-aged man, his young wife, and a partially crippled son from the man's first marriage were renting a room in my uncle's home. The boy was about my age. We were not friends, but due to the somewhat similar circumstances in our lives, the two of us felt a bit of camaraderie toward each other when we occasionally crossed paths. As I stood there in the dark courtyard looking into my cousins' living room, a door suddenly opened to my right and the man's young wife, clearly pregnant, her large belly extending forward, came out. Not knowing what else to do, to avoid startling her, I stood motionless in my spot, but it was too late. She saw my outline in the dark, let out a scream, and fainted. The boy was first to respond to the scream and run out of the room. He recognized me standing in the middle of the courtyard and whispered for me to run before his father came out and got a hold of me. And I did just that.

I bolted out of the courtyard and kept on running, turning my head every few steps, hoping not to see the man behind me. The man had a rough temper and was brutal. I knew this from seeing him hitting his poor son in the past. After a while I did not turn to look for him anymore. I did not feel the pain of my swollen penis bouncing against my bare thigh. In a strange way I wished the man was behind me and could catch up and finish me. I kept on running and could not stop now even when I knew it was safe. My fear transformed into indignation, anger at just about everything, but most of all at God for seemingly condemning me to live this awful life. A lonely life of vagrancy, constant hunger, and a constant state of trepidation. It is a dreadful feeling to know you don't belong anywhere and nobody wants you and, worst of all, you don't know the reason why. I was running in the middle of the dark blacktopped street, tired and with an empty stomach, and didn't want to stop. I felt, like in many of my dreams, that if I ran fast enough somehow I could ascend and leave myself behind. I was trying to outrun myself and get away from me, the source of all of my misery and pain. The cool evening wind was rushing against me, scattering my silent tears over my face as I ran. I hadn't gone to the army depot that day to collect some bread to eat and was therefore very hungry; the salty tears had the pleasant taste of food. Suddenly I found myself airborne, but not ascending into the heavens as I wished I could. Instead I was falling down into the dark depths of a utility ditch dug into the blacktopped road not far from my cousin Jam's home. I had failed to see the orange marking, and soon I was lying at the bottom of the ditch, unable to move. I could feel warm liquid running down my thighs but wasn't sure if it was blood or urine, and I did not care anymore either. I focused on dying and death and hoped it would come soon. For the first time in my short life I began questioning the purpose of life and whether it was worth such a constant struggle.

After a while the desire to die dissipated and gave room to fear. I pulled myself up and out of the ditch and began the long walk to Maydoneh Bar and my aunt's home. One of my sandals was lost in the mud at the bottom of the ditch.

There was not a soul around for me to ask the time, though it appeared to be late. Eventually I made it to the Maydoneh Bar area and my aunt's home. I remember seeing my father's automobile parked in front of his home as I passed the alleyway where he lived. Since it was late, at my aunt's home I used my knuckle to timidly tap on the surface of the metal door and waited. After a long pause

I tried again but no one answered. They were probably asleep and could not hear my knocking, I thought. I did not have the audacity to knock any louder.

Tired and hungry, with my knees scuffed and burning and my pants torn and wet, more than anything I wanted to go to sleep and get rid of the night. I was having great difficulty keeping my eyes open at that point. I could just as easily sit right there in front of my aunt's house and go to sleep, but I worried a neighbor of hers may see me, and that would have tarnished my aunt's reputation. I decided to walk back to the only other place that I could think of— the sidewalk across the street from my father's home. I had slept there many times before, but always during the daytime. After that encounter with my father when he gave me the five-tooman bill, in hope of repeating the event I spent many days sitting across the street from his house and waited to cross paths with him again. As a matter of fact, I can safely say that before I reached the age of fourteen, I spent thousands of hours sitting across the street in front of my father's home without him ever knowing.

I sat next to the entrance of a hammom called Sadaf, across the street from my father's home, lay on the cold sidewalk against the wall, curled my body, with my head pillowed on my hands and went to sleep. The temperature in Mashhad, even during the summer months, dropped sharply in the shade and even more so at night. Knowing, however, that someone with the same blood as mine running through his veins was sleeping just across the street was somewhat reassuring. I dreamed I was sitting on a high plateau overlooking a lush green meadow of tall wheatgrass sparkling under the sun and dancing with the wind. My familiar dream companion, the ancient Greek-looking man with a masculine body, a perfectly trimmed beard, and hair the color of snow, was sitting on the boulder next to me, casting a warm smile in my direction. It felt as if we were the best of friends. Just as in the past dreams, his presence emitted solace, hope, and tranquility. I felt him conveying that everything was going to be alright.

Suddenly the warmth of someone or something's breath blowing against my crotch and the bare surfaces of my wounded knees that were exposed through my ripped pants yanked me out of this peaceful plateau and had me quickly standing up on my feet. Half awake, I was startled as a couple of street dogs, scrawnier than

157

I, were sniffing me and licking the dried blood on my knees. I waved them off and hurried away to look for another place to sleep.

Earlier that night, on my way to my aunt's and back, I saw half a dozen migrant day laborers sleeping in front of a high school on the main road about a block away from my father's home. I decided to go there and sleep amongst them. The wide sidewalk where they were sleeping was well lit and offered the best security. The young country men had taken their shoes off and placed them under their heads, to keep the shoes from getting stolen and also to use them as pillows. Their shovels and picks stood against the wall next to them as they all slept in a tight cluster, I assume to feel safe and to keep warm. Right in the middle of the group there was a spot big enough for me. I quietly coiled my body on the cold cement and went to sleep with my hands beneath my head. I did not have my sandals to use for a pillow since I had lost one in the ditch and thrown the other one away.

Not long after I began to drift off to sleep, someone struck me in my abdomen—not forcefully, I should add. I immediately rose to a sitting position and noticed a policeman playing with his baton while standing over me.

"What are you doing here, kid?" he asked.

"Nothing, sir," I quickly replied.

"You call sleeping on the sidewalk at this time of the night nothing?" he said sarcastically.

"But I am not the only one sleeping here, aqa," I pleaded. Ever since that incident with the policeman who took me home to my mother and demanded a finder's fee, I felt intimidated by the police.

He ordered me to get up and step aside from the sleeping men who were surely awake by now but dared not open their eyes.

He stood under a tall cement light pole, studied me up and down, and asked, "What has happened to you, boy? Have you been raped?"

"No, sir," I answered firmly, insulted by his question.

"Then why are your pants all ripped and bloody?"

"I fell into a ditch, sir."

"A ditch? There are no ditches around here!"

"In Ahmadabad, sir."

"Ahmadabad? What were you doing there? Is that where you live?"

"No, sir."

"So where do you live?"

I shrugged my shoulders and looked at my feet. In reality, I did not live anywhere. All I wanted to do was to go to sleep. Mashhad was practically a crime-free city; nothing ever happened here, especially at night, and that left the policemen with a lot of free time on their hands. Because of the streetlight above his head, I couldn't see the policeman's eyes under the shadow of his cap to read what he was possibly thinking.

"Where do you live, I asked you?" he said again, with a firmer voice this time. "Look, kid, if you don't tell me where you live I have no choice but to take you to the station. It's okay if you have run away from home. Just tell me where you live and I'll take you home and talk to your parents, alright?" This time he switched to a kinder tone.

I did not know how to answer the man. Surely I was not going to give him my aunt's address and have him hustle her for money at that hour of the night. Mr. Rahimi's address was out of the question because the policeman would not have believed the story of my relationship with them. I was about to faint from exhaustion and hunger when suddenly he grabbed my wrist and said, "Okay, kid, let's go. You leave me no choice but to take you to the station."

Station! It sounded frightening. I thought it meant jail, and I had seen in the movies what jails were like. I also knew that one of the stories surrounding my little sister's disappearance involved my father and his brother taking her to a policeman or a police station. I certainly did not want to go to the station, whatever and wherever that place was.

In one last attempt to soften his heart to let me go, I pleadingly promised not to ever sleep there again, and when that did not work, I thought of my father. He lived only a block away, and with him being a staff sergeant in the army, I was certain he could tell the policeman off if the policeman's intention was to extort money.

Without giving it any more thought I said, "My father lives right up the street, aqa!"

"What do you mean your father? What about your mother?"

159

"They are divorced."

"Okay, show me the way. You better not be lying."

Once in front of my father's home, the policeman rang the doorbell as he cleared his throat and straightened his body and uniform. From the other side there came the sound of footsteps approaching the imposing, vast iron door. My heart began to pound out of control against my ribs. Knowing that I was forbidden from nearing my father's home, I began trembling.

The right panel of the door opened and my father appeared, half asleep. "Salam, aqa. Are you Mr. Golmakani?" the policeman said to my father.

"Yes!?" said my father, standing in the partially opened doorway, wearing two-piece pajamas. His hair was uncombed and ruffled to the side and his eyes puffed up. I was standing out of the moonlight in the shadow next to the wall, frightened and shivering like a baby sparrow that had fallen out of its nest and had been touched by a human hand. My mother used to say once a fallen baby sparrow is touched by a human, its mother would abandon it.

"Forgive me, aqa. I found this boy sleeping on the sidewalk in front of the high school down the street. He claims to be your son and gave your address."

My father turned his attention to me standing in the dark and gave me a cold and indifferent look, like the one his mother, Beebee, often gave me when I went to visit my cousins. I put my head down and whispered, "Salam, aqa. Please forgive me, aqa."

Before the policeman could say anything more, my father thanked him as he leaned forward, grabbed my wrist, pulled me inside the house, and shut the door.

I had sat across from the house many times before, but I had never been inside. The door was more of a large gate made of solid sheets of iron. It was designed to allow enough room for an automobile to get through and into the courtyard. We stood silently there behind the door as my father sharpened his ears and listened for the sound of the policeman's footsteps to dissipate into the night.

Still half asleep and in a daze, he looked at me with repugnance for a little bit before looking at the other end of the courtyard where all the lights were off and his family was asleep. Hungry, petrified and tired, I barely stood with my feeble body against the

160

cold surface of the metal door and quivered. The last time I was with my father behind a closed door, my mother was there too and things did not turn out so good.

My father softly asked why I brought the policeman to his home. I had nothing to say in response.

He then bent down and whispered angrily into my face, "Tell me motherfucker, who told you to bring a policeman to my home in the middle of the night?" I looked at the ground, fearing that I may wet my pants, and did not open my mouth. He grabbed my hair and banged my head as hard as he could against the door several times as he repeated his question. Soon his blood came to a full boil and he unleashed his massive anger on me. Punching and kicking me and hitting my head repeatedly against the metal door, all the while cussing in a low voice, calling my mother all sorts of names. I had no energy to protest or to utter even a single ouch. And soon, I could no longer hear him or feel any pain. Time appeared to have suddenly slowed. Like in a dream, my father's punches seemed to land on my face in slow motions, shifting my head from side to side. I remember asking God in my head to help my father at that moment. Help him take back what he had supposedly given me a decade ago—my life. I didn't want it anymore.

When he finally let go of my shirt, I folded to the ground at his feet like a sack of bones.

"Don't move, motherfucker," he said as he walked away.

He didn't need to worry about that.

He returned carrying a folded army blanket, grabbed me by my shirt, and dragged me outside into the alley, where he opened his automobile's door and shoved me in. Slamming the blanket onto my face, he said he would deal with me in the morning and closed the door and went back inside his house.

At last, I thought to myself, a comfortable place to go to sleep. I cuddled on the back seat, covered myself with the coarse and scratchy blanket, and closed my eyes. My upper lip and the corner of my left eye felt swollen and in pain. I wished for this grueling night to come to an end soon even though the other side of it was not going to be any more promising.

Soon my eyelids were heavy again and I was back sitting on the boulder on a high plateau overlooking the lush green meadow of

161

tall wheatgrass sparkling under the sun and waltzing with the wind. The ancient man was sitting next to me with his arm draped over my shoulders, solacing me once again. "Everything is going to be alright, I promise you," I felt him conveying. I dreamed of running, flapping my arms, and eventually becoming airborne. There were men chasing me and jumping up to grab my feet in an attempt to bring me down as I flew low over the meadow. I felt no pain and no hunger.

The sound of the automobile's engine turning woke me up.

"Good morning, aqa," I sat up quickly and said to my father, who was sitting behind the steering wheel. He did not reply. The scent of his aftershave dominated the air inside the automobile as he put it into first gear, released the clutch, and drove out of the alley. His full-dress army uniform made him look very official and attractive. Since he did not order me to get out, I was certain he was taking me somewhere, but where, I did not ask. Gauging by the early morning time and his uniform, he was surely going to work. My aunt's home was just around the corner, and I believed that she still had my old pants, the ones she did not let me wear after the circumcision. I needed to change but was afraid to say anything to my father.

Thinking about his promise to take care of me today, I sat quietly in the back and said nothing, hoping he had had a change of heart. My left eye was swollen shut and my tattered body and clothes stunk. Suddenly and strangely, for no apparent reason at all, I felt as if I was a Holocaust victim and my father, with his pristine army uniform and perfectly trimmed little mustache, was a Nazi officer, driving me somewhere. A surreal déjà vu of a sort.

I watched motionlessly as he drove out of town and passed through Mr. Rahimi's neighborhood. By the mountains, he turned onto a newly carved dirt road still under construction and drove until it ended in the middle of nowhere. There he pulled over.

"Get out," he said, looking at me sullenly through his rearview mirror.

Immediately I got out and stood by the door awaiting his next command. After he told me to shut the door, he put his automobile back into gear, turned around, and sped away, sending a cloud of dust and gravel into the air behind him.

162

I stood in the middle of the unfinished dirt road with the dry and dead-looking Hezar Masjed Mountains scraping the sky behind me like an infinitely tall prison wall, while in front of me stretched a vast and barren land marked by hints of structures here and there in the distance. I was going to ask my father for two rials to buy some bread for myself but never got the opportunity. An eagle, perhaps awakened by the sound of my father's automobile engine echoing against the mountain, circled above, checking things out. The early morning sun was already potent and piercing through my thick black hair. I had been to this place many times before, exploring it both with my friends and by myself. Every spring wild red tulips, often luminous with the morning dew, blanketed the entire rolling hem of the mountains here. I used to come and fill my belly with sweet and juicy tulip bulbs before and after school. I wished the tulips were still here. I sure could use them today.

Before heading back into town, I decided to walk to a little stream I knew just up the hill and wash myself. I stunk with dried blood, urine, and sweat saturating my clothes and body. In the past, during the hot days of summer, my friends and I used to come up here and cool off in the stream. It was very shallow with a bed of small round pebbles, which suited us just fine since none of us knew how to swim.

I walked to a section of the stream where the depth was as high as my ankle and lay there in the water with my clothes on, what was left of them. Usually there were children playing and screaming around here while their mothers washed dishes and clothes. But it was way too early for that and I had the entire vast barren land and the cool creek to myself. I closed my eyes and lay still on my back for what seemed to be a very long time. The cool and soothing clear liquid crested my body as it rushed around me and away in a hurry. Soon I could no longer feel the rigidity of the pebbles on the streambed pressing against my bony back. The hot sun warmed my face as the cold water, rolling over the rest of my body, balanced the heat from the sun and covered my skin with chill bumps. I imagined being in a stream in my grandparents' village where, unlike here where everything was the color of dust, the whole place was lush and green. I could sense the smell of burning tobacco coming from my grandfather's pipe. I could vividly smell the heavenly scent of bread coming out of Modar

Joon's in-ground clay oven and see and feel the sweat beads over her forehead as she folded and unfolded her body in and out of the hot oven.

The pinch and the pain of hunger in my stomach would not let my mind free. Food was all that I could think about. I thought of going to Hajji Aqa's little convenience store in a little while and asking him to give me another bread and put it on Momon Bozorg's account. During the past two months, whenever I could not find food anywhere else, I went to Hajji Aqa's store and bought bread or a little melon here and there on Momon Bozorg's account. I had told Hajji Aqa that Momon Bozorg was out of town and would settle the account as soon as she returned. My plan was of course to find my father and convince him to give me the money and pay the man long before Momon Bozorg was due to return to Mashhad. Like most military wives in that area, Momon Bozorg had an account with Hajji Aqa and settled it at the beginning of each month when she received her allowance from Mr. Rahimi. The total amount that she would owe in any given month would hardly reach ten toomans: two rials' worth of fruit-salt for when she had indigestion, two rials' worth of cigarettes or aspirin for when she had a headache, and two rials' worth of ice and ten rials' worth of grapes for when someone came to visit her unannounced. With what little money she received from Mr. Rahimi, she had to be very frugal.

I took off what was left of my shirt, squeezed the water out of it, shook it in the air, and put it back on before I began limping and walking down the long gravel road toward Mr. Rahimi's neighborhood where Hajji Aqa's convenience store was. Out of shame—shame of owing him money and not being able to pay him back yet—I had not been to his store or even passed in front of it for a while. My biggest fear was Momon Bozorg's returning to discover what I had done before I could pay the man. She would definitely have considered my using her good name and credit in her absence and without her knowledge an act of dishonesty and perhaps even theft.

But today I did not have a choice. I was going to black out soon if I did not get some food inside of me. I thought of walking to the army depot, but I wasn't sure I could make it that far, and if I was going to pass out, I preferred it to happen somewhere where

I could be discovered and not in the barren, snake-infested land surrounding the depot.

Sheepishly I entered the store, where Hajji Aqa stood behind the small wooden counter.

"Salam, Haj Aqa."

"Salam," he answered in his usual way, without smiling or lifting his head and looking at me. Hajji Aqa was a smaller-than-average country man who resembled my grandfather Aqa Bozorg, except that unlike my grandfather, he never smiled. In his mid to late fifties, he had a sunken and serious face that was always covered with a white beard a few days old. Like most country men, he used a small white turban as a cap and was clad in the same clothes almost every day. Hajji Aqa hardly ever said a word, and when he did it was very short and dry.

I apprehensively scanned the little mud-hut store, standing across from him on the other side of the counter where he kept a bulky brass scale and a pile of old newspaper that he used to wrap his customers' purchases in. To my right there were wooden cases of Coca-Cola and Pepsi-Cola stacked against the wall, and to my left all sorts of dry goods were on display inside heaping gunnysacks. The air was saturated with the sweet aroma of golden grapes and melons. As usual he did not ask what I wanted and went on about doing his business. He was that way with everyone, although I could not help but feel he was unhappy with me and sulking. Perhaps he thought of me as a charlatan, I worried. With the amount that I already owed him, it was highly unlikely for him to sell me anything on credit until he was paid, but I was too desperate and could not think of any other way to get some nourishment at that point.

"Can you please give me one bread and put it on Mrs. Rahimi's account?" I said with a faint voice that sounded as if it was coming from the bottom of a well.

Hajji Aqa raised his eyes without lifting his head and studied me for a brief moment and said, "When is Mrs. Rahimi coming back?"

"Soon, Haj Aqa."

"She now owes twenty-one toomans!"

I gasped. That was a lot of money for me to come up with before Momon Bozorg returned.

Feeling small and worthless, without looking him in the eye I responded, "Yes, Haj Aqa." I was hoping that he would not ask any more questions, as swirling emotions were forming a big lump inside my throat. I was too emotional at that moment and knew if I opened my mouth one more time I would burst into tears in front of Hajji Aqa. Despite the fact that I was growing up in a culture where crying was the norm and knew no gender or age, I had always hated to cry.

Hajji Aqa's gaze fixed on the bruises on my face for a brief moment, and then as if he forced himself to look away, he reached behind him as he shook his head and whispered something to himself, grabbed a bread, and handed it to me. As with everyone else in and around Mr. Rahimi's neighborhood, Hajji Aqa knew that I was an orphan.

"Merci, Haj Aqa." I took the bread, left the store, and began crying as I walked back to Maydoneh Bar and chewed on the thin round flatbread. I felt very sorry for myself at that moment and my tears this time were for me, the little ten-year-old boy alone in the jungle of life, and the injustice that I felt. An injustice that I had been conditioned to blame on God.

About a month later, after Momon Bozorg had returned, she and I were going somewhere when she suddenly decided to stop at Hajji Aqa's store and purchase some aspirin. I told her that I would wait outside, but she did not want to go into the store alone and did not give me a choice. I reluctantly followed her into the tiny store and stood directly behind Momon Bozorg by the door, with my head down. Hajji Aqa was standing behind the wooden counter and said hello to Momon Bozorg.

"Salam, Khanome Rahimi."

"Salam, Haj Aqa. Please wrap two rials' worth of aspirins for me."

"Chashm, khanom"

I was filled with shame and fear that Momon Bozorg was about to discover what a cheating and dishonest child I was and how I had been tarnishing her good name and credit behind her back. The already small store was psychologically shrinking even more and suffocating me. The only thing that could have saved me at that moment was death, I thought. Now I wished I'd told Momon Bozorg about the twenty-some toomans that I had charged to her name. "You are just like your father, dishonest and a charlatan. You need to pack your things and leave my home at once," I imagined her saying.

Hajji Aqa wrapped a few aspirins inside a small piece of white paper, folded it, and handed it to Momon Bozorg. Momon Bozorg reached into her little black coin wallet, counted four 10-shahis, and gave them to Hajji Aqa.

With his hand holding the coins still extended in the air, he said what I was hoping by some miracle he would never say: "Would you like to settle your account today, *khanom*?"

"What account?! We owed you four toomans, and I personally paid you that amount before I left for Tehran, do you remember?"

As if Hajji Aqa were a balloon and Momon Bozorg's response a needle, his shoulders and his body that had been standing at attention out of respect for Momon Bozorg suddenly dropped as he placed both hands on the counter and took a deep breath. He then lifted his head slightly and for the first time gazed deep into my eyes— a gaze filled with questions and comments for which I had no answer or reply. Instead of looking down or away, I allowed his eyes to travel deep into my soul and examine the truth for himself and see that I was not a hoodwinker. I gently looked back at him and like a puppy begged for mercy with my eyes.

"You are right, Khanome Rahimi," the wonderful old man suddenly said to my delight as his gaze was still intertwined with mine. "Your account was settled at the beginning of the summer. My mistake, forgive me please."

I will never forget Hajji Aqa.

Chapter Twenty-Four

O ne night I dreamed that I was dancing with a woman in a large, dimly lit room of some sort. We embraced as if the world did not exist beyond the two of us. I felt a maddening affection for the woman as our bodies gently swayed around the room. Even though the man in my dream was much older and clearly did not look like me, I perceived him as myself. It was as if I was standing aside in the dark and watching another me dance. While the woman's face was vague and unfamiliar, the strong emotional connection suggested a deep love affair between the two of us. I appeared to be tall, handsome, and in my thirties, and I distinctly remember that I was wearing a white, somewhat ruffled long-sleeve shirt and a pair of dark-colored pants. When the dance came to an end I did not want to let go of the woman. This wasn't the first time I had experienced this dream. In the past few weeks, however, it had become more frequent and progressively more emotionally intense. The morning after each episode I found myself both perplexed and vividly affected by this apparently unexplainable experience.

"Alireza, don't go disappearing anywhere this week, I am going to need you here."

"Chashm, Momon Bozorg."

School had just ended and I was planning on going to Golmakan at the end of the week. My cousins from Gorgan were due to arrive in Mashhad any time now, and they usually went straight to Golmakan to indulge in eating mulberries while they were at the peak of their season. According to Momon Bozorg, her niece was coming to visit from Kashmar, a small town some few hundred kilometers south of Mashhad, and she needed me around to prepare for her arrival. Because of Momon Bozorg's age and poor vision and everything being so far away from where we lived, ever since we moved here I had been running all of her errands for her.

She barely had enough money to purchase bread or even kerosene for our only appliance, a little Aladdin portable heater. Back when Kia lived here with us, Momon Bozorg used the heater for everything: cooking, making tea, warming water for Kia to wash his face on winter mornings, and heating the iron for Kia to press his pants. But now she only used it to make tea or to create a warm place to thaw my frozen hands and feet when I came home from school during the winter. With an attitude similar to that of a proud queen, Momon Bozorg would never ask anyone for help, nor would she allow people to notice her impoverished circumstances. The two of us managed to get by with one or two meals a day, consisting often of dried old bread, moistened with a little water to get it soft, and a couple of walnuts. Momon Bozorg wore dentures and couldn't chew anything even slightly hard. On special occasions and if she was in the mood, she made some onion soup for the two of us. After what I'd experienced the previous summer, I was grateful with or without any food as long as I had a roof over my head. Under the circumstances, I was not sure how much longer Momon Bozorg would be able to keep me around, even though I hardly imposed any expenses on her. The beginning of every summer renewed my fear that I was going to be asked to leave. You can imagine my delight when Momon Bozorg asked me to not go anywhere.

After Kia moved away, Mr. Rahimi had cut Momon Bozorg's monthly expense money to almost nothing. Once I happened to be out in the courtyard when Momon Bozorg was asking Mr. Rahimi for more money. He just causally pointed his large, tobacco-stained finger in my direction and, without lifting his head or looking at either one of us, said, "You need to see his father for that." When she told him that she had tried but had no luck finding my father, his response was "Kick out his kid, something that you should've done a long time ago if you'd listened to me, you thoughtless woman. This place is not a charitable organization for orphan children. I got plenty of my own to feed."

All of Momon Bozorg's relatives were very well off and lived in nice homes. Once or twice a month the two of us would pay a visit to one of them where we would be served delicious Persian meals consisting of meat and rice. Poor Momon Bozorg … I often wondered how differently her life would have turned out had she not lost her first husband and been forced to marry Mr. Rahimi. Even without any formal education, she was very well informed, had a lot of wisdom, and above all, was a classy lady. She was a clear mismatch for Mr. Rahimi and was definitely miscast for the life she was leading.

On the day of the arrival of Momon Bozorg's niece, per Momon Bozorg's instructions, I put on a clean shirt from the clothesline outside and combed my hair with Kia's old comb before I left the house to meet up with her. I was told that she was going to be dropped off about a kilometer up the road and that I was to carry her suitcase and walk her home. I arrived at the designated spot and waited in the shadows of an adobe wall on the side of the gravel road. The sun in Mashhad was always bright and piercing and the air was dry and pleasant.

When the sun reached directly above my head in the deep blue sky, a shimmering yellow taxicab, trailed by a large puff of dust, appeared at the end of the road on top of the hill. I immediately stepped forward and waved, alerting the driver as to where to stop. Since taxicabs seldom ever came this way, I was certain that it was Momon Bozorg's niece the cab driver was bringing. The taxicab stopped, the back door opened, and a girl about my height and age stepped out with a little suitcase in her hand. Before closing the door she exchanged a few words with a man and a woman still seated inside. She then closed the door and the taxi left and quickly disappeared into a nearby side street.

"Salam! You must be Alireza," the young girl said in a sweet voice while smiling and blocking the sun out of her eyes with her free hand. I suddenly realized that I was still standing there, dumbfounded, looking at her as if I had never seen a girl before.

Once I regained my senses, I immediately jumped over the narrow creek that ran between the road and the long adobe wall and responded, nervously, "Salam." As I reached out for her suitcase, she looked into my eyes, cast a smile, and softly extended her hand for me to shake. It was the kind of smile that could easily

170

melt away the entire drought-stricken existence of a lonely little man like me in one sweep. It was the kind of smile that could force the strongest of hearts to kneel at her feet in total submission.

"How are you?"

"Fine, thank you," I replied. Without daring to look directly into her eyes, I quickly shook her hand and then reached and grabbed her suitcase. It seemed as though an enormous magnetic energy field abruptly rushed through me and rearranged the polarities of my physical existence into an intoxicatingly illogical and unfamiliar pattern. I found myself disoriented between different realities, unable to stay focused where my physical body resided. Where we lived, girls and boys never made any form of physical contact or even spoke to one another. Intimidated by her beauty and assertiveness, I was very nervous. It should have been the other way around, since supposedly I was a big-city boy and she was a small-town girl. Like most of Momon Bozorg's relatives, Molouk spoke a better Farsi, with a more pleasant accent and was elegant.

There is no point in pretending that I fell in love with that girl over time and in an orderly and logical fashion. It quickly became apparent here that the usual protocols of falling in love were not going to be observed by my heart. Something in me drastically changed at the moment of that first handshake and hello. Suddenly I was no longer the same eleven-year-old boy that I'd been only five minutes before. Like the introduction of one element to another, meeting Molouk instantly provoked some chemical and emotional reaction within my core and transformed me into someone new.

Could it be the first time in the history of love that a heart had fallen so swiftly and with so little resistance into the hands of a conqueror? This conqueror just happened to be a young girl with warm, honey-colored, seemingly bottomless eyes capable of giving sanctuary to an entire civilization in their calm and easeful depths. I was certain that she had always existed and would forever exist in the timeless core of my probable pasts and futures. How else could every cell in my anemic body seem to know her so well and have anticipated her coming long before this day?

With her suitcase in my hand and while mumbling and stuttering, I asked her to follow me. Like an idiot, I almost took an

171

embarrassing fall into the little creek when I tried to look cool as I hopped over it. I shook my head in disgust at myself and continued on. I decided not to take the main road home so as to shield Molouk from the lurid stares of the older boys who had nothing better to do during the summer days than sit around and watch time and people pass by. Instead, we took a narrow dirt path that cut through the undeveloped part of our neighborhood, the same path that I had traveled many times before on my midnight moonshine runs for Mr. Rahimi.

Being in no particular hurry, Molouk and I walked shoulder to shoulder down the hill on the dirt path. Occasionally she would say something or ask a question. Every time her body brushed against mine, a jolt of warm and paralyzing current rushed through me. It seemed as if on that bright sunny day some divine invisible hand from an unknown reality had decided to reach way down here and place a dazzling white little daisy by the name of Molouk on the middle of the dusty, dry, and sun-drenched adobe canvas of my world.

"What grade are you going to be in this year?" she asked in her soft voice.

"Fifth," I said proudly. "And you?"

"Fourth. I heard that you are very smart," she said, with the same warm and addictive smile.

I blushed and did not answer.

"How long are you going to be staying here for?" I timidly inquired.

"I am not exactly sure. Perhaps the entire summer."

When I heard that, I began pleading with God to intercede and prevent Momon Bozorg from asking me to go and spend the summer with my mother's relatives so I could be with this beautiful stranger whom I felt closer to than anyone I knew.

"My uncle also lives in Mashhad, so I may go and visit him and my cousins for a while," she added.

Molouk was wearing a white summer dress made of cotton that reached just below her knees and a pair of black leather shoes and white anklet socks with lace ruffles. Her silky shoulder-length hair was the color of dark chocolate. It shimmered under the sun and bounced with her every step, releasing a honeysuckle-like fragrance into the air, a scent that until then I didn't know it to be possible to come from someone's hair. Her voice matched her looks and personality. It was sweet and gentle like a soothing melody, the kind that automatically gains your trust and disarms you. For the first time I began to like my name when I heard it escaping through her lips, tinted with her breath. Maybe, just maybe, Molouk was an angel in disguise who was sent here to rescue me from this wretched life for a brief time.

Small boys with dusty short hair and girls with their heads covered under scarves curiously looked on from a distance as we got closer to Mr. Rahimi's home. Some of the boys I went to school with looked at me as I walked alongside Molouk and smiled approvingly—and, I might add, with just a touch of envy in their eyes. I was instantly filled with pride and covered with goose bumps with the knowledge of their envy.

From that day on I was never more than a meter away from Molouk at any one time unless I had to go to the bakery or the store for Momon Bozorg. When I did have to go, I did so with unbelievable speed that surprised even Momon Bozorg. With Molouk around, I forgot all about Maydoneh Bar, my favorite village of Golmakan, my beloved cousins from Gorgon, and Arg and all its cinemas.

Molouk's presence lit up our lives and brightly colored our tiny gray world. Aside from always smelling femininely enchanting, being radiantly beautiful, and having a permanent smile affixed on her face, she was also positive, intelligent, and open-minded. She had a very strong personality which was uncharacteristic of any of the girls I knew in our family. With Molouk's arrival, Momon Bozorg started cooking again and sent me to the bakery every morning to purchase hot, fresh bread for breakfast, just like we used to have back when Kia lived with us. Instead of the usual smell of dust, the air in our little room was now filled with the scent of cooking, spices, honeysuckle and, best of all, Molouk.

A week after Molouk's arrival, Momon Bozorg received a telegram from Kia for all three of us to pack up and come visit him at his new post in a village near Damghan. He was very specific in his letter to Momon Bozorg that we were not to embarrass him with our appearances when we got there. Kia, like most Iranians, was overly concerned with his image and what other people thought of him. With that in mind, Momon Bozorg took me

173

shopping near the shrine, where most of the stores were at the time, and bought me a shirt and a pair of cotton sneakers to wear on our trip. The shoes were two sizes smaller than my feet but, since I liked them and they were the only pair we found at a price that Momon Bozorg could agree on, I did not want to risk not getting them. When Momon Bozorg pressed the tip of the shoes as I was trying them on, she remarked that they were too tight. I convinced her, however, that they were not tight at all. Outside she yelled at me for acting anxious and showing interest to the shop owner. That cost her a couple extra rials, she said. Apparently I had broken one of the first rules of shopping by not feigning disinterest inside the store.

What an interesting play life is. The stage was the same as always, but this summer's act was already turning out to be in stark contrast to that of the year before. I not only received my first cotton shoes, something that I had been dreaming of having ever since I could remember, but soon I was going to be traveling the farthest I had ever traveled before, and with Molouk at my side. What a fantastic difference a year makes.

By now Molouk and I had bonded well while still maintaining the social boundaries that ruled any relationship between boys and girls—a polite and touchless friendship. More than anything, I wished that I could give her a hug or hold her hand, if only for the briefest of moments. I have come to believe that eyes and hands are the most expressive and conductive parts of the human body. A touch of hands or the slightest gaze can transmit more emotions, in my opinion, than any words. Incidentally, it was not uncommon for two boys my age, or even two grown men, to hold hands while walking in public. This behavior was viewed as a sign of close friendship between two males while at the same time being forbidden between a boy and a girl.

On the day of our departure to go and visit Kia, we arrived at the bus station bright and early. Once the boarding was announced, we took our seats on the bus and soon were on our way to Damghan. The bus was destined for Tehran but, according to Momon Bozorg, we were getting off just outside of Damghan, which was almost halfway to Tehran. Momon Bozorg had purchased only two tickets for all three of us; therefore, we had to snuggle up close and share a seat that was designed to accommodate two adults. Momon Bozorg sat by the window with Molouk in the middle and me by the aisle. Needless to say, I was not going to complain at all about the tight seating arrangements.

By noontime the bus came to a stop alongside a small adobe structure in the middle of nowhere, and all the passengers filed off for a break. The three of us quickly made our way to a boulder by the shallow river, where Momon Bozorg prayed while Molouk and I ate hard-boiled eggs and nan that Momon Bozorg had prepared the night before. Other passengers also ate their lunch or partook of the noon prayers under the shade of a couple of massive trees. People who ordinarily did not pray often did so while traveling, hoping that it would keep them safe in their travels.

Between the lunch and the steady humming sound of the bus traveling on the blacktopped road, soon the passengers could be heard snoozing in their seats—including Momon Bozorg and Molouk. Not me, however. In fact, I had not been able to relax the entire time we'd been on the road, not with Molouk's body so closely attached to mine. I was like a piece of drought-stricken land that had seen very little rain in the past six years, and Molouk was that bountiful rain that brought with it the gift of love and life. How could I go to sleep while every cell of my body was working hard to absorb every hint of Molouk?

From our seats in the third or fourth row behind the driver, I took to looking in the rearview mirror to watch the driver. Once I was certain that his thoughts were somewhere other than looking my way, I turned my head and nervously placed one quick kiss on Molouk's cheek and then another one, something I had wanted to do from the first moment I'd laid eyes on her. If there ever was a heaven, I experienced it when I kissed Molouk.

Just before nightfall, we passed through the little town of Damghan, and soon after the bus pulled over to the side of the road and the three of us quickly exited. The only visible sign of civilization under the early evening's deep violet sky was a single small structure of stone and mud with a brightly burning kerosene lantern hanging in front of it. There was nothing else for as far as one could see except a million stars blinking in sync with the sound of crickets. Momon Bozorg walked directly toward the structure, which turned out to be nothing more than a tiny general store. I had tears in my eyes because of the new shoes being too tight as I slowly walked behind Molouk. The entire time on the bus I had the shoes off, but now I was in agony as I had no choice but to put them back on.

Momon Bozorg went inside the little shack, briefly spoke to an old man, and came back out just as quickly as she went in. According to Momon Bozorg, we were to wait there for Kia. Momon Bozorg sat on some empty wooden Coca-Cola boxes while Molouk and I glued our eyes on the empty road in front of us and waited for a pair of headlights to appear at a distance in the dark.

As we waited, Momon Bozorg told us of this area's heyday. According to her, it was still the pistachio and paper-almond capital of Iran. As is always the case with most little Iranian towns and sometimes even villages, Damghan too had its own history and was not always so small. Its origin dated back to 4000 BCE when the Aryans first moved from Europe and settled on the Iranian plateau. During the invasion of Alexander of Macedon into Persia in 334 BCE, the Greeks called Damghan the Hecatompylos, the city of "one hundred gates"—a title commonly used by the Greeks to underscore the importance and size of a large city. It even once served as a capital during a Persian dynasty before finally being destroyed by the invading Afghans in 1723. By 1967 Damghan was a small town with only a couple of blacktopped streets and a small public park.

After we'd waited for an hour or so, an old Land Rover pulled into the graveled area in front of the store and Kia stepped out of it with his usual big smile on his face. The driver immediately put our luggage into the vehicle as the four of us hugged and kissed. It had been more than a year since he and I had last seen one another. Soon we were being driven on a dirt road snaking through a barren land marked with thorn bushes. We were heading toward the village of Amirabad, Kia's first assignment post after finishing his gendarme training.

The next morning Kia took both Molouk and me on a tour of the village and introduced us to its people. This was the first time that I was seeing my brother in his army-green military uniform. With his signature serious look on his face, a mustache—an indispensable part of many Iranian men—his chest filled with air and expanded outward, Kia walked stiff and straight, as if he had swallowed a sword. His black boots sparkled and his uniform was well pressed. A holster holding a Colt .45 military handgun hung from a pistol belt over his right hip. A pair of Ray-Ban sunglasses under his slightly tilted military cap completed his impressive appearance. If it wasn't for growing up in military families, I would have definitely thought that he was both a general and the leader of the little village. I was proud to be seen with him—just as I was on my very first day of school when he walked with me while wearing his school police uniform. The role suited him well as it gave him what he always wanted, the chance to be a big fish, albeit in a small pond.

The gendarmerie's outposts played a pivotal role in Iran's countryside. The gendarmerie served three major purposes: law enforcement, recording and keeping of vital documents, and managing the draft for the armed forces. The post in Amirabad was also in charge of several other neighboring villages, and that kept Kia away from home much of the time. In addition, twice a week he had to stay for night duty at the post and did not come home.

The village of Amirabad was a small, sun-drenched fortress that contained about a hundred little adobe homes, all clustered together inside its tall ancient walls. Inside the fortress the homes were connected together through a series of narrow alleyways that ultimately merged and ended at a massive wooden gate. As with most Iranian villages, the farmland and the fruit groves—mostly of pistachio, pomegranate, and fig—were all laid out surrounding the fortress. Where there were no orchards or farms, thorn bushes, which were the villagers' main source of fuel, grew everywhere. The villagers cut and folded the bushes into large round piles and then inserted each end of a long wooden bar through the middle of a pile, carrying the burden over their shoulders like weightlifters with giant barbells.

Momon Bozorg spent most of her time cooking and cleaning and left Molouk and me to do our own thing. The two of us explored the village and its many orchards during the days that followed, while during the nights we lay inside a mosquito tent in the middle of the courtyard and talked about everything and nothing. There were many instances of gazing into each other's eyes and communicating what we were too shy and too cautious to utter verbally. With each passing day and each innocent touch of our hands, our souls became more interwoven than the day before.

With the exception of Kia and my aunt Sarvar, no one else had shown me any meaningful and unconditional affection since my grandfather passed away and my mother left. I had little notion of what it was like to be loved and/or to matter to someone. However, by the end of the summer that all changed. Molouk, without having to even say a single word, made me feel loved and relevant. Her physical body was only ten years old at the time, but there was something magnificently mature and ancient about her presence that put me at complete ease when we were together. I felt as if knowing her extended far beyond my current existence, if that was even possible.

The most amazing thing about her, however, was her compassion and broadmindedness. Unlike many spoiled and shallow urban children who visited the countryside during their summer vacations and often privately ridiculed the locals for the way they dressed or spoke, Molouk never looked down upon anyone. In her view, everything and everyone had their own individual uniqueness and beauty. An oak tree was just as magnificent and important as a highly producing fruit tree, she would say, as long as they were not compared based on one criterion. "Different" is the common denominator for all intolerance in the world, be it politically, culturally, racially, or spiritually, she believed. Was she an old queen incarnated in the body of a child? I ponder now when I think of her. In Molouk's eyes, I was never a raggedly dressed orphan boy whom her aunt and cousin had taken pity on and were raising out of the goodness of their hearts. When I was with her, she behaved as if I were a prince, as did my cousin Jam.

Every night, just before bedtime, we helped Momon Bozorg to set up a large square tent made of a very fine, see-through white lace out in the courtyard for all of us to sleep in. Despite the fact that Amirabad was on the edge of a vast desert, at nightfall its mosquitoes were notorious. Momon Bozorg spread two mattresses next to each other where we all slept. On the nights when Kia was home, he would sleep on one side of the tent and Momon Bozorg on the other side with Molouk and me in between the two of them. On those nights when Kia was on duty at the outpost, Molouk and

I slept next to each other and were free to talk and giggle until we eventually fell asleep. Sometimes we just lay there on our backs, looking up at the star-filled black sky through the tent's thin fabric, and softly talked. I remember one particular night when Molouk said, "We will be going back in a few days, you know."

"Yes," I sighed. "Are you happy that you're going back?"

"Somewhat," she responded. "I've never been away from my family for this long before, and I miss them. What about you? Are you glad we're going back?"

"No," I remorsefully responded.

"Why not?" she inquired.

"I am just not." I could have told her the truth. I could have revealed what an uncertain and lonely life was awaiting me back in Mashhad.

Quickly changing the subject, she added, "My mother is going to kill me when I get home. I have turned into dark chocolate from all the walking we did under the sun. She specifically warned me to stay out of the sun!" And then she suddenly changed the subject once again and asked, "Do you think we dream in color?"

"I'm not sure. It's not something I've ever thought about before," I told her.

"I wonder what dreams mean," she said, while continuing to gaze at the sky above us.

Momon Bozorg suddenly moved in her spot. We both turned our heads and looked, but apparently she was still asleep. We looked at each other and smiled. Lowering my voice, I said, "Momon Bozorg thinks that dreams tell a lot more stories than we think or understand." At this point Molouk turned to her side with her back to me, curled up, and softly asked, "Have you ever had a dream that recurs and feels real but does not make any sense when you wake up?"

I too turned to my side, facing her back, and said, "Yes."

Just then a whiff of her hair rushed into my head. I could not remember the last time I had lain this close to anyone. More than anything I wanted to inch my way forward and embrace Molouk tightly. I wanted to sink my face into her silky hair at the back of her neck and inhale her scent until every cell of my body was saturated and high. But I wasn't that daring. What if she misunderstood my intentions and became upset? What if Momon

179

Bozorg opened her eyes and saw what I was doing? Deep down, I knew that I was not about to risk jeopardizing the most beautiful relationship of my childhood by doing something stupid. Most of all, I could not betray Momon Bozorg, as Molouk was her niece and in her care; the act of holding Molouk in my arms, no matter how innocent it might be, would have been an act of disloyalty in her eyes. Molouk's feminine scent and the gentle warmth escaping her body and brushing against mine were slowly weakening the wall of resistance I was desperately trying to hold up, however.

"Every now and then I have this dream that is like that. It feels so real and leaves me affected for days afterwards," she said while adjusting her body a little backward and closer to me.

"Me too," I responded.

"Really?" she asked, turning her head to look at me.

"Yes," I quietly answered, not wanting to wake Momon Bozorg.

"I dream that I am in the arms of a tall and handsome man, dancing in a rather large and dimly lit room. I feel tremendous love for him yet I do not seem to recognize his face, as if my heart knows him but my mind does not. Does that make any sense?" She sighed while at the same time wiggling her body backward and attaching it completely to mine.

I was speechless after not only hearing the account of her dream but also feeling her entire body against mine. I was excited and confused all at the same time. How could it be possible for two people who live in two different cities and have never met before to have the same dream? I pondered but did not speak a word of it to her.

"I feel as if the man is either my husband or my lover, but how? I am only ten years old. What do you think it all means?" she asked, turning her face slightly around and gazing romantically into my eyes with a question mark.

I had no answers for her, just as I had no answer for my own similar and parallel dreams.

"Well? What do you think is going on, Mr. Smart?!" she said teasingly while turning around and gently poking me in the chest. Before I could give her an answer, she looked at my lips and placed a kiss on them. My heart almost stopped. In her kiss I felt God, if that is at all possible.

She turned around once again and nested her curved body completely into mine.

I was in a state of ecstasy and shock and had no idea as to how to respond or what to do at that point. Molouk reached behind her, grabbed my hand, and pulled and wrapped my arm around her, holding my hand tightly against her chest. "Well, what do you think about my dreams?" she whispered as if she was now ready to fall into sleep and take me along with her.

I could not think. "I am not really sure," was all that I could say.

"Then tell me about your dreams."

"Mine are not like yours at all," I said.

Never before had I felt so strongly for anyone except my mother. All the love I had saved up for the past several years with no one to give it to manifested itself at that moment for Molouk. The non-physical me, the one that resides somewhere deep inside of my body and claims it as his own, merged with Molouk and became one that night. Déjà vu, a feeling as if we had been together before and in this manner, took control of me.

Two days later we were at the Damghan train station waiting for the Tehran-Mashhad train to arrive. A train that I wished would never come. I did not want to go back to Mashhad. After experiencing life the way I did in Amirabad and with Molouk, it was not easy for me to go back and readjust to my old life. By making me feel loved and wanted, she'd put me on the map of life and drawn a big red circle around me. How could I ever wake up again without having her large, ever-smiling, beautiful Persian eyes opening next to me and greeting me with adoration? I was feeling very sick inside, just like the day my mother left me.

There I was, standing on the platform with my back to a light pole near the tracks, while Molouk was sitting on a wooden bench nearby with our luggage on the ground next to her. Both Momon Bozorg and Kia were inside the terminal purchasing the tickets. When Molouk signaled for me to come over and sit next to her, I shook my head no. For some reason I felt angry at her and was sulking.

The train whistled as the locomotive emerged from the distance. Once it came to a stop, the passengers got off to stretch and look around. Kia then came out of the terminal and signaled

181

for us to board. Molouk and I grabbed our belongings and followed his command. Once we found an empty cabin, Kia placed our luggage on the overhead racks and left to get Momon Bozorg, who was still in the terminal. I opened the window and began staring at the outside, feeling lousy about going back.

"I will never forget this place," Molouk said softly while standing behind me.

I did not say anything.

"Are you alright?" she asked, playfully shaking my shoulder.

"No," I said without hesitation.

She grabbed my chin and turned my face around to look into my eyes. "What is wrong?" she asked. "Are you sulking?"

"No." I yanked my face away, not wanting her to see that my eyes were on the verge of being flooded with tears.

Unlike now, when expanded satellite television and the Internet can turn any ordinary kid, in any remote corner of the world, into a Romeo or Juliet, at our age we had no practice or framework with which to express our feelings for one another. As close as Molouk and I had become in the past few months, never once did we directly speak of how we felt about one another. For one thing, we were only kids. It was just not customary for us to talk about our feelings for each other. In our culture any expression of affection or emotion toward a member of the opposite sex was immediately deemed as sexual, hence vulgar and taboo. As a culture, we often kept our romantic feelings for someone to ourselves and whispered them only in songs or wrote them down as poems. It was not at all uncommon to be in love with someone without them ever knowing. Why else would Iran, or as some still refer to the country, Persia, have the highest number of poets and poems in the history of the world's literature?

I was ashamed to tell Molouk that I did not want to be left behind to a life that could be summarized as a piece of discarded barley bread at the army depot's trash. I was embarrassed to let her know that, contrary to what she thought, I had no one in this world and that besides Kia, she was the best thing that had ever happened to me. I was not strong enough to break with tradition by telling her that I loved her more than life itself.

Molouk suddenly pulled an ink pen out of her small handbag and asked for my hand.

"If I write something in your palm, would you promise not to read it until tomorrow after I have left Mashhad?"

Without really knowing what to say, I nodded in agreement. She gently began writing something in the palm of my left hand while I looked away. When she had finished writing she quickly closed my fist. "Remember, you promised not to read it," she said with a smile while at the same time blushing a little.

"Do you know why I wrote in your left hand as opposed to your right hand?" she asked.

"Because I am right-handed and would not use this one?"

"No, silly. Because it is the hand closest to your heart!" she said, smiling and gazing at me with her warm and romantic eyes.

It wasn't long before Kia and Momon Bozorg walked in and, following lengthy goodbyes and many kisses, Kia exited the train. He then waited outside by our window until the train slowly rolled out of the station.

The next day in Mashhad, Molouk was packed and ready to be picked up by the same couple who had dropped her off earlier that summer. Momon Bozorg and I walked her to the same spot where I'd picked her up on the day she arrived. While we waited, I stood quietly as Momon Bozorg gave Molouk some last-minute advice on her trip back. And Molouk was being her usual self, kind and composed, with a soft smile on her face and her large beautiful eyes sparkling with vitality.

I felt like I did at the end of every good film I went to see in cinema. After I became attached to the characters and their storyline, the film came to an end and I reluctantly had to leave the theater and go back to my own empty life outside.

All too soon a yellow taxicab came down the hillside on the gravel road and eventually stopped in front of us. While Momon Bozorg exchanged greetings with the couple inside the taxicab, Molouk and I looked into each other's eyes and silently exchanged a thousand emotions of goodbye without having the need to open our mouths. In all of about a few seconds she shook my hand, said goodbye, and climbed into the taxicab. This time her handshake did not seem to be as bold and full of confidence as it did when she first arrived here. And this time I was not about to retrieve my hand as quickly as I did when we first met. The cab quickly took off and disappeared into a side street with a puff of dust chasing behind it.

Momon Bozorg had to ask me to slow down several times on the way back home. Little did she know that I wanted to get away from her. I wanted to get away from everything and everyone and find a place where I could be alone to read what Molouk had written in the palm of my hand. As soon as we arrived at the house, Momon Bozorg went inside while I ran as fast as I could to the top of the hill beyond the side of the house. I sat there and looked in the direction of the city where I knew Molouk's bus station was, hoping to feel her presence. I took a deep breath and slowly opened my fist. There before me, inscribed in the palm of my left hand, were the most powerful words anyone had ever written to me: "I will always love you."

With that, the tears I had been holding back since yesterday finally exploded in my face. I cried as I had on the night my mother left Mashhad. I did not go back into the house until very late when I heard Momon Bozorg calling for me.

That night I had the same old dream that I used to have before meeting Molouk. I was a tall man in a white shirt with long ruffled sleeves, dancing with a beautiful woman that I was passionately in love with. The only difference was that this time the woman had a face I recognized. I could swear that in my dream I saw many of my born and unborn children in her warm, honey-colored Persian eyes.

Chapter Twenty-Five

T he following year, I began searching for a job as soon as
school came to an end for the summer. This meant going
door to door from one shop to another and asking if they
were hiring. I learned quickly, however, that it was difficult to get a
job, especially being only twelve years old, unless I knew someone
who knew a merchant or a businessman and was willing to vouch
for me. My father was in the best position of anyone for that, but I
had been staying clear of him after something that had transpired
between us the previous summer.

It had all started on the train as Momon Bozorg, Molouk, and I
were returning from Amirabad. While Molouk was asleep, Momon
Bozorg had a heart-to-heart conversation with me, telling me that
upon our arrival back in Mashhad she wanted me to find my father
and tell him that he needed to either pay child support or find
another place for me. She explained how difficult it was for her to
feed just herself, let alone me.

"I am old and don't need much to survive on but you, Alireza,
you are a growing boy and need to eat. You need food and clothes,
both of which cost money—money that, as God is my witness, I
don't have. I can no longer bear to helplessly watch you go to
school on an empty stomach or freeze in winter because you don't
have a proper coat to keep you warm. If your father wants to go to
hell for slowly killing you, then he needs to do it somewhere else
where I don't have to be a witness to it. You may think that I don't
notice, but I do. I see how you stay away from home so I don't
have to see your scrawny body and feel bad about not being able to
feed you. I know you are not telling me the truth whenever I ask
you if you are hungry and you say no."

This was the first time that she had actually discussed the possibility of having to let me go. Ever since Kia moved away two years ago, Momon Bozorg would, every now and then, make some threat about getting rid of me. Usually the threats were hollow and came out of frustration over something. This time, however, she was simply stating the facts—she could no longer afford to keep me around. I understood exactly what she meant. Mr. Rahimi's upcoming retirement meant he was going to have even less money to spread around between his three wives. Both Rana and Maryam now had more children than when I first moved with the Rahimis, entitling them to a larger cut of Mr. Rahimi's soon-to-be-shrinking monthly paycheck. And that meant financially things were going to get even worse for Momon Bozorg.

I could not afford to lose the only home I knew, and with that in mind, the day after Molouk left Mashhad at the end of the summer of 1967, I embarked on the mission of finding my father and getting him to pay Momon Bozorg.

My father was now stationed at the army depot on the other side of the hill from Mr. Rahimi's home, and that made the task of finding him a bit easier. I had met with him there a few times in the past and knew which corner of the small, rectangular complex he worked. To keep my promise to Momon Bozorg, I started going to the depot every day to wait by the fence, hoping to get a hold of him. The best place to catch him and the only place that offered some shade and protection from the sweltering sun was under a row of young mulberry trees across from the gate, but I was forbidden by my father to stand there. He was concerned my presence there would have other soldiers talking about him. Given my penurious appearance, resembling a character right out of *Les Miserables*, who could have blamed him?

I camped under the grueling hot summer sun alongside the wire fence surrounding the depot for a few days without spotting my father anywhere. Finally one day a good sergeant came over and offered me some water and advice. After hearing why I was there, he suggested that I should write a letter to the general in command of the Sixty-sixth Division of the Army, headquartered here in Mashhad. After he had me promise not to tell my father about this conversation, he gave me instructions as to what to do and where to go.

That evening I discussed the idea with Momon Bozorg, and she felt that I had nothing to lose by following the sergeant's advice. So, I quickly set about writing a letter to the general, explaining my situation in my own words and asking for his help. After two days of standing on the sidewalk of the residential street where the general lived, I finally spotted his jeep approaching and was able to get his attention by waving the letter in my hand and jumping up and down. As soon as the vehicle stopped, I ran and handed the general my letter. I was very nervous standing there on the side of the road next to the official military vehicle and in front of a god-like general wearing an arresting uniform and dark Ray-Ban sunglasses, with a stern look under his imposing cap. I remember stuttering and shaking throughout the few seconds that I was given to explain why I was there. Feeling weak due to having had no food or water the entire day was not helping any either. All I could remember after the general ordered his driver to drive away was his remark about my excessive use of saliva on the soiled envelope and him instructing me to come to his office the next day. Unable to contain my excitement, I ran all the way home to give Momon Bozorg the good news. Securing the appointment with the general had me imagining all sorts of pleasant outcomes.

The next day I managed to find the general's office located deep within the massive and intimidating military complex. Inside I waited in a rather large reception room with a group of women and children who were also apparently waiting to see the general. Judging from some of the conversations that were taking place in the room, my case did not seem to be as unique as I thought after all.

Eventually, nothing came out of my meeting with the general. There wasn't much he could do except to call my father into his office and admonish him a little for being irresponsible. And that apparently was exactly what he must have done, because a week later when I went back to the army depot to look for my elusive father again, he came out to see me almost immediately, as if he had been waiting for me. Waving and smiling from the other side of the fence, he seemed anxious to want to meet with me. I figured the general had ordered him to take care of his son and he was coming to hand me an envelope filled with cash for all the back pay to take to Momon Bozorg.

"Salam, aqa," I said, smiling at him.

Once he was close enough, his smile vanished instantly and turned into a bitter frown. Without saying a word, he quickly reached and locked his fist tightly around my wrist and began to swiftly walk away from the depot, with me in tow. To prevent my sandals from coming off my feet, I was trying my best to keep up with him. He was squeezing his teeth and fuming with anger. Once we were far enough from the depot where he was sure no one could hear my cries, he stopped next to an eroded rifle pit and unleashed his wrath while still holding onto my wrist, almost cutting off my blood circulation in the process.

"I am going to teach you a lesson, motherfucker, so you never again think of going to the general," he cursed through his teeth as he kicked and punched me. From the corner of my eyes I looked at the distant hill, hoping to see Momon Bozorg miraculously manifest herself there. She used to stand on top of that hill and keep an eye on me when I went to collect bread for her chickens. Unfortunately, except for a couple of wild dogs resting and the summer heat waving and shimmering in the wind, there was nothing else on top of the hill.

Not wanting to fuel my father's anger any further, I did not utter a sound as he delivered his blows. Suddenly, along came the sound of an automobile engine, which caused him to stop and turn his head around, giving me the opportunity to yank my wrist out of his grasp and get up and run like I had never run before. He chased me for a little, cursing and throwing rocks, before finally giving up and returning back to his base.

At home, all it took was one look at my purpled wrist and cut-up and bruised feet and face for Momon Bozorg to realize I had fulfilled my promise of going after my father.

"Your time will also come, Alireza joon. Don't worry, pesaram, the sun does not stay behind the clouds forever, I assure you of that."

This was the first time that she had ever referred to me as *pesaram* (my son), and it felt good. I could swear that also for the first time, I saw tears in her eyes as she squeezed the blood from the corners of my swollen eye and lips. In all the years I lived with Momon Bozorg, I never saw her cry, a practice very common amongst most people I knew. In the presence of such a classy lady, even poverty and hunger seemed graceful. After that incident she did not speak of my leaving, not for a while.

Now, a year later and knowing how he felt about me, I was still hesitant to get anywhere near my father regardless of how badly I needed his help to find me a job.

Getting a job this summer was the only way I knew to feed myself and, at the same time, lessen any burdens that I inadvertently placed on Momon Bozorg. With that idea in mind, when I had no luck anywhere else, I applied for work at a frozen dessert company called Alaska. They did a brisk business during the summer months manufacturing a limited selection of popular popsicles and selling them through an army of men and boys pushing carts around town. At first they said that I was too young for the job, but after some persistence on my part they agreed to hire me, contingent upon my providing a guarantor as well as a cash security deposit for their cart.

Once again Aunt Sarvar came through for me. With her baby in her arms, while holding her chador in place with her teeth, my aunt, my forever faithful solacer, walked with me to the other side of town to the Alaska Company and gave them a deposit of one hundred and fifty toomans—probably her entire savings— along with the birth certificate of her oldest son for them to hold as a guarantee.

"Don't you do anything that would cause me to lose my deposit, khaleh joon. Ali Aqa will kill me if that happens," were her only words to me as she went back to Maydoneh Bar and I ran home to give the good news to Momon Bozorg.

On the morning of my first day at work, following a brief orientation, I received my uniform, some tokens, and a white slim three-wheeler pushcart made of processed wood. The tokens were needed to replenish my supplies from distributors located throughout the city. I haggled with the manager to give me a four-wheel metal pushcart instead, but he said I was too young and too little to push one of those. The man reminded me that my aunt would lose her security deposit in the event I damaged the cart.

I hit the road that day wearing the company's official white cap and shirt, feeling all grown up and proud inside. I was more excited about the fact that I had made it far enough in life to be able to get a job than getting the actual job itself. I had worked before doing

189

odds and ends, pitting and halving apricots during the summer in Golmakan for ten shahis a tray, selling sweets and candies out on the streets, and making and selling kites to the kids in and around the neighborhood. This job was different in many ways, however. It was the mental equivalent of having grown fledgling wings.

Mimicking other Alaska salesmen I had seen on the streets, "*Bastani* Alaska (Alaska ice cream)," I coyly announced as I pushed my little cart on the sidewalks of Mashhad for the first time. All those years of wandering the city streets, either with my mother while looking for my sister and father, or alone by myself, were now paying off. I definitely knew my way around the city very well.

Every morning I passed through a quiet little residential street where once in a while I found a young woman and a small girl silently sitting on the doorsteps of a brick-front house. The beautiful young woman often had her arms wrapped around her arched legs and her head resting sideways on her knees, with her eyes indifferently fixed at the end of the street. I imagined all sorts of scenarios as to why the two of them sat there and who they were waiting for, most of them romantic.

Trying not to disturb her peace, I softly and hesitantly would announce, "Bastaniiii … Alaskaaaa …" as I passed her and the child. It was on my third or fourth trip through that street that she called me over and asked how much each ice cream bar cost.

"Two rials, khanom," I told her, smiling.

"My daughter would like to have one very much but I don't have any money right now, not until my husband returns from his trip."

Without giving it any further thought, I said, "No problem, khanom. You can pay me later. I pass through here every day." And with that I opened the lid to my pushcart and asked, "What flavor does she like?"

"Orange! Are you sure you can do this?" she asked with a faint smile.

"Yes, khanom. The ice creams are mine. I buy them in bulk from the company and sell them and keep the profit," I said as I handed the little girl an orange-flavored Alaska bar.

"Oh, okay then. In that case I want one too! Chocolate, please," she said as she smiled again, and I quickly smiled back.

That was my first transaction on credit. It was very common for people to do business with their local bakeries and stores on credit, especially in the neighborhood where most people were in the military and received their paychecks only once a month. From that day on, going down this woman's street and seeing her and chatting with her for a few moments became the high point of my days. It felt good to see a familiar face happily waiting for my arrival, albeit because of the ice cream.

A month into the job, I already had all sorts of regular customers whom I knew by name, and I made a point of passing by their homes or shops at least once or twice a week and brightening their hot summer days with some cold popsicles. One such customer was a sheep trader who camped in the vacant land across from Maydoneh Bar. The sheep trader was an oversized country man with an impressive handlebar mustache. He wore a long turban and wrapped the excess loosely around his neck, over his shoulder, or let it dangle like a ponytail on his back. Because of my pleasant memories of my grandfather and all the other kind country men I'd met in Golmakan, I felt comfortable doing business with him. All the country men I knew were very honest and trustworthy, so when he asked to start a tab and purchase Alaskas for himself and his crew on credit, I agreed. Each time I passed through the Maydoneh Bar area he would purchase at least ten or twelve Alaskas for himself and his help of four or five teenage boys, pay me for part of it, and put the rest on his tab. Each time my sales to him were big enough to entice me to make a trip there a few times a week. He promised to pay the balance once he sold a few sheep.

Having this job enabled me for the first time to purchase all of my own food, buy a pair of real shoes, and go to cinema often. I was not much of a saver, and even if I had been, I did not make all that much of a profit to save.

It did not take me very long to figure out that selling on credit was a bad idea, especially for a kid my age and without the support of any adult to back me up when I needed one. I was quickly learning that there were a lot of clever people in this world, like the sheep trader. He had me trapped in a loop. In order to get paid for part of what he already owed, I had to give him more Alaskas, on credit. Whenever I brought up the subject of getting fully paid, he

191

would say, "As soon as I sell some more sheep." The larger his tab grew, the more I felt reluctant to give him popsicles on credit. I must add that these were no ordinary popsicles. The creamy frozen delights were heavenly and came in three flavors: orange, chocolate, and vanilla.

Things weren't any different with my young lady friend either, except for the fact that she had never paid me for any of the Alaskas she and her daughter had been enjoying over the summer. On occasion I would casually bring up the subject of her bill, and each time she would cast a sad face and say that as soon as her husband returned she would take care of it all. She appeared both lonely and sad and, for that reason, I did not get carried away by insisting on being paid. Plus, her bill was not nearly as high as the clever sheep trader's.

The adventures of my first real job were not at all incident free. I remember one day, as I was traveling on Naderi Avenue, there happened to be a large crowd of women gathered and demonstrating—for what, I don't know—at the Statue Square. In order to continue on my route, I had little choice but to cut through them. I'd made it halfway through the crowd of women when I noticed a policeman staring directly at me. Something in the way he looked at me said that I had made a big mistake coming this way. He began marching toward me with his face fuming, seemingly with held-back anger and frustrations stemming from his dealing with the protesters. I looked around for a way out but it was too late. The crowd of women was too dense for me to maneuver my pushcart out fast enough.

The policeman's boot was the first thing to come down and hit my pushcart, going right through it and knocking it over. Then a few swift blows of his baton landed on my head and back, sending me instantly to the ground. A young woman quickly rushed to my aid and blocked the angry policeman from hitting me again.

"What has this poor innocent child done to you, you stupid man? You can't take on these women so you're going after a kid instead?" the woman shouted at the policeman while waving her delicate hand with long, slender fingers at him. The policeman would not have dared touch her, for that would have brought upon him severe disciplinary action from his superiors.

While the young woman, now joined by a few others, was still yelling at the policeman, I quickly seized the moment, pulled myself and the cart up, and ran out of there, limping as I went. There was a big gash where the policeman's boot landed on my cart, and I was not at all sure what to do about it. All I could think of at the moment was my aunt. I had promised her that I would not do anything to jeopardize her security deposit. I didn't know how much it was going to cost to replace one of those carts. In addition, I was worried as to what the company was going to do to me once they discovered the damage. Just last week I was severely beaten on the Shrine Circle by a young man claiming to be a field inspector for the company for personalizing my cart and having my name inscribed on the inside of the lid.

After considering all the consequences awaiting me at the Alaska factory, I began looking for someone who could repair the cart and found a man who did just that. After a few hours of going street to street and shop to shop and showing the cart to various people, I came across a man at a carpenter shop who for twenty toomans patched, filled, sanded, and painted the cart for me. Of course, by the time the repair work was done, all of my Alaskas had melted and the entire day was lost.

Summer was almost over, and I decided to get firm with the young woman and the sheep trader and ask for what I was owed. First I went to Maydoneh Bar and found the sheep trader resting in the shade of a wall. As soon as he saw me, his slick tongue began to roll, praising God for my arrival, telling me how I was going to be his savior on that hot day. He immediately asked for a round of Alaskas for him and his crew, to which I said no. Not before he settled his account, I told him. That angered him and brought him up to his feet. He refused to pay and became belligerent and ordered me to leave the area before he cut my throat or had his boys take me to the canal and perform unspeakable acts upon me, calling me an ungrateful bastard who did not know the value of a good customer. I knew then that it was best for me to forfeit my claim, move on, and add the experience to the list of my lessons learned in life.

They say that when it rains, it pours, and that certainly seemed to be the case for me that day. It was early afternoon by the time I made my way to the Ahmadabad area on the other side of town.

Strolling and pushing my cart under a long row of false-acacia trees on a quiet residential street, all I could think of was the sheep trader. The incident had taken away my energy and enthusiasm, and I did not feel like working. Out of habit, however, I made my announcement every few hundred meters: "Bastaniii ... Alaskaaa...." Conscious of the fact that it was afternoon and naptime for many people, I kept the calls low-key. Almost everyone closed shop at noon and went home for lunch and an afternoon nap. Even though there was hardly ever anyone out on the street during those hours, especially in this part of town, there was always a chance that a child or a bored housewife could hear my call from behind a wall and run outside and make a purchase.

To my delight, I heard a door unlatching and opening a few meters behind me, and I stopped, turned my head around, and eagerly waited to see if it was a prospective customer coming out. A man stepped out of a house and called me over. He was in his mid-twenties, wearing a two-piece pajama set in the middle of the day, with his eyes all puffed up, indicating he had just woken up. Excited with the possibility of making a sale, I turned my cart around and paced toward him. As soon as I stopped the cart in front of him, I smiled and said hello, ready to take his order. Without any warning he delivered a devastating punch to the left side of my face, immediately knocking me to the ground. It felt as if I'd been hit with a heavy dumbbell. Lying there on the sidewalk, feeling dizzy and dumbfounded, I watched the man first turn my cart on its side and then launch at me, both kicking and punching me all at once.

"I've had it with you motherfuckers. Every summer I have to go through this with you bastards. A man cannot even take a nap in his own home anymore," he said while continuing to kick me. And then, just as suddenly as he had come out of his house, he turned around and went back inside. The whole incident could not have taken more than a minute or two, but from the way my face felt, it was certain that I was not going to forget it for a while. An air of unreality settled over me, and if not for the fact that my face was bleeding and my cart was still lying next to me with one of its wheels turning, I would have thought for sure that the attack had been nothing more than the sun playing games with my mind.

194

I have to admit that walking and pushing a cart for twelve or more hours a day, seven days a week, did not bother me as much as did the cold-heartedness of some people that I crossed paths with.

The next day I went straight to the house of my favorite lady customer and rang the doorbell. She owed me about ten toomans, enough to cover the cost of all of my upcoming school supplies. Not surprisingly, the lady herself answered the door. This time, however, I sensed that something was different. The tone in her voice when she said "Yes?" gave the impression that we had never met before. For a brief second her eyes rolled over the cuts and bruises on my face, giving me a slight impression that she cared. Ironically, I noticed similar cuts and bruises on her face.

"Salam, khanom. Summer is ending and I am going back to school soon and need to collect my money, please," I said without any preludes.

She nervously turned her head around and took a quick look behind her into the house, as if expecting someone to be watching her, and said, "What money?" acting as if she hadn't a clue who I was or what I was talking about. "Listen, boy, you better leave immediately or my husband is going to come out and teach you a good lesson." She seemed worried and was obviously hurrying to get rid of me. I certainly did not need any more men coming out in their pajamas and teaching me a lesson, and with that, I looked deep into her eyes disappointedly and turned my cart around and left. As Momon Bozorg would have said, I only had myself to blame, both in her case and the case of the sheep trader. With the sheep trader I felt taken, and with her I felt betrayed.

What happened a few days later concluded my first real job as an Alaska salesperson.

It was around four or five o'clock in the afternoon and I was pushing my cart on the sidewalk of an uphill residential street while calling, "Bastaniii … Alaskaaaa …"

A few blocks into the street, I noticed a door opening on the other side and a little boy, about three or four years of age, anxiously waving for me to stop. From where I was standing I could see a pacifier in his mouth, and that immediately made me think of my little brother, Mehdi. I yelled for the boy to stay put as I prepared to cross the street. At a distance I saw a yellow taxicab flying down the road in our direction and decided to wait for it to

195

pass. The little boy, apparently anxious to get to me, suddenly took off running toward me, crossing the street while smiling and waving his bill in his little hand.

By the time I could react, the speeding automobile was already there. It struck the little boy and sent him flying into the air. The driver and his two passengers were immediately out of the taxi and rushing toward the boy as he lay motionless on the asphalt. I too, leaving my cart behind, began to run to him when suddenly the image of an angry mob beating and tearing me apart flashed in front of me and locked my legs. A voice inside told me to run and run fast. I stood there for a brief second and helplessly watched the taxicab driver and his passengers circle around the little boy on the ground—and then turned around and left.

I could not imagine what the people of that house and their neighbors would have done to me once they learned why their little boy was crossing the street. I ran as fast as I could while pushing my flimsy cart up the hill, crying with anguish. If only I hadn't been there at that very moment, if only I hadn't gotten into the business of selling Alaska, if only my mother and Baba had taken me to Tehran with them.

Chapter Twenty-Six

Kia was now married and had a newborn baby. He met his wife while he was stranded in a small town during a snowstorm in the winter of 1968. He and another gendarme had been on their way to Damghan, transporting a couple of draftees, when a heavy blizzard forced them to stay in Sabzevar for a few days. According to Kia, while waiting for the roads to reopen, he stayed at the home of one of Momon Bozorg's cousins who happened to be living in Sabzevar at the time. I remember Kia regularly visited Uncle Kameli, as he called him, while the man lived in Mashhad. He was a charming and witty man, especially after he had a few drinks. By the time the snow had melted and the roads reopened a few days later, Uncle Kameli managed to have Kia engaged to Morvareed, the quiet, tall, and slender girl next door.

A few weeks later, on leave for the Norooz holiday, Kia came to Mashhad and took Momon Bozorg and me to Sabzevar to meet his future wife and her family. It was customary for both parents to accompany their son for such an important occasion, but Mr. Rahimi did not come with us. He was too unpredictable and often became a liability when he drank—there was no telling what Mr. Rahimi would do or say after having a few drinks—and because of that Kia often took steps to exclude him from certain events.

We stayed in Sabzevar for a few days, and after a small wedding ceremony at Uncle Kameli's home, Momon Bozorg and I, together with Kia and his new wife Morvareed, took a train to Amirabad, where Kia still lived. (That trip alone had all the ingredients of a tragicomedy that could be the subject for another book, another time.) Momon Bozorg helped situate the newlyweds

197

in their home, and a few days later the two of us returned to Mashhad in time for me to go back to school.

The fledgling stability I'd experienced during the first few years after moving in with Kia and his mother was replaced with fretfulness and uncertainty soon after my "big brother" joined the gendarmerie and moved away. Considering Momon Bozorg's age and her financial situation, I felt every year was my last year at her home. After Kia moved away, with the exception of the summer of 1967, every year as soon as summer came she latched and locked the fragile wooden door to our little room and left town for months at a time to be with her son, leaving me behind. I was a lost soul in her absence. Like a locked-out puppy whose master was not home, I wandered the streets and slept wherever I was let in, placing all of my hopes on Momon Bozorg's return home. Kia's marriage essentially ended any hope of him returning here and living with Momon Bozorg and me again.

Without Kia, life, and more importantly attending school, got progressively harder for me with every passing year. Lack of food, proper clothing, and adequate school supplies now made going to school an agonizing experience, both physically and emotionally. Thanks to friends, classmates, and the nearby army depot, however, not having school supplies was not as dire as was the lack of clothes and food. At school everyone shared with me their inkwell, pencil, eraser, and whatever other school supplies they had. And at the army depot, not only could I find an ample amount of whole-grain bread in the trash, but also all sorts of discarded half-used office supplies.

The summer of 1969 marked an important milestone in my life. That year I surpassed both my father and Baba in education by receiving a sixth-grade certificate. Considering the circumstances surrounding my short life, that was a miracle in and of itself. But more than anything, finishing elementary school was a moral victory, a repudiation of my father's notion that I was not meant to get an education.

I remember waiting outside the school with a group of boys and their mothers on the day that the final exams results were going to be released. Once the door opened and we were allowed inside, I found the list posted on the wall next to the principal's office, searched for my name, and there it was: "Alireza

Golmakani, passed." The word "passed" written next to my name seemed to carry a herculean meaning, a victory over adversity. All around me there were mothers either embracing and kissing their sons in bliss, or frowning and storming out of the building with their teary-eyed and droopy-faced boys following reluctantly in step behind them. I only wished that my mother were there so that I could see and savor my achievement in her sad and warm brown eyes.

Despite all the hardship I had to endure, I enjoyed attending elementary school. It gave me a place to belong. The teachers and my classmates graciously looked beyond my impoverished appearance and respected and liked me for what I was, a good student and a loyal friend.

Right after school ended I began working for Mr. Rahimi, who had retired from the army and was now driving a pickup truck to supplement his pension. Shortly after he retired, Mr. Rahimi purchased a Japanese three-wheeled pickup truck with the intent of starting a business but without any idea as to what. He'd purchased the vehicle halfway through autumn of the previous year, just as the city was preparing to go into its long winter hibernation. His truck sat under the heavy snowfall for most of the winter, with me and occasionally one of his sons from his second wife sleeping in it at night to deter anyone from trying to steal it (an impossibility, considering the condition of our little dirt road under a meter of snow). Occasionally, using a portable heater to thaw the radiator and with all of his children, including me, pushing, he was able to get the truck started, only to get stuck in the snow farther up the road and return home. It was cold and lonely sleeping sitting up in the tight cabin of the little truck with all sorts of wild dogs waiting to ambush me in the event I decided to step out of the vehicle to relieve myself.

By the time summer came around, Mr. Rahimi finally figured out how to make some money with his little truck and hired me as his help—without pay, of course. Ironically, after the summer of 1963 when I'd first met him and he'd spent some time teaching me the letters of the alphabet while he was recovering from his illness, the two of us had hardly ever crossed paths or spoken again until now. During the six years that I lived on and off in his home, I took every step necessary to avoid running into Mr. Rahimi unless he specifically called upon me to do something for him like make a midnight moonshine run to the mountains or something of that nature. In all the years that I lived with Mr. Rahimi, not once did he look me in the eye. Now, though, we were working seven days a week hauling whatever paid: produce, fruits, farm animals, building supplies, and pilgrims. This arrangement came to an end halfway through the summer when Momon Bozorg once again latched and locked the door to our room and left town to spend time with Kia.

For the rest of the summer I worked as an assistant to an electrician, a job my uncle Abdul-Husain, my mother's older half brother and Jam's father, found for me. My uncle and his family had moved to Mashhad about a year ago after he retired from the army. He knew the owner of a light and ceiling fan store near his home and was able to get me a job there. A few summers back I had attended a two-week camp at a vocational school outside of the city and completed a course in electrical wiring. The program was sponsored by the government in an effort to teach young country boys some skills and trades. Even though I was not officially a villager and my birth certificate was issued in Tehran, I was still able to find a way to take part in the program. If the truth were known, I was more interested in the meals that I was going to receive and having a secure and clean place to sleep for two weeks than learning a trade. The skills that I would eventually learn there were an added bonus.

The day before I was to start work, my uncle accompanied me to the electrical and lighting fixture store and introduced me to the store owner and thanked him for giving me the opportunity. I was hired as a helper to the business's only electrician who worked out in the field, wiring new homes, installing new fixtures, and making repairs.

The next morning I was at work bright and early, eager to meet my new boss and begin working. The job paid two toomans per day, and with that I could easily feed myself. Inside the store, while waiting for the electrician to arrive, and remembering what Momon Bozorg always used to say to Kia, "Never stand around at your job, especially in front of your boss," I quickly volunteered by helping another boy working there to organize and dust the displayed merchandise. A short while later a young man pulled onto the sidewalk in front of the store on a Moped.

The shop owner looked at me from behind the counter and announced, "Your boss Husain Aqa is here, pesar."

My heart felt as though it had quit beating, and a cold sweat covered my forehead as the electrician walked into the store. My left knee began to jerk, as it always did when I became nervous, and my stomach was turning over as a sudden anxiety rushed over me. I could never forget the face of the man who had so savagely beaten me last summer for interrupting his afternoon nap. I immediately excused myself and ran to the bathroom and closed the narrow metal door behind me before the shop owner even had a chance to introduce me to my new boss.

Bewildered, I had to make a decision and make it quick. Feelings of hate, fear, rage, revenge, principles, and pride all kept on bouncing in and out of my mind, until finally the stern image of zealous Uncle Abdul stepped in and stopped the hullaballoo in my head. As much as I wanted to run out of the tight confines of the narrow little toilet and get as far away from the store as my anemic body was willing to take me, I suddenly realized that I could not. I was trapped in the gratitude that I now owed my uncle for finding me the job. You only needed to know my uncle to understand the predicament in which I found myself. Quitting that job before even starting it would have been the ultimate insult and an epic act of betrayal and ungratefulness in his eyes—and like an elephant, Uncle Abdul never forgot and most certainly he never forgave. The slightest disenchantment brought Uncle Abdul's blood to a boil. He was a zealous believer in respect and gratefulness and a crusading paper tiger, roaring loudly at injustice while doing nothing to stop it. While I was growing up, there was no shortage of relatives like my uncle who were sympathetic to my plight and cursed loudly at both earth and sky on my behalf. Unfortunately, however, what I needed was deeds and not words.

Before my uncle moved here I'd known very little about him; therefore, my expectations of him as my mother's oldest brother were very high, especially since he was married to my father's only sister. It was customary to place enormous values and expectations on aunts and uncles. I felt that my uncle could use his position as my father's brother-in-law and influence him on my behalf. He could find a way to pressure my father into revealing the whereabouts of his niece—my missing little sister.

My mother used to tearfully tell the story of how my father put a knife on her pregnant belly while standing in the rain outside of the divorce office, demanding that she hand over all of her gold jewelry and give up her claim to her *mehryeh* (an amount a man agrees, at the time of marriage, to pay his wife in the event he later decides to divorce her). Mehryeh, derived from the word "kindness," was in essence the world's first spousal support social code established centuries ago in the Muslim world.

"Uncle Abdul was my older brother, Alireza joon. He could have stood up for me. He could have intervened," my mother said.

But he didn't. Not on her behalf back then and not on mine now. In the end I decided to avoid a backlash from my uncle, swallow my wounded pride, and keep the job that I needed if I wished to eat that summer.

After a brief introduction, Hussein, my new boss, handed me a small bag of supplies and signaled me to follow him as he left the store. Outside, I reluctantly got on the back of his Moped and he drove off. At the first traffic stop he asked where I lived and I told him. He then told me the name of his street and asked if I had ever lived there before.

"No, sir," I said.

"Strange! You look very familiar," he said as the light turned green and we drove away.

From that day on we met every morning, except for Fridays, at the store, where we picked up supplies and our work orders before leaving for a job site. We were sent to do work in all sorts of places, wiring a new home under construction, installing a ceiling fan, repairing an old air conditioner.

My boss and I ended up not working together all that much. Oftentimes he would drop me off at a job site, show me what he needed me to do—mostly simple and sometimes laborious tasks, like cleaning, digging and what not— and leave. Sometimes I worked by myself for a few days straight, with him periodically checking on me, mostly during his lunch hours.

At times my life felt like a little play, where some of its characters appeared, disappeared, and reappeared in various acts, seemingly by chance and without having anything to do with me. I remember working for a few days at a new residential construction half a block from my father's home that summer. From the second

202

story of the unfinished building I could see my father's wife and children as they walked to and from the store. I even saw my father a few times but made no attempt to get his attention or to run outside and greet him. Somehow it felt as if I was only supposed to witness his appearance on the stage without any interaction. I was also afraid of approaching him the way I looked; covered in dust, looking like a common laborer, would have embarrassed and angered him. With my luck, he would have found a way to translate the location of my work as a deliberate attempt by me to bring shame on him and his family. I don't know about now but back then, unlike here in the United States where work is viewed as a developmental activity for teenagers, many middle-class Iranians would not have their children take on summer jobs on account of their *abroo* (honor). God forbid, someone could have interpreted that as them not having the means to feed their children.

In a similar fashion I also ran into Molouk; more accurately, saw her, that summer. For a week I was working at an old house in Ahmadabad, near where Molouk's uncle lived, replacing an old air-conditioning system. For the first three days I worked there alone, removing clutter and clearing up the attic, preparing it for my boss to run new wiring, plumbing, and duct work. The old attic was dimly lit and its only little window was blocked by dense branches of a tree outside, and painted shut. If it wasn't for a few small cracks on the wall, allowing for thin wedges of light to pierce through, the place would have felt even more claustrophobic than it already was. By attaching my face to the wall I could see the entire length of a narrow residential street that ran away from the house. The street was always quiet—hardly anything or anyone ever passed through it, especially during the afternoons. Without anyone to talk to or a radio to listen to, my working hours there were long and boring. The slightest sound of life coming from the outside broke the monotony and got my attention. The noise of an automobile's engine, the sound of someone's footsteps passing by, a child laughing or crying, even the occasional hullabaloo of crows fighting over their favorite spots on the branches of the tree next to the house had me rushing to the cracks on the wall.

It was in the afternoon of my second day of working there that I heard some footsteps, followed by the soft and subtle laughter of girls, coming from the street below. Immediately I rushed to the cracks on the wall to investigate. Two teenaged girls were chatting and strolling in the direction of the house. Amused and delighted by their sight and sound, I watched them as they walked in rhythm and in sync with the sound of their footsteps. The walls on both side of the narrow street echoed and amplified their voices, and I could almost make out some of what they were saying as they got closer. They were carrying school binders against their chests and talking about school. Summer classes were popular in Iran and I guessed that was where they were coming from. My heart suddenly dropped. I recognized the voice of one of the girls. It was unmistakably Molouk's. Like a small sparrow, my excited heart began to bang itself frantically against my ribcage as she got closer. She had grown but I would recognize her anywhere. Desperately I twisted and turned my face to see as much of her as I could before she disappeared out of sight. I learned later that she was visiting her uncle that summer and while in Mashhad, she and her cousin were taking a class together. Momon Bozorg was out of town that summer, so I had no way of knowing Molouk was in town.

The next morning at work, as soon as my boss gave his instructions and left, I glued my eye to the crack on the wall facing the street and did not move. Convinced that Molouk was taking a summer class, and knowing most classes began in the morning, I was going to stay there until I saw her again. And to my delight, I did. It wasn't long before I heard footsteps and then I saw Molouk as she turned the corner and hurried down the street, away from me. This time she was alone. She was taller now and with her hair hanging halfway down her back. She looked more like a young woman than the little girl I spent one summer with—it looked as if she had even grown breasts. I wanted to run outside, embrace her, and tell her that I had never stopped thinking about her. Tell her how much I missed her. But I couldn't—I didn't want her to see me this way and feel sorry for me. I thought I should wait until I grew up and became a successful man before I showed my face to her. During that entire week I painfully watched through the thin cracks as Molouk came and went. I could swear that on my last day of work there, she somehow sensed my presence as she briefly paused at the corner of the street and gazed at the attic where I was before she turned the corner and disappeared.

A few years later when we met again under much better circumstances, I told her the story of the attic and seeing her. She became upset with me and thought that not going outside to see her was the dumbest thing anyone has ever done.

Summer was coming to an end and so were my working days as an electrician's assistant. Although relatives advised me to give up the idea of going to school and make working there a permanent profession for myself, a little voice inside of me was saying I shouldn't listen.

Working with Husain did not turn out to be as awkward as I first feared. By getting to know him a little, I learned the aggressive behavior that he displayed last summer was more a byproduct of ignorance than him being inherently a bad person. Much like animals, folks suffering from ignorance are often quick to use physical force as a mean to solve problems. At the time the majority of people living in Mashhad were migrant villagers, with no education and little social skills suitable for urban living. Husain suffered from having a limited and narrow perception, influenced by his parents' limited and narrow beliefs.

I remember he showed up unannounced one day and decided to eat his lunch there at site, instead of going home, as he often did. We sat across from each other on empty upside-down buckets in a partially finished room of a house we were wiring for electricity. My lunch consisted of a small melon and a piece of freshly baked bread I had bought from a bakery down the street. Melons and grapes were inexpensive and made for practical meals. They did not require any preparation, refrigeration, or containers. I could break the melons easily using a sharp edge of a rock and bite into it without needing any utensils. Just as I was about to crack open the little melon I had purchased for two rials, Husain offered his pocket knife. I sliced the melon open and began to shake out its seeds as Husain opened his lunch pouch, containing beef patties, chopped parsley, dilled pickles, and flatbread. The fried patties smelled delectable. (My mother used to make the best beef patties.) Husain wrapped a patty with some chopped parsley and a slice of pickle in a piece of bread, extended his hand, and offered it to me.

"Here, have a patty. My mom made it."

Hesitant at first to take his offering, I shook my head and said, "No thank you."

205

As was customary in Iran, Husain would not take no for an answer when it came to offering food to someone. He kept his hand extended, insisting that I take the food. I had learned from Momon Bozorg that once you ate someone's bread, the relationship changes and takes on a different meaning. "You cannot eat someone's salt and then break their saltshaker," she used to say.

I wasn't sure if I was ready to forgive this man, and accepting his beef patty meant exactly that.

"Take it pesar, I insist."

Too uncomfortable to say no again, I reached and grabbed the food out of his hand. "Merci aqa."

The patty was fantastic. I could have eaten several more.

When he finished with his meal, I cut a wedge of melon and offered it to him to have as his dessert. While eating the melon he asked how I liked the beef patty. I told him it was almost as good as my mother's patties. He chuckled and said maybe my mother should get together with his mother so they could exchange recipes. We both laughed. At that moment I suddenly found myself liking him, like an older cousin or a friend. The hard feelings I had saved up for him ever since that infamous summer afternoon in front of his home flew away out of my chest as if they were never there. On the way back to the shop, as I sat behind him on his Moped, it no longer felt awkward holding on to his waist for security.

❖Chapter Twenty-Seven

Morvareed, Kia's new wife, gave birth to her first child here in Mashhad, and afterwards Kia decided that it was best for her and the baby to stay with Momon Bozorg for a while until the baby was a little older and out of the woods, so to speak. Since there was no healthcare available in the village of Amirabad where Kia was stationed and Morvareed was an inexperienced mother, it was more reassuring for Kia to have his newborn baby and wife stay in Mashhad and with Momon Bozorg.

I seized on the opportunity to make myself appear useful to Momon Bozorg and help her with the baby. In addition to my regular chores—going to the store, the bakery, the kerosene shop, and getting water—I was now responsible for getting milk for Kia's baby and Rana's small children. Almost every morning, long before the sun came up, I was awakened by Momon Bozorg to go to Mandali's on the other side of the hill and purchase some milk. With a small aluminum pot and five rials in my hand, I was often the first to arrive at Mandali's mud hut. There were two convenience stores near where we lived, but neither one of them carried any milk. For anyone who needed milk there was only one source, Mandali; therefore, it was important to be there before he ran out.

Mandali, a scrawny widower and an opium addict, lived in a mud hut at the end of the dirt road on the other side of the hill with his three children, a handful of goats, and a dozen chickens. I often saw him at the army depot's trash, where he spent most of his day collecting discarded bread, cardboard boxes, and anything else of value to him. He used the bread to feed his chickens and

207

children and the cardboard boxes to burn for heat. Since his goats were not picky, in addition to eating all the thorn bushes and anything else that was green in the area around Mandali's home, they fed on the cardboard boxes as well.

On this specific morning, while the rest of the house was still sleeping and I was too sleepy to fully open my eyes, I felt around with my feet just outside of our room in the veranda and found and put on a pair of sandals. There were always a few community pairs of sandals by the doorway for everyone to use.

Shivering in the predawn chill, I walked up the hill toward Mandali's place hoping he was already up and had milked his goats. Oftentimes I was too early and had to wait for him to wake up, or even enter his smoke-filled room and wake him up myself. Once on top of the hill, just before reaching his home, I heard a conversation coming from inside a patch of morning fog from twenty or so meters away to my right. I recognized Mandali's distinct opium addict's low-energy nasal voice and decided to stop and wait for him to finish his business and then walk with him to his place. The mist kept on shifting in density, making him and the man he was talking to appear and disappear from view. I recognized the other man as well. He lived down the hill, indirectly across from Mr. Rahimi's home. His boys and I went to the same school, and sometimes we played together at their house. I had never spoken to the man, but I am certain that he knew of me through his boys. In a neighborhood full of snoopy people, it was impossible for someone not to know me and my story, especially since I lived with such a colorful and unusual family as the Rahimis.

The man as usual was dressed in a traditional tribal outfit. A long white shawl wrapped around his head a few times then dangled like a ponytail behind him. I was cold and wished Mandali would wrap up his business soon.

Suddenly I saw the man pull out a dagger and without any hesitation shove it into Mandali's sunken belly and drag it upward, ripping Mandali's upper torso open. Mandali fell to the ground without making a sound and folded at the man's feet. I swallowed nervously and stood still. This was one of those times in my life that I wished I was gifted with some physical dexterity. I thought of dropping the aluminum pot and running, but fear had my feet glued to the ground. Country men and boys were known for their

208

agility and ability to run fast and I would be no match for this man if I ran and he decided to chase me. Like a deer that has encountered a tiger that has just made a kill, I was not sure what to do except to stand still and stare into the man's eyes, whenever the fog allowed, and wait for his move. I was his only witness in that early morning. While Mandali's body lay folded at his feet, the man turned his head and with his piercing gaze looked straight into my eyes for ten seconds or so. My heart was flapping frantically like a startled little bird against my ribcage. A thick patch of fog moved in to where he was standing, and I could no longer see him. Once the fog thinned out again, the man was no longer there. He disappeared into the morning mist and I never saw him again. I returned home dumbfounded and explained the situation to Momon Bozorg with great difficulty.

Now there was no milk and Morvareed's breasts had been clogged for a day or two; both mother and baby were desperate. The baby had had all the warm sugar water he could bear and was now relentlessly crying for his mother's milk. And poor Morvareed, she was in agony with her breasts painfully bursting with milk and no way to get it to come out. The women of Mr. Rahimi's home had all been working diligently to help the young mother and her baby and get the milk flowing again.

I can still picture all three Mrs. Rahimis—plus Mr. Rahimi's mother who was now living in the same house with us and Mr. Rahimi's aunt/mother-in-law from the house next door—sitting on the floor in a circle around Morvareed, each taking a turn and trying different methods to get the milk to come out of her breasts. One woman rubbed Morvareed's shoulders as she moaned in pain while another one held a bowl beneath her breasts as the rest took turns caressing and squeezing them.

Morvareed was sitting straight with her long legs crossed in front of her and her eyes closed, softly wailing in anguish. She was a slender, attractive, and very coy nineteen- or twenty-year-old woman with shoulder-length dark brown hair, large brown eyes, perfectly trimmed thin bow-shaped eyebrows, and skin the color of pure milk. Her small and childlike round mouth resembled a pink rose placed carefully in the middle of her oval face. The light-colored flower-patterned chador that she usually wore around the house had fallen around her waist and on the ground. Her red

209

blouse was fully unbuttoned and pulled open, exposing her two large and stiff white breasts. She had a very narrow waistline, and her unusually expanded breasts made it look even narrower.

Fascinated by all the activities surrounding Morvareed's breasts and on Momon Bozorg's order, I stood against the wall and waited in case she needed me to do something. Just when the women were about to throw their hands in the air and give up, suddenly and to everyone's disbelief, Mr. Rahimi walked in through the door. He went right up to Morvareed, pushed the women aside, knelt in front of her, and began sucking vigorously on her nipples.

Almost never would a Muslim man enter a room full of women without first knocking and announcing his entrance. In a home where most of the women believed that no woman should ever allow any man except those in her immediate family to ever see even one strand of her hair, Mr. Rahimi's act was a cardinal sin. But no one amongst the women present in the room dared to say anything, including the usually outspoken Momon Bozorg.

Momon Bozorg bit her lower lip as she slapped the back of her left hand with her right one, looked skyward, and shook her head—a gesture of disbelief. Her face turned pale as if she had seen a ghost, and Morvareed was not doing any better. I thought she would get up and run out of the room screaming, but just like I froze yesterday as I watched Mandali being slain, Morvareed too was dumbfounded and motionless.

Mr. Rahimi's large, rough hands and tobacco-stained fingers held and squeezed Morvareed's breasts firmly as his powerful jaw vigorously sucked on her crimson and fully erect nipples. Watching the entire event, I thought of Rasputin's faith healing, and I thought of Lennie, the character from *Of Mice and Men,* who loved holding and caressing soft things, like rabbits, in his powerful, large hands.

Soon the milk began to shoot out of Morvareed's breasts. Mr. Rahimi victoriously looked at everyone in the room, said, "A bunch of incompetent women," and left the room with his alcohol-tainted breath lingering behind.

"If you ever tell a word of this to anyone, especially to Kia, I will cut your tongue off and feed it to dogs," Momon Bozorg warned me, her eyes bulging.

"Chashm, Momon Bozorg."

❖*Chapter Twenty-Eight*

For many children in underprivileged and working-class families, completing elementary school and receiving a sixth-grade certificate was a dream come true and, oftentimes, the end of their formal education. I was determined, however, to find a way to continue my education beyond elementary school. It wasn't because I was hungry for knowledge and wanted to learn—not at all. School to me was simply a road that I needed to take in order to get to where I wanted to go; a better tomorrow with a home and a family of my own and plenty of food to eat. For some strange reason I seemed to already know most of the subjects they were teaching at school. I hardly ever had to study for anything and still did very well. Learning seemed to come easy for me, so I chose education as my escape route out of my situation.

I had my mind set on attending high school that coming autumn but, under the circumstances, I was not sure if that was at all possible. As in the past, Momon Bozorg was the key here. If she decided to leave Mashhad to be with Kia or if she told me that she could not afford to support me through more than a sixth-grade education, then this was the end of the road since I had nowhere else to stay. After all, her own son stopped at sixth grade and got a job, why should I be any different? Halfway through the summer, I discussed with her the idea of me going to high school, and to my delight she was receptive and suggested that I should talk to my father about tuition and enrollment. I translated that as meaning I still had a place in her home, and with that I began searching for my father once again.

I needed to act fast if I wished to get enrolled in school. High school registrations were on a first-come, first-served basis, unless of course, as with everything else in Iran, you had connections. Most schools, especially the ones with better educational reputations, were often filled quickly. I was not too concerned about the quality of the school, as long as it was close enough that I did not have to walk more than a couple kilometers to get to it. With Momon Bozorg's blessing now in my pocket, I took a few days off from work and went looking for my father to see if he would be willing to help me out with the tuition and the cost of initial school supplies. My father was the last person on earth I wished to ask for anything, but unfortunately I had no other alternative.

This time it did not take long for me to find him and, when I did, I was elated to learn that not only was he supportive of my plan to go to high school but he also agreed to help. The same man who six years ago balked at the very idea of my receiving an education was now on my side, at least in principle. Perhaps it was my imagination, but I could swear that I detected a nuance of pride in his eyes when he looked at me that day. Maybe he saw in me the same resilience that helped him get through his own difficult childhood. He asked for the name and the address of the school that I wished to attend and offered to register me personally. I supplied him with the information of the school nearest to Mr. Rahimi's home where most of my classmates were going to attend, and we went our separate ways.

With the opening of school only two weeks away, I had not heard from my father and was becoming anxious. Frantic, I started camping across from his house again, hoping to get lucky and run into him soon. When I finally did catch up with him a few days later, he admitted that he had not signed me up as yet, saying he was looking into a better school for me. That told me he had not acted quickly enough and the school near Mr. Rahimi's home was no longer accepting more students. When he mentioned the location of the school that he had in mind for me, I shook my head in protest and sighed in disappointment. Even though I did not know anything about the school, just hearing its location made me sick—it was on the exact opposite side of town from where I lived. But, as the saying goes, beggars can't be choosers, and at this late point in the summer, and given my circumstances, I was glad to be enrolled anywhere.

Just two days before the opening of school, I quit my job at the electrical and lighting fixture store, collected my pay, and went to meet with my father. He confirmed my enrollment and gave me ten toomans for school supplies, in addition to a partial booklet of bus tickets—good for thirty rides or fifteen days—then he left in a hurry.

On the first day of school, just before daybreak, Momon Bozorg was apparently in the middle of her prayers. I sat quietly on the edge of the window niche and waited for her to finish so that I could thank her again for the opportunity and say goodbye before I left for school. I was dressed and ready to go, holding my new notebook and used textbook—courtesy of Rahim, Maryam Khanom's oldest son—on my lap. As I sat there looking at Momon Bozorg, I thought of my mother and how I missed her. She too never missed a prayer. When I was little, I used to sit across from my mother and as she folded and unfolded her body, praying, I wondered what she was telling God and why in a foreign language. She and my grandmother used to speak in Zargary in front of me when they didn't want me to know what they were talking about. Perhaps my mother did not wish for me to know what she was saying to God either, I used think. Sitting there looking at Momon Bozorg, I wondered if God was pleased with the way humans have ritualized and systematized what otherwise should be spontaneous and natural intimate spiritual moments between the created individuals and their creator. I wondered how God felt about the millions of people like my mother, pledging the same allegiance and telling Him the same thing each morning, over and over again. I was curious as to whether or not God actually bought any of what my mother was saying to Him in her broken Arabic. What if God was not like humans? What if He did not suffer from any form of narcissism and was not at all interested in people fawning over Him a billion times a day? What if He cared more about people spending that time doing something useful for humanity and doing the right things? My mother's prayers and promises were monologs of obligation fulfillment rather than genuine conversation with God.

Momon Bozorg always prayed in Farsi.

One morning six years ago, I'd sat similarly holding my school supplies on my lap, waiting in my new grey Soviet Union suit for Kia to accompany me to school for the very first time. I remembered that special day in the fall of 1963 as if it was yesterday; the radio was broadcasting the morning news as the heavenly aroma of hot, freshly baked bread, brewed black tea, and sharp Bulgarian feta cheese filled the room. Now, six years later, I found myself once again sitting on a window niche, but this time in an unassuming, semi-dark room, looking at a fragile old lady praying on a tattered rug spread over a hardened dirt floor. This time there was no radio playing and no bread of any kind in the room. Just me and the feeble old lady who for whatever reason had decided to share her roof with me. I could hear God whispering into my mind's ear how blessed I was.

On the first day of high school in the autumn of 1969, there weren't enough adjectives to describe how I felt—honored, lucky, excited, motivated, eager—as I waited anxiously at the crowded bus stop. All around me were men dressed in formal business attire and high school girls in their gray uniforms standing in clusters much like doves seeking safety in numbers. And there I was, packed with so much pride I could hardly fit in my skin.

I got off the bus at Statue Square and ran the rest of the way to school. My new school was a converted old residential home located, of all places, on Naderi Avenue, just a few blocks north of Imam Reza's shrine. My memories of this avenue formed a mosaic of some of the most unforgettable moments in my life. Before going inside the school building, I stood against the wall on the sidewalk, closed my eyes, and whispered my gratitude to the Creative Force of the universe for providing me with the opportunity to be here at this very moment. For a brief instant I recalled the image of my mother holding my hand as we walked on the same sidewalk to the shrine on Fridays. Then there were our rides with Moosa, the scrawny horse-drawn carriage driver, one of my mother's many admirers. Just down the road from here, on the other side of Statue Square, I was picked up by a policeman who took me home and demanded a finder's fee from my mother. And up the road, my stepmother fed me tainted soup while we were visiting her sister. I thought of Baba returning me on his bicycle to the carpet weaver's family, whose home, ironically, was just around the corner from my new school. I visualized the policeman who broke my Alaska cart a couple hundred meters away on Statue Square. My world suddenly appeared small, like a local morality play, with Naderi Avenue one of its main stages thus far.

At the time, high school in Iran encompassed grades seven through twelve and the standard for passing was set very high, especially in the areas of math and science. Many students ended up repeating at least one or two grades before they graduated, a situation that caused a wide age gap between the students. To my amazement, my new school was packed with students that I considered grown-ups, which intimidated some seventh graders, but not me.

One day several months into the school year, the assistant principal poked his head through my classroom's door and said, "Golmakani, come outside. I need to talk to you."

I had just arrived at school after two hours of walking in the snow and ice and was still shivering and thawing. The wonderful warmth emanating from the large black coal-burning heater in the corner of the classroom had just begun to find its way to the surface of my frozen bones.

"Now!" he said, rounding his eyes, looking directly at me. Reluctantly I left the room and met him in the narrow stairway.

"Where is your jacket, Golmakani?"

"I forgot to wear it today, aqa."

"How can anyone forget to wear their jacket on a subzero-temperature day like today?" he quickly responded.

I shrugged my shoulders while looking down at the floor.

"I am not as stupid as you think I am, Golmakani! Don't think that I don't notice you sneaking into the building without wearing your jacket! You know the rules: no jacket, no school. This is my first and last warning to you."

"Chashm, aqa."

It was mandatory for students to wear a jacket to school, and mine had come apart recently after one of my classmates pulled on it during a recess. If it wasn't for Momon Bozorg continually patching and stitching the old jacket over and over again, it would have fallen apart two years ago. I had no idea how and where I was going to find a new one, given that I spent six days out of a week in

215

school and when I was not at school, I was on the road walking to or from it. That left only Fridays for me to look for a solution.

At this particular time I was living with Momon Bozorg's young niece and nephew. A few months after high school started, Momon Bozorg locked her place up and left to stay with Kia for a while. Her sister's two oldest children, who were attending high school here in Mashhad, agreed for me to stay with them until she returned. Bigger cities had better schools, hence many small-town, middle-class families sent their children to places like Mashhad to complete their final two or three years of high school. Iranian middle-class families took their children's education very seriously and went through great pains and personal sacrifices to ensure that their children had every opportunity to succeed.

Momon Bozorg's niece and nephew were living in a partially finished home that their father was slowly building in Mashhad in anticipation of transferring here someday. Being high school junior and senior students, and living on a limited monthly budget provided by their father, they were hardly in a position to feed me, let alone buy me a new jacket. I did not have the impudence to ask them even if they could afford it. Just sharing their small room and bread with me allowed me to continue to go to school, was more than enough and, for that alone, I was eternally grateful to them.

The only person who could get me a jacket was my father, and I had not seen or heard from him since last summer when, just before school started, he handed me a booklet of bus tickets and disappeared. Incidentally, the booklet only had thirty tickets, each valued at two rials and good for one ride. During the first week of school, I used some of the tickets and exchanged the rest for lunch money and had been walking ever since.

Moving in with Momon Bozorg's young relatives on another side of town did not shorten the distance to my school any. Even on a good day, it took me two or more hours to walk to school. During snowstorms, the trip was even longer. On average I spent five hours a day, six days a week, walking to and from school. During the winter months, when the days were much shorter, it was always dark when I left for school in the morning and dark by the time I made it back home. Since I did not have a school bag, I placed my books under my shirt and then tucked my shirt into my

216

pants, thereby freeing my hands to cover and protect my ears and nose from the cold as I made my way.

I wondered if life was insisting on playing a cruel game by throwing as much adversity at me as possible. This winter would be no different than any other. My worn shoes had large holes on their soles, thus allowing for snow, slush, and rainwater to get in. The one set of clothes that I owned hardly qualified to be categorized as clothes and proved very inadequate to protect me against the Siberian-like cold. My stomach was always growling for food and my soul longing for love and companionship as I walked the city streets day after day, back and forth to school, in hope of a better tomorrow. Sometimes I badly craved a hug or a simple touch by another human. My parents might as well have been dead and my heart filled with loneliness, and now, as if all of that were not enough, I had to travel farther than anyone I knew just to go to school. I was mightily tired of slogging through purgatory in this divine comedy called life.

It was mandatory for all students to leave the school building during the lunch hour. Most of the boys who attended my school lived in the surrounding areas and were able to go home for lunch to enjoy a little warmth and be fed by their mothers. I spent the lunch hour sitting in the afternoon sun on the sidewalk across the street with ice-covered gutters above me. Next to where I sat there was a small sugar-bread bakery. Whenever its door was opened, an aromatic sweet steam escaped the little shop and filled my lungs, teasing my empty stomach and driving me crazy. I sometimes found myself standing, Charlie Chaplin–like, in front of the shop staring at the large round sugar-bread inside and letting my imagination go wild; all the while wishing I could get my hands on one of them. Other times I would walk to the shrine and spend my lunch break there inside one of the many nice warm halls.

Wishing for the best and hoping I wouldn't get caught, I kept on going to school without attempting to find myself a jacket. I took all sorts of steps to avoid running into the assistant principal. Knowing he always stood by the school's entrance at eight o'clock sharp to catch the latecomers, I arrived at school half an hour early every day. In addition, I stayed out of trouble and did not leave the classroom for recess. Sometimes I had to enlist the help of a large friend to hide behind when I had to move around school to do such a simple thing as go to the bathroom. I was able to evade the assistant principal for a good while, until one bitterly cold winter day when an incident in the math class brought me face-to-face with.

I hadn't cared much for my math teacher from the very first day I set foot in his class. He seemed to be more interested in promoting his twisted personal views and propaganda, mostly religious, than in teaching math. Finally one day, being the self-appointed defender of the truth that I have always been, I simply could not keep quiet any longer. All throughout elementary school and later high school, I was well known for speaking my mind, even when it was not in my best interest. Under duress of hunger and a long and exhausting walk to school in heavy snow that day, I snapped and decided to challenge the poor primitive soul.

On the day in question, this short and stocky math teacher started his sermon halfway through the class period. His subject, as always, was Baha'ism—at the time a relatively young minority religion with a very small number of followers. Baha'ism is a monotheistic religion founded by Baha'u'llah in nineteenth-century Persia. It emphasizes the spiritual unity of all humankind and the underlying unity of the major world religions. In 1960s Iran, the Baha'is enjoyed government protection to freely assemble and practice their faith. But as is often the case the world over, opposition to the group formed among many uneducated, dogmatic, and unenlightened souls who perceived anything different as a threat. I am sure that jealousy also played a role in fueling such uninformed and misguided opposition. Baha'is were well educated, very well-mannered, outstanding citizens, and most of all, honest (which I liked most about them), and they selflessly loved their country. Their presence was refreshing in a culture where for the most part manipulating the truth was accepted as a way of life. Baba used to say that no other country in the world has as many words for affirming the truth of a statement as Iran. Why would there be a need for such a large volume of words to use only for swearing, if people simply told the truth? he would say. People swore to God, to the graves of their dead ancestors, the lives of their dear ones, the twelve imams, the Fourteen Innocents, the king's crown, their grandfather's white beard, and a thousand other things to persuade someone that they were telling the truth, often under no pressure and during the course of a casual conversation. I must emphasize that this practice was widespread only within a certain segment of society to which my zealous math teacher happened to belong.

At my age I was hardly an expert on any religion, and because of my free and unstructured upbringing, I was not at all religious and did not care one way or another if others were. But I didn't need to know anything about religion to recognize when a fanatically deranged man clad as a math teacher was wasting my time by telling stories about subjects that were not relevant to the class. The poor bastard seemed to be trapped inside a dark, long, and narrow tunnel of extremist ideology, and as with the blinding nature of all tunnels, he was unable to see any version of the truth other than his own. He told fantastic tales of the different tactics Baha'is used to lure young Muslim men into their religion, including the use of naked women.

"Permission to speak, aqa," I asked, raising my hand.

"Yes!"

"How do you know all of these things about the Baha'is?"

"I just know!" he said firmly, caught somewhat off guard.

"Forgive me, sir. But how do you know that the Baha'is use naked women to convert Muslim men?"

The class suddenly became quiet and all ears, waiting for the teacher to respond. Perhaps they were waiting to learn how they could benefit from this alleged generous offering by the Baha'is, or perhaps they were simply startled by my bold behavior.

Challenging and questioning authorities of any kind, including parents and teachers, was not done in our culture. Not only was it considered rude, but doing so often bore unpleasant consequences.

"I just know!" he responded with a twisted grin on his face.

"How many times have they offered naked women to you, sir?"

Seemingly agitated, he stumped his oversized feet on the floor, marched to my desk, and ordered me to stand up. His rather large and excessively white and repulsive bald head was covered with sweat beads, accenting little blemishes that covered his scalp.

"What are you, a Baha'i?"

"No, sir."

"Then you are a Muslim?"

219

"No, sir. I am too young to have a religion."

"What are your parents?"

"Dead, sir."

"Are you making fun of me?"

"No, sir. To tell you the truth, sir, I don't care much about math, but I have to take it and pass it in order to pass the seventh grade. So I figure since I walk for two to three hours every morning to come here, it might be nice if you could stay with teaching me math instead of your personal propaganda. Frankly, sir, if I was a Baha'i and had the means, I would offer people like you all sorts of naked women not to become a Baha'i."

With that the class burst into laughter, and the next thing I knew I was being dragged out of the classroom by my ear. Once in the hallway, the stubby little man relieved his anger by slapping my face and head and slamming me against the wall. I just glowered at him and said nothing. When he was done, he ordered me to go and wash my face and return to the classroom. As I walked down the stairs I found myself face-to-face with the assistant principal.

"Where are you going, Golmakani?"

"I am going to wash my face, sir."

"What happened to you? Why is your lip bleeding?"

I looked down and did not answer. He was quickly able to figure out what had happened. And since beating students was an acceptable practice he did not inquire any further. Unfortunately, in some segments of our society beating a child was seen as an act of kindness; it was viewed as teaching a child a lesson. For instance, if a child reported to his parents that he had been beaten by a teacher or a man living a few doors down, the first reaction of the parents was "Tell me what you did." And almost always their response after hearing your story was "Good for him! If I was there I would have beaten you as well for being disrespectful."

"Don't bother with washing your face; the water faucet is frozen outside. I hope your jacket is upstairs in the classroom!"

I did not respond.

"Well, is it?"

I was about to say yes, but I feared he might check on it. If he did and found out it wasn't there, which it wasn't, I would have gotten in even deeper trouble for lying.

220

"No, sir. My mother washed my jacket last night and it wasn't fully dry this morning so I couldn't wear it."

"Don't you have another jacket?"

"No, sir."

"Why wouldn't your mother wait till Friday to wash it?"

"She thought it was too dirty, sir, and couldn't wait."

"Well, you know the rule and unfortunately leave me no choice but to suspend you until you learn not to come to school without your jacket. Go back to your class, get your things, and come to my office. I need to talk to you about something else as well."

"Chashm, aqa."

I grabbed my books from the class and left to see the assistant principal in his office.

"Golmakani, when are you going to bring the rest of your tuition in?"

"What do you mean, sir?"

"I mean the rest of your school tuition. When your father signed you up here he promised to send the balance within a month, and now it has been almost six months!"

"I was not aware of that, sir. I will talk to him and get you the money."

"Okay, son. But remember: jacket is first. Tomorrow I want you to come and show me that you have your jacket on before you go to your class, alright?"

"Chashm, aqa."

I obviously had no idea that my father had not paid my school tuition in full. I wished that I had never asked him to help me in the first place but I had no other choice. My first year of high school was turning out to be a painful experience, to say the least. I was living with two teenagers who were hardly old enough to be anyone's caretaker. And without exaggeration, I hardly ever had lunch while at school and only had two or three breakfasts per week—often a piece of bread and, if I was lucky, a slice of cheese to go with it. And worst of all, I couldn't even complain as I had no one to complain to.

But like the assistant principal said, first things first. My first priority was to come up with a jacket. Unless I could find someone to lend or give me one, I was going to be out of school for a while, and if I didn't go to school, I wasn't sure where I was going to stay

221

during the days. Money couldn't help me at the time. Even if I could miraculously come up with the money, there was no place in Mashhad where I could purchase a premade jacket.

From school I walked straight to Mr. Rahimi's, hoping Maryam Khanom could help me. She and my uncle Abdul were the only people I could think of who had boys my age and could perhaps lend me a jacket until I could come up with one of my own. Right away I decided I was not going to ask my uncle for help—I just didn't want to be indebted to him—and that left Maryam Khanom as my only hope and option.

I arrived at her house late in the afternoon, explained my predicament to her and asked if I could borrow one of her sons' jackets until I found my father. She swore to Imam Reza and the Koran that her son, the one that was about my size, had only one jacket and he was wearing it to school that day.

Disenchanted, I left Mr. Rahimi's house. I was faint with hunger and cold. I thought of walking to the army depot and looking for some bread there, but the amount of snow on the ground and the distance discouraged me. Out of desperation I decided to stop at the home of my best friend from elementary school, hoping he was home that day due to the heavy snowfall. I was cold, starving, and hardly had enough energy to walk through the waist-high snow that blanketed the entire vast barren land between Mr. Rahimi's house and my friend's. I prayed that my friend would be home and, more importantly, that he would be able to invite me inside for a little while so I could warm up before embarking on the long trip to the other side of town where Momon Bozorg's niece and nephew lived.

I had not been to my friend's house for a couple of years now. His mother, a very serious and proper lady, had forbidden her son from associating with me. According to my friend Reza, his mother thought she had seen me smoking cigarettes when I was in the fifth grade, and therefore she thought of me as a bad influence and did not want me near her son. Even after I explained that what his mother saw was me pretending to be a movie star and smoking a cigarette by using a rolled-up piece of paper, she did not change her mind. Reza and I kept our friendship at school, but not in the neighborhood where his mother could see us together. And now, perhaps to his mother's delight, I was living in another part of town and going to a different school.

Nervously I knocked at Reza's door, and his mother immediately answered. I said hello to her and asked if her son was home. As usual her eyebrows were pulled together and she was not smiling when she informed me that Reza was at school. I knew before I came here that the chances of finding him at home were not all that good, but I had to at least try. At that point, overwhelmed with hopelessness and the events of the day, plus feeling humiliated for stopping by Reza's house, I felt my eyes suddenly fill with tears as I apologized to Mrs. Zareef for taking her time.

She looked at me as I stood there in front of her with dried blood and bruises on my face, wearing no jacket, shivering, and covered with snow. With her usual puckered face, she asked, as if confirming her low opinion of me as being irresponsible and not worthy of her son's friendship, "Did you get in a fight? Aren't you cold? Where is your jacket? Why aren't you at school?"

For the first time in a long time, I felt very cheap, pitiful, and more alone than ever. As tears sprang to my eyes I began to turn around and walk away before she saw me crying. Just then Mrs. Zareef grabbed my arm and with a stern and motherly tone told me to come inside for a little bit and warm up. Her maternal instinct must have told her that I was at the end of my rope.

Inside, Mrs. Zareef sat me on the floor next to a hot kerosene heater in the living room and gave me a piece of cloth to dry my hair and face with while she went into another room. Her children were all at school at that time and her husband was at work. Her husband was one of the kindest men I had ever met. Often when I used to witness his interaction with his son Reza, I wished he were my father too. Reza's father was a delivery driver for the Pepsi-Cola Company. Every time Reza and I spotted his truck on the road somewhere, he would give us each a large ice-cold bottle of Pepsi. We had to finish the sodas right then and there and give him back the empty bottles.

Mrs. Zareef's house felt like a home. This was a sensation that I had very little experience with. There were pictures of the entire family on the wall, and the place smelled heavenly: lamb fried with cinnamon and steamed rice. Moments later, Reza's mother returned with a tray holding a bowl of hot food. She placed it in front of me on the carpet and told me, "Eat." I could only whisper, "Thank you." I would have burst into tears if I'd said another word. Like a stormy sea, waves of emotions were smashing in every direction inside of me. I was not sure if it was her unconditional kindness that had me all choked up or the shame and desolation that I felt for having had to go there in the first place. Maybe it was envying my friend Reza for what he had and I did not. For whatever reason, I was very sensitive that afternoon, sitting on the floor of a woman who in her son's best interest did not want me around, but who would nevertheless feed me in the interest of humanity and kindness. I quickly finished the bowl of hot steamed rice and fried lamb with the piece of bread that she gave me. I even licked the bowl when she was in the other room and couldn't see. It was, without question, the best meal I had eaten in almost two years.

Soon my belly was partially full and I was warm and comfortable. It was then that I began telling Mrs. Zareef the truth about why I was not at school and not wearing a jacket. In her abbreviated way and with her Isfahanian accent (the family had moved here from the city of Isfahan only a few years earlier), she briefly inquired about where I was staying now and where Momon Bozorg was, and I told her. Once she learned that Momon Bozorg was out of town, she left the room again and returned with a jar of Vaseline and without asking my permission, began rubbing the ointment over the backs of my hands. Ever since I could remember, the backs of my hands had always been cracked and covered with lines of dried blood in the winter. Momon Bozorg used to rub Vaseline over them a couple times a week to moisten the dry skin and reduce the pain. A pair of gloves would have prevented all of that, of course. I was both embarrassed and happy as Mrs. Zareef held my hands in a motherly way and caressed them with the oily substance. I had not been kindly touched by another human for a long while now. Until one experiences it firsthand, it would be difficult to understand what it means to suffer from human-touch deficiency.

I had to head back into town before it got dark and colder outside, so I got up and walked to the front door to end my awkward visit, thanking Mrs. Zareef the entire time. The wonderful woman had placed my riddled shoes upside down on a piece of newspaper to drain. Just as I reached for the front door to open it and leave, she signaled me to wait and ran into another room, emerging moments later, carrying a pair of socks and a jacket in her hand.

"You are going to freeze out there. Take those wet socks off and put these on. The socks are new and the jacket is Reza's but it is too small for him now."

When I promised to return them she said that I did not have to, they were mine to keep. I was speechless. All I could do was look at her and thank her with my gaze. I quickly put on the new socks and the jacket before leaving her house. She disposed of my tattered wet socks for me. The jacket was a little old but fit me just fine and, more importantly, gave me the opportunity to return to school the next day.

The Zareefs were Baha'is, just as was Momon Bozorg and her teenage niece and nephew who were now looking after me for free, only a few blocks down the street from my devout Muslim uncle. Just as nothing else was ordinary in the colorful Rahimis' home, neither was the ethnicity and religion of the Mrs. Rahimis. Except for Momon Bozorg, everyone in Mr. Rahimi's home, including Kia, was a Muslim and did not seem to have a problem with Momon Bozorg's being different. Ironically, my parents and all of my relatives were hardcore Muslims who never missed a Namaz (the daily practice of formal and obligatory prayer in Islam. The ritual prayer has prescribed times, conditions, and procedures, conducted in Arabic only) and made pilgrimages to Makah once they had the opportunity. I could not see for the life of me why the math teacher would think that a Baha'i like Mrs. Zareef would ever wish to contaminate her gentle and compassionate world by luring someone like him into it.

Thanks to Mrs. Zareef, my feet and heart were warm, my belly was almost full, and I had a jacket that was my ticket back to school. I walked home feeling grateful and inspired as I indulged in a fantastic dream that perhaps someday all the people in the world would evolve to be like Mrs. Zareef and Momon Bozorg, the silent solacers of orphans like Mandali's daughter and *me*, the discarded son of Assad-Banafsheh. A year after Mandali's death, his daughter found a suitor—I cannot recall clearly whether the suitor was an orphan himself or just did not have anyone in Mashhad—but she had no one to help her with the wedding arrangement and to give her away. When no one in our area stepped forward to help the poor girl, Momon Bozorg rolled up her sleeves and rushed to her rescue. She borrowed some money and paid the wedding mullah and sent me to purchase five toomans' worth of cookies and sweets on credit from Hajji Aqa, just in case any of the neighbors decided to attend the wedding. I still remember the teenage bride and groom standing against the wall in a small adobe room lit by an oil lantern, in their wedding clothes, with Momon Bozorg and me and the bride's two younger siblings as the only guests of honor.

Ironically—and contrary to the twisted beliefs of the math teacher—I do not remember Momon Bozorg, not even once, speaking of or advocating her religious beliefs, either to me or to her son Kia. I recall once when childish curiosity compelled me to ask her about Baha'ism and the process of becoming a Baha'i, she smiled softly and said; Baha'i is not something that one becomes or changes into. It is a way that one chooses to think and to perceive the world and everyone and everything within it.

I believe those who have spiritually evolved—and by that I do not mean religiously—perceive the world and everyone in it as "us," as did Momon Bozorg, while the unenlightened souls view the world as "me" and "not me," like the math teacher did. In his instinctively driven mind, the "not me's" were different, and hence, a threat and enemy. While in Momon Bozorg's spiritually driven view, we were all waters of the same ocean separated only by a physical bottle called the body.

❖Chapter Twenty-Nine

Summer, my savior season, was here again, and with it I turned fourteen. Just before school ended, as I was about to take my last test of the final exams, the assistant principal walked into the classroom and asked me to leave until I could pay off the past-due balance of my tuition. He was a kind and good man, only doing his job, and I understood that. I could read the regret in his eyes, but his hands were obviously tied. Out of compassion he purposely chose to stop me from taking the test on a subject he knew I was strongest at—composition. He knew that I would have no trouble passing it and would not have to study over the summer before I returned to take the test in August. I owed the school twenty-eight toomans, roughly about four American dollars at that time.

After a month of vagrancy and unsuccessfully looking for a job, I came up with the bold idea of finding a way to go to Tehran and visit my mother for a week or two. I did not have the stamina to live through another summer of aimlessly wandering around the same places and imposing on the same frowning faces. I wanted to be like the Little Black Fish and venture out of the small puddle I had come to know as home. *The Little Black Fish* was a well-known children's book written by an Iranian writer, Samad Behrangi. The story was about the adventures of a little black fish that lived alone with its mother beneath a small rock in a little stream that ran along the side of a rocky mountain. As the story goes, the Little Black Fish grew tired of swimming in the same old spot and circling the same old rock, day in and day out. One day, in spite of its mother's protest, the Little Black Fish decided to leave and follow the stream to see where it would take it. With both wisdom and courage, the

227

Little Black Fish traveled far indeed and had an adventurous journey along the way.

I discussed my intentions with Aunt Sarvar, and she thought it was a splendid idea; she even offered to pay for my bus fare. A few days later, one fine early morning, she and I walked to Maydoneh Bar and stood on the side of Naderi Avenue while waiting for any bus that would be willing to take me to Tehran for ten toomans. Ali Aqa, my aunt's husband, recommended that I catch a bus at Maydoneh Bar instead of going to the station and paying the full price for a ticket. He also suggested we offer the driver fifteen toomans; reducing it to ten toomans was my aunt's idea.

Naderi Avenue was Mashhad's only arterial to the northern parts of Iran. The buses destined for Tehran, via the scenic Caspian Sea route, had to pass through here. They were easy to tell apart from the rest of the buses that went to the surrounding villages and the nearby small towns every morning. Tehran's buses were large, modern, and chic, free of any writings except for the logo of the bus line. Buses going to the countryside, on the other hand, were smaller, often with a distinct country flavor in their appearance, colorful, and with religious slogans written on them to ensure a safe journey.

The drivers of the first few buses that stopped considered my aunt's offer of ten toomans to be too low and drove away. After a while the sun was beginning to come up and cover the tips of the single-story buildings across the street, and I was starting to get worried. From hanging around the Maydoneh Bar area during the previous summers, I knew most buses left town early in the mornings; therefore, with every passing hour my chances of catching one were petering out. I was not the one paying for the fare, so I was in no position to ask my aunt to increase her offer a little. My aunt was like my mother—tighter than the clutch on a ten-ton truck. She would go through great lengths to save ten shahis—half a rial.

She told me not to worry, that if we could not find a bus to take me that day it was probably God's will and we would try again tomorrow. But I couldn't wait until tomorrow. I was all pumped up and anxious to be on a bus that morning and found myself unwilling to spend another night here. If only she were willing to increase her offer to fifteen toomans, like her husband suggested, I was certain that God in turn was willing to change his will in my favor.

While we continued to wait, my aunt seized the opportunity to do what Iranians are best at—giving advice. She told me all the do's and don'ts while traveling and during my stay with my mother.

"Tehran is not like Mashhad, khaleh joon [dear nephew]. It is so big that a camel can easily lose its owner there. Be very careful, Alireza joon. Watch out for child molesters; they are everywhere waiting for handsome boys like you to take advantage of. I want you to come back safe and marry my daughter someday. I don't want anything bad to happen to my future son-in-law." She said this with a sly smile.

I blushed in embarrassment with her last remark, which made her chuckle. Marrying one's cousins was still practiced here.

"Remember not to tell anyone at Mansoor Aqa's work that you are his stepson. They don't need to know that his wife has been married before. Should anyone ask, tell them you are a relative of his wife visiting from Mashhad."

"Chashm, khaleh."

Finally a bus pulled over in which the assistant driver agreed to take me to Tehran for ten toomans. Of course, not without my aunt first embarrassing me by haggling for a while before using her ace in the hole: "He is an orphan boy and God will reward you someday in heaven for giving him a break."

My aunt and I embraced, kissed, and said goodbye before I stepped up into the bus. As the assistant driver closed the door I could see my aunt's face, one eye full of tears and the other eye full of joy. The look on her face confirmed what I was feeling inside; this moment was the last paragraph of the last chapter of our story together. I did something that I had never done before; threw a kiss for my aunt, my old solacer, as the driver put the bus in gear and drove away.

I was directed to take the only seat available at the back of the bus amongst four or five young men, two of whom were Western tourists. The men quickly adjusted themselves to make room for me. I sat holding on my lap all my worldly possessions, including some little gifts I had previously purchased for my brother and sisters along with two hard-boiled eggs and half a nan to eat on my trip.

229

The bus glided away northbound on the same blacktopped road that I had so often taken to my grandparents' village in the past, except this time I was traveling a greater distance to reunite with my mother. She too was about my age when she first left her village and embarked on this very same road to meet her destiny. I just hoped that unlike my mother's journey, mine would bear a better outcome. A little voice deep down inside of the forever-optimistic me said that it would. For one thing, I was starting out with a better hand than the one my mother was dealt. I was literate, much more experienced and, more importantly, I viewed the world with a far more optimistic outlook than my pessimistic mother. I strongly believed that our lives were a direct reflection of our own thoughts and personal beliefs, while she saw herself as a helpless instrument in the hands of some unexplainable powers and destiny. I am not sure if I would have fared any differently, however, if it hadn't been for Kia, growing up in the city, and having the opportunity to go to school. Being a boy, and for the most part, free to choose my own destiny, was the main reason for the contrasting outcome of our lives, I believe. How can you expect a dove to fly when they trim its wings at an early age before it has a chance to learn to fly? my mother used to say when she complained about her upbringing. I believed in destiny also, but one that was imagined and formed exclusively by me and no one else.

Baba and my mother had no idea that I was coming to visit them. Once we reached Tehran tomorrow I was to get off the bus at a certain intersection. According to Ali Aqa's directions, the tailor shop where Baba worked was somewhere near that intersection. My aunt made sure that the assistant driver knew where to drop me off as she was paying him. I prayed that nothing would go wrong as I only had ten rials to my name. That was hardly enough should I encounter any problems finding Baba's work, since I had no idea where they lived.

The next day, not long after we entered the city of Tehran, the bus pulled over to the side of an intersection as the assistant driver shouted from the front. "Pesar, here is the end of the line for you!"

Upon hearing his words, I said a hearty goodbye to my fellow travelers in the back of the bus and ran out. I had become friends with the two young men sitting to my left and right, one a

European and the other a Tehranian. As the bus pulled away, I began to miss the two young men already, as if they were my brothers and I had known them all my life.

The street sign confirmed that I'd been dropped off in the right place. I had to walk only half a block before I found the tailor shop where Baba supposedly worked, just as Ali Aqa had described. Suddenly the magnitude of what was happening and where I was at the moment came crashing down on me. I was about to face the man whom I had not seen since I was a little boy, the only father figure I had ever known and loved unconditionally. My emotions were out of control: my left knee was shaking badly and warm tears were silently rolling down my face. All of the things I had bottled up since I was five years old, everything I wanted to tell Baba if I ever saw him again, took hold of my body: the complaints for leaving me behind, the thoughts of missing him, and how I always remembered and cherished our wonderful times together. To prevent myself from crumbling to the ground, I found myself next to the tailor shop crouching on my heels with my back against the wall. Over the years, seeing panhandlers and migrant day laborers crouch on the street corners of Mashhad had made me detest crouching; I perceived it to be a pathetic gesture, a sign of weakness.

Once all the clouds of emotion poured out of my system and vanished, I wiped my face dry with the corner of my shirt, took a few deep breaths, collected myself and nervously walked into the tailor shop. Inside, and with a quivering voice, I said hello to a man sitting behind a desk located at the front of the shop.

"Salam, aqa."

"Salam. Can I help you?"

"Yes. I am here to see Mansoor Aqa please."

"And you are?"

"I am a relative of his wife from Mashhad."

Baba must have heard his name, because no sooner had I finished my last sentence than he leapt out from the back room and strode across the shop toward me. His face was one huge smile and his eyes were flashing with ardor. He hugged and kissed me joyfully and told the man that he was taking the rest of the day off, and with that he put his arm around my shoulder and we left. He was genuinely happy and excited to see me, which instantly made

231

me feel both good and welcomed. It had been a very long time since anyone besides Kia had shown any joy in seeing me at his doorstep.

Once out on the street, Baba impatiently paced back and forth as he attempted to wave down a taxicab, clearly excited. While waiting, he kept looking at me in disbelief and studying me up and down, shaking his head saying how much I had grown and changed. With the exception of a few extra kilos around his waist, along with some footprints of time on his visage, Baba was still the same Baba. He still had the mustache and the same full set of fine hair greased and combed perfectly backwards and to the side. Without grease, his hair was too fine to stand in any style.

"Momon is not going to believe this! I can't wait to see the expression on her face when she sees you!" Baba said with glee.

Finally a taxi pulled over. "Nezamabad," Baba told the driver as we got in.

Sensing my anxiety, he updated me every few minutes as to how much longer before we arrived at our destination. We got off at an outdoor market where Baba purchased some fruits to celebrate my arrival. He walked the rest of the way towards home with the fruit in his arms as I tried to keep up with him, just like the old days. It was exciting for me to know that perhaps I was walking on the same ground as my mother did on her way to the market every day. My heart pounded harder with every step that we took. I prayed that it would not burst before I had the chance to see my mother one more time. My face was burning hot and my brain was numb from all the excitement I was feeling inside. Before I knew it, we had suddenly turned into an alley and stopped in front of a half-opened metal door.

"Here we are, Alireza," Baba whispered as he pointed to the door. "Momon is not expecting me home at this time of a day, so let's go in quietly and surprise her!" He chuckled.

I nodded in agreement as I quietly followed Baba into a tiny, damp brick courtyard shaded by a two-story structure. We tiptoed through a narrow hallway, up some stairs, and into a small corridor on the second floor. In front of an open door a little girl wearing a white cotton summer dress was playing on the marble floor. Her fine and straight hair and facial features were unmistakably Baba's.

232

Seeing Baba, she jumped up smiling and was about to say something when Baba signaled for her to hush.

He waved at me to stay behind as he went inside the room. The adorable little girl, about two or three years of age, stood against the wall with her hands behind her back, all the while biting her lower lip. She just stared at me with an understandably puzzled look on her face. I obviously knew who she was already— my youngest sister, Nasrin, Baba's and my mother's fourth and, at that point in time, youngest child. Over the years Ali Aqa had been keeping me informed as to how many children my mother had given birth to. More than anything I was dying to lift her up into my arms and hug and kiss her, but I did not want to spoil Baba's plan.

"Salam, Mansoor Aqa! What are you doing home?" I heard my mother's unmistakable voice, but with a completely different accent than the one I was familiar with, coming from the room that Baba had just entered.

"I brought home a guest with me, Soory joon."

"Oh my God! For lunch? Who?" my mother asked worriedly, lowering her voice.

Before she could say another word, Baba stuck his head out into the little foyer and winked at me to come in. I walked into the room and saw my mother with her back to me, scrambling to get her chador. She let out a scream after turning around to see me standing in front of her. After all those years, it only took her a second to realize who I was before she ran over and embraced me, kissing me while at the same time crying out of control.

"I hope your mother dies for you, Ali *joon*. You are my gift from God today, pesaram. You don't know how every day, when I am home alone, I sing your name and weep for you, momon. You don't know what my life had been without you, Ali *joon*. The pain of being without you had been shredding my heart, pesaram." She went on and on repeating this as her arms remained locked around my neck.

I took in the familiar scent of my mother and filled my hungry lungs with it. Like a little lamb that had been lost in the mountains and was now reunited with its mother, I clung to her and rested my weary soul in the fold of her arms. It felt so good to be held against the bosom of a woman who uttered my name with love and

233

emotion and whose scent was so wonderfully familiar. Someone whose resemblance to me suggested that I indeed belonged to her.

"Okay! Okay! That's enough, you two. You are scaring little Nasrin," Baba added playfully as he unlocked my mother's arms from me.

"This is our little caboose, your youngest sister, Alireza," said Baba.

I dried my eyes with the back of my hand and picked up the little girl into my arms and kissed her a dozen times over.

"Do you know who I am?" I asked. She nodded her head yes. "Well, who am I?"

"You are Alireza," she responded.

And with that Baba quickly added, "Bravo! And Alireza is your oldest brother, Nasrin joon."

Soon my other two sisters and Mehdi came inside and we all went through another series of hugs, kisses, and tears. Mehdi could not remember the details of our common past, but he knew well who I was. I reached into my pocket and pulled out a fistful of raisins and toasted chickpeas and gave them to Mehdi. Baba and my mother laughed, but Mehdi could not remember the ritual.

About a week after my arrival, Baba suggested that I should live with them and attend high school here in Tehran. His offer was beautiful music to my ears. I had been dreaming of a day when I could have a family of my own and here, finally, was my chance. For a rent increase of fifteen toomans a month, my mother was able to get the landlord's approval and add me to her household.

Within days of arriving in Tehran I went through a complete transformation. Baba bought me some new clothes and shoes more appropriate for my age and sewed a chic and fashionable pair of bell-bottom pants to go with them. I had my hair cut Beatles style—the hairstyle of the day—and soon I was feeling like a brand-new person, both inside and out. New clothes, new look, good food, and a family who loved me, they all helped bring color back to my cheeks and sparkle into my eyes. For the first time since I could remember I began to pay attention to the mirrors, and out on the streets I enjoyed seeing young girls turning their heads around and looking at me with desire. As a matter of fact, by the end of the summer the landlord's oldest daughter, two or three years older than I, volunteered to teach me how to French kiss and showed me how to caress her firm breasts on the secluded rooftop.

Fashionably dressed young men and women colored the busy sidewalks in upscale and popular parts of the city. Young men with thick boot-shaped sideburns wore bell-bottom pants and shiny patterned shirts revealing their bare chests, and young women had on maxi- or miniskirts or whatever else they wished.

To a fourteen-year-old boy like me, Tehran, the capital and the largest city in Iran with a population of almost three million at the time, could not have been any more exciting. It was a massive city of tall buildings, double-decker buses, bigger-than-life billboards, and cabarets. I had never seen double-decker buses or billboards before, and the tallest building in Mashhad stood only four stories high. Tehran was filled with stylish men and women who dressed in the latest European fashions and drove automobiles I had previously seen only in the movies. I could not believe my eyes when I first saw women in miniskirts riding roaring motorcycles and driving fancy sports cars. To state it in American slang, the people of Tehran were "cool." They spoke with a romantic and beautiful accent and seemed to be always smiling and happy. The sound of music came from everywhere: the automobiles, the storefronts, and the open windows of most homes. The thing that impressed me the most about Tehran, however, was television. I had never seen a television before, and the idea of being able to watch a film at home was mind-boggling to me.

Everything here was in stark contrast to where I came from. Mashhad was a cold religious city with conservative people who spoke with a bad accent and rarely smiled at strangers. It was a city of intolerance that prepared lavish daily feasts and fed its foreign pilgrims for free, while thousands of its own little citizens went to bed hungry every night and froze a thousand times every winter. In my mind, Mashhad was symbolized by my father. Just like the city, my father too was now wealthy. He too took great interest in his mosque and nourished his faith, while his own child remained invisible right under his nose. I peevishly wished that the people who were responsible for the character of Mashhad would stay there and never find their way to Tehran to ruin this beautiful, lively city.

235

Two weeks after my arrival in Tehran, I was on the train bound for Mashhad, accompanied by Mehdi. We were going to pay off my school debt with money that Baba had given me and to pick up my school records.

❖*Chapter Thirty*

I was enrolled to begin the eighth grade in a high school a few kilometers away from where my mother lived. There was another school only two blocks away from her home but Baba's brother happened to be the principal there, and since Baba was not on speaking terms with his brother, he decided not to enroll me there. For one thing, Baba never got over the fact that his brother was able to go to school and he was not. He was also unhappy with him for divorcing his first wife of many years and marrying a younger woman. His first wife could only produce girls and he badly wanted a boy, my mother said.

For the first time in a long time, I got the opportunity to be somebody's child. I didn't have to do anything except go to school and play. No longer did I have to worry about where to find my next piece of bread. No longer was I shadowed by the constant shame of imposing on others. Baba and my mother had very little, but I was content with just having a family. Baba's income would hardly have been sufficient to support a family of six if it wasn't for my mother's tightfistedness. I don't remember any of us ever getting up from the sofreh full, but having a home and a family more than made up for any deficits. When there is love, sharing the have-nots feels just as good as sharing the haves.

We all lived together as if all of those years of separation had never happened; in other words, we never talked about it. No expressions of hard feelings or regrets, as if I had been there with them all along. My mother never asked about my past without her, and I never brought it up, at least not in detail. Judging from when I was first placed with the Rahimis in 1963, seeing I was taken care of, happy and enrolled in school, my mother left for Tehran believing I was in good hands. I saw no reason to tell her otherwise. She was already carrying the heavy coffin of her unfulfilled dreams, lost and deceased marriage and children, on her frail shoulders— adding the dead weight of my recent past to it would have been unfair. She still had small children and a marriage to worry about.

It is only recently, some forty years later, that the two of us have begun slowly, over the long distance phone, to fill in the old but unforgotten blanks for one another, unveil what really happened to us while we were apart. Her heart-wrenching tales of poverty and hardship after she moved to Tehran eerily parallel mine. The beatings that she received from Baba, all of her forced pregnancies and subsequent abortions, and the emotional toll they took on her. The memories of her evictions, living shamefully with her six children in the tiny backroom of Baba's tailor shop, the recent deaths of her two youngest sons and, missing me, her oldest son—all this haunts her every night, she laments. We take turns and pause on the phone as we are overcome with emotions while listening and talking. Now, our roles have reversed. I am the parent and she is the child. I still have not told her my whole story, past or present.

I fell in love with Tehran, the city of my birth, right away. Everyone living up and down the alley where my mother lived, including her landlord and the other tenant who shared the house with my mother, was very nice to me. My mother and her family shared the second floor of the narrow two-story, four-room townhouse with two wonderful young brothers from Qum, a small town near Tehran. They were here working and attending school. The brothers occupied the larger room with a balcony in front, and my mother and her family lived in the smaller one in the back with a small window that opened to a tall brick wall a few meters away. A wall-to-wall French door with frosted glass separated our room from the room of the two brothers from Qum. At nights when everyone was home and the lights were on, we could see the silhouettes of the next room's occupants as they moved about; we could also hear everything they said. Baba was constantly eyeballing the kids, reminding them to keep their voices down, out of respect for the two brothers on the other side of the French door. We seemed to be always whispering, even when the two brothers were not home.

My mother did not have a trunk room or a closet here, so all of her belongings were out in the open. Every morning she folded the sleeping cotton mattresses and covers, stacked them neatly against the wall, and covered them with a large decorative sheet to make room for the breakfast sofreh. In winter a portable kerosene heater was enough to warm the little room. The heater also served as a stovetop to make tea and for my mother to produce all of her culinary masterpieces on. There was only one light in the room, hanging from the ceiling. The landlord did not allow for the bulb to exceed forty watts, so the room always appeared to be hazy and dim.

Seven people packed into a room the size of a matchbox with all of their clothing, school supplies, and other personal belongings made for a very tight space. There was hardly enough room for anyone to roll over in bed at night. In early autumn and late spring when it was warm outside, the size of the room was not so much of an issue since all the children slept on the rooftop at night.

My mother thanked God every day and considered herself very lucky for finding this place. Not many people were willing to rent to a family of six, now seven, she always pointed out to the kids when they complained about the size of the room. Not much seemed to have changed over the years for Baba and my mother. He was still without his own shop, and she without a home of her own. She was still working relentlessly to cook, clean, and look after her family. Without a refrigerator, she had to go to market every day to purchase what she needed to make a meal.

Personal time and privacy were foreign concepts that had no meaning in my mother's life. Baba's life wasn't much different, except he was able to leave the little room and the dampened little courtyard and breathe a freer air. Night after night, tired from a long day at work, Baba came home with a big smile on his face and a melon, a bag of oranges or grapes, or a box of fantastic Persian pastries under his arms. This was his way of showing his love for his family, and his reward was seeing his children's faces shining with delight when he walked into the room.

Now that I look back, I realize the magnitude of the sacrifice Baba made that year by inviting me to live with them. He was hardly in a position to feed and clothe another person, I learned shortly after I moved to Tehran. With the little money that he made, my mother, as savvy as she was, could barely put enough food on the sofreh. "Leftovers" was not a concept we were familiar with.

An interesting thing happened in winter of 1971. My school was located in an area of Tehran called Heshmatieh, a long distance from home, and the roads from home to school were steadily ascending, which made walking slow. Because of the long uphill walk, I was regularly late for school. On this particular day I was running late as usual, and as I got closer to school I noticed a man impatiently pacing back and forth and looking at his wristwatch. I was used to seeing the school's custodian there, getting ready to close the gate at eight o'clock sharp, but from a distance I did not recognize the man in the suit. Once I got near the gate I found the man to be my father, apparently waiting for me. We exchanged a short greeting while he waved down a taxicab and asked the driver to drive us around for a few minutes. He used the short time to inquire about how I was doing. Before I could ask any questions, the taxicab was back in front of my school where my father gave me one hundred toomans, the largest amount of money he ever gave me, said goodbye, and left. (After an argument with my mother about how to spend that money, and despite Baba's opposition, I used twenty toomans and bought myself a pair of boots I had adored for a while, and cannot remember what I did with the rest. Baba thought with summer approaching, the boots were impractical and a waste of money. It turned out that he was right, of course.)

This was the first and the last time my father initiated seeing me for no other reason than to see me. And that was the end of Assad son of Banafsheh's role as a character in my life. Of all the things that my father did and did not do to and for me, the one I remember the most was the fact that he never once called me "my son."

❖*Chapter Thirty-One*

I finished reading the rest of the book *Papillon* by the time the train reached the station in Ahvaz. I was on my way to visit Kia in the city of Abadan. About a month before, miraculously and against all odds in a city as vast and as populated as Tehran, I happened to run into him out on a busy street. He had recently been transferred to Abadan and was in Tehran on official business. He was in a rush to catch a train and could not spend any time with me, but he gave me his telephone number at work in Abadan and asked me to give him a call if I decided to go and visit him.

I had completed the eighth grade and was taking advantage of the summer break, exploring Tehran, while at the same time assessing my situation at my mother's. As it turned out, living with my mother did not seem to offer any more stability to my life than when I lived in Mashhad. As generous and as kind my mother's family were to me, especially Baba, I knew that for many different reasons I did not belong there. The honeymoon of reuniting with my mother fizzled away quickly beneath the pressure of everyday life.

My mother and I were not able to bridge our two separate pasts and did not get along all too well. Not so much because I blamed her for the sordid life that I was left to lead in Mashhad, but because we had nothing in common. We were two strangers, linked by a thin and faded biological thread. I think of relationships as structures that people build together, and over time. With every shared day and every common experience, they add a new block to

241

the structure, henceforth expanding it and making it bigger and stronger. All that my mother and I had in common was a hazy and distant past filled with sorrows and a lot of unrealistic expectations.

As in the past, Baba was struggling to make ends meet, and I was clearly the straw that was added to an already heavy load on the camel's back. He felt bad for leaving me behind some years ago and was now trying his hardest, struggling to make it up to me.

At this point there was no place for me in Mashhad to go back to even if I wanted to, and I wasn't sure how much longer Baba would be able to afford to keep me here in Tehran. Running into Kia that day was a godsend in more ways than I could realize at the time—it opened a whole new set of doors for me that I did not even know existed. As the summer neared its end, I decided to take Kia up on his offer and pay him a visit in Abadan. He was elated when I called his work one day and quickly arranged for my train ticket.

This was not the first time that Kia had "coincidentally," if there ever is such a thing, run into me and consequently redirected my path in life. I remember one summer after he first joined the gendarmerie and left Mashhad, when I tried to lessen my burden on his mother, Momon Bozorg, by keeping away from her home for as long as I possibly could at a time so she wouldn't feel obligated to feed me. Since I had no particular place to go, I did what I did every summer: wandered the city streets and ate whatever I could find. One afternoon, tired and hungry, I was standing in front of a sandwich shop in Arg and looking at the mouthwatering sandwiches behind the glass window. Suddenly I heard my name. "Alireza? Is that you, dadosh?"

My heart fell. It was Kia. My first reaction was fear. I had been busted and was definitely going to be punished, I thought. Arg was no place for a small boy to be hanging around, he probably was going to say. I looked squalid, like a long-lost sheepdog. My skin had turned dark from being outdoors and in the sun, my soiled hair was overgrown in no particular style, and I stunk. Except for an occasional dip in the local creeks, I had not bathed or changed clothes for a while. Angry, not with me but with the condition that he found me in, Kia took me home. He was here on leave and could not have come at a better time. At home, he cut my hair down to my scalp to get rid of the lice and then took me to

242

hammom, where he paid the dellock and instructed him to double-scrub me. Momon Bozorg submerged my lice-infested clothes in boiling water and washed them good before I was allowed to bring them inside. By the time Kia's leave was over, school was about to start and I was blessed with having a place to live and the opportunity to go to school for another year. I am not sure if I would have gone back to the Rahimis' if I had not run into Kia on that fateful summer afternoon in Arg.

I got off the train at its last stop in Khorramshahr and met with Kia, who was standing on the platform next to the track jubilantly awaiting my arrival. The sparkling love in his eyes when he saw me stepping off the train reassured me that I was still his little brother. The feeling of belonging was always comforting to me. We took a taxi and crossed the bridge over the Karoun River that stood between the cities of Khorramshar and Abadan.

During the first few days after my arrival, Kia showed me around and proudly introduced me to all of his new friends—mostly bragging about how smart I was and how well I always did in school. He'd felt that way about me ever since we first met. I was a trophy that he was proud of showing off and claiming as his own. He was the type who celebrated all good things and victories, no matter how slight.

By the week's end he had made up his mind that I was going to go to school there in Abadan, a decision that his wife Morvareed also welcomed. She was an inexperienced and unassertive young woman who was afraid of her own shadow. In a city where she knew no one, and especially since Kia's work often took him out of town, it was reassuring for her to have me around. Kia had no idea how grateful I was for his timely manifestation in my life and did not have to twist my arm to convince me to go along with his plan. After I turned five, nothing in my life seemed to have any rhyme or reason. But when Kia entered my life, he gave it structure, showed me a path, held me accountable and above all, made me feel I mattered to someone. In addition to everything else, Kia was the wooden mold during the crucial years of my childhood when my personality was still like wet cement. I learned to respectfully fear him, like a son would his father. He was the only figure of authority in my life that I felt accountable to. Up until I was nine years old, Kia spanked and grounded me when I misbehaved or failed to complete my homework on time. Most of all, he pressed me to be mindful of a higher system of balance and justice. "Never forget, Alireza," he would tell me, "you will reap tomorrow what you sow today." Like most young people at the time, he was not religious at all but believed strongly in God. Persians believed that discipline was as necessary for a child as a stick was for a sapling. If a young tree was not tied to a stick during its early stages, there was a good chance it could grow crooked, they said. Kia had been my stick.

In a two-day trip back to Tehran, I picked up my school records and said goodbye to my mother and her family before returning to Abadan. Baba and my mother made no attempt to persuade me to stay, and who could have blamed them for that?

I knew very little of the city I was about to start my new life in. "Abadan is an industrial city," I'd learned from a small photograph in my elementary school textbook. In the photo, men in overalls and wearing round metal helmets carried lunchboxes as they entered a refinery plant. That was the extent of my knowledge of Abadan.

Chapter Thirty-Two

I believe that nothing in life is an accident, not even the slightest and seemingly least significant events.

The night before moving to Abadan, I had an emotionally packed dream in which I saw my old friend the ancient Greek standing on the deck of a ship. He was sailing away towards a beautiful sunny, blue horizon, waving for me to join him. I stood on a beach looking on while a storm approached from behind. Massive black clouds tinted with red were rapidly forming and darkening the sky. The man kept on signaling for me to get on board and sail away. At the time I did not know what to make of it, but like most of my other dreams in the past, I knew that it was a clue of what was to come and that I should be on the lookout for more clues.

Located in the extreme southwestern corner of the country, no other place in Iran stood so opposite and so far apart from Mashhad as did Abadan, and I do not mean only geographically. In Mashhad almost everything was owned and influenced by religion. Razavi Foundation, a 1,200-year-old religious organization responsible for managing Imam Reza's shrine and its assets, held the title to almost everything there, including most of the land that people's homes were built on. Baba always talked about the irony of the situation in Mashhad whereby the Persians did not own their own land and had to lease it from a deceased Arab. In Abadan, on the other hand, almost everything belonged to the refinery and was defined by oil and the British. The constant odor of processed petroleum hung in the sultry air, and the specter of a fairly recent British past lurked everywhere in the city. The culture, the way people spoke, the city's structural design and style and its infrastructure, they were all influenced by the British. English vocabulary, often taking a Farsi connotation, was embedded within every aspect of the local language and life.

The discovery of oil by the British in the nearby area in 1908 and the subsequent building and commissioning of the world's largest oil refinery in 1913 transformed this little island of sand and salt into a beautiful subtropical European-style paradise. The British modeled Abadan after one of their own cities and employed a diverse group of people, mostly of Western European descent, to work at the refinery. By the time Iran nationalized the country's assets in the Anglo-Persian Oil Company and expelled the Western companies from the oil refinery in 1951, Abadan was well established as a major city, albeit a small one. By nationalizing oil production, Iran essentially ended some forty years of a lopsided partnership with the British. Naturally the British were not at all happy with their eviction, but thanks to the Americans, the Iranians' new best friends at the time, they decided to forego taking any military action and move on. Incidentally, Iran received a total of $67,000 from the sale of all the oil that the British pumped out of the country for almost half a century.

With its warm climate and many unique attributes, Abadan was a popular vacation destination, especially during the Norooz holidays and in winter, when most of the rest of the country went into a deep freeze. Well-off Iranians from the north and rich Arabs from the neighboring Gulf States all flocked here to shop for European goods—smuggled in by the crews of oil tankers— and to have a good time. Abadan offered an exciting nightlife with its clubs and bars, not to mention a gated community of brothels.

About two-thirds of Abadan was comprised of segregated residential neighborhoods, designed and built by the British exclusively for the refinery's employees. Where an employee lived and what type and size home he was assigned depended on his position and rank at the refinery. The majority of the oil refinery's over thirty thousand employees were laborers, and they and their families all lived on the eastern side of town in Ahmadabad and its surrounding neighborhoods. The management, engineers, and other white-collar employees inhabited the western part by the Arvand River. Both sections were very well maintained and manicured by the refinery. The sun-drenched blue-collar neighborhood of Ahmadabad where Kia lived at the time, was vast, flat and symmetrically designed. Uniformly trimmed evergreen shrubs and scattered small trees marked the area. Almost all the homes there were enclosed by brick walls and seemed to have been built from only a handful of blueprints. Braim, the area where the managers lived, on the other hand, was a collection of prestigious quarters with luxury homes, green lawns, and romantic secluded streets shaded by rows of tropical trees and foliage. Life was very good here in Abadan.

A week before school reopened, I moved in with Kia and his wife and little boy. We all shared a rented room inside a single-family home. One early morning I left the house and embarked on enrolling myself in school. I was advised by Kia to try and return home by noon. The temperature here reached well above one hundred Fahrenheit by the afternoon, and with the high humidity, being outside was unbearable during that time.

It was not too difficult to find Ahmadabad's high school for boys since it was the widest building sitting by itself on the side of the main road. I walked in carrying my school records and birth certificate, ready to register.

"Can I help you?" a man sitting behind a desk asked without raising his head or looking at me as he continued writing on a file in front of him.

"Salam, aqa. I am here to register for the ninth grade, please."

"You are in the wrong school. The girls' high school is up the road by the circle," he said, still not looking at me. He was an average-looking man with a stern face, an authoritarian tone of voice, and of course, a mustache.

"I don't understand, sir," I said, while I knew perfectly well what he was doing. He was trying to tell me that my hair was too long and he did not like it.

"This place is the high school for boys only, and boys do not need to have any hair. When you cut your hair, you can come back here and see me."

Just before moving to Abadan I had spent one tooman getting my hair cut Beatles-style again, and now I had difficulty letting go of it. Long hair was very fashionable at the time amongst young men and teenagers, and I was at an age when fashion mattered to me greatly. As disappointed as I was for the way the man treated

247

me, I had no other choice but to comply, especially since I had assured Kia that I was capable of taking care of my registration myself. We had not lived together since 1966, and this was my first chance to impress him and show him how much I had grown up. I found the area's only barbershop in a nearby shopping strip and reluctantly walked in, took a seat, and waited.

When it was my turn, I asked for my hair to be cut with a number-four clip, a standard cut for elementary school boys in Mashhad. A number-four clip would have left my hair about two or three millimeters long.

"Are you cutting your hair for school enrollment?" the barber asked.

"Yes."

"Well, number four will not do it. I have to use a number-two clip or you will be back here again, wasting five more rials."

"But number two is almost like shaving my head!"

"Don't tell me, tell the school's assistant principal," the barber said, shrugging his shoulders.

I refused to have my hair cut that short, and the barber declined to cut it at any other length. According to him, that was the assistant principal's instruction. Frustrated, I stood up to leave when a boy much older than me, also waiting to have his hair cut, said that I had no other choice if I wanted to go to that school. He spoke bitterly of the assistant principal and said how detested the man was by many in the area, parents and students alike.

"The man is the school principal's brother-in-law so he thinks he owns the school and makes up his own rules. He thinks that he is God," the boy sneered. According to him, the assistant principal was responsible for a dozen or so suicides and attempts of suicide amongst the students at that school.

"Why doesn't anyone do anything about him?" I asked the young man.

"What can anyone do? Everyone around here is a laborer and without connections. If you piss him off, he will quickly report you to the secret police as a political agitator and you are finished."

While feeling angry and bullied, I came to my senses and realized that Kia's generosity of bringing me here was worth much more than my hair, and with that, I allowed the barber to do as he wished with my hair.

248

I will never forget my first day at the new school in the new city. Finding my classroom was easy since the one-story school building had no hallways and all the classrooms and offices faced each other around a rectangular courtyard. A large solid metal gate at one corner of the courtyard served as the school's main entrance for students to ingress and egress. The gate was kept locked while school was in session in order to prevent the students from leaving prematurely. There were only two places for students to be while in school: classrooms or the courtyard. Like all the schools that I had attended thus far, there was no gym or cafeteria or any other hall where students could gather if they were not in class. A narrow window in the school's bathroom was the main escape route for those who wished to skip a class. Over the years I witnessed numerous students getting wedged halfway in the narrow window and requiring assistance to get freed.

No sooner had I entered my assigned classroom than I found myself in the middle of a furious fistfight taking place between two boys, with everyone else circled around them and watching. The two boys seemed both older and bigger than an average ninth grader—often an indication that they had repeated some grades in the past. I noticed one of the fighting boys was wearing white bandages around both his wrists. I was told that he had just been released from the hospital where he had been staying for a failed suicide attempt. The brawl came to an end once the teacher entered the classroom and gave a good beating to the two involved students. The boy with the wrapped wrists later became one of my best friends.

I became popular in my class almost immediately, made a handful of friends, and received a few invitations to go to their homes after school, all on my first day. You see, during the introduction, I presented myself to the class as being from Tehran. After moving away from Mashhad, I relinquished my history with that city and never again claimed any ties to it. That included giving up the Mashhadian unpleasant accent. Starting that day, I told everyone that I was from Tehran, and my birth certificate, together with my last completed grade and my newly acquired accent, supported my claim. To be from the capital meant being sophisticated and a novelty.

I found the people of Abadan to be warm, friendly, happy, and very loyal to their own city. Perhaps the warm climate had something to do with their warm nature. I also found them to be the least religious folks of all the Iranians I had come to know thus far.

Besides oil, Abadan had plenty of date fruits and people who spoke Arabic, two things that up until then I had learned to associate with death and religion. In the religious city of Mashhad, Arabic was the official language of funerals and religious ceremonies and date fruits were the official snack of such events. Living in Abadan changed my perception about both. Here I learned that Arabic is also the language of love, music, poetry, and happiness, and the date fruit … I'll tell you about that later.

❖*Chapter Thirty-Three*

A few months after I started school in Abadan, we moved to Braim, the prominent and upscale neighborhood by the Arvand River. Kia had been on a waiting list with the gendarmerie for a unit to become available in that area since he had first transferred to Abadan. He and his wife Morvareed, like most fledgling middle-class Iranian married couples, had very little in terms of household goods and furniture; therefore, we were able to pack everything and move to the new location in one trip. We decided that it was best for me to stay in the same school in Ahmadabad and finish the ninth grade there. I commuted on public transportation; at the time it belonged to the oil refinery and was free to ride.

We moved into a room in a flat located in the Date Palm Groves section of Braim. The small residential neighborhood consisted mostly of condominiums, one-story flats, and a few houses here and there. It was originally constructed by the British for the refinery's bachelor, white-collar employees. The navy and the gendarmerie leased some units from the refinery and in turn rented them to their personnel at a subsidized rate. Enlisted men lived in flats and were given the option of renting one or two rooms, and the officers lived in condominiums or houses, depending on their rank and marital status. Like the rest of Braim, here too was a lush tropical heaven but with significantly more date palm trees.

Our flat was the last of six at the end of a quiet cul-de-sac, adjacent to Arvand River. Each flat had a common area at the end of the hall where there was a kitchen, a shower, and a bathroom for everyone to share. Kia was next on a waiting list for a second room once it became available.

Our little room had a window that faced the river, a ceiling fan, and a very small and shallow reach-in closet for us to hang our clothes. The fan was hardly a match for Abadan's sultry nights. There was a space under the window for an air-conditioning unit, but Kia could not afford one at the time. A folding military bed, a small monochrome television set, and a dresser for Morvareed to store her things in were the only furniture in the room. When it was time to sleep, Kia, Morvareed, and their little boy slept on a mattress on the floor, and I used the military bed on the opposite side of the room. For two or three nights out of a week Kia had night duty at the base or was gone out of town on official business and did not come home.

We lived in the last structure on Iranian soil on that particular spot. From our window I could see Iraq—the Persians' ancient and most loyal Arab enemy—on the other side of the Arvand River. The edge of the river's bank was less than ten or fifteen meters away from where I went to sleep every night. It was exciting and felt sophisticated to be living in Braim and on the border with a foreign country, albeit a less sophisticated one than Iran.

The Arvand is formed by the confluence of the Tigris and Euphrates near Basra in southern Iraq, and farther down the Karun, merging into it from Iran. The southern end of the river, where we lived, constituted the Iran–Iraq border all the way down to where the mouth of the river discharged into the Persian Gulf. In Middle-Persian literature and the *Shahnameh*, the name Arvand was used for the Tigris River. (The Shahnameh, the Persian epic *Book of Kings*, was written by the Persian poet Ferdousi in 1010 CE. The Shahnameh tells mainly the mythical and to some extent, Iran's historical past prior to the Islamic conquest of Persia. The work is regarded as a literary masterpiece.

The shark-infested Arvand was a major passageway for massive oil tankers, military, and cargo ships. The area on both sides of the river was believed to hold the largest date palm forest in the world, about seventeen to eighteen million palms. To most Iranians, history, even ancient history, mattered very much. The past offered them a sense of identity. I, however, hardly ever cared much for history and viewed it as a lesson learned and a river long gone. But still it was thrilling for me to learn that I was now living on the edge of lower Mesopotamia where some thousands of years ago Western civilization took its first baby steps.

Our small room offered little privacy to any of its occupants. Understanding that, on the evenings when Kia was home, I stayed out as much as possible to give him and his wife some private time together. And when he was not home, I was often forced to leave the room to escape the relentless nagging and crying of Farshad, my little terrible-two nephew.

The river's bank was our backyard and soon became the sanctuary where I spent most of my time when I was not at school or with my friends. During the day, a couple of immense shade trees—just outside our window, with their lush branches spread over our flat—extended to the edge of the river, providing plenty of shade for me to escape into. It was always a few degrees cooler out there than it was inside of our room. And at night, a lone light post, faintly illuminating a narrow spot on the river's edge, providing just enough light for me to study and do my homework. The area was out of the way and at the end of our secluded street, and because of that, hardly anyone ever came by there, especially at night. Since this was a border area, there was always a soldier assigned to patrol it, but almost always they chose to spend their shift talking to other soldiers at a camouflaged foxhole farther up the river. There were only a dozen or so soldiers on tour of duty there at any time, and I had become good friends with all of them.

Living next to the river was exiting. Not only did it offer peace and tranquility, it was also a source of food for me, but only for when I was desperately hungry and couldn't find anything else to eat. I learned from a local boy how to catch fish using a date-palm twig, a piece of string, a safety pin, and bread as bait. Sadly, the fish tasted as if they had been marinated in petroleum. Eating this oil-infused bounty was difficult but sometimes necessary; there was rarely enough food at home on account of Kia's limited income.

Kia often ate at the base, where the food was much better and free, before he came home. Naturally his wife was seldom obligated to cook any meals, and when she did, it was often during the daytime when I was at school and she made just enough to feed her and her little boy. After what Kia had done for me, I did not have the audacity to bring up the subject of food and eating with him. Having a roof over my head and being able to go to school was more than I could have wished for, and for that I was eternally grateful to Kia and his wife. He rescued me and brought me to this wonderful place where, besides its many other fantastic attributes, it was always summer. In Abadan a pair of sandals, a T-shirt, and a pair of slacks was all I needed to look and feel good. And for food, there were plenty of date palms around and many wonderful friends who were willing to share their bread with me.

What I was starving for the most, however, was not food. More than ever I yearned to be loved, and I am not talking about the kind of parental love that I used to wish for as a child. When I was little I used to pray for a nice couple to come along someday and adopt me as their child. Now at age sixteen, I yearned for the warmth of a woman's heart and arms to take sanctuary in. All of the old melancholy feelings of missing my mother were now replaced with longing for a woman—a woman whom I had never met but was certain I would.

Packed with the fervor of puberty and haunted by the specter of a sorrowful past that did not seem to wane easily, I ran to the secluded arm of the river's edge with every opportunity. I sat there for hours at a time, listened to music through a little transistor radio, daydreamed, and searched for an interpretation of the events in my short and perplexing existence. I sat there and craved the feeling of being loved and in love. Reading and writing poetry became a way of venting and dealing with the newly manifested emotional dramas that were taking place within me. My poetry was mostly about love and loneliness. Is there any other kind?

Persia had many things that uniquely identified her: rugs, cats, colorful culture, beautiful women with the most romantic eyes, hospitality, epic friendships, epicurean cooking, and a rich and ancient history. I, however, chose to remember it as the land of poetry. Writing poetry, besides being a national hobby for many, was also a common and inexpensive way of dealing with emotions and expressing oneself. Many sappy Iranian adolescents—just like me, hankering to be loved and to be in love, or suffering from the pain of a first unrequited love—often escaped to poetry. Soon some of what I wrote by the river's edge was being published in national periodicals and broadcast during a popular nightly local radio program.

It all began when my friend Parveez, without my knowledge, submitted one of my poems to a nightly radio show. The hour-long program was dedicated to playing contemporary music and reading poetry, very popular amongst young people. I was shocked when for the first time I heard one of my poems on the radio—not so much for hearing my own work, but because the host of the program mentioned my friend Parveez as the poet, dedicating his poem to a girl! I immediately got on my bicycle and pedaled as fast as I could to Ahmadabad to confront Parveez for stealing my work. Instead of apologizing, he accused me of being cheap and stingy. He argued since I had written so many poems, I shouldn't care if he used one of them to impress a girl.

"Are all the Tehranians as snobbish as you?" playfully asked a girl in a white cotton dress, standing a few meters up the river from me.

"Forgive me, are you talking to me?"

"Do you see anyone else here that I could possibly be talking to?" she said, smiling and shaking her head as if in disbelief.

"How do you know where I am from?"

"I just do!" she said, without looking in my direction.

The warm afternoon wind carried her pleasant scent in my direction and made me wish I could hold the source of it tightly in my arms. She was new to our neighborhood. About a month ago I watched her and her family moving in as my friends and I were playing a card game of trumps on the grassy ground across from her flat. Almost every day since they'd moved here, she had come to the river's edge to watch the sun set—perhaps also to escape the confinement of her family's small living quarters or perhaps, like me, to search for herself in the depth of the river's tranquility.

She usually sat silently on a large rock or stood leaning against a tree not far from where I always sat. Her eyes were often closed, and she was seemingly thinking pleasant thoughts as she occasionally sighed and smiled at no one in particular. An errant breeze swirled and danced around her, every now and then lifting the lower section of her light, floppy dress and exposing her shapely and seductive bronze bare thighs, sending a thousand volts of paralyzing electricity into my senses. She made no serious attempt to stop the wind from moving her dress about. I studied

255

her during the intervals when she closed her eyes. She did not seem to have the slightest worry about anything in the world.

Secretly, I celebrated her sudden and mirthful manifestation into my quiet corner. After a while I became so accustomed to seeing her there that in anticipation of her arrival, I often became restless and clumsy. And when she was late or did not show up at all, my thoughts frantically ran in every direction, searching for her, leaving me with little concentration. Unknown to her, she had become the inspiration for many of my new poems.

But I showed no interest and pretended as if I had not noticed her presence there at all. As a child I learned to feign disinterest in food and anything else that I felt people may be hesitant to share with me. As I grew older, I practiced not showing any interest when I found myself in the presence of a girl, no matter how badly I wished to be with her. I felt that sniveling for a girl's attention was just as pitiful as begging for a piece of bread. And now, somewhat blessed with my parents' good genes, I received plenty of attention from girls, and didn't need to behave in ways that were contrary to my personality.

"What do you write about, sitting here every day?" she asked.

"Have you been spying on me?"

"No, but I see you here all the time writing. What do you write about anyway?"

"Poetry."

"Oh, I love poetry! Who is your favorite poet?"

"Forouq."

"Oh my god, mine too!" she said with excitement as she moved closer. "Have you read her poem called 'The Girl and the Spring'? That is one of my favorites!"

"Yes."

"Can I read some of your poems?"

"No."

"Why not?" she asked, curving her lower lip, pretending to be sad and giving me a puppy-dog face.

By now she was sitting almost next to me. I could nearly feel the warmth of her body and her aromatic breath. It was clear from her complexion and accent that she was an Abadanian. Her slightly bronzed and moist skin resembled expensive imported silk, and her hair was cut just short enough to reveal her beautiful neckline and partially exposed shoulders. A set of perfectly aligned white teeth delightfully accented her lovely face every time she smiled. The pheromone of a woman is the most intoxicating fragrance that nature has to offer, in my opinion, and the air around me was saturated with hers.

After a while, she convinced me to read a couple of my poems as she quietly listened.

A drop of silence
The impish talkative little sparrows,
the ones that never stand still,
and nest just outside my window
in the dense branches of the tall tree.

The bullish immense river,
the one that never forgives
and rests just outside my window,
in the deep brink of history.

And my heart,
the one that never ceases
thumping in your name,
just outside your window,

all stood still
in anticipation,
as the gypsy wind,
ahead of your arrival
rushed your scent to the river's edge.

"My name is Sarah," she said after a long pause.
"I am Ali."
"I know. I'd asked my brother."

From that day forward we met almost every evening by the river's edge, and as the time went by and we grew closer, we ventured out into the beautiful and verdant Braim, taking long and romantic walks together.

257

Every Thursday evening the two of us shared a dish of ice cream and a bottle of soda at a popular neighborhood café called the Milk Bar before going to see a film at the refinery's romantic little alfresco cinema. The private movie theater sat back behind a row of date palms and shade trees in a secluded residential street near where we lived. It was open only one night a week and offered one showing, often featuring an American film. Iranians loved everything American; blue jeans, cigarettes, automobiles, and films were top among them. Thursday nights at the cinema was more of a social event, an excuse for the young people to get together, than anything else. Most people knew most everyone else there, since we all lived in Braim. Teenage boys and girls dressed in fashionable clothes arrived early and gathered in the beautifully landscaped open courtyard to wait for the show to begin.

I remember one night as we were returning home from the cinema, walking under a row of date palms, Sarah asked if I liked date fruits. I told her that they reminded me of death and religion and explained how on Fridays some people in Mashhad offered date fruits to the passersby at the gates of the cemeteries in hope of bringing salvation to the souls of their deceased relatives. She laughed at my story as she picked a ripe fallen date from the grassy ground, placed it between her teeth and with a mischievous glint in her large dark brown eyes asked me to bring salvation to her soul and try to take the fruit away from her without the use of my hands.

She ran in circles around the date palm, laughing and dodging me as I took her challenge and attempted to catch her and take away the fruit. Finally, out of breath, her face blushing and moistened with the humid air and perspiration, she leaned with her back against a date palm and pretended to surrender. As I placed my lips around the date fruit extending from her lips, she wrapped her arms tightly around my neck, sighed, and kissed me for a long while like I had never been kissed before. The sweetness of the creamy date fruit, mixed with the amatory fragrance of her hot breath and soft and tender lips forever changed what I thought of date fruits that night.

❖*Chapter Thirty-Four*

I dreamed again of my ancient friend. Once more, he was standing at the stern of a ship sailing away into a calm, clear horizon, waving for me to join him while behind me an immense storm was forming over land. With my mind's eye I saw the storm moving over Braim, darkening the sky, and eventually setting ablaze all the date palm trees and turning the Arvand River red. I was very disturbed and affected by the dream and could not get it out of my mind for a long while.

Over time I had become rather good at paying attention to and translating my dreams. What I experienced in the night as I escaped beyond the boundaries of my sleeping physical self often offered clues to my many pasts and probable futures. I was getting better at understanding the symbolism and the emotions that each dream represented, and I used them like a small window through which I could glimpse what was to come. This was a practice I learned from Momon Bozorg, who had translations for all sorts of dream symbols.

I had failed to pass the ninth grade on account of algebra. Now the end of my second year of ninth grade was approaching fast and I was not doing any better in algebra than I'd done the year before. Frankly, I was not trying very hard either. But I knew people who had failed a grade three times, and I did not wish to fall into that category.

Living in Abadan had introduced me to the navy, and I had planned to finish high school and become an officer in that service. I learned about the sort of life a naval officer led through a young man I met by the river's edge. He was a country boy from somewhere in western Iran, completing his two years of compulsory service in the navy here in Abadan. Like most young men from the countryside he was shy, simple, polite, soft-spoken, honest, and overly kind. He knew no one in Abadan, so I decided to befriend him. Ever since I was very little, I tended to gravitate the most toward those who I felt were alone and in need of a friend.

The young man was an eighteen-year-old *gomashteh* (a military servant) for a naval officer. It was mandatory for every young man coming of age to complete two years of service, either in the military or in one of the three corps. Those who did not have a high school diploma could not join the corps and had to serve in the armed forces. Some in the latter group were selected and given the choice to serve as a servant or a chauffeur in the homes of mid- to high-ranking officers. As degrading as it may seem to an outsider, many preferred being a gomashteh or a driver and living in a nice home to spending two years wearing military boots and uniform, living in a barracks and standing guard at odd hours, while carrying a bulky M1 rifle over their shoulders.

My friend Hussein was lucky. The captain that he was assigned to was a bachelor and spent most of his time away at sea or in Western countries, studying. Nevertheless, Hussein kept the large and beautifully furnished home of his boss organized and spotless at all times. During the day when it was the hottest, I spent a lot of time with Hussein at the captain's home, where we drank ice-cold sodas, snacked on European cheese and crackers, and played Dean Martin, Frank Sinatra, and Paul Anka records on the gramophone. I used to browse through the captain's photo albums from when he was studying at the military bases in the United States and picture myself being there. (The majority of the Iranian air force and naval officers were educated in the West.) The more time I spent at that house the more I was drawn to the idea of joining the navy and going to the United States, until the idea turned into a mission for me. Looking at the captain's photos taken in downtown San Antonio, Texas, I imagined myself standing in front of the Alamo and posing for the camera.

It was all suddenly clear to me. I finally understood the message behind the dream of the ship sailing away into the bright horizon. I was to join the navy and go to the United States, I was certain.

Immediately, I had an unstoppable yearning for the United State of America, like a person coming out of a long coma and remembering home. The photo album and the music at the captain's home seemed to have triggered something deep in my subconscious mind, a memory of some sort. From then on I devoted my every free minute to learning the English language, and I found that it came to me naturally. I carried a small notepad with me everywhere I went and wrote down any English word or phrase that I came across and began to memorize them.

But first I had to graduate from the ninth grade if I was to have any hope of finishing high school and becoming an officer in the navy. After the ninth grade, students were not required to take any algebra if they chose to major in literature, which was exactly my plan.

With final exams just over a week away, I worried as to how I was going to pass the algebra class and began my usual monolog with the creative force, the one I have when I feel lost and in need of direction. At the time I had myself completely convinced that I was never going to be able to learn algebra, no matter what.

A few nights later I had a dream in which Mr. Haydari—my algebra teacher—and the familiar ancient Greek man of my dream were in a room together, looking at me with friendly smiles on their faces. Suddenly the dream shifted scene and I found myself inside a prison or a cage of some sort, with Mr. Haydari standing on the other side of the bars, holding in his hand a large old skeleton key. There seemed to be a great deal of emotional emphasis placed on the key.

I took that dream as a clue and did something that I had never done before. That weekend I got on the bus and went to see my algebra teacher at his place of residence on the other side of town. He did not seem at all surprised to see me when he answered the door.

"How did you know where I live?" he asked after he invited me in and began walking across the small brick courtyard and into a living room.

"I asked around at school, aqa."

He was a quiet man with very little expression on his large, dark brown face or in his deep smoker's voice, as if something had died inside of him a long time ago. The reticent Mr. Haydari rarely looked anyone in the eyes as he went about apathetically teaching algebra, and he never smiled. A small tattoo on the back of his hand near the base of his thumb was the subject of many rumors and speculations amongst his students. It was very rare for a teacher to have a tattoo in a culture where, outside of some tribal societies, tattoos were often associated with crime, hoodlumism, and illiteracy. At school the common speculation was that he had been a political prisoner and tortured by SAVAK—the dreaded Iranian secret police at the time. Not too farfetched a scenario either, I must add. He exhibited some of the behaviors that were all too recognizable to those who knew someone who had been the victim of the secret police: staring out with hollow and lifeless long gazes and often being very quiet and into himself. Of course the truth could have been something entirely different, but for a group of teenagers it was much more romantic and exciting to think of their teacher as a former political prisoner than a common criminal. In that part of the world, like the rest of the Middle East, people saw conspiracy in everything, even when there wasn't any.

During my brief visit, I explained my predicament to Mr. Haydari and told him how badly I needed to pass his class in order to graduate that year and move on with my life. I did not come out and directly ask him to take any specific steps on my behalf, nor did I suggest a solution.

Sitting on a Persian rug on the floor across from me and looking down at a string of smoke escaping the tip of his filterless cigarette as it burned over a glass ashtray, he softly asked, "Let's assume you passed algebra this year, what are you going to do next year?"

"I am going to major in literature for the rest of my high school years, aqa, and would not need to take any more algebra."

He nodded his head in agreement and said, "I see. Well, all I can tell you is to do your best in the final exam. And this time do not write any more poems on your answer sheet! If you don't know the answer, just leave the space blank."

"Yes, sir," I said in embarrassment. Last year I filled the answer sheet with a poem about how little room there was for algebra in my future and how jealously algebra was sulking and refusing to let me go. I guess Mr. Haydari was not amused.

262

The week of final exams arrived, and in preparation I was studying day and night. Every evening I sat under the little light by the river and studied until the early morning hours or when I fell asleep. Sarah accompanied me every now and then, and we studied together. During final exams, outdoors offered the best studying environment to many high school students with small homes and large families. I remember when I lived in Tehran it was a tradition there for boys and girls to congregate in the neighborhood parks during the last weeks of school and study in little groups or alone.

While I was studying for the exams, my friend Parveez—the one fighting with the cut wrists at the beginning of the last school year—was preparing the logistics of cheating his way through the exams. I had several close friends in Abadan, but four of them were like brothers to me; one of them was Parveez. I had made a promise to Parveez to do whatever I could to help him get through the ninth grade. Since he was not interested in any tutoring from me, that meant only one thing: helping him cheat (except for algebra, for which he had made arrangements with another student).

Poor Parveez had difficulty with almost all of the ninth-grade courses. This was his third year in that grade, and his father had promised to kill him if he did not pass this time. He blamed his father, a brutal man who beat him regularly for his inability to grasp the subjects at school and for simply being a teenager. Parveez's head was out of form in several places from years of receiving blows from his father. Once or twice I was there at their home waiting for Parveez when his father lost his temper and cruelly assaulted him with his large fists and oversized knuckles. Ironically Parveez was the strongest and the most fearless boy in the entire school, and if I wasn't around to control him, he often got into fights with very little provocation. The assistant principal passionately disliked him and often referred to him as a calf or a "thick skin," both insults in Farsi.

I'd nearly made it through final exams, doing well in every test except algebra, and for that I did what Mr. Haydari asked me to do: worked and answered what I knew and left the rest blank. There was only one exam left, and after that I would be done and free for the rest of the summer. On the day of that last exam Parveez and I met outside of school, where we shared a cigarette and went over the logistics of having him copy my answers during the exam. Once inside I took a seat in a row of chairs set up out in the courtyard and Parveez took the one directly behind me. To escape the hot and poorly ventilated classrooms and also to have more space to spread the students apart, the school set up chairs in different parts of the courtyard during the final exams.

I finished the test almost immediately but stayed seated to give Parveez the opportunity to copy down my answers. The sound of the footsteps of the teacher who was monitoring the session periodically broke the silence as he slowly walked back and forth in between the rows of seats. At a distance the assistant principal stood by the school's main entrance with his usual stern face and puffed-out chest and kept an eye on everything. One could not help but get the jitters when forced to cross his path. The petulant man seldom had anything nice to say to anyone and easily became infuriated, often resulting in clobbering and belittling the poor soul who happened to be his victim at that moment. There was nothing more painful and humiliating to a young man than reluctantly swallowing his pride and controlling his rage while getting beaten or verbally insulted in front of his peers. I was glad that I would not have to lay my eyes on him for the next three months. In fact, I was contemplating changing schools for the next year.

Parveez kept on wiggling, hissing and whispering which way I should turn my body in order to give him a better view of my answer sheet while at the same time I was trying to remain inconspicuous and avoid drawing attention. Parveez was always that way, impatient and careless in every aspect of his life. All the hissing and wiggling finally got the attention of the teacher monitoring the session. As he walked firmly toward us my heart fell, thinking he was going to kick Parveez out and that would have been the end of him. His father would have used the incident as an excuse to kick him out of the house for good.

Instead, the teacher stopped at my seat, took my answer sheet away, and ordered me to leave the testing area. I protested that I had done nothing wrong and refused to leave when he charged me with cheating. He taught seventh grade in the afternoons and did not know me all that well. I was well respected by my own teachers and viewed as someone with integrity, especially by those who read my published poetry. This teacher thought that I was shifting my body to look at the answers of the boy in front of me. Parveez, knowing what would happen to him at home if he was to be kicked out, kept his silence.

I was confident that once my own teacher got the news he would vouch for me and fix everything; therefore, I was not worried until I saw the assistant principal come over. The teacher explained the situation to him as I protested and disagreed.

"That is not true," I said angrily.

"Shut up, you imbecile. We are not talking to you," the assistant principal snapped, pointing his finger at me without turning his head in my direction.

I did not like being called an imbecile in front of my classmates and thought about saying something in response, but then thought better of it. The two men whispered a few more words before the assistant principal came over, stood in front of me and, holding my answer sheet in his hands, he ripped the paper in my face and asked me to leave at once. Reluctantly I got up and walked away toward the school's main entrance, but not without grumping and calling the incident stupid. My remarks did not mix too well with the assistant principal's huge ego, and he began to follow me, challenging me to repeat what I just said. I ignored him, hoping he'd back off so I could go home and return to school in a few days and set the record straight. I was certain that my own teacher would allow me to retake the test.

The assistant principal was not that forgiving, however. He took any little remark by any student as a challenge to his authority. I had seen him in action many times before and knew where this was going if I did not leave at once. As was his style, he was going to make an example out of me in front of all the students who were still taking the test. I decided to deny him that pleasure and increased my pace. Agitated by my ignoring his demand to repeat myself, he ordered me to stop. Knowing, however, that my best bet was to leave the school grounds, I kept on walking as he followed more quickly behind me.

Unlike my friend Parveez, I'd had very few confrontations with the assistant principal during the past two years that I had been attending school there, chiefly because he was under the false assumption that I came from an influential family. We lived in the upscale neighborhood of Braim, and periodically he saw me arriving at school in a military vehicle, which was enough for him to reach such a conclusion. No one at my school had an automobile, including the faculty. In fact, in the whole area of Ahmadabad where my school was located there were very few people with an automobile. Since the military had a lot of clout in the society, it was natural for him to assume that I must belong to an important family in order to be chauffeured in a military vehicle.

The truth, of course, was something entirely different. I was given rides by a corporal friend of Kia's as a favor to him. During my second year in Abadan the refinery stopped operating its free public bus service, so I walked to school, despite the long distance. I had walked all of my life and was accustomed to it. After a few months Kia began to feel sorry for me and arranged for a corporal friend of his to give me a ride whenever possible. The corporal was assigned to drive the sons of an officer to and from school, a different school from mine. They lived in another section of Braim and had to drive past our neighborhood on their way to school. The driver agreed to take me to school after he had dropped off the two boys at their school, so long as I was ready at Alfi Circle when he drove by. He was not able to wait for me if I was not at the designated spot and he could not pick me up from school. Alfi Circle was only a short walk from our home, and I was very happy with the arrangement, but not for long—I was regularly tormented and put down by the officer's snobbish boys and decided to forego the humiliating free ride and walk instead.

I figured if I was going to get beaten by the assistant principal that day, I'd rather it take place outside and away from the view of my classmates. No sooner had I put my first step outside the school's partially opened gate than he caught up with me and smacked me on the back of my head and asked me again to repeat what I said inside. I continued to ignore him and kept on walking. The more I did not respond the more belligerent he seemed to become. He finally began calling me names and saying slurs that involved my mother.

The temperature was well above one hundred degrees that sultry day in early June of 1973. The assistant principal increased the intensity of his slaps against the back of my head and I kept on walking. Weighing less than one hundred pounds, I was small for a sixteen-year-old and no match for this man. But what I lacked in

266

physical stature I made up for in guts. If I sometimes chose to keep my silence or decided not to respond to a particular situation, it was because of a simple cost-versus-gain analysis that quickly took place in my head —not because of any fear. Throughout my entire life, I was rarely prepared to pay a price higher than the value of what I was about to gain.

Like an angry animal whose ego had been wounded, it seemed this man was not about to give up until I was on the ground begging for his mercy, and my blood began to boil as he intensified his verbal and physical assault. I remembered Parveez always talking about how he was able to take on guys twice his own size by surprising them and striking first. I watched the assistant principal's shadow on the ground next to me, and once I knew exactly where he was behind me, I suddenly turned around and delivered a punch right on his nose with everything I could muster. Blood began to shoot out of his nose as he screamed and called for help. I stood for a brief second and looked on as blood, like a large red peony stemming from his face, blossomed and spread on his white short-sleeve shirt.

I did not know then that at that moment I had sealed my fate.

A group of students led by the school's custodian rushed outside through the gate. I took off running like I had never run before as the group, led by the assistant principal and the custodian, took off after me. In an attempt to lose them, I ran through a few residential lanes—short, wide alleyways with houses on both sides—without any success, before running back to the main road. There was nowhere for me to run and hide. The main road ran on a straight line through a vast flat, open area with nothing to obstruct the view. One could spot a cat walking on the ground from half a kilometer away here. There were no pedestrians at that time of the day in the scorching heat, no shops or businesses nearby for me to run and hide inside, and no automobile driving by. My only hope was to try to outrun the mob and wish for a miracle at the same time as they got closer and closer.

Just as I was about to run out of hope and out of breath, a public bus pulled alongside me, slowing down as its automatic doors swung open.

"Jump in … jump in … hurry … hurry!" yelled the driver, signaling me with his hand.

I ran and grabbed the door handle and jumped into the moving bus. The driver shut the door and sped away, without stopping at any more stops.

"Who is trying to mess with my hometown boy?" the driver asked with his heavy southern Tehranian accent—a tough street style of talking.

I was running high on adrenaline and short of breath. "Thank you, *aqa*," I said to the driver and briefly explained the situation.

"Don't worry, champ, I'll take you home. We Tehranians have to watch each other's back in [qorbat], dadosh."

I had met this driver before and did not have a very good feeling about him, but today he saved my life, and for that I was grateful. He had been working this route ever since they unveiled the new busing system. In the past he had tried to use being from Tehran as an excuse to get close to me. I was very aware of his interest in young boys and impure intentions and felt uncomfortable riding on his bus; therefore, up until today, I had done my best to avoid running into him. Sometimes when I had no choice but to take his bus, he refused to let me pay.

Despite my opposition, the driver insisted on taking me straight home. The handful of young passengers on his bus seemed to enjoy the adventure and his cavalier attitude and did not object. With the passengers' blessing, he abandoned his route, and by way of a shortcut through some residential street and the refinery, he took me to Braim and dropped me off at Alfi Circle.

At home I hurriedly changed my sticky shirt that was soaked with sweat and humidity, told Morvareed where I was going to be, and bolted out. It would only be a matter of time before the authorities came knocking at our door, and I did not want to be there when they did. I ran and took refuge at the small gendarmerie outpost hidden behind a dense wall of trees just a few flats away from our home. All the boys in our neighborhood were friends with the young soldiers stationed here at the outpost. We all played soccer or trumps together when they were not on watch duty patrolling the river's edge. Coming from far corners of the country and being away from home, many of the gendarmes treated my friends and me as a sort of surrogate family.

268

Just as I expected, it wasn't long before two policemen arrived at the outpost and asked the guard to take me away to the police station. Morvareed, unaware of what was going on, had unknowingly informed the policemen of my whereabouts when they went to our home and questioned her. The young guard at the little makeshift gate clung tightly to his Uzi—an Israeli submachine gun—and asked the two men to leave the restricted area. The policemen, realizing that they had no jurisdiction there, gave up and left.

Soon after the policemen left, a group of my friends and classmates, including Parveez, arrived. They brought me a couple packs of Marlboro cigarettes—I had been smoking for a year now—and some cash that they had collected for me. According to them, the story of what had happened was changing by the minute and taking on epic proportions. I had become an instant hero.

About a week later, Kia—with the help of one of Momon Bozorg's relatives who happened to be a gendarmerie colonel and lived in Abadan at the time, a case of Johnny Walker Red, and a case of Winston cigarettes—was able to persuade the assistant principal to drop all charges against me. As part of the agreement, I was allowed back into the school, escorted, to retake the infamous test. Also as part of the agreement, I was to be expelled from all the schools in that city. I passed the ninth grade that year thanks to Mr. Haydari, my algebra teacher. He had given me a ten, the lowest passing score.

❖Chapter Thirty-Five

The bus stopped for a late lunch at a roadside restaurant next to a roaring river on the lush foothills of a rocky mountain. After a quick briefing by the petty officer in charge of our group, we got off the bus and made our way into the restaurant. The sound of the river water smashing and rolling over large boulders and the chirping of sparrows coming from the nearby bushes and dense treetops echoed in the air. The scenic narrow road winding around the mountain, together with the white smoke tinted with the smell of charred lamb kebab and burning lump charcoal escaping from the rooftop of the countryside restaurant, made for a fantastic image.

As soon as we took our seats in the large dining room inside the restaurant, a couple of young waiters began hurriedly bringing out plates of grilled kebab and steamed rice and placing them in front of us.

We were new navy recruits traveling on a charter bus to Gilan, a province in the Caspian Sea region, to attend basic training. Gilan was famous for its verdant forests, rich rice fields, masterful fishermen, and gorgeous women with skin the color of imported white silk.

For many in our group, this was their first time journeying out of their hometown and away from their families, and it showed. Persians by nature are very sentimental and family-oriented people, and this group of young men was no exception. All through the trip they took turns singing melancholy songs that spoke of separation and qorbat—foreign land.

The young man who sat next to me on the bus hardly spoke a word during the entire trip. He was last to board the bus at the station in Abadan and had no choice but to take the only available seat next to me. I watched him from the bus's window as he was trying to free himself from the arms of a large crowd of his relatives circled around him, crying and kissing him as if he was going to a war somewhere and was never coming back. I had Kia and my girlfriend Sarah accompanying me to the bus station.

I used to see this boy and his brother coming to our neighborhood, but we never spoke. They lived in another part of town and came to Braim regularly to visit their aunt. I could never forget his brother, who broke my nose about a year earlier in a brawl that wasn't even mine. I never saw his brother after that incident, but this young man continued coming back to our quiet little neighborhood on account of a girl he was infatuated with. He was always dressed in fashionable polyester bell-bottom pants, colorful shirts that were left mostly unbuttoned to expose his hairy chest and the little gold chain that always hung from his neck, and a pair of bulky shoes with even bulkier high heels. He stood for hours at a time under a tree across from the house where the girl worked as a live-in nanny, hoping to get a glimpse of her. Unfortunately for him, she never gave him the time of day. My friends and I thought he was crazy and left him alone. And now, here we were, reluctantly sharing a seat on a bus to our future.

After lunch, before getting back on the bus, almost all of us took our clothes off and jumped into the fast-moving river wearing only our underpants. I didn't know how to swim, but that didn't matter. It was in the blood of every Iranian boy not to waste a good body of water when he came across one; we had a compulsion to take a dip in it. I quickly realized that I was no match for the fast-moving river, after I got smacked around a few times and swallowed a good amount of water.

As you may have presumed by now, I had to forego my plan of becoming a naval officer after the incident with the school's assistant principal. That summer after school ended, Kia found me a job working at an attorney's office across from the courthouse. The attorney was very impressed with my performance and offered me a career in his office that he said would eventually lead into practicing law someday. But I had seen the reflection of my future in the mirror of my dreams, and what he was offering, as good as it sounded, wasn't it. I had already made my mind up. I was the Little

271

Black Fish, and the United States of America was the ocean that I dreamed of reaching one day. Working in a law office was not going to get me there.

Summer was almost over when I discovered through a sailor neighbor that I did not need to become an officer in order to be eligible to go to the United States. The navy also sent some of its enlisted men to study abroad. Once I learned that, I rushed to enlist. Those who knew me well advised against joining, reminding me of my independent personality and how incompatible I was with military life. But, like the Little Black Fish, I was deafened by my extreme desire to find a way to go to the United States. What no one knew was that ever since that night when the policeman found me sleeping on the streets of Mashhad and took me to my father's home, the feeling of Iran being my home died inside of me. It dawned on me that night that I didn't even have an address to give to the policeman when he asked where I lived—from that point on I felt like a stranger in a foreign land. To me home is a place where there is always someone who is happy to see you when you knock, no matter how late and how often. My conviction of not belonging grew stronger once I began reading and writing poetry. I found my thoughts and my ideals to be incompatible with my environment as a whole and that, more than anything else, strengthened my conviction to leave. I kept my plan to myself for many years, not because I worried people might try to change my mind, but for fear of being laughed at and ridiculed. At the time, traveling outside of the country, especially to Europe or the United States, was a dream only those with certain financial means could afford to have. And I seemed light years away from having those means.

"Sorry, the Imperial Iranian Navy does not enlist girls, at least not yet and hopefully never!" grumbled the balding, small-statured petty officer sitting behind the gray metal desk with a frown on his face as he chewed the corner of his mustache. The man obviously did not approve of my long ponytailed hair.

Gaping in astonishment, I turned my head to my right and looked for the reaction of a young officer working behind another desk in the corner of the registration office. He must have heard the petty officer's remark, because without lifting his head and with a wry smile across his face, the officer looked at the man, then at me as if waiting for my response.

Pointing to a portrait of a long-haired Arabian religious figure hanging on the wall behind the petty officer, I said, "So you mean to say that it's all right with the navy to worship foreign men with long hair but it's not all right to enlist a long-haired Iranian who wishes to serve his country?"

The young officer, clearly impressed with my quick response, chuckled and told the petty officer that he lost and ordered him to get a sign-up package for me. Looking at the religious portrait on the wall, the officer also reminded the man that he was not permitted to display personal artifacts in the office.

I was qualified to join the navy, and with my ninth-grade high school certificate, I could become a petty officer second class after completing one year of training. There was one big stumbling block, however, that could spoil my plan. The navy required a deposit of a large sum of money or a title deed to some real estate property as a form of guarantee that I would fulfill my contract once enlisted. My aunt Sarvar did not live here to come to my rescue, and even if she did, she did not have that kind of money to put up for me. Kia had no real property, and the amount of money that the navy was asking would have taken him at least twenty years to accumulate.

When I discussed the matter with Kia, he asked me how badly I wanted to join the navy. After hearing my answer, he said that God was great and that I should not lose hope. A few days later Kia, my old steadfast comrade-in-arms, came to my rescue once again. I remember the two of us driving in his used VW Beetle and meeting with a man somewhere far outside the city. There was nothing around but hilly and barren dry land sweltering under the scorching summer sun for as far as the eye could see. Kia and the man, an Iranian-Arab in traditional clothing, talked for a little while, pointing to a small hill in front of them as I waited by the automobile and watched. A few days later Kia came home smiling and handed me a title deed to that hill, which I gave to the navy, and enlisted.

The bus finally pulled off of the lush main road, entering a secluded camp and stopping on the top of the hill overlooking the entire place and the Caspian Sea. The Hassan Rood camp was

273

located halfway between the city of Rasht and the small port town of Bandar Pahlavi. I am going to like this place, I thought to myself. The beachfront camp consisted of undisturbed sand dunes, grassy patches of land here and there, a large oval-shaped field with paved tracks wrapping around it, and a total of four buildings.

The driver received instructions to drive down the hill where we were told to get off. A chief petty officer resembling Mr. Rahimi ordered everyone to assemble in columns in front of him on a concrete pavement next to the beach, with our suitcases on the ground next to our feet. I did not have a suitcase, just a small hand bag with some shaving tools and a white bottle of Old Spice, Kia's going-away gift to me, inspired by the drawing of a sailboat on the packaging.

Large white-topped waves, contrasting with the deep blue sky above, were chasing each other in and out of the sandy beach next to us. The moist and pleasant sea breeze felt good as it brushed against my face and hair as I waited with the others on the hot pavement under the sun. It seemed as if the Caspian Sea, together with the snow-white seagulls, had put on a welcoming performance in our honor.

"Listen up!" were the opening remarks of the enormous chief petty officer as he stood facing our group. He was larger and taller than any of us, and his words were delivered in a deep tone.

"I'd like to welcome you all to your new home, but before we get started here we need to do some housecleaning first. So listen very carefully and do exactly as I say. I want you all to reach inside your suitcases, pockets, and bags and pull out any utensils, salt and pepper shakers, ashtrays, and anything else that belongs to one of the restaurants where you were served meals during your trip here."

What a crazy man, I thought. Why would anyone want to steal salt and pepper shakers and bring them here where they know they have no use for them? I did not at all appreciate the fact that he assumed we were all a bunch of thieves.

"Obviously not only are you dumb but also deaf," he said to the group as he repeated his original command once more.

To my disbelief, one by one many in the group reached into their suitcases and pockets and pulled out all sorts of things, the very things that the chief named on his list—ashtrays, salt and

274

pepper shakers, etc.—and placed them on the ground in front of them.

"Now, I want you to reach into your pockets again and this time empty out everything, including any knives, brass knuckles, and any other thing that hoodlums carry when they are out on the streets, and place them in front of you on the ground."

Suddenly the sound of metal hitting the pavement began to come from every direction. Fearing they were somehow going to be implicated for possessing knives and whatever else they deemed to be illegal, many of the new recruits were discreetly pulling different objects out of their pockets and disposing of them away from themselves.

"Now pick up your cigarettes, your lighters, and wallets and put them back in your pocket; everything else stays on the ground for now. My name is Master Chief Petty Officer Mohammady. I have just transferred here from the army, where men work for their salaries, on a special request by the navy to come here and turn you ladies into respected sailors to serve in the Imperial Iranian Navy. I am here to crush you into a powder, then mix you with discipline and mold you into a military man that your mother and your country could be proud of. To all the mommy's babies present here, I have bad news for you: Your mothers do not live here, and you are mine now. You will get up with the sound of the first bugle call and go to sleep with its last. Here you will clean your own toilet, wash your own clothes, sweep, mop, and wax your own floors, and obey whatever command comes out of my mouth and the mouths of the petty officers in charge of your company. And those of you who are already contemplating escape and returning back to your mommies, I am sure that on your way here you noticed there is nothing around but forest, sand, and the sea. There is nowhere for you to run away to."

I was astonished by the number of salt and pepper shakers, eating utensils, ashtrays, and knives scattered on the pavement as we left for the two barracks buildings on the other side of the oval-shaped field. Mostly, however, I was humbled by the chief petty officer's cleverness as I discovered my own naiveté.

About an hour or so later, we were taken on military buses to a naval technical school in the town of Bandar Pahlavi where we received our military haircuts and showered. As I was waiting in the hammom's long and narrow steamed-up corridor for a shower to become available, I noticed Masood, the young man who sat next to me on the bus. He was the last one coming out of the barbershop, rubbing his now bare head in disbelief. Despite my aversion to his brother for breaking my nose a year earlier, I cast a friendly nod of acknowledgment his way as he took his place at the end of the line and waited. He did not look so ferocious now without his afro and mustache. In fact I even felt sorry for him, standing there looking vulnerable and alone. In memory of Braim, my home for the past two years, and he being a part of it now, I moved to the end of the line and kept him company.

Back at Hassan Rood camp, we were given uniforms, boots, mattresses and other sleeping gear, and assigned to barracks. Masood and I ended up in the same barracks and decided to bunk together.

Within the next few days more buses arrived delivering more new recruits from other parts of the country. We were told that heretofore our class was the largest to attend boot camp in the history of the Iranian navy.

Right from the start, the students, as we were referred to, for the most part clustered together according to their place of origin and the tongue that they spoke. For many of them Farsi was their second language. At the beginning—when the feeling of melancholy and missing home ran high amongst some of the students, especially the younger ones—staying in groups that spoke the same dialect offered some comfort. In addition to Farsi, the official language of Iran, we had almost every other tongue that was spoken in the country represented here in the camp: Urdu, Turkish, Kurdish, Arabic, Armenian, Gilak, and many other sublanguages that were an extension of Farsi. It was very rare to find two cities in Iran where people spoke with an identical accent. At the time, only less than half of the population of the country was Persian.

I, on the other hand, had no regional identity and mixed with everyone. I was a Tehranian Mashhadi from Abadan who because of Baba had a fondness toward the Turks. Growing up in Khorasan Province amongst many folks from the neighboring Baloochestan Province also brought me close to those for whom Urdu was their main language.

276

Soon Masood and I became best friends. He was a quiet and reserved young man in addition to being unusually polite. Unlike most students from Abadan who were loud and jubilant by nature and who listened to Bandari music, an upbeat and rhythmic dance music unique to the southwestern shores of Iran—Masood enjoyed listening to love songs by Googoosh, an iconic female singer worshiped by many adolescents, including myself. He revealed that he was in love with the girl who was a nanny in our neighborhood and had joined the navy because of her. He was hoping to be stationed in or near Abadan after his training so he could ask the girl to marry him. Now that we were the best of friends, I too shared my life story with him and revealed that I had only joined the navy because it offered the best opportunity to leave Iran.

Masood's parents wrote to him regularly and sent him dried edible goods, prerecorded music cassettes, and money, and he shared everything with me. We were not going to receive any salaries until we successfully completed basic training, so at the time I did not have a rial to my name. The only thing I needed any money for was to purchase cigarettes, and fortunately I had made a few friends who were willing to share theirs with me. None of my relatives besides Kia knew where I was at the time and even if they did, I don't think they would have sent me any money.

At the end of each day, just before we were released to go to the mess hall to have dinner, the chief petty officer made some motivational speeches and recognized some folks for their performances. In one of those gatherings, he called up a young man and praised him for finding a wallet and turning it in. "The navy needs good men like him. I would not be at all surprised if he gets to be selected to go to America or England right after boot camp."

A few days later Masood approached me with an idea that he believed could help me secure a spot on the list of those who were going to be sent to America for schooling. He handed me his wallet and told me to turn it in and say that I had found it. I thought it was a brilliant idea and thanked him. I took the wallet to the chief petty officer after Masood removed most of his money from it.

That evening as we assembled in front of the mess hall listening to the chief speak, Masood smiled at me as the two of us anxiously waited for the chief to praise me and announce my name

277

as a possible candidate to be sent abroad. Instead, at the very end of his speech, he called on Masood to go up to the platform. As Masood made his way through the columns of students, the chief went on saying how the navy did not need incompetent men who could not hold on to their own wallets! Once Masood reached the platform, the chief showed him the wallet and asked if it belonged to him. Masood nodded yes, by now his head hanging in front of him as he faced the crowd. The chief then angrily slapped Masood on the face a few times with the wallet, before telling him in disgust to get lost.

The chief forgot to mention my name, which was probably just as well, under the circumstances.

While boot camp was difficult in many ways, especially for those for whom this was their first time away from the comfort of their homes and their mother's unconditional love and care, I enjoyed it very much. For the first time in my life I was receiving three meals a day, had a little metal locker with my name on it, and a bed to sleep on at night without apprehension. I had also become a member of a large band of brothers whom I grew to love dearly.

❖ *Chapter Thirty-Six*

Wearing my newly acquired winter black uniform, a round white cap with the words "Imperial Iranian Navy" stamped in gold on a black ribbon wrapped around its base, and a pair of shiny black shoes, I proudly walked through the gate of the naval technical school in the small seaside town of Bandar Pahlavi. As if I were an admiral with the entire Iranian navy under my command, I was feeling bigger than life and covered with goose bumps.

Perhaps for many in a similar situation this would have been an ordinary event, but for me it was huge in more ways than one. Being here now meant that a long and difficult road had finally come to a good end and the future and the adulthood for which I had been longing all of my life was now just around the corner. It meant that I was a man of my own now and no longer needed to hesitantly ring anyone's doorbell for a place to sleep for the night or reach on anyone's sofreh for a piece of bread that I constantly felt I was not entitled to. More than anything, however, I saw walking through the gate of this naval school wearing my handsome uniform and smelling like Old Spice cologne as a slap on the face of my father, the man who in my mind stood to symbolize everything that was wrong with humanity. Hope is the most wonderful remedy for an afflicted soul, and I could not have been more hopeful at that moment.

The relatively small military school was manicured and nicely landscaped, resembling a French palace. At the center of the compound was an oval-shaped grassy area the size of a soccer field, marked by a large flagpole. A wide blacktopped track encircling the field was used for marching and going from one building to another. All the classrooms, administrative offices, and barracks were constructed around the oval-shaped field. The jewel of the place, however, was an overpowering, contemporary multistory building that served as the headquarters. The building sat on high ground all by itself overlooking the entire complex and the Caspian Sea.

The headquarters building evoked feelings both of pleasure and of fear amongst the mostly adolescent students. More than a few dozen attractive young civilian women worked there in various offices. Throughout history Iran has always been famous as a land of beautiful men and women. It was a pleasure to watch those civilian women go in and out of the building or cross the campus wearing the latest in fashion and showcasing their seductive and heavenly bodies as their hair danced with the gentle sea breeze. Young, handsome officers, educated in Western Europe and the United States, walked at their sides, complementing the women's beauty and making the place appear even more romantic.

All that beauty was in stark contrast to the mysterious and dreaded school commander, who also had his office in the headquarters building. The commander was a stumpy man of average height with skin darker than the average Iranian. He had bushy black eyebrows and thick black hair just above his cheekbones and extending to his ears and around his dark and turbid eyes. We were led to believe that he was always watching our every move, and very few students ever dared to look up at the commander's all-glass office on the top floor as they hurriedly ran from one building to another. One could never be sure when he was going to be summoned there for not walking in a proper military manner or chewing gum or whatever else irritated the commander. I had the displeasure of looking him in the eye once and received in return a few lashes on my face from his leather whip; it was not at all pleasant.

Life here was like life at any other military school: a lot of running, marching, saluting, standing guard, mopping and waxing floors, cleaning the latrine, doing laundry, being bullied by the more senior students, and attending classes. Five and a half days a week we were in classes, learning mostly English. Guard duty was my least favorite activity here, especially if my shift happened to fall after midnight. Carrying around the heavy and bulky American-made M1 rife during guard duty was not a joy either, especially when I had to climb up an observation tower with it. I often prayed that I would never have to go to war with an M1 as my weapon. Weighing around forty-six kilograms (about one hundred pounds), I was no match for that rifle.

The highlights of my stay at the naval school were attending English classes—on account of my teacher, a lovely young lady educated in New York City—and eating at the mess hall. There I was introduced to all sorts of fantastic Persian cooking, dishes that I had mostly only heard of heretofore.

My entire company had been assigned to a beachfront barracks here after boot camp, and once again Masood and I were bunking together. Almost once a week a list of names was announced by our company petty officer during the assembly to prepare to leave for the United States or Great Britain. Every morning I woke up with the excitement of imagining that today was the day I was going to be called to receive my orders to go to the United States. Ironically, my friend Masood was here for less than two weeks before he was sent to the United States. He did not get the chance to learn any English here, and I feared that was going to work against him in the U.S. Many students failed the English school in the United States and were sent back home after only a few months. Time was actually working in my favor here. With every day that passed without my being selected to go abroad, my English became better, which eventually proved to be a blessing. (In life, there are no accidents. Even the most seemingly insignificant events, like stopping for a brief moment and saying hello to a passerby or asking for directions, have their significance and impact our lives somehow, somewhere farther down the road.) Only a small percentage of the students were selected to study abroad, and I was hoping to be one of them soon.

Incidentally, my friend Parveez also joined the navy a few months after I did and was now in Hassan Rood completing boot camp.

On the weekends we were free to leave the base, unless of course we had guard duty or for some reason had lost the privilege to leave. Those who were from the nearby towns or even Tehran went home for the weekend, and the rest stayed in town or went to the city of Rasht and spent the night there going to cinemas or night clubs and getting drunk.

For a while I did not have any money to go anywhere and stayed in Bandar Pahlavi, mostly window shopping or hanging around a popular park by the river with friends. In the early evening hours the park was always packed with winsome girls and young sailors in uniform. There was often music playing from loudspeakers mounted on the tall trees all over the park, enticing the young hearts to hanker for love. Popular love songs by contemporary artists such as Googoosh, Sattar, and Ebi blasted throughout the evening, making tender and inexperienced emotional adolescents want to take out their heart and hand it to the very first member of the opposite sex who crossed their path. Boys and girls, men and women, young and old, they all strolled up and down the picturesque park in pairs and in groups, chatting, laughing, timidly sharing gazes as Googoosh poured her heart slowly out, like fairy dust, over the daffodils, the tulips, and the many young souls who were there to celebrate life and living.

The very first weekend after the navy opened a bank account for me and deposited my first pay, I bought a couple boxes of walnut cookies and a jar of orange-blossom jam—popular gifts from that region—and got on the first bus to Tehran to visit my mother. I had not seen or heard from her for a long time.

I knew that she had moved from Nezamabad, her old neighborhood, but did not know where to. From the bus station in Tehran I took a taxi to Shoosh Square, where I knew Baba had been operating his own tailor shop for a year or two now. He was flabbergasted when he saw me walking in wearing a navy uniform. We hugged and kissed before Baba locked up the shop and excitedly took me home, just a half a block down the street. My mother and Baba were renting one very small room in a large multi-family house and now had five children.

As usual, my mother cried and shook her head in sadness and regret, as if remarking on how much I had grown without her being there to see. From then on, I made regular weekend trips to Tehran to visit my mother and each time I made sure I had a few boxes of goodies under my arms for my brothers and sisters. Baba was very proud of me.

282

One early April day in 1974 our drill petty officer announced a list of names that were selected to go to the United Kingdom. The list included my name.

"No! It is a mistake! I am supposed to be going to the United States," I disappointedly exclaimed.

"Sorry, Admiral. Maybe the navy did not receive your memo!" said the petty officer, and with that everyone chuckled. Our gay petty officer's overly feminine tone and posture only added to the hilarity of his reply to my sudden outburst.

Once the assembly was over, he released everyone except for me. I thought I was going to have to do some pushups or run around the oval field for a few hours because of my outburst. I was punished regularly and more than anyone else in my company, mostly for questioning the purpose of certain orders or speaking what I perceived as "the truth." All the punishment that I received came from the senior students, however. Our company petty officer never punished anyone. He was a sensitive and kind man and acted more like a mother hen than a boss when it came to his company. I was not surprised when instead of punishing me he comforted me by pointing out how privileged I was to be chosen to go anywhere, adding that he had never been out of Bandar Pahlavi. He knew how badly I wanted to go to the U.S.—he had been listening to me talk about it ever since I arrived here.

The news spread quickly, and I was being congratulated by all who knew me. But I was disappointed and unhappy. In my dreams I had seen myself many times taking photographs inside the hollow tree in front of the Alamo in San Antonio, Texas. A few days later I was informed that I was no longer on the list to go to England. As much as I wanted to go to the U.S., the news was not only embarrassing; in a way it was also disappointing.

As it has always been in the story of my life, every time I felt like I had either missed a bus or been kicked out of one and was depressed about it, shortly thereafter a limo showed up for me instead. Exactly two weeks after I was told that I was not going anywhere, my company petty officer, swaggering his hips and shoulders and smiling ear to ear, came to where I was standing guard and excitedly said, "Admiral Golmakani, I have good news for you, sir! Looks like the navy finally received your memo, because you are going to America, my dear."

❖Chapter Thirty-Seven

I arrived at the Tehran airport long before my scheduled departure time, accompanied by my mother, Baba, and my brother Mehdi. This was the first time any of us had been to an airport. The thought of being in such close proximity to airplanes was thrilling and glamorous.

I was holding tight in my hand a cherished envelope containing my traveling documents, including my passport and a set of airline tickets to the United States of America. Never before had I possessed anything more precious and more meaningful to me. They were evidence of my conviction that my life is what I think and imagine it to be. That I and only I am in charge of my destiny, regardless of any circumstances.

At age seventeen I could not get any more sophisticated and lucky than that. It wasn't every day that an ordinary person, especially at my age and with my background, was gifted with the opportunity to travel outside of the country, especially to the United States. And I owed it all to Kia and Momon Bozorg.

At the time it was the ultimate dream of every young Iranian that I knew to visit the United States someday, the land of our surrogate culture. There were even movies made about that very subject. Being a nation of predominantly Aryans or Indo-Europeans, many Iranians identified more with their ancestors in the West than with their neighbors in the Middle East. The West, the United States in particular, had a strong footprint here, especially in the city of Tehran and the southwestern regions of the country. The most important aspect of the Western influence on Iranian culture could be found in television and cinema. Syndicated

American television shows, cartoons, and soap operas accounted for a high percentage of the national television's total programming. There was also a separate American television station in Tehran that regularly broadcast in English. People here grew up in front of their television sets watching *The Days of Our Lives, Ironside, Mission Impossible, The Fugitive, Little House on the Prairie, Flipper, The Six Million Dollar Man*, and hundreds of other similar shows. John F. Kennedy and Muhammad Ali were national heroes here, and some major avenues in the capital city were named after famous American presidents. Children, those who had access to television, were growing up as Americans without realizing it. The Iranian military was equipped and trained mostly by the Americans. The majority of air force officers and all of the naval officers were educated in the U.S. No other people in the Middle East identified as strongly with the Americans as did the middle- to upper-class Iranians.

My mother had hardly uttered a word all morning long. Her silence was her surrender to the circumstances and, as she believed, God's will. Her eyes were red, indicating that she had been crying and was now all out of tears. She stood against the wall, hands hanging in front of her, head tilted downward, looking at me and sighing every now and then. The last time I saw that particular posture and expression was on that evening in the winter of 1962 when Baba told her that returning me to the foster home I had just run away from was the right thing to do to.

"You are not coming back, are you, Ali joon?" my mother asked sadly and rhetorically.

She caught me off guard with her question. I looked at Baba as he briefly looked at me and then looked down, as if he already knew the answer.

Not knowing what to say, I looked into my mother's sad eyes and said with a faint smile, "I love you, Mom, and will always love you. You know that, right?"

"I had a dream the other night that you were a white dove, flying out of a cage, spreading and showing off your beautiful wings as you flew away," said my mother before she burst into an intense cry. "I am so sorry, pesaram. I know that I was not a good mother to you. I know that God will never forgive me for that, but I hope that someday you could, Ali joon. I wish you could know

285

how much I too suffered for not having you and Shahnaz in my life."

"That is enough, Soory. You are embarrassing Alireza," Baba said in a low but firm tone. I was shocked to hear the name of my lost sister, Shahnaz, come out of my mother's mouth in front of Baba, for he was not supposed to know of Shahnaz. I guess after all the years they had spent together, there were no secrets left between the two of them.

I hugged my mother and placed a kiss on her wet cheek and asked her to be happy for me. "The past belongs to the past, and if it is not pleasant, I am never going to look back at it and you shouldn't either," I told her. "The important thing is that you are my mother and always will be and nothing will ever change that."

The time finally came for me to say goodbye to this family that I so briefly known. My mother and Baba knew deep in their hearts, as I did, that these goodbyes were the closing acts of our intertwined lives' final play. I was my mother's only memento from her first marriage, and now she could forever put away the painful memories of that life. She no longer had to look at me and find the reflection of her heartless first husband in my face.

As I walked away, my heart pounded with the bittersweet knowledge that I, too, was soon to close one chapter of my life and start a new one. I had already packed everything unpleasant about my short life in Iran into a make-believe bag that I left by the door as I walked out of the terminal. This bag included any thoughts of ever becoming a son to my father who was now a wealthy and influential businessman. The pleasant memories and all the things I loved about that land I kept in my heart and took along with me. Most of all, these were the memories of all the wonderful solacers, large and small, who held my hand and walked with me from one point to another when the road of life seemed lonely and cold. Now, just like the Little Black Fish, I could feel the ocean on the other side of the airport's terminal waiting for me.

Epilogue

❖

I remember that after Kia moved away and Momon Bozorg and I were alone, she put out the lamp shortly after dark to save on kerosene and we went to bed. When she was in the mood, to help both of us fall into sleep, she would tell a story, some long enough to stretch three to four nights. All of her stories seemed to underscore two main messages: hope and integrity. The protagonists of her stories all did the right thing and were triumphant in the end, much like the characters in Fardin's cinema.

Like all of Momon Bozorg's stories and most of the films I grew up with, as improbable as it seemed when I was little, the story of my childhood too had an unbelievable ending. Everything, more or less, turned out as I envisioned it would. The path of my life took me from the little elementary school on the dusty and barren foothills of the Hezar Masjid Mountains in Khorasan Province to the College Conservatory of Music on the seven hills of Cincinnati, Ohio, where I received a degree in fine arts. It took me from waiting by the army depot's trash in Mashhad for the soldiers to finish with their meal so I could pick out their discarded bread for my dinner, to waiting for a table at a romantic restaurant on the beaches of Maui. From Maydoneh Bar in Mashhad to the sushi bars of Washington, DC. From selling Alaska ice cream in the quiet residential streets of Mashhad to co-owning a chain of frozen yogurt shops in the Midwestern U.S. From sleeping on the sidewalk across the street from my father's home and dreaming of someone uttering my name with kindness, to singing lullabies and watching my cherished children asleep in my home in the suburb of Dublin, Ohio. Everything that I yearned for as a child I came to have as an adult: a home and a family of my own and all the resources that I needed to take care of them and be the best father I could be—as I promised I would if I ever made it to fatherhood.

Almost four decades have now passed since I first boarded a flight destined for the United States. The start of the Iranian Revolution in 1978 brought to an end the last chapter of my life as an Iranian citizen. Up until then, even though I was living in the

United States, I was still a member of the Iranian navy and lived and attended school at various military bases around the country with my Iranian navy buddies. Due to the circumstances, my experience with the United States at that time was still very limited and narrow.

Unlike some of my friends who decided to stay in the U.S. because of the Iranian Revolution, I was never going to go back, revolution or not—a decision that I had made and planned for back when I was in high school. This is not to say that I never contemplated the idea of going back; indeed I did. I had a lot of wonderful memories of Iran and many dear friends there, but there were just way too many horrid ghouls lurking in my Iranian past, making it difficult for me to return there and have a normal life.

Do you remember my math teacher from my first year of high school? Well, besides wanting to leave my painful past behind, another reason I did not wish to go back was because of people like him. A sizeable segment of Iranian society was comprised of uneducated people who thought like he did. Their narrow and fanatic way of thinking and viewing the world, perceiving anything and anyone different as a threat, was disturbing. I could not imagine myself living amongst people who in my view lived in a dark and narrow mental tunnel. At the time, the government of Iran did a good job of keeping a leash on them and making Iran livable for all Iranians, but the news clips coming out of Iran in late 1978 and throughout 1979 were not promising at all. The leashes seemed to be coming apart and the wolves of extremism, hungry for blood, were on the loose. Long before I left Iran I had dreams about a dark and bloody storm forming over Iran and destroying and setting the country ablaze. I had already had my share of dark clouds and needed no more.

During Christmas of 1978 I celebrated a new beginning as a civilian in the United States. A wonderful American family in Cincinnati, Ohio, took me proudly into their home as their son, treated me as if I were a Persian prince, and helped me start my new life. And it did not stop there. In this land of solacers, almost everyone I encountered, even perfect strangers, immediately and without my asking offered me a helping hand and opened a new door for me. I was overwhelmed by the outpouring of kindness and the degree of humanity I was experiencing here. I was loved

288

and tended to as if I were everyone's long-lost son or brother who had finally returned home. What made it all so magnificent was the fact that everyone treated me as if I were some precious and exotic gift from the great land of Persia and better than they were, instead of the other way around. Pity or piety or hope of being rewarded in heaven someday did not seem to be in the minds of anyone here as they extended me their helping hands.

I felt as if suddenly I had inherited all sorts of brothers, sisters, and mothers, all at once. I remember during the Iranian hostage crisis I was working as a bartender at a very popular night club in Cincinnati. One very late night as I was leaving work and walking to my car, I found three young men, seemingly drunk, waiting for me in the parking lot. I could tell from the look on their faces that they had no good intentions. One of them asked if I was an Iranian, to which I answered yes. The three of them exchanged gazes, and the one who was vocal began calling me names and making threats as he inched his way closer. "Why don't you let our people go?" he asked angrily. I wish I could, I wanted to say to him, but he was drunk and not in the mood for reason. I suddenly found myself cornered with my back to my car at way past two in the morning. Suddenly two male customers I recognized from the club showed up and asked if I was all right, and before long I had a dozen young men and women standing by my side. The situation took a turn when a beautiful woman in a fashionable disco dress and high-heel shoes walked to the man who seemed to be the angriest and said, "I am an Iranian too, so what are you going to do about it?" And soon almost everyone around me was saying, "Me too. I am an Iranian." It did not take long for the three outnumbered men to get in their car and drive away. The kind lady in the disco dress apologized to me as she placed a long and warm kiss on my lips while everyone cheered. As I drove home, touched by what transpired in that parking lot, I could not help but cry and feel very good about life and people.

What I immediately liked the most about the United States was the level of optimism and joy that existed here. Unlike my birthplace where national lamentation days—often for ancient and foreign events and entities—far exceeded the number of celebration days, here people use every occasion as an opportunity to celebrate life, even when the occasion is to commemorate death. Optimism is to fear as light is to darkness, I believe.

Baba used to compare America (most Iranians referred to the United States simply as America) to Noah's ark. He used to say that God had purposely set aside that land to be discovered later when humanity needs a place free of its tangled past to begin anew. A place free of all the ancient ghosts and tribal differences that have divided mankind for far too long. Baba, like most Iranians back then, was in love with the United States and its concept. He believed that eventually all sorts of people from all over the world would leave their differences and their ancient animosities behind on the shores of their motherlands and climb aboard this ark and sail away together toward a better and different future. And right he was. Many Persians, Arabs, Jews, Kurds, Turks, Armenians, Greeks, Spaniards, Irish, British, Italians, Koreans, Russians, Polish, Germans, French, Africans from all African countries, Latin Americans, Chinese, Japanese, Pakistanis, Indians, Cambodians, Vietnamese, and on and on, now call this ark home and themselves Americans. The same folks who back in their motherlands were forbidden to utter the name of a certain ethnicity group, a rival nation, or to recognize the validity of another religion not endorsed by the authorities —now, here in America, all live as neighbors, work as associates, and have their children attend the same schools. Christians, Muslims, seculars, Hindus, Buddhists, Sikhs, spirituals, Jews, Baha'is, Jains, Shintoists, Zoroastrians, Taoists, agnostics, atheists, and more—all are neighbors, co-workers, classmates— Americans first and everything else second. Nowhere else in the world is this possible. Nowhere else is one as free, despite his or her accent, color of skin, religion and place of origin, to achieve as much as he or she aspires to achieve as here, in the United States of America. Your only limitations here are the ones you set for yourself.

Of course I am not so naïve as to suggest this land is perfect —far from it. This land too has its share of dark and painful past. Here too there have been and still are unenlightened, zealous little souls who are trapped inside dim and narrow tunnels of dogmas and feel compelled to keep the tribe, and subsequently the fear and the conflict, alive. How else could those folks spend all of their cherished negative energy that is bursting inside of them?

Author, 1974 —San Antonio, Texas

Author, 1984 —Cincinnati, Ohio

★ Author's journey through Iran